The Bratva's Bride

Volkov Bratva Series Book 1

Rose Chase

CONTENT WARNING

THIS BOOK IS A contemporary dark romance that contains content that some may find triggering and/or disturbing.

Contents include: explicit violence, sexual violence, abuse, alcohol and drug use, explicit sexual scenes, dub-con (dubious consent)/CNC (consensual non-consent), BDSM elements and tones, mentions of assault.

IF SUCH CONTENT TRIGGERS YOU THEN PLEASE DO NOT CONTINUE ANY FURTHER!

P.S: There is a glossary in the back of all the foreign terms used.

BLURB

ANGEL

"I do."

Words I never thought would escape my lips.

Now they bound me to the charismatic head of the Volkov Bratva, Nikolai Volkov.

His mesmerizing blue eyes, charming smile, and silky-smooth voice would be my downfall, and yet, also my salvation.

The two simple words would also be a personal vow to destroy my stepmother and enemies.

If I'm forced to be bound to the mafia life forever then I'll show them all.

I'll show them how far this 'angel' has fallen.

I'm not a pawn like they all think.

I'm the damn queen.

And I will rule with my king.

THE
BRATVA'S
Bride

ROSE CHASE

Contents

Chapter 1

Angel

SCREECH! CRASH!

Great, of course a crash would happen today where I had to stay way past my unscheduled double shift. Some hulking SUV decided to T-bone a sedan in the dead of night where—unfortunately—I was the only other living being around who could help. The apartments around remained dark and oblivious; their occupants were either ignoring the commotion outside, dead asleep, or possibly not currently occupying the space. The very few people who were in the streets scattered like cockroaches when the impact happened.

Fucking hell, you have got to be kidding me! Maybe if I—no, I can't.

I was somewhat tempted to keep on driving, but my conscience would eat away at me if I turned a blind eye. Not like one more round of CPR would kill me if any of the victims needed it. Besides, I already had all kinds of bodily fluids on my scrubs, and the caffeine running through my blood the past sixteen hours hadn't died out completely yet. "I swear to god..." I muttered to myself as I rushed over to the crash after throwing my car in park and turning it off.

Since the SUV was closer, I went over to it first, throwing the door open and scowling when my eyes landed on the driver. Oh, hell no. My oath of helping others no matter what was shoved out the window the moment I opened the car door of the SUV and saw who had fallen out. I instantly recognized the man, one of my stepmother's

1

very shady associates who liked to partake in unsavory business with minors. Scum like him made some hardened criminals seem like saints in comparison.

I quickly checked the man's pulse and went over to the sedan after seeing he had a pulse and was only unconscious. The sedan's driver-side door was smashed in from the impact, so I could only reach through the shattered window to assess the driver. The driver remained eerily still between the airbag and his seat, not even the subtlest of chest rises. A quick check of his—nonexistent—pulse confirmed he was dead. So, I moved down to the back seat and threw the door open—after it budged with my initial pull—and saw the second man slumped over and groaning. At least he was alive, for now.

Moving an injured person from a wreck was never a good idea, but fuck it, he needed professional help, and that was me currently. After a quick once over and deeming he was safe to move, I hooked my arms under his and pulled him out with a grunt. "Oh, fuck you're heavier than I thought," I said with a grunt of effort.

Based on his appearance, I had expected him to have some weight to him, but it's clear my initial assessment was off the mark. He appeared remarkably well-built. At first, I thought his suit was oversized, but upon laying my hands on him, I could see it was expertly tailored to fit his muscular physique snugly. If I weren't in a professional mode, I might have admired this strikingly handsome man for an extended period.

Dragging the man over to the sidewalk and into the alleyway entrance, I laid him down flat on the ground. "Sorry about this." I apologized quickly before pushing his suit jacket off his broad and strong shoulders.

So far, I didn't see too much external bleeding, just some from where shards of glass had embedded into him. Pulling out my scissors from the pocket of my scrub pants, I quickly apologized. "And sorry about this." His dress shirt looked expensive, so I somewhat felt bad about tearing through it with my safety scissors to get a better view of his front side.

Hot damn!

At that instant, I couldn't tear my eyes away from his incredibly toned body. His jawline was like a work of art, his chest all sculpted, and those 6-pack abs? They were like something out of a movie. Even Leonardo's statue of David would've had nothing on this man. Luckily, no one was around to catch me practically drooling over him because I couldn't help but ogle his inked and scarred body.

Whoever he is, he had it rough. I had seen enough scars working in the emergency department to tell what items left what kind of scar. The knife scars across his torso stood out as the most noticeable due to their clean and straight cuts against the broad surface, while the burns followed closely. The distinct shapes of the burns hinted at the methods used, making cigarette burns, for example, easily identifiable because of their small, circular shapes.

Mentally slapping myself, I recentered my attention to the task at hand. Laying my hands on him, I did a quick physical assessment to the best of my abilities. I might not be a doctor, but I knew what I was doing as a nurse.

If it weren't for this situation, my hands on his body would be a lot more intimate. Even though my task was to examine him, the thought of letting my hands slowly take in every dip and curve of his muscles dangled in the back of my mind.

"Fuck!" The stranger's hand shot out and grabbed my wrist, sending a wave of heat through my body at the initial contact before I shook the feeling away to remain professional.

"Hey, don't worry. You were in an accident, and I'm just making sure you're okay before I call for an ambulance." I wasn't sure how conscious he was or if the grab was just a reflex from me touching a potentially broken or fractured rib.

"No! No ambulance. No hospitals." He grunted while letting go of my wrist.

"You need medical help. You probably have, or do have, a broken or fractured rib or two. You need imaging to make sure a lung wasn't punctured or that you're not bleeding internally." I didn't want to send him home to die of suffocation from a punctured lung or an internal bleed.

Unfortunately, it would seem I had a stubborn one. "No. My phone." He gasped, holding his ribs with one hand as he sat up despite my protests.

"Fine." I won't argue with him any further. If he didn't want to go, then I couldn't force him. Well, if he happened to pass out, then I could use implied consent and the good Samaritan law.

Quickly, I searched his pockets, being mindful to not let my hands linger longer than needed. Seconds later, I pulled out a phone with a shattered screen from his pocket. "Sorry, it's busted." The thing wouldn't turn on. "You need to call someone?" Okay, that might have been a stupid question. Of course, he needed to call someone,. Why why else would he ask for his phone?

"Yes." He replied with another grunt before groaning softly as he leaned back against the wall with his hand holding his side.

Pulling out my phone, I shoved it into his free hand after unlocking it. "Call whoever you need. I need to make sure you're not injured elsewhere."

Top side, probably a few busted ribs from what I could tell. Now, onto the bottom area. Again, no major external bleeding from what I could see and feel. At least, his pants weren't saturated with blood, so that was a good indication of no external bleeds. Everything seemed good until I touched his left calf, causing him to release a pained groan.

Pushing the fabric up, I could see his crooked lower leg. "I gotta straighten it a little and stabilize it. Not going to lie, it's going to hurt like hell." I told him before looking around the area to see if there was anything I could use. "Stay." I probably didn't have to tell him. Doubt he was going to hobble anywhere with a broken leg.

Leaving his side, I went over to a pile of wooden pallets and pulled one off before stomping and snapping away two of the long pieces. "Mother fucker!" I hissed in pain when I felt the broken wood slice at my ankle and lower leg when I stomped on it to break it.

Returning to the man with two lengths of wood in hand, I sandwiched his lower leg between the wooden pieces before pushing them together to straighten his leg back out as much as possible, earning another groan from him. "Sorry!" I apologized as I pulled some medical tape from my scrub pocket and used it to wrap around and secure the pieces of wood to his leg. "You're probably gonna need a cast. Are you sure no hospital? You really—"

"I told you." He interrupted with a grunt, locking those hardened blue eyes at me, "No hospitals or ambulances." That was the first clear sentence not riddled with grunts of pain that he uttered to me.

Holding my hand up in defeat, I said, "Okay, okay, whatever you say, boss man." Again, no point in arguing with him.

"Here, thank you." He said, holding my phone towards me.

I was too busy to notice if he successfully made his call or not. I was going to assume he did because he returned my phone to me. Although, one quick glance at my call log had me questioning him a bit because there was no unknown number in the list.

Did I hallucinate him talking just now? No, I couldn't have, right? It's just us in this damn place right now, so it had to be him I heard.

Chapter 2

Nikolai

THE CRASH DAZED ME for a moment. I could barely register the sensation of my body being moved against my own will, let alone form a coherent thought. I probably would have been out of it if it weren't for the shooting pain that pulled me back from the depths of unconsciousness.

Then, I heard it—a faint voice of a woman mumbling to herself. Or maybe I had died, and the soft voice was a hallucination, attempting to pull me to the other side. But then I heard it again, this time more clearly. The voice was gentle and smooth, yet filled with conviction. It sounded surreal, almost angelic. Perhaps it was an angel beckoning me, though I couldn't help but doubt that someone like me belonged beyond the pearly gates. My eyes focused on the scene in front of me, and just as I was about to ask for her name, I heard her say 'ambulance,' which jolted me back to reality.

No way I was heading to a hospital; too many questions. I just needed to reach out to my people and get back to our private doctor.

It was unfortunate my phone was busted, probably due to the crash, but thankfully, she lent me hers. While I waited for the person on the other end to pick up after dialing, I couldn't help but watch the woman work.

In a different situation, I'd fully enjoy the feeling of her hands working down my body. There was a slight roughness to them, but still soft—a hard worker. I wanted nothing more than to grab her hands and place them on my bare chest again, wanting to feel her warmth there when she moved on. Unfortunately, this wasn't the time for that, and the harsh pain from her contact against my lower leg kicked any desire for her to the back of my mind. She spoke, but she didn't look at me as she seemed more trained on my broken leg.

"Hello?" The other end finally picked up.

Switching to my native tongue, I responded, "Finally. Arseny, send a car to the intersection of 45th and Carth. We've been hit. Call the doctor too, the crash busted a rib or a few, and this nurse is saying I have a broken leg." I could see she was a nurse from the badge that hung at the front pocket of her scrub top. At least I could read, so that meant my brain wasn't scrambled in the crash.

My eyes followed the woman down the dark alleyway when she left my side, but my ear remained trained on the phone. "Shit. On it. I'll be with you in ten. Stay alive until then," my brother responded before hanging up.

I didn't think the woman noticed my phone call; she was too engrossed with breaking apart a wooden pallet for pieces, along with the fact she was at a distance. I could hear her curse and hiss, but I couldn't fully see what was going on because the area she was in was too dark.

It wasn't long until she returned and tended to my leg, and I wish I had taken her warning a little more seriously because it hurt—a hell of a lot—when she did her best to straighten my leg and stabilize it.

Afterward, she tried to convince me to seek medical help again, but I shot down the idea before giving her phone back after deleting my call from her history. At least she dropped the topic. I had expected her to push for it more. Maybe she was smarter than I gave her credit for.

"Thank you. Does my little guardian angel have a name?" I couldn't make out the name on her badge because of the angle it was at. The only part of her badge I could clearly see were the initials of her profession at the very corner.

Her soft chuckle sent a chill through me. "Ironically, Angel. What about you?"

Ironic indeed.

I couldn't help but let out a strained chuckle in response. "Nikolai. Thank you, though, really. Not just anyone is so eager to drag someone out of a crash and help them." Getting a good look at her now, I started to wonder just how the hell she managed to drag me all this way.

From a quick glance, she was slightly built but small, probably no more than 5'3. The petite Asian was small compared to my burly 6'4 figure, and I knew for a fact I was heavy as a sack of cinder blocks.

Leaning back against the wall fully, I drank in her image, letting my blue eyes run down her body. Her long, black hair was tied back in a loose ponytail, with a few strands falling gracefully, giving her a somewhat disheveled and tired look. Her scrubs concealed most of her figure, making it hard to discern, but I could tell she had a curvy silhouette. The most prominent feature accentuated by her scrubs was her well-defined and rounded bottom.

"Hey, stay with me." She lightly shook at my shoulders, grabbing my full attention. "How many fingers am I holding up?" Her question was followed by her hand being held inches from my face.

"My head is fine. You're holding up four fingers, your index, middle, ring, and pinky, if you are wanting specifics." My head was mostly clear at this point, and I had no trouble recounting things.

"Good. Well, no need to thank me. My conscience wouldn't have let me live it down if I just drove off. Though, sorry about your buddy, he was gone when I got to him. He bled out." She nodded towards the driver of my car.

"Don't worry, I'll make sure he is given his dues along by way of his family." Losing people in my line of work wasn't uncommon. It just sucked that it was one of the ones I trusted. "What about that man?" I couldn't help but have a nasty tone as I lightly nodded towards the unconscious man next to the SUV.

"Him? I will have no problem leaving for dead. He deserves it. He had a pulse when I checked, unfortunately." The detest in her voice was clear, and the way she glared in that direction made me wonder just why she hated him so much.

"You know him?" That much was clear, but maybe I could get some information out of her.

"Only in passing and by some family association." She said through gritted teeth before turning her attention back to my body.

Maybe it wasn't a coincidence she was here during the crash. What if she had been a part of it? But that wouldn't make any sense if she saved me and left that man for dead. I was probably overthinking it, but I had to be on edge and think about every possible angle in order to survive in this lifestyle.

"You're injured." I noted out loud when I saw the discoloration at the bottom of her pants from the blood seeping through.

"I'll be fine, it's nothing deep. I'll bandage myself later when I get home. You're the one who needs medical attention right now." Her face twisted with worry as she looked up at me with those soft, warm brown eyes of hers.

Reaching out, I brushed away some stray strands of her hair and tucked them behind her ear to try and get a better view of her face in the poorly lit alleyway. "I'll be fine, my help is coming in a few minutes. Don't damage that pretty face of yours with worry for me." Her features were soft and delicate, but her eyes were strong.

Carefully, I studied her face and took in the slight slant of her eyes, which gave her an exotic look, the soft bridge of her nose ending with her small button nose, and those heart-shaped lips that fit perfectly on her roundish face. She truly lived up to her name in my opinion.

"I'll stay with you until I see that you are safe." She sounded determined and stubborn.

Her words made me chuckle because I was never safe, even if I knew what she meant. "You don't have to, you have done enough. I owe you."

"I won't be able to sleep unless I see that you are safe, and you don't owe me anything. I'm just doing what's right and needed, so I don't need to have anything in return." Generous too. People like her were too good for this rotten world.

Even if she was just doing her job and what was right, she still had a choice in the matter. So, she should be rewarded. "Whether you like it or not, I owe you." Slowly, I reached into my pocket, fished out a business card, and snagged a pen from her pocket, scribbling down my personal number before tucking everything back into her front pocket. "Keep it. If you ever need anything, and I mean *anything*, reach out to me."

Sighing softly, she looked at me with defeat. "Fine, I'll keep it, but don't expect any late night calls any time soon." The playful edge to her voice made me smile a bit.

I quipped back, "That's what your lover is for, not me." Though it could be me, and I definitely wouldn't mind one bit.

Laughing softly, she looked at me with a half-smile, "If I had a lover, yes. Or is that your way of finding out if I'm single or not?"

"Damn, you caught me. Guilty as charged." I joked back with a strained laugh and a few coughs.

Before she could say anything else, a car pulled up and a familiar face popped out of the driver's side. "Oh, thank the heavens you're okay." Arseny said with a sigh of relief as he ran over to me.

"Okay? Do I look okay to you?" I bit back with a harsh glare.

"Damn, I was hoping you'd have a major head injury to make you less of a dick," Arseny joked with a chuckle.

If it were anyone else, then a comment like that would have gotten them in deep shit. Luckily for Arseny, he was my brother, so I let him get away with some—a lot of—things. "Maybe I should break your leg and see how you feel," I grumbled, hissing in pain when he helped me up with Angel.

"Grab him too." I told Arseny, nodding towards the unconscious man on the pavement.

"I got him, just do what he wants," Angel said to Arseny with a soft and reassuring smile.

"Uhh are you sure? You know how much he weighs right? And you know how tiny you are?" Arseny seemed wary, which I didn't blame him for. I probably look like I could flatten her if I fell over onto her right now.

"Oh please, I've handled bigger." She replied in a confident voice with a roll of her eyes.

Warily, Arseny left my side to go collect the man, stuffing him into the trunk before returning to the driver's side. "I'm assuming you're the one that helped him, so thank you, really." Arseny gave Angel a grateful smile before turning his attention forward.

"You don't seem bothered by any of this." I noted out loud, looking at Angel with furrowed eyes and a raised brow, because anyone would be freaked out by such an order.

"I've learned to not meddle with these things if I want to keep my pretty head on my shoulders. Besides, one rat off the street is better than none. Just, take care, okay?" Even though I was being passed off into good hands, she still seemed genuinely worried for me. Although, I guess it might just be second nature given her line of work.

"I'll be fine, it's going to take a lot more than a crash to take me down. Just, remember what I told you, I'm one call away." I told her with a brief smile before shutting the door and watching her disappear as the car drove off.

Though it should have been the end of it, her words bugged me a little along with her comfort about the whole situation. I couldn't help but get a little paranoid with my thoughts again as I let my mind ponder.

Was it just an odd coincidence she was here?
Or did she have some hand in all of it?

Chapter 3

Angel

"Hey, are you sure you don't want to go out for that drink? You really
seem like you need it," my brother said with a lopsided smile.

As much as I wanted to catch up with my older brother, I was on
hour sixteen of my shift after pulling a twelve-hour shift the day before.
I was beyond exhausted because this shift was only supposed to be
eight hours—not double! Hell, I still hadn't clocked off. Still stuck
at the nurse's station waiting for my replacement. "Greg, I'm way too
tired for a drink. I just want to clock off then go visit and talk to *ba* for
a bit before heading home and crashing."

"How is he? I haven't been able to go see him because of work, and
because of those stupid goons our dear stepmother has posted around
his room." I could hear the apprehension in Greg's voice as his face
hardened.

Unfortunately, the guards—goons according to Greg—were
more than happy to give Greg trouble. Greg wasn't involved or tied to
the triad business in any way. Actually, he stood on the other side; a
detective for the police department. No one knew of Greg's connec-
tion to our father though. He just played it up that his visits were part
of a case involving our father. It was better to keep it this way, to keep
my stepmother's attention away from Greg as much as possible so he
could continue to help me unnoticed.

"He's still in the same condition, stable but still in a coma. Both you and I know that *she's* not going to let up on the guards, if you can even call them that. Have you found out anything else?" I kept my voice lowered as I continued to speak to my brother.

"No, damn bitch is good, but I'm not giving up. She's bound to slip up, people like her always do, just a matter of time." Greg sighed heavily as he ran a hand through his dark hair. "I just hate that it's taking this long. I might not have been close to dad, but I remember how great he was when he was there before everything changed. So, I hate that she finally got her fangs into him. I just hope we can save him if there's any possibility of it."

Clutching the pen in hand, I could feel the plastic give a little from my hard grip. "She won't get away with it, not if I can help it. I'm tired of her ruining everything she touches, if we can't get her on anything then I'll take care of it myself, personally," I said sternly.

"No, you're better than that Ange, you and I both know it." Unfortunately, he was right, but when push comes to shove, I know what I want and will have to do.

Besides, I have another option, one I don't want to think about. The card from Nikolai still sat in my nightstand, practically calling to me every night when I would come home and think about my stepmother's demise. He said *anything*, but would what I have in mind be too much? There's no way he would risk so much for a simple favor.

I wasn't stupid; I did my research, and had Greg do his due diligence on Nikolai, Nikolai Volkov. On paper and to the eyes of the media he was an owner of multiple high-end, successful clubs and casinos. Also he was known as one of the hottest bachelors in the state of California. I couldn't agree more to that last statement. Just seeing his pictures from the articles I dug up made me sweat a little. He was downright handsome with his cropped honey brown hair and sky-blue eyes which popped so much against his fair skin and hair. His tall nose had a slight kink in it, no doubt from a few fights, but that only added to his dangerous charm.

I knew not to stop at the surface media though, my father taught me better, and I knew better at this point. Even if I weren't fully involved in the family business, I still had my hand in the pot for personal reasons. Nikolai Volkov was so much more than what the media portrayed. His name struck fear around the city, just as much as my family's name did.

The Volkov Bratva weren't one to be trifled with. I knew about the damage they could do, and I knew about what they did. My family had been in a tug-of-war battle with them ever since they rose up and took over nearly half the city of Nespin, California. Although things have been at a stalemate for a long while since my father took over the Qing Triad, things were starting to go down the shit hole ever since he fell into his coma and my stepmother stepped up.

Nikolai definitely would have the means to execute the favor I would ask of him, but it would be stupid of him to do so in his position. So, his card sat idle in my drawer, for now, and possibly forever. I knew better than to get involved with any mafia activity, even being associated and barely involved with my father's business was more than I could handle.

I wanted nothing more than to leave it all behind and just live my day-to-day life as a nurse, live a relatively normal life. Unfortunately, it wasn't simple. Even if my dad never pressured me or pushed the idea of me taking over the triad onto me. Actually, he fully supported me wanting out and helped me before he fell ill suddenly. As a hardened leader as he was, he cared for his children, and even if it wasn't known, he was done with the mafia life and wanted to retire. He told me he had someone good in mind to take over the business, someone with the same ideals and morals as him, but he never got as far as telling me who, nor had he started the process of transfer.

There was no doubt in my mind that my stepmother had something to do with my father falling ill. She was always a slimy bitch. There was no way she would give up the lifestyle of being the Dragonhead's—the head of the Qing Triad—wife. She was too used to the luxury the life afforded her, and she was too narcissistic to give it all up.

That's why I turned to plan B. While my father had hoped plan A would succeed, he also wanted me to execute the backup plan in case it didn't.

Tear it all down.

Finally! My stupid shift was over!

I couldn't stop my excitement as I rushed to my father's room a few floors above in the geriatric center of the hospital I worked at. The goons my mother set in place glared at me softly as I approached and went through. They knew better than to mess with me, for now. Even if they were on my stepmother's side, they still knew better than to pull any shit with me until she said otherwise.

"Hey *ba*, I missed you." I greeted him with a sad smile as I went over and sat next to him on the bed, taking his limp hand in mine. "I hope this passes soon, and for you to get the peace you deserve." Whether it be retirement or death, I wasn't sure what I wanted for him right now. "I spoke with Greg, he misses you too."

"You wouldn't believe the crazy shift I had today." I continued to talk to him for a while, for nearly an hour, just telling him about my day as if he were still conscious and here.

"I'll see you another day *ba*. I'm sorry I won't be able to see you tomorrow. Bye *ba*, love you." Even though I knew full well what he did for a living, he was still a wonderful father who never gave me anything but the best.

"Lady Qing wants to see you tonight." One of the goons told me the moment I exited my father's private room.

"Then she can ask me herself to get the answer she already knows." Like hell I was going to meet with that woman willingly unless necessary. "Whatever she has to say to me she can do it in a voicemail or come seek me directly." I'm not her dog who came to her beck and call.

I didn't say anything more and left briskly after. Although, I couldn't help but wonder what she wanted as I drove home. The answers were endless. Money? Power? My life?

Honestly, if it wasn't for my father's request, or the fact I loved my father dearly, then I would just let her have full run of the damn triad. Unfortunately, both my father and I had the foresight to anticipate how disastrous that would be, although he realized it a little too late. I decided to let her run the place, let her think she's in charge, but everyone who was none the wiser knew better.

Sighing heavily, I brushed my anxious thoughts from my mind as I made my way up and into my apartment. Standing there at the entryway, I scanned my studio apartment. Something felt off, and it wasn't because I was paranoid. Nothing was out of place from a quick scan, but it was a gut feeling. I knew better to trust my gut now, and it told me to hightail it out of here.

Unfortunately, before I could make much of a run, or a step, someone grabbed me from behind with a grunt. "God fucking damn it!" I hissed under my breath as I quickly dropped my weight and threw my assailant forward. Swiftly, I gave him a kick to the face before bolting it down the hallway to the exit in hopes to get into my car and go.

"Oof!" A pained grunt left me as I felt the wind get knocked out of me. I had made it just outside the complex and someone tackled me to the ground.

Quickly, I recovered enough to grab one of my pens from my pockets and stabbed it into my attacker's back, not caring about where the makeshift weapon punctured. Usually, I'd be mindful about avoiding vital spots, but that was hard to do with all the tumbling around we did. All I was sure of was that I didn't get his heart because I stabbed him well over into the right side of his chest, so unless he was an oddball where his organs were flipped, he'd have a punctured lung at most.

The man let me go, and I scrambled to my feet. "What the..." My car was just right there, but I could see it fading. "Shit..." I could feel it now, a pinch in my leg. Looking down, I could see a needle sticking out of my thigh. The words on the label of the syringe were starting to blur, but I could make out some of it. "K..eta..."

Fuck.

Chapter 4

Nikolai

"So, who's the lucky man that's going to get hitched tonight boys?" The comment from my youngest brother earned him a smack to the face with the magazine from his twin.

"Lucky? If you think it's so lucky then why don't you volunteer as tribute then?" His twin shot back with a playful scowl.

Great, the night has barely started, and I could already feel a headache coming on. Maybe it wasn't a good idea to have all of us in a car together. "Would you all shut up? Alexei is not going to be the one wedding whoever this mystery bride is, he's too young and has little in the family business. He's only here because he's our brother and to play peacekeeper with Arseny."

Middle aged men or not, get the five of us in a room together and I swear we revert to rowdy teenage boys after a while. That was one of the charms of our family dynamic I appreciated. I could always be comfortable and free around my brothers, and I could always count on them to have my back and keep me grounded.

"Why the hell are we even agreeing to this old ass tradition? We've more than enough manpower to overtake their territory if push comes to shove, and we've been at a stalemate with them." Lev—the middle brother—spoke up with a disgruntled grunt.

Our second brother spoke up. "Not all of us are trigger happy like you, you asshole. Besides, it doesn't hurt to hear this proposal out.

Worse to come from it is that one of us gets the ball and chain. Having a truce in place would be good for all of us. A stalemate is too unstable, and the latest push from the Qing Triad is making it clear that it's not going to stay a stalemate for long. If we can avoid a massacre, then that would be ideal." I could always count on Stepan to be the voice of reason. Sometimes I wonder why he stuck around the family business given his passive nature.

Sighing heavily, I ran a hand through my hair as I looked out the window from the passenger seat. "We will hear what they have to say. Old tradition or not, sometimes going old school isn't a bad thing. Stepan is right though, I would rather avoid a bloodbath and have some kind of mutual peace between us and the Qing Triad. There would be too much of a power imbalance if we were to take them out. No doubt the other mafias would appreciate our instant growth if we just overtook the triad's area of control."

I had no intentions of going along with this proposed marriage. I'm not one for senseless violence and would rather avoid a nasty confrontation of bullets if possible. As soft as it may seem, it was efficient and effective for me and my brothers. Respect goes a long way more than fear and mindless murder.

"This still feels wrong though. We shouldn't even be entertaining this archaic idea after what happened with—"

Before Alexei could finish his sentence, I cut him off with a harsh glare, sending the whole cabin into a dead silence. It was a subject all of us agreed to never bring up. It was too sensitive, too deep. Even if the event was one of the main reasons why we ran things how we did, it was still a sore spot for all of us after all these years.

"We're here sir." The driver announced as we arrived at the designated warehouse at the docks.

"Thank you. Make sure everyone is in position just in case." I couldn't afford to not be cautious with dealings not in a populated area. We were going to be alone with the rival mafia, just us and them. If this meeting were in a restaurant or a park, where there'd be witnesses around, then I would be slightly more lenient, but this wasn't the case.

"Already on it boss. I'm on standby as always, be careful." The driver replied with a soft nod of his head.

Exiting the car, I made my way into the warehouse with my brothers. Stepan and Lev, my second and third in command, flanked either side of me while the twins, Alexei and Arseny, were behind me along with some bodyguards.

"Ah, welcome, welcome! I am so pleased that you accepted my invite for tonight. I am Lady Qing, lady of the head." A woman dressed in a red and gold Chinese dress with matching heels greeted us with a fake smile. I could tell it wasn't genuine and was forced from how much she strained her face. Also, it was too sickly sweet, like a cake that made your teeth ache with just one bite.

"Nikolai Volkov, head of the Volkov Bratva. These are my brothers and commanders, Stepan, Lev, Alexei, and Arseny. Your invitation stated that you wanted to discuss a truce between us with a marriage proposal?" I just hope this won't be a complete waste of time or manpower.

"Yes, yes. As you are aware, both of us control great parts of the city, and the violence between us has spanned on too long and has grown tiring, no doubt for both sides. So, don't you think it is time that we put everything aside and just live with how things are without any encroachment on each other's territories? The marriage is a way to assure that this truce stays between us, an agreement on both sides." Lady Qing spoke with her head held high, and a bit too much confidence for my liking.

"And how can we trust you to keep your end of the bargain once this marriage goes through? That you won't amass with other marriages on the side and expand and overthrow us? One marriage could mean nothing to you." Stepan spoke up in a voice filled with caution and slight apprehension. He also made a good point. This marriage could just be a ploy to keep us dead in the water while she gathered her army for a strike. She had other children to wed off, so what's to stop her from using them?

Arranged marriages or marriages for the sake of truce weren't uncommon in the day, and in some parts of the world it was still a common practice. It required a vast amount of trust from both sides, that neither would harm the other because of the harmony and sanctity of the marriage, and the lives of those involved. I hated the archaic practice, but I also knew it was a necessary evil when push came to shove. I would never force any of my brothers into an arranged marriage, nor would I partake in it myself if it can be helped. But, I was willing to be a sacrifice if necessary.

"We would dare not to harm you while you have our precious heiress with you. My husband adores his daughter and would never dare try anything to bring harm to her or her family, which would include you all once the marriage is done. He is a good man, one of his word." Lady Qing replied, almost sounding rehearsed.

"Then why isn't he here then? Too good for us?" Lev scowled, his fists clenching as his body tensed. He needed to calm down before one of the jumpy guards mistook his actions as threatening and started a shootout. Thankfully the glance from me was enough of a sign for him to ease back, for now.

"He would if he could. Unfortunately, he has fallen ill and has been in a coma for quite a while now though. But, before he slipped into his state, he was talking to me about making a truce with the Volkov Bratva, knowing how important peace is to avoid unnecessary bloodshed between our families." Again, another precise answer which sounded a little too smooth.

Some people were good at communication and negotiations, like Stepan, but something about Lady Qing and how she spoke kept my nerves on edge. It wasn't something I could call her out on though, it was just what I picked up without any solid evidence to what she could be hiding. Baseless accusations are an easy way to get a bullet through the head. Even if she lied through her fake smile almost too perfectly, any amateur would easily fall for it if they couldn't pick up the nuances. Lady Qing was good, I'll give her that, but I'm no amateur at this game.

"And a part of that truce included offering his daughter as a bargaining chip? Some father he is then." Lev scoffed once more, this time with disgust.

"Consider it a gesture of good faith on our end. You have something precious of ours, we would never dare to wrong you." The sickly smile on her face made me want to call off this meet and deal. A smile of a snake as it remained coiled, ready to strike when we least expect it.

I was torn. My gut screamed at me to not trust this woman or anything that came out of her mouth, but a truce between us would benefit everyone. "Give me a moment to speak to my brothers." Their input was important to me. Even if I was the head and my say was final, I wanted to hear their thoughts on everything.

"What do you guys think?" I switched to my native language—Russian—to prevent the possibility of the other side getting anything from this talk.

"I say we light them up and just take it by force." Okay, maybe I should include everyone but Lev because he was always going to choose the most violent route.

My gaze filtered over to Stepan, the unofficial advisor of the family. "I don't trust this lady, but a truce is a truce. They aren't some small mafia, they can be formidable against us if we are to go to war. I say we take the truce with extreme caution." Stepan inputted with a soft sigh. "Very extreme caution." At least I wasn't the only one wary of this woman.

Then, my head tilted a little towards Arseny. Even though he was the youngest, he was wise and thoughtful beyond his years. "As much as I don't like it either, I agree with Stepan. It might be a ploy to tear us apart from the inside using the girl, but a truce, even if it is short lived, is better than none. We can always plan in the meanwhile too." Arseny tossed his penny of a thought into the pot.

I had a good hunch as to what the last brother was going to say, so I looked at him knowingly. "You already know I hate senseless slaughter. I say we take the truce and play our cards right later." Alexei sighed with a soft shrug of his shoulders.

"You guys are no fun." Lev spat with a scowl as he crossed his arms, clearly unhappy about being outnumbered.

Nodding softly, I turned back towards Lady Qing who remained on the other side of the table with a somewhat twisted smirk on her face. "We will go through with the truce." Why did the words weigh so heavily on me? As if I just signed my death certificate.

"Perfect." Lady Qing cheered a little too chirpily as she clapped her hands and shouted something in her native tongue.

All our attention turned towards a pile of crates when we heard footsteps along with the sound of something dragging.

Sucking in a deep breath, I struggled for a second to keep myself composed when I saw the limp body of the woman they were dragging out. Those beautiful raven locks and soft face couldn't be mistaken, nor the undeniable fire that burned within me at the sight of the angel before me. My eyes raked her nearly naked body, clad only in a pair of white lace panties and a matching bra. I could clearly see her delicate body now, those subtle curves that flared out with her hips, and her toned legs and stomach. She was more than I had imagined in my fantasies of her. But this was no time to get horny for the hot nurse though, this was the worst time.

"Is this a joke?" Lev seethed, his hand twitching, probably itching to grab his gun from its holster.

Scowling, I breathed deeply through my nose to suppress my rising anger. "What is the meaning of this?" I asked in a harsh voice, glaring at Lady Qing.

"This is—"

Before she could finish, chaos broke out. Out of the corner of my eye, I could see Angel spring to life, grabbing a knife off the belt of one of the men holding her and using it to stab him in the back of his knee before stealing his gun from the waistband of his pants and shooting the other person next to her in the leg, crippling him as well.

The other men charged at her, but I watched with amused and amazed eyes as she fought back, her body dodging and striking back with precision to effectively knock back her attackers before rendering them useless with a well-placed shot into their knees. She was tiny, but one hell of a fighter and shooter.

I could hear Lady Qing shout—what I assume—were, orders at her men who were trying to gang up on Angel who made a run for the exit at the other end of the warehouse.

I watched as a man grabbed her from behind while she tried to make her escape, only to have his face meet the back of her head in a headbutt followed by an all-familiar cracking noise. His hold loosened enough for Angel to snag his knife from him and give him a stab in the leg, making him release her completely. Then, she directed her focus to a man a few feet away and hurled the knife, piercing it into his midsection before resuming her attempt to escape. However, her progress was halted by a gunshot near her feet.

"I'll volunteer as a sacrifice for the greater good." Lev spoke in awe, not taking his eyes off Angel.

Gritting my teeth, I shoved the bubbling anger that clawed at my chest. How dare they drag her out like some piece of property like that? If that's how they presented her then I didn't want to imagine the treatment. Then the fact they had their disgusting hands on her earlier.

They dared to lay their hands and eyes on what is mine.

Chapter 5

Angel

STUPID IDIOTS, THEY SHOULD have done what they wanted faster or sedated me more. The moment I could feel my senses and control return to me, I waited until—what I deemed—a good moment to strike and make my escape. I was nearly successful too.

Scowling, I spun around and pointed the loaded and unlocked gun at my stepmother. "This is some shit you're trying to pull. I'm going to walk out of here, and you're going to let me. Like hell am I going to be some stupid pawn that you can wed off for your sick games you bitch. Go marry one of your airhead daughters, they need the help more than me." Unfortunately, the apple didn't fall far from the tree with her daughters. Good thing they were too stupid to be on my threat radar.

"If you take one more step, I will shoot you." Lady Qing threatened, cocking her own gun to point at me.

Smirking arrogantly, I held my arms out, "Go ahead, kill me. You know you'll lose it all." All of my father's assets were in my name, at least eighty-five percent of it was. She would lose a lot more than she would gain with my death. Besides, I had a lot of contingencies in place in case I met an untimely demise by her hands. "You already know I don't give a damn about it all, it can all burn for all I care." It wasn't as if my father wanted to return to all of this, so why would it matter if it all fell.

"Then who will take care of your dear old father if you are gone? Hm? If you don't do as I say, then you can kiss your father goodbye when you bury him at his funeral tomorrow. I'll have him dead the moment you set foot outside the exit." Lady Qing smirked evilly while lowering her gun. She knew where to hit me, and I hated it.

Scowling, I disarmed the gun and threw it on the ground. I hated how she had me pinned, but at least I knew now that she had a large grasp on my father's health if she could make such a threat. I have to figure out how to pry her claws off my father.

I watched as she turned her attention back to whatever guest she had, switching back to English as we had been speaking in Mandarin. "Gentlemen, I am so sorry about that, just a slight misunderstanding between my daughter and I." Then, she turned to me and beckoned me over with those horribly manicured fingers of hers.

What utter lies. I wanted nothing more than to cut her tongue out. It was rare for me to feel violent towards anyone nowadays, but my stepmother was one of those exceptions. Gritting my teeth, I reluctantly went over to the table, glaring at her the whole time and refusing to look at who stood on the other side until she grabbed my arm and forced me to turn around.

"You..." My voice barely came out as a whisper when my wide eyes landed on the familiar figure. I could feel the goosebumps rush down my body as I quickly took in his hulking figure clad in a flattering black suit with a dark blue dress shirt underneath.

I instantly recognized the dashing man, Nikolai Volkov. If he was here, then he was a major player. I knew he was a part of the Volkov Bratva, but I never dug far enough to figure out his status and standing within it. I was determined to *not* get involved with him, so I saw no point in digging further than needed.

Also, why the hell did he make my body burn so much? I shouldn't be feeling hot and bothered being all exposed and traded as some commodity.

"This is Angel, the eldest, and heiress to the Qing Triad." I could feel her fake nails dig into my flesh as she tightened her grip on me, her way of warning me to behave.

Wrenching my arm away from her, I tossed her a harsh glare as I bit my tongue to hold myself back from ripping her a new one. "Listen, I'm sorry if she troubled you with this meeting, she—"

My words were cut off with a small hiss of pain when I felt her nails dig into my shoulder after she placed her hand on it. "So, I have the papers ready, who will it be to solidify the truce?" She didn't bother to pay me any attention. How rude.

Opening my mouth, I was about to say something as I watched one of the men take a step forward, only to be stopped by Nikolai holding his hand out. "I will wed Angel."

"What? *Bratok*, are you sure?" Another man spoke up, looking at Nikolai with concern. Then he quickly switched to another language, Russian I think. The conversation was brief though, due to Nikolai cutting him off with a hard look and wave of his hand.

"I—!" Before I could question things further or make a scene, Lady Qing digs her nails deeper into me.

Two simple words; a reminder, "Your father." Was all she needed to say to get my compliance.

The nerve of this treacherous snake.

Taking in a deep breath, I watched Nikolai with wary eyes as he rounded the table and stood next to me. "Things stay as they are, we mind our own business and do not interfere with each other. We have no business to conduct with you otherwise nor will we go into any business with you. This marriage is only a means to keep the peace and truce between us, nothing more." He was cold and to the point. I should be turned away by his tone and works, but my body had other ideas for some goddamn reason.

"Fine, give me a moment to get all those details amended to the truce." Lady Qing turned away and went over to some of her men who scrambled to write things down on some papers.

"Here." The feeling of something soft and warm engulfing me startled my body into a jerk. When I realized it was a harmless jacket, I relaxed a little. Breathing in deeply, the intoxicating scent of aftershave along with pine and soil warmed my body as my senses were invaded by him.

Shivering, I grasped at the lapels of his jacket and pulled it close to my body, covering myself as much as I could to remain decent and warm. "Thank you." I didn't know what else to say in this situation.

The two of us stood there in silence, just looking into each other's eyes, trying to read one another. It didn't take long for everything around me to fade into the background as I got lost in his enchanting blue orbs. If the situation were different, this moment could have been a lovely one.

It felt like a long moment but not. When my stepmother returned with some papers along with some officials in tow, a lawyer and an officiant, everything shattered back to reality. So much for our little moment.

Well, maybe this won't be so bad...

Oh, who am I kidding!?

The Pakhan—the head—of the Volkov Bratva!? In no way was this good! He was downright handsome, I'll give him that, but beyond physical appearances, I knew very little about him. From what I read in the articles, he immigrated here from Russia with his family at a young age, he owned successful businesses—no doubt fronts for bratva activity—and was charming, charismatic, rough around the edges, and clouded with too much mystery.

"I hope this treaty is to your liking," Lady Qing said with her sick smirk as she slid over the documents that were just written up.

Looking down, I let my eyes scan the documents before I was disrupted. "Nah ah, not for your eyes girl." Lady Qing chided, covering the documents with her hand and sliding it away when she saw my eyes reading it.

Taking a deep breath, I puffed my chest out, ready to say something but then Nikolai reached out and took the documents back. "She is involved in this as much as all of us, especially since she is to be my wife."

My wife.

Those two simple words made me want to clench my thighs together to dull the aching between my legs. My dream of having a man call me his wife became long forgotten once I came to accept that

I was forever doomed to stay single. Yet, that distant dream would now become a reality, in a twisted way through this arrangement.

Sighing softly, I clicked my tongue as I placed my hand over Nikolai's, shivering a bit at the contact as I slid the papers closer.

Glaring over at Lady Qing, I clicked my tongue softly again before throwing my words at her. "I might not be around much, but don't you forget your place." If I really wanted to, I could take over fully and everyone would bow to me. One big problem: I wouldn't know how loyal everyone would be to me considering how many have already turned their backs on my father in favor of my stepmother.

Gritting my teeth, I leaned in close to Lady Qing and glared at her. "You may think that you have won, but mark my words, you will regret everything. If you so much harm one hair on my father, I will take it all from you within half a blink of an eye. You may just hold the title of head lady for now, but that's only because I am allowing it. Do not forget your place, snake." I seethed at her in Mandarin, watching as she glared back at me.

"You do not forget your place girl." She threatened back in Mandarin.

Smirking, I replied, "Oh, I know my place, but I'm not sure you do." Two could play at this game, and this game was one I would always win.

Carefully, I read over the treaty agreement, taking in every single word, line, and clause multiple times to make sure it was what they had just agreed on with nothing slimy in between. I had to bite my cheek to hold back my smirk when I saw the loopholes in it though, ones that would benefit me in the future regarding my plans. "Almost as good as my charting, good to see you didn't skimp on the lawyer this time." I remarked in English with a smirk, watching as my stepmother scowled at me in annoyance.

I watched as both sides signed all the copies of the treaty agreement in silence. Then, much to my surprise, Nikolai held the pen out to me. "Like I said, you are as much involved as all of us now. You're going to be my wife, therefore part of it all."

Sighing softly, I took the pen and signed my name under his on the documents before sliding one back to the nervous looking lawyer and the other towards my seething stepmother. At least her displeasure brought me some joy out of this fucked up situation.

"Ahem, I'm to officiate the marriage." The officiant spoke up with an awkward and forced cough.

Groaning internally, I repressed my eyes from rolling as I remembered why I was drugged and dragged here. How the hell was I going to get out of this? I didn't want to be married yet, let alone with a stranger who was head of the Bratva! Well, again, at least he was handsome. I could have been carted off to some fat slob who's a wife beater. Oh god, I hope Nikolai wasn't some abuser behind closed doors. I can't make myself a widow at twenty-four. Hell, I didn't want to kill my own husband, period.

Gripping his jacket tightly, I stared at the ground as the officiant went on with the impromptu ceremony. "Do you Nikolai Volkov, take Angel Qing to be your lawfully wedded wife, to live together in matrimony, to love her, comfort her, honor and keep her, in sickness and in health, in sorrow and in joy, to have and to hold, from this day forward, as long as you both shall live?"

"I do." Nikolai replied bluntly.

Wow, so much for the wedding bliss and excitement. Full sarcasm intended.

Then, the officiant turned his attention towards me. "Do you Angel Qing, take Nikolai Volkov to be your lawfully wedded husband, to live together in matrimony, to love him, comfort him, honor and keep him, in sickness and in health, in sorrow and in joy, to have and to hold, from this day forward, as long as you both shall live?" Truthfully? No, I don't. Too bad I couldn't say it without signing my father's death certificate.

Gritting my teeth, I swallowed my pride and answered, "I do."

"Before these witnesses, you have pledged to be joined in marriage. By the authority vested in me by the great State of California, I now pronounce you husband and wife! You may kiss each other if you wish." I feel like the last bit was altered by the officiant given the circumstance.

Did I want a kiss from him? Yes! In any other situation, yes! Right now though? Through a forced marriage? I wasn't so sure.

Well, guess Nikolai made the choice for us. "No, we'll take our leave now. We have other business to attend to." Reaching down, Nikolai picked me up in his arms unceremoniously.

Uhh, okay, rude.

"H-hey, put me down, I can walk by myself." God this was embarrassing! First, I get kidnapped after a long ass shift, then get my ass sedated, wake up from said sedation in nothing but my undies, get pushed into an arranged marriage, and now I'm being carried out like some helpless damsel. Just fucking great.

"I know you can, but you have no shoes on. I'm not letting you walk anywhere but our home barefooted." Nikolai responded, tightening his grip on me when I started slipping a little.

"Our home..." The words sounded so stiff and foreign to me.

Remaining quiet, I clung onto the front of his shirt with one hand while using the other to keep his jacket secured around me. I let him carry me to the SUV and set me inside in the backseat before climbing in next to me, letting himself be squished by one of his brothers because he took the middle seat.

Did all of them have to cram into this suffocating car and make things more unbearable? I saw the other cars on the way out, so why couldn't they fill those and leave the newlyweds alone? Also, this just felt so awkward, being shoved into a car with all these big burly men. Hell, I'm surprised they all managed to fit into the damn car without being pressed up against the windows like some overstuffed cartoon car.

But just fucking great.
I was stuck in the middle of a pack of wolves.

Chapter 6

Nikolai

"How come Stepan gets shotgun?" Arseny grumbled in the very back row.

"Because I'm older, so shut it." Stepan chuckled while turning back to look at Angel who sat in her seat with her legs curled up to her chest. "Welcome to the family! Sorry if this wasn't how you planned to spend your night, but I can assure you that we're all surprised as well. I'm Stepan by the way, the second oldest. Mister lucky tonight is Nikolai, the oldest. The scowling menace next to him is Lev, the third oldest. Lastly the twins in the back, Arseny and Alexei."

"Hello! Welcome to the family! I promise we're not all *that* bad!" The twins said in unison, popping their heads up towards Angel.

"Nice to see you again!" Arseny threw a friendly grin at Angel, reaching over and patting her shoulder.

"Also, probably a rude question, but where are your clothes?" Alexei asked, earning a soft glare from me.

"They cut them off me, apparently scrubs aren't appealing for a marriage proposal." Angel replied in a low voice as she turned her attention to the floor. "They caught me at the end of a long ass shift. Didn't even have time to change before they jumped me." She grumbled with a cute little pout on her lips.

A moment later, she looked up at me with mixed eyes I couldn't fully discern. I could see some wariness, hesitation, and lust...?

Reaching up, I tucked away her stray strands of hair behind her ear. It was so tempting to bring her up to me and kiss her right now. Then I could finally taste those luscious lips that have haunted my dreams for the past months. The temptation to kiss her earlier was hard to resist, but I knew if I did, then I wouldn't stop. I also had an image to uphold.

"You're in good hands, you have nothing to be worried or scared about. Besides, you should be used to this life already." I don't know why she seemingly made a big deal out of this. This was the life she was born into, and grew up in.

Rolling her eyes, she crossed her arms loosely. "No, I'm not. This isn't the life I chose for myself, and it definitely isn't the one my father wanted for me either." She responded with a soft scowl.

"Is that why you were fine with that guy we tossed in the trunk months back?" Arseny questioned, bringing up the fateful night.

"Yeah, I could care less what happens to half those shit heads. Besides, that guy deserved whatever he got for what he's done. Please tell me he's dead." Her eyes eagerly searched mine for an answer. Her eagerness caught me off guard.

"He is." I answered her flatly.

The corner of her lips twitched softly, but she hid the smile. "Good." She sounded somewhat satisfied.

"Well, you don't seem too loyal to your people." Lev piped up with his own scowl, his hostility taking a bit of an edge. He probably still felt a little butt hurt over the fact I took Angel for myself rather than let him wed her.

"I'm only loyal to my father and those who are loyal to him and me... And now my husband..." She didn't seem to be lying about being loyal to me, even if she did sound a little hesitant, I didn't detect ill will from her. She was probably still adjusting to the fact she has a husband now.

"Besides, that man was not one of mine, nor would I want a serial child abuser to be in my ranks." She clarified with a soft glare at Lev.

"Fine, that aside, how can we know you're not lying? Obviously, your loyalties sound very questionable." Lev did pose a good question, and it was one that hung in the back of my mind as well.

"My loyalty might be to a select few, and even if this marriage wasn't by conventional means, I've sworn myself to Nikolai minutes ago. Believe it or not, that is up to you, and that is nothing I can force you all to change your minds on, but just know that I would never betray Nikolai or his family, which includes you all." She seemed defeated, but genuine. If she lied, then she was very good at it.

Yawning, she rubbed her eyes softly and leaned against the window before letting out a small chuckle. "You know, when I heard that she wanted to clean her hands of me with this marriage, I thought about calling in that favor from you. Guess there's no point in doing that anymore." Her eyes drifted to me out of the corner as she kept her head planted against the glass.

"You still remember?" A part of me thought she'd thrown it out the window the moment she got home, and as the days stretched on and I heard nothing from her, I figured as much.

"Mhmm. Never had a use for it, until now, but I can't use it now because you can't exactly get rid of yourself or me out of this marriage." She chuckled softly while glancing at me.

"You were going to have me get rid of your husband?" I asked with an amused smirk. I could see how that would be impossible with this situation. There was no way in hell I would let her go now that I had her in my grasp.

"If I wanted to be in a committed relationship then I would, alright? There is a reason why I am single, err was single. Besides, if it was a forced marriage to anyone else, then yes, I would have called in that favor to have his body in a body bag." She replied in a low voice.

"Anyone else? So, you're fine being married to Kolya here is what I'm hearing?" Stepan teased Angel with a playful smirk, making her blush.

"Well, I mean, he wasn't a dick to me when I met him initially..." Then she muttered something under her breath I couldn't quite catch.

Soon, questions started to get tossed back and forth, and I let it go on for a little while until I noticed Angel getting overwhelmed. "Alright, quiet down." Not one peep after I uttered those words.

Reaching over, I pulled Angel against me, inhaling her sweet scent with a deep breath. It didn't smell like she wore any perfume, but she had a clean scent to her, like fresh water with a hint of citrus, a nice fresh breeze. It was so refreshing and nostalgic. "Rest, Angel, you deserve it."

Angel gave me a faint moan in return before settling against me, making me suck in a deep breath as I felt my body awaken. I've longed to hold her in my arms, have her body against mine. Ever since she saved me that night, I haven't been able to get her out of my mind.

The thought of tracking her down had occurred to me, and it wouldn't have been hard given how I knew her name and her profession. Yet, I refrained from it. She was too kind when I met her, there was no way I could drag her into my world. I might be selfish and driven, always getting what I wanted no matter what, but I couldn't bring myself to steal her away for myself. She was an angel, and I the devil.

So, it was much to my surprise when I saw her being dragged out earlier. Granted, I was angry at the sight of her in such a state, but beyond that, I was happy to see her again. I just took it as a sign from the universe we were supposed to meet again. I wasn't going to complain about this marriage, forced or not. I volunteered for it, so I really can't complain. But only because it was to Angel.

Once I was sure Angel was out, I began to speak again. "I'm going to drop Angel off first then head to the club. Stepan, I need you to go see what the problem at the High Wind Casino is about. Lev, there's some trouble with one of our apartment complexes, seems like the 99th Street Gang is trying to take it from us. So, teach them a lesson, but you know the rules, Lev." I paused for a moment to glance at him from my phone.

With a roll of his eyes, he looked at me like a child whose fun got spoiled. "Yeah, yeah, just scare them, no children or women or anyone innocent, just broken bones, no lethal shots unless necessary, keep damage to a minimum, yeah, yeah, I got the spiel at this point." Lev grumbled with a wave of his hand.

Nodding my head in response, I quickly sent him the address before addressing the twins. "Alexei, you're going home. Arseny, I'll drop you off at Guilty to handle business there."

"Oh good, thought you were going to send me somewhere, not that I would argue with that, it's just I've another shift and am on call tomorrow." Alexei gave a sigh of relief as he sat back in his seat.

Alexei was the least involved with the family business. He never was interested much with it growing up, always just sticking around because of us. It's why we always cut him the most slack and never involved him unless we thought it was necessary or unless he demanded to come.

I would never force any of my brothers to be involved with the family business. I knew how dangerous and stressful this life could be. So, I always gave my brothers the option to partake in the bratva life or not. They've all made their choices at this point, but I always let them know they always have an out if they choose so.

Another small moment passed before some more words filled the car. "Who would have thought that you'd end up marrying the hot nurse that patched ya up." Arseny chuckled and patted my shoulder. "Lucky bastard."

"Wait, she's the one who saved you from that car crash?" Stepan asked with a surprised look, bouncing his eyes over to Angel for a split second before returning them to me. "Nah, no way she dragged your fat ass out of that car by herself." His playful laugh filled the car, making most of us smile and chuckle in response. I still found it hard to believe she dragged me out as well.

Giving out a small hum, I nodded my head in response as I held her tightly against me. I finally had her, and there was no way in hell I would let her go.

"Damn, you are one lucky bastard getting your little guardian angel." Lev grumbled, slumping in his seat a little.

Damn right I am.

My sweet angel, all mine.

Chapter 7

Angel

"Ugh... My fucking head..." Groaning, I sat up in my bed.

Wait.

I could feel the panic set in when I realized this wasn't *my* bed. It was too soft, the sheets too comforting and warm, and *that* intoxicating scent.

Panicked, I scrambled out of the bed and looked around at my surroundings. "What the..."

It took a few moments for my mind to be set straight as my adrenaline died down. Then, the memories of last night flooded in like a broken dam. "Fucking hell." And here I thought it was some weird, sick dream.

Groaning softly, I ran a hand through my flattened bed hair to fluff it out some while walking over to the dresser in the room. Then, I started opening the drawers one by one. The drawers were filled with tee shirts, socks, boxers, shorts, and sweatpants. Closing the drawers, I went over to the walk-in closet that—no surprise—was filled with expensive suits, shoes, ties, slacks, and button up shirts. Now, the emptiness of one side of the closet did surprise me. Strangely, half the drawers of the large dresser were empty as well.

Humming softly to myself, I left the closet, shutting the door behind me before going back over to the dresser and pulling out a white t-shirt from it and throwing it on. No way in hell was I going to march out of this room in my undies.

Carefully, I opened the room door and peered my head out to check the area first, but the sight of the two guards at the door stopped my head from turning. "Uhh hello..."

"Hello Mrs. Volkov." One of them greeted me back with a curt nod of his head.

The sound of it made me wince a little, serving as a stark reminder of last night's events. "Please, Angel is fine." Being called Mrs. Volkov sounded too foreign, and just being called miss or missus in general made me feel old when I was only twenty-four. Also, I did not agree to change my last name from what I remembered.

"If that is what you wish, Miss Angel. I am Benjamin, and this is my partner," he gestures to the man on the other side of the door frame, "Tim. We're assigned as your personal guards by Mister Nikolai."

Sighing, I pinch the bridge of my nose to hold back my tongue. I wanted to dismiss them, tell them I didn't need them because I really didn't. I could take care of myself just fine, but I knew it would be useless to argue with them. If Nikolai assigned them to me then they weren't going to leave me alone unless he told them otherwise. I could argue with Nikolai about this later, after I find him.

"Could you two lead me to Nikolai, please." We had a lot to talk about. A lot.

"Yes, this way Miss," Benjamin said, gesturing for me to go ahead of him.

Tim led the way with Benjamin covering the back, and me in the middle.

The huge hallway was lined with many doors on one side while the other were just windows. From the looks of it, it seemed like we were on the second floor, or maybe a third judging from the distance to the ground, but I couldn't be sure.

Upon exiting the hallway to a grand staircase, I could see the hall I came out of was one of few on the second floor.

Just how huge is this place?

I could count four long and large hallways including the one I came from, and I could see the other hallways were lined on both sides with doors and skylines.

Following the guards, I continued down the stairs into a foyer before turning away from the front door to a spacious living area where all the brothers, minus one, were spread around the area. One of them stood by the window while two of them were seated at different couches. Then the man I was looking for, my *husband*, was seated in a black leather armchair.

The four of them stopped their conversation the moment my presence was noticed, all of them giving me friendly—or what appeared to be—smiles. "Angel, how are you feeling?" Nikolai asked as he beckoned me over with his hand.

Chewing my bottom lip, I cautiously walked over, shivering a bit at the way he eyed me hungrily. "I didn't have anything else to put on... So sorry for borrowing whoever's shirt this is." I assumed it was Nikolai's because why would I wake up in anyone else's room.

"You can wear my shirts whenever you want Angel." His deep voice came out low as he wrapped his arm around my waist and brought me close to him.

"How long was I out? What time is it? What day is it? Where am I?" It was obvious it was daytime from the brightness shining through the huge windows of the living area.

As I remained standing next to him, I kept my curious and wary eyes trained on him. "Just a few hours, you have been asleep ever since the car last night. It's only a little past 9 AM right now on Friday, August tenth. You're at the Volkov Estate." He answered calmly while rubbing my waist with his thumb.

Letting out a deep breath, I calmed myself a little. "Any chance you can ditch the guards on me? I don't need them." It was a long shot, but I had to try.

"So, you can run away? Get your nose into things you shouldn't and report back to your side?" One of the brothers, Lev, I think his name was, spoke up. He had a rugged appearance, shorter than Nikolai but with a wider, more muscular build, and scars on his forearms visible through his black button-up shirt with sleeves rolled up to the elbow. He also had a nasty scar running from his hairline down past his lips.

"I'm not going to run away, as tempting as it is. I value my father's life too much to risk it. And you don't have to worry about me sharing information with my stepmother; she's the last person I want to inform unless it's about her children suffering a horrible death. Like I said last night, you don't have to question my loyalty to any of you. Unconventional marriage or not, it's a done deal. Unless Nikolai gives me a reason to think otherwise, I'm loyal to him." The enemy of my enemy is my friend at the very least.

Once again, at least it was Nikolai I would be stuck with until the end of time, so it couldn't be too bad. So far, he didn't seem like a domestic abuser, but if he did turn out that way then I'd handle him myself. I might not have known him long, or at all, but I got a sense he was a good man. Well, as good of a man as a man can be in this profession.

"Wait, stepmother?" Stepan questioned. At least I could tell him apart from the others easily because his hair was the lightest amongst the brothers, almost blonde.

"Yes, stepmother. Honestly, you guys should have said no to the deal unless it was one of her actual daughters being promised." Using me as a bargaining chip would be her undoing, I would make sure of it.

I didn't even correct them last night when I saw they had the wrong name down for me. Qing wasn't my last name, it never was. My mother wanted me to be kept out of my father's business, so they had both agreed I would take on my mother's maiden name instead. So, technically, the marriage could be considered null and void if I argued enough.

"So, this truce is moot then? You're just a useless body?" Lev sneered, walking away from the window and stalking towards me with angry eyes.

Clicking my tongue out of annoyance, I glared at him and took a step towards him. I wasn't afraid of him, even if he was more than twice my size. One well-placed strike and he would be out for the count. "Call me a useless body again and you'll wish you'd never did. The truce is not nulled or anything, it's rocky at best though because I'm not her legitimate daughter, so she had no right to do what she did. The truce is intact because I am the heiress to my father's empire, and I still hold my title as temporary head of the triad in my father's absence."

"Isn't Lady Qing the one in charge while your father is unable?" Stepan questioned with wary eyes.

"Only because I let her, but I'm still technically the right head currently on my father's orders. As much as I don't want to be head in my father's absence, I rather grit my teeth and stave through it than give it all over to my stepmother. If she had full control, then this city would be on fire. Only reason why half the shit she does goes through is because she's bought most of the men's loyalties and employed her own. I've stopped what I can, but it's getting hard to keep a hold of things when barely a quarter of the men there are still truly loyal to me." Which is why I started to try and tear down her twisted empire before it can fully bloom.

If there was any indication it was all salvageable then I would have done so in order to carry out my father's wishes of succeeding his mystery successor—after figuring out who the fuck it was. Unfortunately, with how things were going, it seemed more beneficial to burn everything to the ground. I didn't want my father's successor to take over with the number of dishonest members there were. Even if we did do some house cleaning, the few left would leave the triad more vulnerable than a newborn child to a pack of hungry wolves.

"She's also going to keep the truce up until she can effectively find a way to get rid of me and my father. As of now, if my father dies, I am to take up the mantle of Dragon Head officially. She also can't kill me right now because nearly all of my father's assets are in my name or to be given to me upon his death. So, she's kind of stuck in a tough spot right now, which is why I think she'll keep up the truce until she can figure out some other twisted plan to get her nasty claws into everything." She needed this truce to ensure the Volkovs won't try a takeover, that's my sense of this whole arrangement.

If the Volkovs made a move, the triad would be doomed to fall to their mercy. Lady Qing would lose everything. I hated to admit it, but she was a conniving and smart bitch when it came to getting what she wanted.

"Either way, I'm not going to run, doubt I'd get very far before I get my ass hauled back here and get put in lockdown. I ain't going to stick my nose in anything and report to whoever. Why the hell would I want to tear down my own husband's empire? I'm not going to do any wrong to or by Nikolai." Divorce was an option in the future possibly, but who knows, maybe this will work out without blowing up in my face. So, until death do us part, or divorce do us part. I intend on being by Nikolai's side through everything and do right by him.

"Besides it being a trust issue, which you can understand, they are also for your protection, Angel. I know you can handle yourself, last night being a very clear example, but no one here goes anywhere without at least one guard. You're going to have a lot more enemies once word gets out that you are my wife, Angel. So, no, the guards stay, no compromise on that." The seriousness of Nikolai's voice made it clear to me that this was one of those things where compromise would never happen. His word was law on this matter.

Groaning out of annoyance, I turned my head towards Nikolai. "So what? They're just going to follow me around the hospital too?" Because it wouldn't fly one bit. "I'm not going to give up my job just because I'm married to you now. If you think that I'm going to sit pretty at home and play housewife, then you've got another thing coming for you bucko." He won't compromise on the guards, and I won't ever compromise on my job because God knows it's the only thing that keeps me sane.

"I figured a little firecracker like you wouldn't be the housewife type. You can keep your job, for now, the guards will stay outside unless told otherwise by you or me or any of my brothers." Well, it seems like that was it. I won't argue or try to argue with him on the matter since it wasn't too bad of a solution.

Honestly, I should be used to having guards around since I've had them most of my life growing up, but I convinced my father to drop them during late high school and have gone without one ever since. Besides, my friends who hung around me were as good as any guard, and at least they were around my age and were my friends.

"Alright, thank you." I was more than willing to take any slack he was willing to give me.

"Oh, a few people have been blowing up your phone since an hour ago." Arseny spoke up after a moment of silence, fishing out a phone from his pocket. "Asshole 1, Asshole 2, and Best Bitch. Interesting people you got." He teased me with a snicker as I snatched my phone from him with a soft glare. "Wonder what my name in your phone is gonna be."

"It's going to be Asshole 3 if you don't shut up." I grumbled as I watched my phone light up with another call.

"Go on, answer it, on speakerphone," Nikolai said in a way as if he gave me permission to answer my own calls. "Whatever you say to them you can say to us."

As much as I wanted to argue with him, I had to earn their trust, show them I could be trusted. So, scowling softly, I answered the call. "What?" I answered bluntly in an unamused voice.

"Oh my god, finally! We thought we were going to have to fish for your body at the bottom of the Garth River at this rate! Hold on, let me patch in Hanna, she's been trying to get ahold of you too. I already got Bao here with me, so give me a moment." The familiar voice of my brother soothed me a bit. At least I've got some close people out there who cared about me enough.

Soon, a soft beep could be heard as my other friend joined in on the call. "She's alive! Man, getting hitched without inviting us? Rude. But seriously, it's good to hear your voice Ange. You have no idea how worried I was last night. Sorry you have to be in this situation. If we'd figured out what she was trying to do sooner, then we could have warned you and come up with some plan. Guess we're just getting a little too careless with her." A woman's voice could be heard on the other line now.

"Oh please, I'm pretty sure she wouldn't have had any problem if she knew who she was going to marry anyways. Hey, at least now you get your handsome hunk. Tell me, is his ass as nice as the pictures we saw?" Greg teased with a snicker, making my face pale with embarrassment.

"Oh my god shut the fuck up Greg." I wanted nothing more than to chuck my phone into oblivion and lock myself in a closet to hide my embarrassment and from everyone who snickered and smirked at me teasingly. Even my own husband seemed to be enjoying it a bit too much.

"What? You never shut up about him for weeks! 'Oh, maybe I should have pretended he needed CPR and given him mouth to mouth, bet he would have tasted manly as fuck.' Or what was the other thing you said uhhhh..." I could hear Greg drag on a little.

Fucking kill me right now God, and save me from this embarrassment!

Groaning, I started to sink down to the ground, but I didn't get far before a pair of strong hands grabbed me and pulled me backwards. Looking back, I could see Nikolai's smirking face, making my blood rush more with embarrassment and lustful want when I realized he pulled me into his lap, giving me a good opportunity to feel what he had going on under his pants.

"Oh! Wasn't it something about cutting his pants off?" My other friend, Bao, chimed in.

"Oh yeah! Should have pretended that you needed a better look to shred through those pants so that you could—"

"Shut the fuck up! Moving on!" I didn't let Greg finish his sentence because I was damn sure I would never be able to face any of them in this room ever again if he did.

"Oh no, we're not moving on from this girly. You go from single to being married to one of California's hottest damn bachelors overnight! Who you were practically drooling over when we were doing research. Man, why can't I get myself a hot man like that? Maybe I should start dragging people out of cars too." I could hear the pout and perfectly picture it on Hanna's face.

"Oh please, you already do pull people out of cars, the only difference is you beat the shit out of them while little miss sexy nurse over here saves them." Bao laughed.

"Well, I never get anyone hot to drag out, they're all slimeballs that deserve it." Hanna grumbled.

"Considering how they're your targets, when are they ever going to be hot and good enough for you? I mean, do you really want to go out with any of the people I send you after girl?" I groaned, pinching the bridge of my nose.

"I mean, you could try to put in a good word for me with one of your new brothers in laws, yeah? I mean, come on, help a sister out girl. You know how I like 'em." Hanna snickered.

"Oh my God kill me now. I'm going to go crawl into The Catacombs and die after this call. Just what the fuck do you guys want? Why the hell are you calling? And don't say it's to check up on me and mister handsome." Oh god, did I really say that last part out loud? I mean, I have to keep things up so they don't think something is up. But fuck me for my slip up.

"Well, half of it is us wanting to know that you're alive and well. Also, how mister handsome is, because, well, come on, who would have thought that you'd be the first of us to get married, much less to one of the hottest men in the state? The heavens really answered your damn prayers girl." Bao laughed softly, making me groan internally.

"In all seriousness though, how are you? I mean, a forced marriage with a Bratva member? The head, nonetheless. That bitch really out did herself this time with this stunt of hers. What is she even hoping to achieve with this? We all know she's been eyeing their territory for a while, so a peace treaty doesn't make any sense." Greg's tone took a serious edge to it, changing the mood of everyone on the call and in the room.

Sighing, I shook my head softly while running a hand through my long locks. "I don't know, I really don't. She has something planned though, and I don't like the feeling I'm getting. That bitch aside, I'm fine, really, just adjusting. Nikolai isn't that bad, so far." I've only interacted with him for not even an hour before knocking out in the car last night, and not like I've done much before the phone call either.

"Have you consummated the marriage yet?" Hanna's voice had an edge to it, and I knew she had to be smirking right now.

"Oh please, why even put it nicely? Did you fuck the dude yet?" Bao laughed loudly, followed by a loud smack, probably from Greg.

"Come on girl! I need to know the deets! You know how boring my bed has been of late! I need some juicy excitement! Come on, spill the beans! Was he good? Oh, who am I kidding, a man like him is probably amazing. How big was he?" Hanna giggled, sounding a little too interested in my nonexistent sex life with Nikolai—well, nonexistent for now.

"Stroke his ego more, why don't you." I grumbled, hiding my face in my hand, not wanting to face Nikolai or his brothers right now who were a little too closely gathered around me.

"Nah, stroking him is your job girl." Hanna laughed, making me groan more in embarrassment.

"You get drugged with some ketamine, go on an adrenaline rush, then let me know if you want to fuck after that. I've been out since last night." I wasn't one hundred percent better just yet, but a lot better than last night after everything died down.

"Are you going to tell him?" Greg asked, sending everyone on the call and in the room into a still silence.

"About?" There was a lot to tell Nikolai about, so Greg needed to be more specific.

"Our dear old stepmother of course, and how much of a bitch she is, and what your plans are for her and the triad." Greg specified.

Well, I had to now since they all heard it. Granted, I planned to tell them, eventually. "He's my husband, of course I'm going to tell him. Just wanted to settle a little more before telling him. Not like it's the best first conversation to have on day one or two of my marriage. Besides, I'm pretty sure he trusts her as much as I do, which is none. Also, I don't know what to do now. Before this mess it was clear, clean up loose ends, stir a shit ton of trouble for her, watch it all burn around her, and tear it all down. Now though..."

"Hey, it'd be a great honeymoon present! Well, besides you in some nice red lace, or whatever his favorite color is. I mean, think about it, merging the triad to him would be the best thing probably. Not like he's some tyrant from what I've seen and what my sources have told me, so it'd be better to just hand it over to him and let him expand rather than leaving it open for anyone's grab. Last thing we need is another Lady Qing to stake her claim to a third of Nespin." Hanna might seem like an airhead sometimes, but that's the image she gives; she's quite smart at the right times.

"That or I was thinking about going with *Ba's* original plan of succeeding his choice to head of the triad. We all know they'd run things right like how *Ba* wanted. Plus, they would want to keep the treaty and who knows, maybe form an alliance like *Ba* wanted too." I'd rather get rid of it all so I wouldn't have any ties left to that part of my life, give everyone under the triad's thumb some peace.

"Well, whatever you decide, you know we'll always have your back." Bao reminded me.

"Thanks, I know you guys will always have my back. Family forever. Either way, anything new?" Maybe some good news will help me forget the embarrassment I am suffering.

"Unfortunately, no. Still working the leads we got right now, and nada. Sorry sis." Greg replied with a defeated sigh.

"We might have to force our hands more too. I think Lady Qing is starting to tie up loose ends on her side. If we aren't fast enough then we're not going to have anything." Hanna sighed as well. "I overheard her men saying something about clearing out a warehouse in the next week or so, as in completely clear it and trash it to the ground."

"Shit... Get a jump on that warehouse then and report back to me when you get something, anything. Keep me updated." I gritted my teeth and growled softly out of anger.

"We will, you take care in the meantime too. Stay safe. And sis, if he lays a hand on you, I'll let him have it. I don't care if he's head honcho, you're still my little sister, and it's my job to beat the shit out of anyone who lays a hand on you," Greg said.

Laughing softly, I smiled to myself as I let my finger hover over the end button on the screen. "I appreciate the gesture Greg, but we all know that's bullshit." Nikolai could probably drop kick my half-brother a whole football field without breaking a sweat.

"Ha ha, well, I gotta go, shift is gonna start soon and the chief has been breathing down my neck about *that* shooting. Love ya sis. Good luck and stay safe," Greg said with a long sigh.

"Well, I'll continue digging on my end. Good luck and stay safe ya'll," Bao said with a sigh.

"I got an idiot to beat up then I'll look further into the warehouse business. Good luck and stay safe everyone." Hanna sounded a little too excited with the first bit, but that was no surprise to me.

"Good luck. Stay safe." I sighed softly before hanging up the call.

Chapter 8
Nikolai

Well, it would seem my little Angel has a lot she still has to spill.

Smirking, I tightened my arm around her waist, pulling her flush against me. "If you wanted a taste then all you had to do was beg like a good girl." I whispered deeply into her ear, making her shiver against me.

My brothers weren't going to let this opportunity pass either. "Handsome hunk? Do you like our dear Kolya more than you're letting on little Angel?" Arseny teased with a grin and snicker.

"Can you all pretend the last half an hour didn't happen? Just erase it from your memory, forever?" Angel groaned as she shrunk into me, trying to hide away from my brothers.

"And give up all that ammunition? Even Kolya found it amusing, and it's rare for him to find things amusing these days." Arseny laughed softly, giving me a pat on the shoulder.

It's true, I did find her phone call amusing. I couldn't hold back my smirk and chuckles the more embarrassed she got with each teasing comment from her friends. It was a good call to make her take it on speaker, although it was a test on her end to see if she could be trusted, which she passed.

Well, I guess I should save my poor little wife and save some of her dignity. "Alright, give her a break all of you. Pretty sure you all have

"

other things to attend to, so go. I'd like to have a moment alone with my wife." I dismissed the others with a stern look.

My wife.

Those two words were so foreign to me. I never thought I'd say such words in my life. As strange as they are, they flowed off my tongue like nectar.

My Angel.

My wife.

The thought of it felt just as natural as breathing.

Leaning onto the arm of the chair, I propped myself up on an elbow while reaching up with the arm I had around her waist and gripping her face, forcing her to look at me. "Let's play a game."

"I'd rather not, thank you." She replied shyly while trying to move her head away.

Gripping her face harder, I brought her closer until we were a mere inch apart. "It wasn't a question or a suggestion. So, either you ask the first question, or I do. Which will it be, Angel?"

My thumb lightly brushes across her bottom lip, making her tremble as she lets out a shaky breath. Her rosy pink lips were so soft, so kissable. It would take less than a second to press them against mine and devour her. A part of me was tempted. I could only wonder if she'll taste as good as she smells as I held my temptations at bay.

"Why are you hard?" She asks shakily, placing a hand on my chest before twisting her body around so she sat across my lap comfortably.

Chuckling softly, I shake my head, "That's your first question?"

The look of realization hit her, and I couldn't help but chuckle more. "I'm sorry, I didn't think I said that out loud." The way her face flushed red was so adorable. It amused me to watch her squirm on the phone earlier. The way she tried to hide herself into me or with her hands as her friends blurted out some rather interesting, and embarrassing, things was rather cute.

"Why would I not be hard seeing my sexy wife in nothing but my shirt and having her in my lap? You know, I haven't been able to get you fully out of my mind ever since that night." I admitted as I slowly trailed my hand down the side of her face, neck, and body to her waist, resting it just on the curve of her hip. How I've longed to settle my hand on her body like this. I could only imagine the feel of her delicate skin in my dreams, the ones where I'd have her pinned under me at my mercy.

"You think I'm sexy?" Her voice came out breathy as she let her eyes wander my body, a small smile gracing her face.

"This isn't how the game is supposed to go, Angel." I chuckled deeply as I reached out with my other hand and twirled a lock of her hair around my finger. "But, since I'm feeling generous right now, I'll give you a pass, this time. But yes, I do find you sexy, from your looks to your skills. You have no idea how impressed and amazed I was watching you last night. I love a capable woman."

The thought of sparring a few rounds with her to get our adrenaline pumping before getting down and dirty while in our highs was a riveting thought that made my cock ache more in my pants.

"You know, you didn't kiss the bride last night." She teased in a sultry voice, leaning in just enough to where our lips were just a thread apart.

"Do you think you've earned it?" I growled softly, letting my hand slip into her hair and fisting it to keep her head still just in case she tried to push forward to seal the deal.

"Yes, I've been good so far." She pouted, making me chuckle deeply.

"So far? Were you planning on misbehaving later on?" I gave her hair a firm tug, pulling her head back to expose her lovely neck to me fully.

"No, sir." Angel trembled with her words when I leaned in and ghosted my lips along the length of her neck.

Sir.

I've been addressed that many times, but coming from her gave the title a whole new feeling. I could feel my cock throbbing painfully in the confines of my pants when she said it. "When we're alone or in bed, you're going to address me as that from now on, got it?" Just the mere thought of her uttering the word made my chest swell with pride and gave me a rush of pleasure straight down to my member.

Shuddering, she gripped the front of my shirt tightly in her balled up fists. "Yes, sir." She moaned softly.

Fuck, she would be my ruin, and I was more than fine with that. "If you behave like a good girl for the rest of the day, then you can get all of this," I paused for a brief second to thrust my hip up against her clothed sex, gritting my teeth together to suppress my groan when I felt her heat, "Tonight."

Pouting, Angel pressed herself down against me, making me suck in a sharp breath. "But I need you now, please, sir." She whimpered needily while not letting up with her gyrating hips. My little vixen knew how to play the game.

Growling deeply, I let go of her hair so I could use both hands to grab at her hips, stopping her movements and holding her firmly against me. "No, if I take you now then I'm not stopping until well into the night, and we have things to talk about and do. So, behave, and I'll reward you well tonight. If not, well, consequences and punishments are there for a reason, Angel."

A part of me hoped she would give me a damn good reason to bend her over and spank her. I've wanted nothing more than to grip her plump ass cheeks and spank them red when I saw her from behind the first night. If she'd let me then I'd love to take it a step further and use my belt, leaving nice welts she could feel for hours.

With careful eyes, I watched her torn face as she seemed to debate with herself on what to do or how to respond. A few seconds go by before her lips stick out in a pout as she looks at me defeatedly. "Fine." One stern look was all she needed to correct herself. "Yes, sir."

Smirking triumphantly, I leaned in and placed a kiss on her cheek. "Good girl." My grip on her hips tightened when I felt her shiver at my praise. Breathing deeply, I leaned back fully in the armchair, hands still on her hips. "Now, let's start this game again. Question, Angel."

I watched her take a deep breath while she shifted in my lap until she straddled and faced me fully. "Why did you choose yourself? Why not one of your brothers? I mean, I'm not complaining, I'm happy that it's someone I'm barely familiar with, but you are the head of the

Bratva, surely you have other use for your time and energy on other matters than a wife."

"True, I do have a lot on my plate, but I stepped up because it was you. You have plagued too many of my nights, and I held myself back so much from seeking you out and trying to make you mine. I saw it as a sign from the heavens when you were basically delivered to my feet last night. You are mine to have Angel, only mine. I let you fly away before, but now that I have you in my grasp again, even God can't save you from me now." No one can take her away from me. This beautiful little thing was mine to have and hold for all of eternity.

Smirking softly, I let my eyes take in her delicate face, wanting to burn it into my mind so even when I closed my eyes, I would be able to picture her perfectly. I couldn't wait to watch her pretty face twist with pleasure tonight and every night after.

Fuck, maybe I shouldn't have stopped myself. She begged me to take her, yet my stupid self didn't take that opportunity. So, what if I had important business to attend to? Nothing should be more important than giving my wife the best pleasures of her life with me buried deep in her hot cunt.

"Sir, Nikolai, it's your turn." Her soft voice tore me away from my thoughts before they got too dirty.

"Kolya, only people who aren't family call me Nikolai, and you're family now. Though, I much prefer 'sir' from you." I corrected her with a playful smirk.

"Kolya... Well, that answers one of my questions that I was going to ask. If I address you as 'sir' then we're going to get nothing done, so Kolya it'll be. Well, either way, it's your turn for a question, and you were just kind of staring." Angel replied with a soft giggle.

Honestly, I'm not sure if my name was any better coming from her lips. Hearing it didn't bring out that dominant side of me much, but it did bring out a passionate side I didn't think existed. A passionate yet possessive side; the one that got jealous and angry at the mere thought of any other pair of hands on her body that weren't mine.

Chuckling softly, "Not starring, admiring." I corrected her while running a hand up her side into her hair. I don't think I'll ever get enough of her black locks. They were so smooth and silky. I could probably spend a good portion of my day running my fingers through them while having her in my lap. "But you're right, it is my turn." I had to take a moment to think of what to ask her first. "Last night, what was the exchange that you had with Lady Qing?"

"Oh, that? I basically told her that I was going to walk out of there and she wasn't going to do shit. Reminded her to not forget her place too. Then she pulled the father card, which is how she even got an ounce of compliance from me. At least the marriage was to you, if not then I would have had to make myself a widow at twenty-four. It was more so a personal exchange, so don't worry, nothing scheming or anything." Angel's assuring smile put me at ease a little along with those soft eyes of hers. "I can promise you, swear to you on my life and my father's, that I will never wrong you Kolya. You will never have to question my loyalty or worry about me betraying or playing spy for the other side. I will always be truthful to you no matter what, I swear to it."

I'm not one who trusts people easily, trust would only get me easily killed in my line of work. "I trust you and will hold you to it. You and I both know that in this line of work, there are no such things as second chances. Even if you are my wife, if you ever betray me in any way."

I didn't need to finish the rest of that last sentence for her to respond to me with a firm nod. "I understand, and the same goes for you." It was the life we were born into, unfortunately. "Why didn't you reach out to me sooner?"

Chuckling softly, I moved my hand from her hair to cup her face, stroking her cheek softly with my thumb. "Believe it or not, I wasn't a selfish bastard for once and kept away from you for both our sakes. You seemed too good, too innocent, to drag into my life. Also, I knew that having you around would just be a huge distraction for me, give my enemies more of a means to get at me. Guess all that can't be helped now, not that I mind."

"I'm a big girl, I can handle myself, and last night should have been a good indicator as to what I can be capable of. Thank you for not being a selfish prick, even though I wish you had been." Angel chuckled softly as she started to play with the collar of my shirt.

"I was really hoping that you would call in the favor, or at least call in to try and spark something." I wasn't going to lie to myself or her about that fact. I remember staring at my phone on some nights, hoping for it to pop up some strange number I didn't recognize and to have her voice be on the other end.

"I actually thought about it, but after finding out that you were involved with the bratva, I knew I couldn't unless it was truly an emergency. I already kept myself uninvolved with the crime world and mafias in general. So, no way in hell was I going to get tangled with a bratva member, no matter how hot and tempting he may be." Her reddened cheeks didn't go unnoticed, even if she did try to hide her face by turning away.

Chuckling, I grasped her chin and turned her head back towards me. "How much truth was in your friends' words?" Did she have it bad for me as I did for her? Could she feel the fire of lust every time she laid her eyes on me?

Even right now, all I wanted to do was rip my shirt off her and lay claim to her, fuck her like a rabid beast until she was broken, until I was more than satisfied before taking the time to admire her naked beauty. Even if she had almost nothing on last night, I worried too much about her well-being to ogle her like a horny teenage boy.

"I am still waiting for your answer Angel." I reminded her with a smirk as I watched her squirm in her spot.

Pouting, she glared at me softly in a playful manner before answering, "All of it..." She was embarrassed, and it was adorable with how red her face got. "But only because it's true, even the articles I read through praised your physique and charming personality, and I'm not blind to deny the truth."

"Even the stuff about mouth to mouth and cutting my pants off?" I teased with a chuckle, watching her face get more heated.

"H-hey! That's more than one question mister!" It would seem like my little angel caught her footing again.

"Caught me." I hoped I could slip it past her with her embarrassment, but she was still sharp enough to push through.

"What do you usually deal in? I should probably get an idea if I'm going to be involved as your wife." Guess she started to feel a little bolder.

"The typical stuff that I'm sure you are used to. Besides, you of all people know that empires like ours aren't built on clean money or by decent means. It'll be easier to tell you what we don't partake in, which is forced prostitution and human trafficking. I abhor such things and anyone who partakes in such activities. Other than that, we have our hands in a little of everything." Though there were some things that netted us more profit than others, we didn't want to close off any avenue unless it proved too risky.

Aside from the family business, my brothers and I did have legitimate business that didn't serve as fronts. If it ever came to the point where we had to shut down the family business indefinitely, which I will never see happening, then at the very least we had our own businesses to fall back on. If we were careful, which we were overly so, then we had nothing to worry about.

"What skills are you going to bring to the table?" I wanted to glance at her strengths and weaknesses, see what use she would have for the family business if she was going to partake.

"Well, I'm a nurse, so I'm usually patching my own men up. Surprisingly I'm good with interrogation, even though I hate getting my hands dirty most of the time. I'm a good leader since I've been taught to be one growing up." I feel as if she wasn't giving herself more credit for what she can do.

Humble. I like it.

With a small hum and tilt of her head, she asked in a curious voice, "Are you going to let me become involved?"

"Only if you wish, and even then, it's up to you on how much you want to be involved. Just because you are my wife doesn't mean I am going to force you to partake if you do not wish. I'm not the kind of person who forces these things upon people. All my brothers, all my men, are all here of their own volition. I'm also not going to keep you completely shut out and oblivious either." Forcing my hand only meant a bigger headache and less trustworthy people. If I had my own men hating me then the chances of them turning against me or questioning my authority would increase significantly.

I was forced into this life, and it was by my own will that I chose to stay and run the Volkov Bratva after my father's demise. I could have ended it all, but I saw an opportunity to make the shitshow my father created better. I never forced any of my brothers to work with me either, they wanted to support me because I'm their brother, which is why some of them aren't as involved as others.

"You seem to care for your father a lot, but it's obvious that you'd rather watch the devil drag your stepmother down to hell. Why?" Was this Lady Qing really that bad? Or was it some personal grudge between stepdaughter and stepmother?

Sighing softly, Angel leaned in and settled her head on my shoulder. "Besides her being a total bitch?" She forced a dry chuckle out as she settled more against me.

"There's no love lost between us. She's hated me ever since I could remember, way before becoming my father's wife after my mother's accident. To be fair, I always hated her too, just a gut feeling when I was younger, but as I grew, I put reason to the hatred. She's a narcissistic, greedy, arrogant, and twisted bitch. She's with my father for the power of her position and his money, his empire. My father, the way he ran things, there were things that were off limits to him when it came to how we got our means, but she didn't care about it. She had been dabbling in everything my father stood against for years, and by the time we figured things out, she struck us. She's the reason my father's health tanked, because of the stress and bullshit she placed on him. She's the reason behind the deaths of so many innocent people. She's the reason why I'm so guarded." A heavy sigh followed the end of her words.

I could hear the subtle crack in her voice, even if she tried to hide it. No doubt there was something more and deeper—a sore subject. Sensing she was upset made me frown as I wrapped my arms around her fully and held her tightly. As much as I wanted to pry, this wasn't the moment. "You're giving her her dues." I stated is a low voice as I stroked her hair.

"Her long overdue dues, yes. I hate that I want to though. I shouldn't be stooping to her level, I should take the higher road. I mean, would I be any better than her if I went as low as her?" I could feel her conflict as she squirmed in my arms.

Breathing in deeply, I fisted her hair and tilted her head back. "You and I both know there's no such thing as a higher road in this life. We're already damned to hell, so might as well make the trip worth it."

Slowly, her soft features twisted with her little frown. "You're not going to have mistresses or other women, are you?" Her worried voice tugged a little at my heart.

"No. I'm not the kind of man who indulges in such things. I have seen how my mother suffered with my father and his indiscretions, and I was taught better by my mother. You are the only woman that is going to be in my life from here on out." I assured her with a firm voice and look. The marriage may be a business transaction of sorts, but I still agreed to take her when I could have refused. I didn't want or need anyone else in my life but Angel.

She looked at me for a moment, the broken look in her eyes shifting to one of need. "Kiss me, please." Those pleading eyes paired with her whispery voice nearly broke my resolve.

"Please, I need to feel your lips on mine Kolya, I need to know how my husband tastes, just a little." She continued to beg, leaning up until our lips were nearly touching.

Growling softly, I pulled at her hair more, moving her head back so her neck was exposed to me. "I already told you, tonight." I breathed heavily against her neck as I ran my teeth down the length of it, making her shudder and whimper.

"I can't wait until tonight, please, just a small taste, please, sir, please." She was persistent, I'd give her that.

Too bad she wasn't in charge, but who am I to deny my sweet wife such a request?

"On your knees." I could feel my low voice rumbling against her neck before my teeth sank into her supple skin, making her squeak and jump.

"What?" She looked as stunned as she sounded, which I found very adorable and amusing.

Chuckling deeply, I pulled back and looked deeply into her eyes. She had a knowing look with a mix of denial. She was a smart girl, I'm sure she knew what I hinted at but didn't want to accept it. "I don't like to repeat myself Angel, but I'll forgive you this time. Now, on your knees."

Chapter 9

Angel

I THOUGHT I MISHEARD in my lustful haze, but his deep voice was real enough.

Swallowing the lump in my throat, I whimpered softly when he gave my hair a firm tug towards the floor. "Wait, but."

The growl rumbling from his chest made me shiver with delight as my pussy clenched uncontrollably. "I'll indulge you this one time. You said you wanted a taste, so that's what I am going to give you." He gave me no room to argue as he pushed me off his lap and forced me to the floor between his legs.

With bated breath, I watched as he worked his zipper down with his free hand, still keeping a firm grip at the base of hair with his other. "Oh fuck." The thought slipped my tongue the moment I saw his monstrosity appear from the depths of his pants.

Shit. All I wanted was a kiss, so how did I find myself on my knees before his cock?

Fuck he's huge.

I couldn't help but admire him with hungry eyes as I reached out to grasp him, only to be stopped short by a grab to my wrist by his free hand.

Pouting, I looked up at Nikolai with confused and pleading eyes. I attempted to make another grab at him, only for him to grasp that wrist into his large hand too. "I might be indulging your need for a taste of me, but that's where it ends. We are doing this my way, and I don't remember saying you could touch. Now, behave."

Before I could protest, he pulled me forward until the tip of his swollen length pressed against my soft lips, where the bead of his pre-cum smeared against them. Shivering with pleasure, I let my wanton eyes drift to his blue orbs as I slid my tongue out and licked his swollen tip teasingly.

Maybe I shouldn't have begged him. My core ached painfully with the need for him to fill me with his girthy member. Scratch that, my whole body starved for him, his touch. I could see what he meant by us not getting anything done if we started something.

Just a small taste of him and I could feel my hard nipples scratching against my bra that started to feel way too tight. Hell, even his loose shirt felt suffocating on me. God, I wanted more of him, I wanted him in my mouth. I wanted him to bathe my tongue in his cum.

"Open, and no biting, or else." There was a threat in his eyes. No, not a threat. A promise, for if I dared to disobey.

Swallowing, I opened my mouth, letting Nikolai shove my head until he had himself in my mouth with a soft groan. "Fuck." He sucked a deep breath through gritted teeth as he started to move my head, using me to get himself off. "Hands on my thighs. I am going to fuck your mouth, stuff myself fully into you. If it gets too much then tap my thigh three times, understood?"

Moaning, I nodded my head and moved my hands to his thighs when he let go of my wrists, gripping him tightly to brace myself when I felt him hitting the back of my throat. Breathing deeply through my nose, I fisted his pants to keep myself centered, and to keep my hands from wandering down my own body to pleasure myself.

"Fuck you're taking me so well, *lisichka*." I could barely hear his strained words through the pounding of my heart along with the lewd sounds of his length moving in and out of my mouth.

His words made ripples of pleasure tingle at my already aroused body, loving his praise. Of course, just when I thought he couldn't get any sexier, he threw that curveball at the end. Did I have any idea what he said? Fuck no. But did it sound hot as hell right now? Fuck yes.

Just something about men with accents and switching to their native tongue was a turn on for me.

"You like that my dear wife? You like it when I praise you for being a good little slut for me?" His husky voice with his sexy smirk, and the way his dark, lustful eyes looked at me with such desire was almost enough to make me have an orgasm right then and there.

Fuck me.

Did he know how much of an effect he had on me? Damn him, he was going to make me jump down a few rungs on the ladder of gender equality if he kept this up.

Sucking in a deep breath, I felt his grip on my hair tighten as his pace picked up. "Fuck I'm close." I rasped heavily with his breaths. "I'm going to cum in your mouth." He stated with a hard thrust. "And you are going to swallow every last drop."

He didn't have to tell me twice. I was more than happy and prepared for him to blow his load in me and give me a mouthful. I was eager for his cum, and I've been eager ever since I got a taste of his pre-cum.

Moaning softly, I started to work my tongue more along the underside of his length to coax him to his release faster. I grew impatient for him.

With a soft grunt and few jerky movements, I started to feel him throb as a delicious salty taste coated my tongue, making me moan with delight. Eagerly, I swallowed and sucked, milking him for everything he had to offer.

"Shit...! You are going to be my fucking ruin, *lisichka.*" He groaned with a soft growl at the end. His hold on me didn't ease for a few moments, holding me firmly in place as he breathed deeply and recollected himself.

Smirking down at me, he pulled me off his cock and forced me to look up at him by jerking my head back. "Open your mouth, I want to see that you got everything."

He's going to be my undoing at this rate. Without hesitation, I opened my mouth and stuck my tongue out for him to see there wasn't a trace of him left.

Looking deeply into his eyes, I could see his eyes sparkle with proudness and adoration. I couldn't help but smile as I allowed myself to relax against him while remaining on my knees. Leaning against his leg, I reached back to his hand that was still tangled in my silky hair and placed my own over it, stroking the back of his clenched fist with the tips of my fingers.

God what has happened to me? Why was I so eager to let him man-handle me like that? I would have stabbed anyone who tried to do what he did. He may be my husband by law, but that didn't mean I had to be so eager to let him use me so easily.

'It's because you're nothing but a little whore.'

That stupid little voice was still there after all this time. A stern reminder as to why I clung onto the single life.

Chewing my bottom lip, I averted my gaze from Nikolai as I let my hands drop to my lap. Out of habit, I started to fidget with my fingers as the intrusive thoughts started to filter in.

Snap! Snap! Snap!

Chapter 10

Nikolai

OUR MOMENT OF SOLACE was short-lived, too short. I could feel my eyebrows furrow with concern when I saw the shift in Angel.

She was fine one moment, living in the high, then like a flipped switch, she shut down almost.

Did she regret what just happened? I might have been stern and rough with her, but she could have stopped it any time.

Releasing her hair, I reached down and picked her up to pull her into my lap when she started to snap at some kind of rubber band on her wrist. "Hey, what's wrong?" It was hard to not sound concerned as I grasped her chin and tilted her head up at me. "Did I push you too far?"

"What? No, no, no you didn't, everything was perfect, I loved it." My concern ebbed a little when her twisted face softened with a small smile full of content. "Don't worry about me, just you know how we can remember the stupidest things at the worst times. Sorry for ruining our little moment."

It seemed to be a lot more than that, and I could sense it when she avoided my first question. There was something wrong, and she wasn't wanting to let me in. "You are my wife, and I am your husband. I know we haven't had a chance to go through the typical timeline of forming and building a relationship and the feelings and emotions involved with it, but you can trust me as I will you. Whatever is bothering you,

I want you to tell me. I want you to let me in. It's going to take some time from both of us, but I am never going to keep anything from you, and all I ask is the same from you."

"I want to, and I will... I just need some time. There will be things and parts of my life that I can give to you easier than others. I just—can you be patient with me? Please? I promise I will tell you when I am ready. I will never keep anything extremely important from you though, like anything threatening to you or your family." She practically begged me with her eyes for that request.

Sighing softly, I reached up and petted her head. "Of course, I am going to be patient with you, my *lisichka*. I will give you all the time you need, but I just hope you will tell me before I end up six-feet underground." I chuckled softly with smile when I saw her chuckle and smile at my little crack at the end.

"I will. Thank you." She gave me a grateful smile as she leaned in and placed her forehead against mine. "We should probably get a start on our plans for the day before we end up naked." She giggled softly.

The sound made shivers run down my spine at how delicate and soothing it was. "Let's go get some food in you then we'll head out to your place so you can change and pack. Then we'll grab some lunch before going to the jewelry store. After our outing we'll come back here to get settled after I give you a quick tour. I won't be able to stay with you the rest of the day though because I have some business to attend to, but we'll have our fun once I'm back."

I laid out the plan for the day, looking at her to see if she had any input or objections. She took a moment, her delicate face scrunching in thought. "That all seems fine to me, but why do we need to go to the jewelry store? You need a new fancy watch or something?" She laughed softly as she tilted her head and waited for an answer from me.

Chuckling, I shook my head softly as I picked up her left hand and held it up for both of us to see. "Your finger is looking a little empty as my wife." There were no rings exchanged last night, just signatures on papers.

"You can just get me a white gold or platinum band. I don't need anything flashy or big. I'm a simple person. Besides, with my job, I prefer lowkey. It's always amusing watching my friends rip their gloves on their big diamond rings, and I don't want to join that club." She replied with a quick lopsided smile.

Even though the situation was one neither of us could have predicted, I still wanted her to be happy to have the symbol of our marriage around her finger. It was also a way for the world to see she was taken. "I still want you to be happy with what's around your finger. Besides, this will be a temporary ring until I actually propose to you after I get you to fall for me."

Angel deserved so much more than this quick sham of a marriage. I wanted to follow the typical tradition of being sappy, getting down on one knee and popping the question. She deserved to have an actual proposal along with a lavish wedding many would describe to be a fairytale come true.

Laughing softly, she let out a sigh. "Funny how we're doing this all backwards. You don't have to propose to me Kolya, we're already married."

"No, you deserve to have that moment in your life. I don't care that we are married on paper, I still want to give you everything that should have happened. I want to see your eyes light up while you smile uncontrollably when I get down on one knee out of nowhere one day and spill all the sappy shit to you before asking for you to marry me. Then, I want to have an actual ceremony with you, the one of your dreams." My Angel deserved everything, and I intend on giving it all to her.

"As long as you don't stick the ring in my food, I'll let you propose to me." She laughed softly with a defeated shake of her head and smile.

"Please, I have much more class than that. Now," I patted her bubbly ass to get up, "Kitchen."

"Yes, sir." She replied with an attitude and roll of her eyes.

"Keep that up and you won't be able to walk or sit after tonight." I chuckled deeply as I took her hand and led her to the kitchen.

"This is Anna, she's the chef around here." I introduced Angel to the old woman who busied herself in the large kitchen area. "She's been our chef for as long as I can remember, anything you want just ask her."

Then, my eyes drifted to Anna who had paused her activities to greet us with a smile and small bow of her head. "Anna, this is my wife, Angel, she's going to be living here from now on."

"Your name suits you well my dear, you do look like an angel." Anna smiled warmly at Angel who blushed at the compliment and smiled back.

And I couldn't agree more with the old chef.

My little angelic wife.

Chapter 11

Angel

I FEEL LIKE I should just chop my hand off and pass it around to my coworkers to save my hand from all the yanking as they admired my ring. It was a cute platinum ring with a 2.0 carat heart shaped diamond as the center and tapering round diamonds on either side of it. I wanted an encrusted band, but Nikolai demanded I get something more because no wife of his was going to walk around with a plain old sparkly band.

Even though he said I had control over what ring I wanted, he butted in too much. If it were up to him, I would have left the place with the hugest and flashiest ring they had there. Well, at least he wasn't too pushy once he realized it wasn't really my style. Still, he wanted some nice rocks on the ring.

"How the hell did you get hitched on your two days off?!" One of my coworkers asked as she admired the ring.

"You'd never believe it." I half joked with a snort.

Oh, my evil stepmother drugged me and married me off to the head of the bratva using my father as a threat, nothing fancy.

Well, it was definitely going to be an interesting story for the kids.

Wait, kids? Did I want kids with Nikolai?

"Who did you marry girl? Were you even dating anyone?" Another one questioned after yanking my hand in their direction.

"It was a big spur of the moment thing. I knew him through my father's business with him." It wasn't a total lie. We did meet because of our mafia businesses.

"Who is he? Name girl, name, we need a name to stalk." Another pushed with a laugh.

"There she is!" A somewhat familiar voice broke our little group huddle. It wasn't long until I felt an arm slung around my shoulders. "There's my favorite sister-in-law."

"Alexei, I'm your only sister-in-law." I replied with a roll of my eyes while shrugging his arm off.

I still had trouble telling the twins apart whenever they were together at the house, but there was only one who was a doctor.

"Sister-in-law?! You're married to one of Dr. Volkov's brothers!? Oh my gosh, which one!?" Now they were all ganging up on me again.

"Does it matter which one? They're all drop dead gorgeous and successful as hell. I'm surprised our little one here snagged one." One of the older nurses chuckled and patted me on the shoulder.

"Dr. Volkov, to what do we owe the pleasure of your ED visit?" I directed the attention back to him, changing the subject so I could avoid being grilled for answers I didn't know how to give yet.

"Oh, I'm on my first break of the day and thought I'd drop down and pay ya a visit. Also, wanted to ask if you wanted a coffee or anything from the café, my treat of course." Alexei replied with his usual friendly grin.

Out of all the brothers, the twins seem to be the least weighed down. I could still see their playful youth and outwardly friendly behavior. Everyone else was friendly, but just one look and you could tell their shoulders were burdened in a way.

"You mean Nikolai's treat? Considering how most of your money is from him still." I joked with a chuckle.

Residency didn't pay much, and Alexei didn't have a vast fortune from the family business because he rarely dipped his toes in it. All his brothers pitched in though, always tossing quite a few chunks into his bank account for him to spend as he pleased.

"Even if you paid it'd still be on Nikolai considering how you have access to his funds now." Alexei shot back.

"You're hitched to Nikolai?! Girl, I knew you like 'em older but damn!" My coworker piped up, smacking me on the arm.

"He's not *that* much older than me." It never occurred to me to ask for his age this whole time, though I assumed he was maybe thirty's or early thirty's based on his appearance. So, just a few years older than me? Maybe? Honestly, I sucked at age judging any ethnicity beside Asian.

"He's thirty-nine, going on forty in a few months." Alexei answered.

Oh shit. That's about a fifteen year age gap between me and him then. Surprisingly I didn't find it off putting. Actually, the fact of it made it a little more fun. He was a well-seasoned man who knew what he was doing. No doubt he'd know all the ways to my body without much guidance. I always did try to pine for older men because I wanted a man in bed, not an inexperienced boy. That and the hope an older man was actually mature and not entirely stupid.

With a smirk, my coworker leaned in. "Oh? Guess you got a new da—"

Not letting her finish her sentence, I lightly smacked her with a chart. "Okay, that's enough out of you missy, you've got a patient in bed five to tend to." I shooed her off along with the others to have some peace to myself before shit would hit the fan.

"Oh," Alexei had an 'ah-ha' moment as if he remembered something. I watched as he fished around his pockets, trying to find something. "Here," he held out a black metal looking card to me, "Your new credit card. It came after you left this morning."

"Well, at least now I know what he meant by grab something nice after work for tonight." I hated how the card felt like a few hundred pounds in my pocket. I hated having access to basically unlimited funds through Nikolai.

My dear husband was insistent I was given a black card to his funds, not that I planned on using it. Husband or not, I didn't want to dip into his finances unless necessary. I made good money on my own, and it wouldn't feel right spending money I didn't earn by my own hands.

For the fifth time, I checked my reflection in the full-length mirror again, smoothing my hands over the white sequined silk dress that stopped a little below midthigh. Nikolai wasn't home yet, having to deal with business as usual. So, I was left to my lonesome self to get ready for our dinner date tonight.

"Tonight's the night." I told myself.

Much to our disappointment, we never did get to have sex or do anything sexual in nature that night two days ago. By the time Nikolai got home, it was so late I was already deep asleep. The next day when I woke, Nikolai was already gone. Once again, when he had returned home at night, I was deep asleep. So, we were determined to make this first date night work with a happy ending—the one where we'd end up in bed naked.

The sounds of heavy footsteps approaching our shared bedroom made me turn my attention to the door. "Sorry, things ran later than I expected, just give me a moment to wash u—" Nikolai stood there with a stunned face, not even trying to hide the fact he checked me out with his hungry eyes after he stopped midsentence. "Maybe I should cancel our reservations and eat you up instead." He said with a cheeky grin as he approached me.

The way his hungry eyes filled with a dark lust made my stomach tighten with anticipation of what's to come later. He practically stripped me with his eyes, no doubt he would make good on it with his hands later.

I couldn't deny the burning desire in his eyes, and I couldn't deny the same fire that consumed me. I'd seen my fair share of men's lustful eyes, but seeing them from Nikolai made me soaking wet. I had never wanted a man so badly in my life, nor had any other man had such an effect on me. I wanted him to do all kinds of sinful things to me. Whatever reserved inhibitions I had were thrown out the window in his presence alone.

Even before our marriage, I had desired him. There were many nights when I would pleasure myself with thoughts about him, how his deep voice would spew the dirtiest things into my ear while he'd take me like an animal.

Blinking my thoughts away, I mentally slapped myself to snap out of it, "I'm just dessert, you wouldn't be satisfied with just me." I tried to keep firm, but those dark eyes of his were making my knees weak. I could already feel myself aching with need.

"You have to give yourself more credit, *lisichka*." Nikolai chuckled as he reached out and ran his hand up my arm to my neck, grabbing me by it and bringing my body flushed against his before anchoring me by my hip with his other hand.

"What does that mean? *Lisichka*. You've been calling me that a lot lately." I couldn't have easily Googled a translation because I had no idea how to even spell the word. Then none of his brothers wanted to answer me when I asked, telling me I should ask Nikolai instead.

"It means little fox because you, my darling, are a little vixen." His lips were right there, just barely an inch away. "But I mean it, you need to give yourself more credit. You are more than just dessert, you are a whole feast, my feast, and only mine."

Then there was that snap.

A moan clawed out of me when I felt the surge of pleasure from the feeling of his lips against mine. "Finally." I giggled against his lips before resuming the heated kiss.

Damn, maybe I should have just kissed him that first morning and taken the punishment. I thought his touch was dangerous, but his lips on mine brought a new kind of fire to my body I didn't think was possible. The desire I felt for this man right now was otherworldly. I wanted him to lay his claim to me so badly, to show me what other things his mouth was capable of.

Moaning, I gripped at the front of his shirt, anchoring him to me, afraid if I didn't then he'd pull away fully. The feeling of his strong tongue sweeping against my bottom lip made me giggle with delight as I parted my lips for him. His dominating tongue was enough to make me shudder as I weakly attempted to fight back using mine. Fighting back against him was pointless, but it was a fun try.

The feeling of his hand on my hip moving didn't go unnoticed because it felt like a trail of fire wherever he touched. He hasn't even spanked me, yet I could already feel the burn of his hand on my ass cheek as he gripped and molded it in his hands. "Can't wait to watch this pretty ass of yours bounce while I take you from behind." His words should have brought another moan out from me, or a string of teasing words.

Instead, I found myself chilled to the bone with unease as I looked up at him with wary and far out eyes. I couldn't control it, those cold and haunting thoughts flooded my system before I knew it.

Maybe this was a mistake. What if this turns out like last time? After all, this marriage is more so for business than love. Maybe it was silly of me to think this could go beyond some marriage of convenience.

Chapter 12

Nikolai

THERE WAS THE SWITCH again, the iron door dropping between us. Her hands that had been gripping my shirt dropped down to her lap where she fidgeted with her fingers for a bit before snapping at the hair tie around her left wrist. "Was it what I said? Or was it something I did?" What had I done to trigger this effect?

It concerned and broke me to watch the strong and independent woman before me fall apart within moments. How badly were her demons to have such a hold on her? "No, well, yes. It's nothing you did, and what you said was fine, in a way, just I didn't think it would affect me like it did." Her voice was cold and distant as she shut herself off again, just like the other day.

"Do you not like being taken from behind?" Everyone had their preferences, but there was something more than preference with her if this was how she reacted. Was it a bad experience? We all had our fair share of bad fucks, but this reaction from her meant something else.

"I don't know. I haven't... It's complicated. I don't want to ruin our night before it starts, maybe some other time. I also don't want to talk about it yet." She avoided it again, but I didn't want to pry open a bad can of worms if she wasn't ready. Whatever it was, it was her story to tell, not mine.

"I won't push, but I hope you will let me in sooner than later." Wrapping my arms around her, I held her for a moment, attempting to soothe her. "You really do look lovely in that outfit."

When I thought she couldn't get any better, she takes my breath away. Seeing her dolled up in a sexy dress tested my control so badly. I was still for the idea of canceling our plans so I could rip her dress off and ravage her body. Even now, my cock strained against my pants to be let out and buried in her hot walls.

Taking in a deep breath, I placed a kiss on her forehead before pulling away completely. "Go fix your makeup while I get ready." I told her with a chuckle before making my way to the bathroom.

"Wha? My makeup is—oh shit, never mind." I could hear her shuffle around. No doubt she saw her reflection in the mirror and changed her words. Her ruby red lipstick was smeared messily—a nice look in my opinion. I couldn't wait to get her on her knees again and have her wrap those pretty red lips around my hard member.

Shaking my head softly, I pushed my thoughts back into the depths of my mind as I went to the bathroom. It didn't take me long to wash up and throw on a clean navy suit with a white button up. Then, thankfully, we made it out to the car in one piece. Seeing her eye me lustfully made me want to ruin her lipstick again, and possibly her clothes. I almost went through with my plan to cancel our outing again, but she slipped from my grasp in the nick of time before I could capture those soft lips between my teeth.

The need I felt for Angel was intense. I don't think I've ever felt so close to the edge of losing my self-control with any other woman. Hell, I don't think anyone before her came close to making me feel the raging inferno of lust by just being in the same room as me.

I'm a man with needs, and I've had my fair share of bed partners. Yet, I've never felt such a spark with anyone but Angel. It wasn't even a spark at this point, just an electrifying feeling that went straight to my nether regions. Angel started to make me lose myself. Just seeing her fucked out face the other day made me want to bust another load at the sight of her. She made me feel like my teenage self discovering porn for the first time.

Fuck, I must have done something right for the heavens to reward me with such a lovely wife.

The lovely wife who remained concerningly quiet in the car, staring out the window seemingly deep in thought. "Something on your mind darling?" I asked, reaching over with one hand and placing it on her thigh.

"Hm? Just wondering where you're taking us, you just told me dinner and to dress nice and fancy." Her attention turned towards me when she spoke, and her body shifted into my touch.

Smirking, I glanced at her for a quick second as I slipped my hand under her dress. "Then there would be no point in it being a surprise. Don't worry yourself too much, I have a lot planned for tonight besides dinner and taking you to bed later. Just enjoy yourself, you deserve it." In all honesty, she deserved so much more. She deserved the simple life she desired so much, and I wish I could give that to her. But I can't. Not fully at least. Nothing about us was simple, that was a hard and sad fact.

Slowly, I rubbed her inner thigh, squeezing softly when she let out a sigh of pleasure. "Open your legs more." It was at least a half an hour drive into the heart of the city from the estate, and nearly another fifteen to the restaurant. No harm in having some fun.

"No." She defied me with confidently with a smirk I caught when I tore my attention away from the road briefly.

"*Lisichka*, if I have to repeat myself then that pretty ass of yours is going to pay the price tonight. Now, open your legs." There was an edge to my voice to let her know I wasn't playing nice. I wanted to feel her, and I wanted it now.

I could feel the defiant energy roll off of her as she giggled and remained firm in her seat. "Oh? What are you going to do? Bend me over your knee and spank me?" As if to egg me on, she closed her legs tightly, crossing them and clamping my hand between her plush thighs. And I can picture her cocky little smirk clearly as I kept my eyes on the road.

"It's not going to be the fun spanking that you are thinking of, *lisichka*. Your little act has already racked you up ten for tonight, and if you keep pushing my buttons enough then it will be more than my hand marking that sweet bottom of yours." My grip on her thigh tightened, my fingers digging into her soft flesh. "Open them. Now."

"You're not the boss of me." She bit back confidently, making me smirk at her spunk.

The damn brat.

"You're right. I'm not your boss." The temptation to pull over to the side of the road and pull her out of her seat got hard to resist.

"I'm your fucking husband."

Chapter 13

Angel

Shit.

The dark edge to his voice made me soak my thong. God, I wanted to beg him to break me right then and there.

Swallowing the lump in my throat, I slowly uncrossed my legs and opened them until they were at the edges of my seat. Unable to help it, I shivered at the feeling of the cool air hitting my arousal, and I had to bite my tongue to hold back my whimper when I felt myself throb.

His strong, deep voice sent another shiver of pleasure to my sensitive nipples and pussy, making me clench at nothing but the thought of him later tonight. "That's going to be thirty later tonight. Your attitude the rest of the night will determine whether it will be my hand or my belt that will be marking that sweet bottom of yours." His eyes never left the road as he spoke, but I didn't need to see his dominating eyes as I could hear it in his voice.

"What? Thirty?!" What happened to ten?! He made it clear this wasn't going to be some funishment, so I was fucked.

I was tempted to shut my legs closed again, but the warning squeeze from his hand was all I needed to keep them parted. "You gave me attitude, defied me even further by closing your legs, and I had to repeat myself. I am being generous right now with you, so I suggest you don't push your luck the rest of the night, *lisichka.*" Was it a warning or a threat? It was hard to discern which from the edge in his voice in my hazy mind.

Shuddering, I swallowed my defiance before it could slip from my mouth and get me in more trouble. "Yes, sir." I doubt he would pull his punches. He said this would be a punishment, so I could only imagine the infliction later.

"Having naughty thoughts already?" There was a playfulness to his voice as he trailed his hand up my thigh and cupped my pussy. The thin lace of my thong did nothing to protect me against his hot touch that made me gasp. "Fuck you are soaking wet already." His voice rasped.

Gripping the sides of my seat, I sucked in a sharp breath when I felt his fingers slip under the thin fabric and stroked at my wet slit. "Kolya." I whimpered, bucking my hips softly against his hand to get more traction and hoping maybe it'll be enough to get the slightest slip of his finger inside my aching cunt. "Ah!"

The pinch came out of nowhere, jolting my body with a painful pleasure. "Try that again." It wasn't an invitation or a dare; it was a warning. He didn't ease up on my throbbing clit, keeping it pinched between his strong fingers while he rolled it to keep the stimulation going.

Whimpering and shuddering, I pulled myself together as best as possible. No man has ever touched me like this before, so harshly right off the bat. But I lived for it. "I'm sorry, sir." Fuck this man made me unravel faster than I wanted.

"Are you going to be a good girl the rest of the night?" He turned his head to smirk at me as he teased my clit with slow strokes of his finger. His tone challenged me to argue, to give him more reason to add more to the counter.

But I won't give it to him. "Yes, sir, I'll be good." For the sake of my sanity and ass later, I would force myself to behave.

A deep moan left me as my back arched in my seat from the feeling of his thick finger penetrating me. I could already feel the pleasure buzzing at my ear, fading nearly everything out. "I don't know how you're going to fit that big cock of yours in me later, but it's going to feel so good." Maybe I should just tell him to turn the car around and take us back home. I would need more than his fingers to sate this burning need for him.

"I will be gentle, don't worry." Nikolai chuckled as he slowly thrusted his finger in and out of my tight cunt, his palm rubbing against my little love button with each movement.

Whimpering needily, I lightly stomped my foot out of frustration. "I don't want you to be gentle, I want you to ruin me, sir." I wanted him to fuck me until I couldn't walk for days, until I couldn't feel my legs. I wanted him to make me be at his mercy.

God what is wrong with me? I shouldn't be wanting those things so strongly from a man this early on. Granted, he was my husband, so a part of it has to be alright, right? It's normal for me to want my own husband, my chiseled god of a husband.

The deep growl from Nikolai made me flutter and clench around his finger as I bit my bottom lip with a delighted smile. "Be careful with your words darling. I am not the kind of man that you should be saying such things to." I wanted to unhinge him, make him lose control.

"I always say what I mean and want. Make me your slut tonight, sir." I have no idea where such filthy words came from, but the primitive desire for him to dominate me and make me his won over my logical side.

Another soft moan was ripped from me when I felt his finger curl into my sweet spot. "This is the only time I am going to warn you, Angel. If we go down this route, there will be no turning back. I am going to ruin you, break you. If you are not ready for that side of me then I suggest you stop your little games before I lose what control I have around you." The deep rasp to his voice only turned me on more as I bucked my hips at him, drawing myself to a small orgasm which caused me to shudder; it wasn't enough though, I needed more.

Was that what I wanted? What I craved? For a man—no, for Nikolai to dominate me like that? I was a woman who always had control over my life and choices, and I enjoyed that aspect. Yet, deep down, no matter how much I denied it, I wanted a man to dominate me. I wanted Nikolai to break me down to nothing and build me up however he wanted.

It felt so wrong and sickening though, how I wanted that. The independent part of me made me hesitant to throw myself at him fully.

'You need to live your life again girl. Show those demons whose boss.'

Hanna always pushed me to get past my trauma, always telling me to move on and conquer it. Maybe if I push myself hard enough I could. But... If I did push myself and things went the other way, it could ruin something good between me and Nikolai.

Do I dare play it safe? Or should I finally give into my desires to chase after what I truly needed and wanted?

"I know what I am capable of, Angel. I have hard tastes. I will use you to my pleasure. I will abuse, ruin, and break that heavenly body of yours, ravage every last thought of yours until all you can think about is when I am going to fuck you next. I have locked that side of me away, and if I let it out then there is no caging it again. But just know, I may mark up that flawless body of yours and abuse it, but I would never truly harm you. I will always do right by you in the end, and I need you to trust me. Trust me enough to give yourself up to me fully. For you to place your life in my hands and trust that I won't abuse that power. So, before you go down this route with me, I implore you to think about it carefully and deeply before deciding. I won't be upset or mad at your decision as long as you have thought long and carefully about it."

Could this man get any more perfect?

I might be falling hard for him, and fast.

I watched as his chest rose and fell with each deep breath. He was recollecting himself. He was usually so put together, professional, and cordial at times, but just now, I have a feeling I've gotten a glimpse of the dangerous man underneath it all. I was terrified. Not of him, but of me. I should run for the hills, find a way out of this marriage, yet hearing all of that compelled me more to stay. I started to wonder if I was insane at this point. I wanted and needed someone to tame me. No, not someone. Nikolai. Only Nikolai.

"Kolya." My voice dripped with lust as I grabbed his hand to urge him to continue. "I'll think about it before I give you my answer, promise. But please, I need you right now." I was so close again, just teetering torturously on edge.

My little orgasm before did nothing to curb my desire for more.

"If you want something then beg for it, *lisichka*." He purposefully moved his fingers at a slow pace, brushing against my sweet spot with every thrust.

Huffing, I gave him a pout as I bucked my hips at him, hoping maybe I could just fuck myself into an orgasm on his fingers. Unfortunately, he saw through my plan. Pulling his fingers out, he rested them against my aching folds. Then, he pinched my clit, hard, making me squeal softly from the sudden pain.

"Beg, and if you try that again then you are not going to be coming tonight no matter how much I take you." No doubt he would make good on that promise. The thought of going against him dangled in front of me like a carrot on a stick, but I didn't want to test him tonight.

Chewing my bottom lip, I sat there stubbornly for a moment. Thinking maybe if I held out long enough then he'd just pull his hand back or maybe my arousal would die down. I highly doubt the latter though since being in the same space as him was enough to get my blood rushing in all the right places. Definitely won't be simmering down any time soon either because he toyed with my love button while he drove.

Swallowing my stubbornness, I gave him what he demanded. "Please, sir, I need to come, please." Begging for my own orgasm, how embarrassing.

"Only when I say so, but not a moment sooner. Understood?" The tips of his fingers lingered at my entrance, circling it but never breaking past to tease me.

"Yes, sir." I whimpered needily, moving my hand back to the sides of my seat to grip at them.

Two if his fingers entered all the way to the last knuckle without warning, making me jump a little in my seat. "Fuck your fingers feel so good." I could already feel my tight walls stretching from his thick digits as he pumped them in and out of me hard and fast.

"You are so tight, *lisichka*. You're not a virgin, are you?" I could see his eyes glancing at me for an answer as he continued to work his fingers.

Sucking in a deep breath, I shook my head, "No. Not by choice." I could feel myself wanting to shut down as the nasty feeling started to claw at my chest, but the pleasure Nikolai gave me did well to keep that feeling at bay.

It was hard to see in the dimly illuminated car, but I could see the muscles in his neck tense as his jaw clenched. "We will touch on that later. For now, I want you to come. Now."

I didn't even have a second to think about the icky feeling because of the rush of euphoria washed over my body. "Fuck." I moaned deeply as I dug my fingers into the leather seats. My body writhed with pleasure as I rode my orgasm out with his moving fingers. It was only when my walls stopped squeezing and fluttering around his fingers did he slow to a stop and pull out.

Breathing deeply, I let out a shaky breath I didn't even know I held until the rush started to die down. God, when was the last time I came like that? I was no stranger to self pleasure, but I don't think I ever came that hard before by my own devices. That or it had been so long I've long forgotten about it.

His deep chuckle made me shiver along with the feeling of his warm hand leaving my body completely. Looking over, I couldn't help but feel a wave of heat hit my cheeks when I saw him suck his fingers clean and smirk at me. "You taste so much better than I imagined. I'm going to enjoy burying my face between your thighs later tonight."

I could feel the heat pool at my cheeks upon hearing his words. "Kolya! Don't say such things, it's embarrassing...!" I lightly slapped his shoulder and gave it a soft shove.

"Too bad, get used to it, *lisichka*." He laughed softly before resting his hand on my thigh.

Rolling my eyes, I wrapped my arms around his outstretched one and leaned in for a moment, enjoying the feel of his bulky arm under his expensive suit. "Quit showing off." I snickered, pulling back and smacking his arm. It was obvious he flexed his muscles as I held him, I could feel it clearly through the fabric.

Nikolai laughed in response and gave my thigh a few squeezes before blindly feeling around for my hand, grabbing it when he finally succeeded. Slowly, he brought my hand up to his lips and gave the back of it a chaste kiss before letting our hands rest on the center console.

A peaceful silence fell between us for a while before Nikolai broke it. "What you said before, when I asked if you were a virgin, what did you mean by your answer?"

Chapter 14

Nikolai

THE EDGE TO MY voice when I questioned her would have been hard to not pick up. A part of me told me to wait to bring it back up, but I needed to know now or else it'd eat at my mind until I snapped. Another part of me hoped I had misheard, which was highly unlikely.

There was a tense silence from her as she played with my fingers on the hand that held hers. "The last guy I was with..."

Out of the corner of my eyes, I could see her opening her mouth and closing it, struggling to get the rest of her story out. It didn't take a genius to piece things together though. "Hey, you don't have to finish it if you don't want to, darling. I'm sorry for bringing it back up this soon." She started to snap at the band around her wrist again too, a clear indicator of her extreme discomfort.

My grip on the steering wheel tightened as I felt my anger rise. It didn't take a genius to put two and two together. Just the thought of anyone touching a woman without their permission was enough to get the anger rushing through my blood. So, the fact someone forced themselves onto Angel sent a new kind of anger through me. This rage, I hadn't felt anything close to it since my parents and sister.

"I'm sorry. I want to tell you, but I can't bring myself to right now. It's too painful." The crack in her voice, though subtle, didn't escape me.

Glancing over at her, I shook my hand free of hers and moved it to the top of her head, petting her softly. "It's okay *lisichka*, you've told me more than enough. You did good." She didn't shut down, so that was some progress. "Never apologize for that or anything that is not your fault."

"But it was my fault, I should have been more careful." Her sad whimper clawed at my heart.

"No, it's not your fault, something like that is never your fault. If I ever catch you thinking otherwise, I will bend you over my knee where we stand. There are things that unfortunately are out of our control, so never apologize for that." It wasn't a threat, I would punish her for such thoughts, and I intend on keeping to it.

Taking a few deep breaths, I calmed myself back down, easing my grip on the steering wheel before I broke it. " I need you to understand that what I will do is for the benefit of us both. I would never harm you nor do anything beyond what you are comfortable with, darling. I may drag you around like a ragdoll, fuck you brutally within inches of your life, give you a firm hand when I see necessary and when you need it, but I would never harm you or go beyond your limits. I need you to understand that Angel, alright? Understand, and trust me."

Reaching down, I picked her hand back up and brought the back of it to my lips, placing a long and gentle kiss against it. I wanted to throw her in the back seat and show her how much I would cherish her. Kiss and touch every inch of her body to replace all the bad memories with good ones of us.

"As insane as it sounds, I do. I shouldn't because I still barely know you besides what I've dug up, but strangely, I feel safe around you. I probably am insane to be feeling safe around a ruthless killer." Her lighthearted chuckle brought a smile to my own face.

Chuckling softly, I held her hand against the stubble of my chin as I spoke, "Are any of us sane? And I am only a ruthless killer to those that deserve it. Gone are those days of the savage wolves of the Volkov Bratva. My brothers and I are not my *father*, nor will we ever be." Thinking about my father made my rage boil again.

"Tell me more about your family, Kolya." She sounded so pure and curious.

"My parents and sister are gone, so it's just me and my brothers left. We immigrated to the U.S. from Russia when I was fourteen and have remained here in Nespin ever since." I was being vague, not wanting to go into detail yet as I could feel my rage building from digging up the past.

The only thing keeping me grounded right now was Angel. Having her hand against my face like this let me inhale her scent so easily. The crispness of her intoxicating scent was enough to cut through the anger and keep my mind present.

"You're upset, you don't have to continue if you don't want to." Her soft voice continued to work away the fog that threatened to cloud me.

"It's fine, you need to know." As long as I had her right here then I would be fine. "My father was a twisted bastard, there was no love or affection given to my brothers and I from him. He trained us ever since we were young, but his methods were brutal. We were forced into bratva life at a young age, nearly all of us having been forced to kill before we hit our teenage years. The twins managed to escape most of it because we had moved to the states when they were around four. Thankfully the public school system here was enough to keep us away from our father for the bulk of the day. It also kept my father in line because he couldn't beat us like he usually did otherwise the authorities would be called."

Pausing for a moment, I breathed deeply to keep myself fully rooted. "It took him a while here in the states, but he managed to build a branch of our family's bratva here in Nespin. My brothers and I tried to make ourselves scarce with college and making a life for ourselves, but he never left us alone. He wanted and planned for us to work alongside him, to take over once he was gone. We didn't want any part of it, and if it weren't for our mother and sister, we would have left completely. He used them against us to keep us in compliance."

The things I've done to keep my mother and sister safe, to keep my father appeased; they were things I weren't proud of or wanted to dig back up. Those actions weren't a reflection of me. My reputation was bathed in blood and violence, something I tried to clear up to this day.

"Sounds more of a sperm donor than a parent." Angel joked with a chuckle as she reached over with her other hand and grabbed mine, bringing it over to her own lips and placing a kiss on it.

The feeling of her soft lips made a shiver run straight down my back to my manhood as I thought back to that first morning. I couldn't wait to have those pretty lips of hers wrapped around my hard cock again. God, she looked so arousing and felt so good.

"Long story short, he overstepped a line and fucked himself over when he got rid of his means of controlling us, and we overthrew him. Ever since I've taken over as Pakhan, we've been correcting our father's shitshow." That was by far the most exhausting part, but at least it was mostly settled now after the years.

"You said your parents are dead..." I could see the thoughts tumbling around in her eyes when I looked at her.

"My father killed my mother, and I returned the favor." I would never regret that moment in my life, ever. Of all the kills in my life, I took the greatest pleasure in taking his life. He caused my mother's death, and my sister suffered greatly before meeting the same fate because of him.

Shockingly, Angel didn't seem to be thrown off by my statement, or if she was then she did a good job at hiding it. "You seem like a reasonable man, so anyone you kill probably deserved it. Just because you're related by blood doesn't mean shit. I probably sound like a psycho, and to a normal person probably, but you and I both grew up in a fucked-up life."

Two psychos fit for each other, what are the odds. The thought was enough to bring a soft laugh out of me as I pulled her hand back and kissed it. "Well, our kids will never go through anything like that, I swear on it."

"Our kids?" I could tell she was probably blushing by the little uptake in her voice.

"Eventually I want to start a family with you. Don't you?" I didn't care about having an heir to my legacy or having kids for that matter until Angel happened. "You have no idea how much it turns me on to think about knocking you up and watching our love grow inside you, then the image of you taking care of our little ones, to be able to come home from the office to a house full of our children." I wanted all of that with Angel, and only her.

Chapter 15

Angel

God, please don't let this be some fucked up dream. This husband of mine started to sound too good to be true. Sure, he has a really fucked up past from the sounds of it and a very fucked up childhood, but it amazed me to see him go against his upbringing. Not many people could defy their environment like that.

My childhood was nowhere close to his. Hell, compared to his, it might even be considered lavish. My father may have forced me to partake in some aspects of the triad, but he was never harsh about it or went to the lengths Nikolai had been put through. Then, when I hit my teen years, my father stopped all together to give me full reign of my life. I was lucky compared to Nikolai.

The notion of children was always an iffy subject to me given the triad would always be a part of my life, and I was afraid to bring my own children into such danger. Even if I wasn't directly involved, my life was always in danger, and I knew my child would be no different.

Sighing softly, I replied to him, "I gave up the idea of having children of my own a long time ago, but maybe one or two with you wouldn't be too bad down the road. Just as long as you promise to keep them away from the family business. I want our children to live the life they want without any exposure to our fucked-up world of crime. If they choose to partake when they can make such choices then I won't

"

stop them, but I don't want any pressure on them to succeed in any of our positions."

Yet, the thought of children with Nikolai was wonderful as long as he was fine with the terms I set forth. The thought of him being a father brought a warmth to my chest that spread down to my core, making me clench.

"Where are you taking us?" Maybe he'll slip in this sweet moment.

Chuckling, he twisted in his seat to face me when he stopped at a stop light. Reaching out, he trailed his finger down the side of my neck to my chest, then slipped his fingers under the sweetheart neckline of my dress where my hardened nipples were being hidden.

"Ah!" The sudden sting of pain from his fingers pinching down on my hard bud made me lurch forward in my seat as I clenched my legs together.

"Nice try." His smug smirk was the last I saw before he removed his hand and sat straight in his seat again to resume driving as the light had turned green.

"Fuck you." I grumbled, sinking down in my seat and crossing my arms across my chest.

"Oh, you will later, but that makes it forty now." I wanted to reach over and slap him for being so smug.

"How the hell did ten more get added?!" Was it because I said 'fuck you' to him just now?

"You're going to have to be more mindful of your attitude around me, *lisichka*. I don't want to punish you more than I have to." He replied with a chuckle.

Scowling, I glared at him. "That's bullshit, if that were the case then you wouldn't be hard right now." The tent in his pants was hard to ignore when I raked my eyes over his body.

Then, a wicked little thought occurred to me. "How much longer until we get to our destination?"

"About twenty minutes." He replied, still focused on the road.

"Good, gives me more than enough time." I giggled, shifting in my seat so I could lean over the center console.

"*Lisichka*, what are you doing? Sit back in your seat." The edge to his voice should've been a clear warning to behave.

"Don't worry about it, sir, just focus on the road." I giggled deviously as I quickly worked the front of his pants open and pulled out his rock-hard cock.

"Don't you—ah fuck!" I could hear his grip against the leather steering wheel as he sucked in a sharp breath.

I couldn't help but smirk to myself when his tone changed the moment I took him into my mouth. Moaning softly, I bobbed my head up and down his thick rod, using my hand to pump what I couldn't fit in my mouth yet.

Fuck he tasted so good. I love the feeling of having him stuffed in my mouth. I don't think I could stop working my tongue along the underside of his length if I wanted to as I continued to bob my head. It was a bit of an awkward angle, but I managed to work him down my throat once I found a good tempo to work at.

I only pulled off of him fully when I felt his hands in my hair. "Nah ah," I swatted his hand away and placed it on the steering wheel while giving him a smirk, "Both hands on the wheel."

The glare he shot me sent shivers down my spine as I lowered myself back down to his crotch. No doubt he would get me back later for this little stunt of mine.

Opening my mouth, I took him back in, deepthroating him in one go and earning a deep groan from him. Hollowing out my cheeks, I started to suck him more as I resumed taking him.

Carefully, I reached down between my legs with one hand while I used the other to steady myself using his thigh. Unfortunately, I didn't get very far with touching myself because he pried my hand away.

"Naughty girls don't get rewards." The growl in his voice only made me more aroused as I kept up with the blowjob.

It wasn't too long until I started to feel him pulse in my mouth, pushing me to pick up my pace to coax out my creamy treat from him. "Shit, Angel, if you keep doing that—fuck!" His body tensed as his breathing became jagged, and then the salty and tangy taste of his seed flooded my mouth.

Delighted, I smiled happily to myself as I used my hands to help milk his cock for every last drop while I eagerly sucked him dry.

Reluctantly, I pulled off with a soft *pop* and giggled softly as I returned to my seat fully, straightening myself out and looking at him innocently as if I didn't just give him road head just now. Licking my lips, I savored his lingering taste as I looked at the road ahead, trying to see if I could figure out where he would stop.

I was about to bug him again until we stopped at another stoplight.

"Eep!" I was suddenly yanked by my neck, and I found my lips pressed against Nikolai's by the time I processed what happened.

I instantly melted into the kiss and his touch, moaning softly as I fought against his tongue with my own when he shoved himself into my mouth. Shakily, I reached up and grabbed the lapels of his jacket to keep him planted against me.

"Don't think that little stunt of yours is going to save your ass later." He growled against my lips before taking my bottom lip between his teeth and pulling as he pulled away. "Now behave, we're almost there. Maybe if you're good enough the rest of the night then I might knock some off, if I feel generous enough based on your behavior."

"Yes, sir."

As easy as that sounded, I was too much of a troublemaker to do much good.

Chapter 16

Angel

"Wʜᴀᴛ ᴀʀᴇ ᴡᴇ ᴅᴏɪɴɢ here? I thought we were going home after dinner?" I questioned Nikolai with a raised brow as he pulled the car into the parking garage of his club.

"What? Eager for your punishment already, *lisichka*?" He teased with a chuckle as he pulled into his designated parking spot. "I just have a meeting then we can go," he said while turning off the car.

"Oh, I wasn't aware you had business tonight." Well, what was I doing here then? Unless he intended on pulling me into this meeting of his, which I really hope wasn't the case because I would have no idea what it would be about.

"It was last minute, I apologize. It shouldn't take long though, but I have something planned to keep you occupied and entertained in the meantime." He told me before exiting the car and rounding to my side, opening my door for me and helping me out.

"I don't know if I should take that as a good thing or not." There was a playful hint to his smile, but that could mean so many different things. Was he just going to let me have free roam of the club or something? Or was he going to stick me in a corner with other means to keep me distracted?

"Don't worry, *lisichka*, you'll love the surprise." He assured me with a soft chuckle.

Moments later, we were on the third floor of his club where all the offices were at. We avoided having to go through the whole club because the elevator opened into the hallway directly. Nikolai's office was at the end of the hallway, and it was huge.

His office was equipped with a mini bar, shelves filled with expensive liquor, a fully furnished area with couches, a coffee table, a meeting table with chairs, and a big wooden desk which got some ideas running through my mind. One whole side was a floor to ceiling window where you could see out into the club, and you could faintly hear the music being played down below.

"Welcome to my office, this is where all things business, legal and not so legal, get done." Nikolai led me over to the window as he spoke, keeping his hand at the small of my back the whole time.

"Wow, this place is amazing." I gasped in awe as I took in the floors below me. On the main floor was the bar area, DJ stage, a stage with poles, a huge dance floor, tables and chairs, and booths. The second floor was a wrap-around balcony with ambient lighting, couches and lounge chairs, small dance stages with poles. Of course, the third floor was just filled with offices of all kinds from the manager's office to security to Nikolai's.

The club was packed with high profile attendees from what I could see from a quick glance; kids of high profile politicians, young celebrities, and other famous people whose presence paired with their social media would blow this place up. "Well, I can see why it's one of the most popular ones." His club made top ten in the whole state and top three of Nespin. "I'm guessing you only have the good stuff here then."

"Of course, only the best. It's one of my tamer clubs, and this is the first club I opened." Nikolai sounded proud, and the way his face lit up when he spoke carried his point through.

"How many do you own exactly? And what do you mean it's your more tamer one?" I was aware he owned a few from my search before, but I didn't look into the details much.

"I own five in the city, including this one and the newer one I co-own with Arseny. I started Guilty in the recent years, and it picked up more than expected. Arseny was showing interest in starting his own, so I offered Guilty to him. He runs basically the whole show, and I'm just the co-owner that barely pops in." Nikolai answered as he slipped his arm fully around my waist and brought me closer to him.

"Wait, Guilty? As in the sex club Guilty? That's your club too?" It was a surprise to hear because it was a little hard picturing him running a sex club. Arseny though, I could somewhat see, barely.

"Partially, yes. Don't worry, I've got plans for us in the near future at Guilty." His confident and smug smirk meant he wouldn't take no for any answer.

"What makes you think I want to go to a sex club with you? Hm?" Okay, the question sounded silly when said out loud because who in their right mind wouldn't want to go to a sex club with someone in the top ten sexiest men alive list?

"What makes you think you have a choice, *lisichka*?" He shot back smugly while grabbing my neck with his other hand.

I opened my mouth to answer him but was silenced by his hungry lips devouring mine. Without a thought, I reached up and grabbed his shirt, pulling myself flush against him as I kissed back eagerly.

With a few steps, he backed me up into his desk, his lips never leaving mine as we moved. With one arm wrapped around my waist, he lifted me onto his desk as his lips started to leave rough kisses along my jawline and down my neck after forcing my head back with his fingers.

Sucking in a sharp breath, I reached up and placed one hand on his shoulder while grabbing at his hair with the other. Sparks of pleasure lit up my body like a Christmas tree as he continued to rain kisses down on my sensitive skin. The feeling of his stubble scratching along his path added more stimuli to my aching body. "Kolya, more, please." I begged with a breathless moan, arching my body into him more when I felt his lips at the top of my outfit.

Nikolai's hand grabbed at the front of my dress, ready to rip it down when the doors to his office suddenly burst open.

"THIS PLACE IS AMAZING!"

Unlike Nikolai, who remained cool and collected, I panicked and scrambled off the desk like some startled cat. Quickly, I patted myself down to fix myself as I turned around to face the familiar voice with a big smile.

"Go." Nikolai whispered in my ear, patting my ass to urge me towards my friends.

"What are you guys doing here?" I could barely contain my excitement as I hugged all of them.

Hanna, Greg, and Bao were all here and nicely dressed. I was so happy to see them! I hadn't been able to leave the house ever since I was brought back there because I was too busy getting settled around the place. Also, everyone was much too busy to schedule a get together.

"Nikolai invited us here, said you were getting a little too crazy to deal with." Hanna joked with a laugh, making me roll my eyes at her. "Seriously though, he just called us this morning and told us to free our schedule for tonight to party at the club with you."

Looking back at Nikolai, I gave him a big, appreciative smile which he returned with a nod. "Don't get too crazy down there, but go have fun. Drinks are on the house." Nikolai said with a chuckle before going over to his minibar and pouring himself a drink. "Just have her back up in about two hours, alive and unscathed."

"You got yourself a bossy one. Didn't even ask if I was free, just told me to be free and that I was going to get carted away at 9 o'clock sharp tonight." Greg said with a friendly smile, throwing his arms around me and hugging me tightly. "You okay? He hasn't hurt you or anything right?"

Rolling my eyes, I gave my brother a soft shove. "I can kick his ass better than you would be able to."

"So? I'm still the big brother, I have to make the effort." Greg said with his hands on his hips.

"So that you can end up in a body bag floating down the river?" Bao joked with a laugh, earning a punch in the arm from Greg.

"Also," Greg turned his attention to Nikolai who peered at him over the rim of his glass, "I would have appreciated a warning beforehand as to who the hell was going to pick me up! Thought the big burly ass Russian dude was there to murder me or some shit!"

It was barely noticeable, but I caught a glimpse of the small smirk on Nikolai's face. "You have other big Russian guys knocking on your door at 9 PM?" Nikolai chuckled as he came up next to me and wrapped his arm around my waist.

"Man, he has all kinds of weirdos knocking at his door at 9 PM, from people mistaking him as their grandpa from space or someone wanting revenge." Bao replied with a roll of his eyes.

Bao and Greg were roommates and lived in a rather sketchy place where the tenants were very questionable and high off their asses ninety-percent of the time.

"Didn't know being a cop made you that big of a target." Nikolai replied with a raised brow.

"He just pisses off the wrong people." I chimed in as I leaned into Nikolai a bit.

"Unfortunately, the most dirty often have means to stay dirty. Whatever, no more talking about work and shit. We have a whole club to enjoy and endless booze, so let's gooooo!" Greg grinned excitedly, grabbing Bao's wrist and dragging the smaller man behind him as he took off.

"Go have fun, *lisichka*." Nikolai leaned in and gave me a kiss on the forehead before patting my ass again as he pushed me forward a little.

"Come girl, let's go!" Hanna giggled, grabbing me and dragging me away. "I want that good shit after the bozo I had to chase down today. Damn idiot tried to run me over with his ratty ass car after I shot at him."

"People tend to not like getting shot at Hanna, especially when they are on the run already." I replied with a chuckle as I trailed behind the boys with her.

"I gave him a chance to surrender, and I only shot him once in the knee... And maybe a concussion with the coffee pot, and a few minor burns to his face..." No assignment was ever a simple shot with Hanna. Anyone she had her sights on always ended up with a few broken things. She was hell rolled into one little tiny Asian lady with how crazy she can get.

I don't know how long we were on the dancefloor for because time became irrelevant after a few shots of hard liquor. By the time we retired to the second-floor lounge area to try and catch our second wind, we were all hot, sweaty, and tired. "Hey, do you think it's time we head back to Nikolai's office?" The thought finally occurred to me after the alcohol somewhat left my fogged mind.

"Eh, if it's time then I'm pretty sure he'll send one of his people to snag us. Just loosen up, drink some more, dance some more." Bao said with a dismissive wave of his hand.

"Ugh I'm getting too old for this shit." Greg groaned before downing the rest of his drink.

"Greg, you're younger than Nikolai, so shut up, you don't get to complain." I laughed softly with a roll of my eyes. Greg wasn't too much younger than Nikolai, about two or so years, but I had to make a jab.

The four of us sat there a moment drinking and laughing, talking about the fun memories we've had throughout the years together. They were definitely enjoying the unlimited alcohol, courtesy of Nikolai. I didn't indulge much though, not going beyond a buzz because I wanted to keep a clear mind for later. Everyone else though, they were drunk.

A bathroom break was finally needed after a shit ton of drinks. The two males took off first while Hanna took a phone call. So, I was left there in the lounge area with Hanna turned around away from me in a corner on her phone.

"Excuse, miss." A waitress leaned down to me, presenting a tray to me with a drink on it, "The gentleman over there wanted you to have this." Her head nodded towards someone in a sectioned off VIP area a little ways from us.

Looking over, I caught the man's eyes, not like that was hard to do because he stared right at me with a predatory gaze. With a polite smile, I took the glass off the tray and tipped it at the man before taking a small sip. No surprise the drink was smooth like butter.

God, I hope it wasn't drugged. Why didn't I think about that before drinking it?!

Fuck. Well, I don't feel funny, yet.

Getting up, I made my way over to the roped off area, nodding at the guard who stood at the entrance. "Mrs. Angel, is there something I can help you with?" The guard greeted me with a curt nod.

"Not at the moment, no. Just coming over to thank our guest here who bought me a drink. Although, don't give me away quite yet." I smiled kindly at the guard as he let me through.

Smiling, I approached the middle-aged man, "Thank you, you really didn't have to spoil me with such a delicious drink." My eyes gave the glass in my hand a quick glance as I tipped it at him. "I appreciate the kind gesture though." I was honestly being polite. Although, now that I stood before him, my gut told me this was a bad idea.

There was an accent to his voice, similar to Nikolai's. "Only the best for an angel like you. You look stunning in that outfit by the way." His compliment wasn't what made my skin crawl, it was his crooked smile with this bad edge to his eyes. A bug getting caught in a spider's net, that's what this felt like. Sadly, I was the bug in this situation.

"Thank you, you seem rather generous tonight." I gestured at the various bottles of expensive drinks at the table along with the people around him—who were mostly women—with my head.

"I am a generous man my dear. I love to give to receive." I have to get out of here before he strikes and things get ugly. "Why don't you come a little closer and see what more I have to give." He leaned towards me and took my wrist into his sweaty hand.

Struggling to maintain my smile, I took a step back and yanked myself away from him. "That's fine, I've gotten plenty from you. Thank you again for the drink, it was really nice." I spun around and tried to quickly exit the area, but I didn't even make it a step before my body was pulled backwards.

A small grunt left me when I felt myself land against someone. Then goosebumps crawled along my body when I felt an arm anchor itself around my waist and a hand grabbing my chin. "I wasn't asking my dear." His gravelly voice made me shrink in disgust as I wrench my face from him.

Throwing my elbow back, I caught his face and stunned him enough to where his arm around me slackened so I could escape. Freeing myself from him, I spun around to face him and threw my drink in his face before setting the glass down on the table and turning to leave.

Once again, I didn't get far before I was grabbed again. My body was spun around this time, and I was met with a backhand to the face which threw my head to the side. "Stupid bitch, do you know who I am?" The alcohol reeked from his breath as he seethed inches from my face.

Scrunching my face up in disgust, I glared at him before giving him an open-handed hit to his pudgy neck. I watched as he stumbled backwards and fell into his seat while clutching at his throat. "I don't give a single fuck. I don't care if you're the fucking president, no one is allowed to touch me without permission let alone hit me. You fucked with the wrong bitch. I suggest you fuck off before you make it worse for yourself."

As I turned around to leave, the man shouted something in Russian and the guard turned around, hesitating. "What are you waiting for, grab her and throw her out!"

Unable to help it, I let out a small laugh as I turned back around and strutted up to the man. Crossing my arms, I leaned down towards him with a smirk, "Wow, can't even be man enough to take care of a little bitch like me? Pathetic." Straightening back up, I stared down at him for another moment before turning away and looking back at him. "Also, you can't kick me out, I belong here."

"We'll see about that." He was angry, which meant it was time for me to fully take my leave now.

Unfortunately, the plan of escaping went out the window the moment he grabbed my upper arm and started to drag me out of the VIP area and up another flight of stairs.

Now, I could have easily escaped him, and maybe thrown him down the stairs, but once I saw where we were headed, I decided to let this play out. The hallway he dragged me down was all too familiar at this point. I watched as we passed each door until we were at the end of the hallway.

This is where he fucked up.

He didn't even bother knocking on the door, just barging through the guards and through the door as if he was *that* important. I had to bite my tongue to keep myself from saying something snarky when I saw it was a full-blown meeting he interrupted along with one pissed off Nikolai.

"You need to better control your staff Nikolai, this bitch just assaulted me." The man threw me forward, keeping his deathly grip on my arm as he presented me like some wanted criminal before a judge.

"Take your fucking hands off my wife. Now!"

Oh shit, he's beyond pissed.

Chapter 17

Nikolai

I SPENT A GOOD while standing at the window watching my sexy little Angel enjoy herself down below before sitting down at my desk to get some work done before the meeting with Ivan Petrov, a leader of a small upcoming mafia.

Although, the temptation to march myself down there and glue myself to Angel's side was hard to resist. Especially at the thought of how other men were having their beady little eyes and disgusting hands on her.

My possessive side wanted nothing more than to join Angel on the dancefloor, make her dance against me before claiming her lips voraciously for everyone to see she was taken. I wanted the whole damn place—no, the whole world—to see she belonged to me.

God I wanted nothing more than to rip the hands off of those men who I saw grabbing at Angel's hips for a dance.

I nearly did act on the thought if it weren't for Angel handling herself. Seeing my little vixen bite back amused and reassured me. She made it damn clear she didn't want to be touched. The unwanted hands were harshly thrown away by Angel, some got a good hit if they didn't get the hint with the first warning.

About an hour went by before Ivan showed up with his own guards in tow and a blonde-haired woman and man, both looking to be in their thirty's. "Hello, you must be Nikolai, I am Ivan and this is my daughter," he gestures towards the female, "Natalia. And my son," his head turns towards the man on his left, "Nikita."

With a friendly smile, I greet them with firm handshakes. "Hello, nice to meet you all. This is my brother, Stepan. He'll be joining us for the meeting as well." Stepan was always involved in every meeting. Both him and I were good at reading people, so I always trusted him to pick up what I missed. Also, though I rarely admit it out loud, he has better social skills than me, and a bit more brains.

"Please, have a seat and we can get started." I gestured at the couches as I took a seat at the armchair with Stepan standing next to me.

I waited until everyone was settled before starting some small talk to get a good setting in place before bringing up the subject of the meeting. "So, you are wanting my assistance in protecting your product?"

"Yes. You see, we are finally starting to expand, and our enemies have started to see us as a threat. We thought it would be fine, some vandalism of our goods here and there, not too much loss in profit, at first. Things the past few months have been very rough. Our ports and warehouses need extra protection against our enemies. We have been having nearly everything coming in or staying within our storage taken from us. We just need some extra manpower from someone strong and formidable to aid us for a few months." Ivan confessed with a heavy sigh.

"And how do we know you can afford our services if you are not able to keep up with your profit? How do we know that our protection means that your products will be successful at gaining profit? That the net gain will meet and exceed your current threshold? I wouldn't want to waste your time or mine if the profits aren't going to gain their traction and exceed expectations." I could probably afford to not have their money in my pocket, but if it was an easy enough job then who am I to decline easy money? Still, I have to see if it was even something worth the time and effort.

"Our products are the best on the street right now, and we are the only ones able to provide it. So, once we can push it back out then our profits will rise back up at a substantial rate. The gangs that have stolen from us have been trying to stretch what they have, diminishing its quality and value. Once people see that the real product is back, they will return to it." Ivan sounded confident, and if what he said is true then I can see why. If he had monopolized and no one has been able to replicate so far, then his profits would sail through the roof once he gained his traction again.

"What is that you push?" Stepan questioned, having stayed silent so far.

"LSD, pure and good stuff, not the typical ones you find on the street. I have a team of chemists who make it out of state and transport them here to me. Ever since I started dealing with LSD, people have been flocking my dealers for mine because of how it stacks against what else is around. What the competition has is nothing compared to mine." Ivan replied honestly and proudly with a confident smile.

He wasn't lying, but my gut told me there was more.

"We also deal other drugs, but our LSD is our main bread." Ivan added.

Still, there was something amiss, but what?

"Ten-percent. I will give you twenty of my men for the duration of our deal, and if you need more then I will be willing to give more within reason and depending on the situation. I will also have those in my pocket turn a blind eye to your dealings to give you more leeway to push your product out." It was a small cut, but my intention wasn't the profit. There was something else going on, and I wanted eyes on the inside to figure exactly what it is I am not seeing.

"Ten? That's—" Ivan's son started to speak, but he was silenced by Ivan's hand.

"I agree. It's a deal." Ivan stretched his hand out to me, and I took it in a firm shake.

That was too easy. Something was definitely not right. Now to just wait and see what was in the snake's lair.

"Thank you for this meeting. I am glad we were able to work something out. Before we take our leave, my daughter, Natalia. I have been trying to find a suitable man to care for her, protect her properly. I knew your father once long ago, and he had brought up that her hand could be brought to yours." Ivan didn't need to continue. I already knew where this conversation would go.

Was this what I missed? No, this didn't carry the same weight. There is something hidden, deeper.

Smiling politely, I held my hand up for him to not continue. "My father is long gone, and he and I have different views on such matters. Last I checked, there was no contract or binding deal regarding your daughter and I. I have no doubt that Natalia is a lovely woman who will have no trouble finding a suitable partner, but that person cannot be me. It's still fairly new, and there has been no formal announcement, but I—"

SLAM! BANG!

Pure rage.

It was one thing to barge into one of my meetings, but this man had a death wish. I couldn't focus on anything as everything turned into a haze when I saw who he had in his clutches. I never knew what people meant by the veil of anger, seeing red, all those sayings. I had been angry many times in life, gone into fits of rage, but never had it ever been this intense. Not even earlier in the car when I figured about the abhorrent act Angel was forced into.

Clenching my jaw, I balled my hands at my side, afraid if I didn't then they'd end up bashing the bastard's skull in. Slowly, I stood up and turned my body to face him.

"You need to better control your staff Nikolai, this bitch just assaulted me." The man spoke, practically throwing Angel forward like some ragdoll.

"Take your fucking hands off my wife. Now!" My anger echoed throughout the room, and not even the muffled music was enough to touch the tension in the silent room as my anger rolled off in suffocating waves.

Realization hit his face faster than a train, and he released Angel who immediately ran to my side while rubbing her arm where his grubby hand had been. "I didn't assault him, he grabbed me first." Angel said with a soft glare at the man.

I instantly wrapped my arms around my wife, holding her tightly in a protective manner. Even if she could handle that man in her sleep, I was still going to protect her and do my duty as her husband.

Upon a quick inspection, I could see her reddened cheek that started to get discolored. The temptation to reach for my gun and put a bullet through his head became hard to fight. Death would be a mercy though, something he didn't deserve for laying a hand on Angel like this. No, he needed to suffer for his insolence.

"Wife?!" A shrill voice sliced through the air.

"Who's the plastic Barbie?" Angel whispered, earning a muffled snicker from Stepan who had to cover it up with a cough.

"Igor, explain yourself." Ivan demanded of the man.

"Do you know this man, Ivan?" My voice carried a sharp edge to it, showing the seething anger that boiled within me.

"Nikolai, I apologize for his intrusion and for him laying his hands on your... Wife. This is my other son, Igor." Ivan answered me almost shamefully while avoiding my gaze.

"I should cut your tongue out and feed it to you for calling my wife such an insulting term. Your hands should be cut off as well for touching her. Your eyes gouged out for even looking at her. Then maybe, just maybe, if I am feeling merciful enough, then I will put a bullet through your brain." I would make good on my words if Angel so wished. I was not a man to be trifled with, nor would my wife. If anyone dared lay a single finger on what is mine then they shall lose that finger.

Igor paled and shrunk with each seething word that left my mouth until he practically hid behind his father who looked equally as panicked. "I'm sure he is very sorry about his actions. Please, Igor can be a little mindless after some drinks. Please forgive him, he never would have even glanced in her direction if he knew that she was your wife."

"My wife or not, he should not be treating any women in my establishment like he did. I think our business here is done. The deal is off." Working with a man who has a son like that, a son who dared to harm my Angel, was something I won't agree to. If he couldn't control his son, then what's to say he could control his own men?

"Nikolai, please, we need your protection. Listen, you can have him, do whatever you want with him, kill him if you want to, just please reconsider." Ivan was quick to turn on his son who blabbered in protest besides him.

"Enough!" I barely raised my voice, and the room went into a dead silence again.

Taking a deep breath, I looked down at Angel. "They need our protection to continue their business. Original deal was ten-percent, twenty of our men with more if needed, and a blind eye. What do you think, *lisichka*? What do you want to do? Do you want to do business with them? Do you want me to take care of the trash?"

"What? She has no business in this." Natalia spoke up in protest.

Angel's lips curved in a twisted smirk, one that made my chest swell with pride. "I am his wife, I am very much involved in his business. I was going to say, ask for a twenty-percent cut, but now I'm thinking forty-percent is better, the men that you get is based on our discretion, and you'll still get the blind eye. Oh, and I get one minute with Igor."

"What? Forty-percent?! We can't—" Natalia was cut off by her father's hand, and probably for the best too.

"We'll agree to those terms." Again, no hesitation from Ivan. Holding his hand out, we shook on it.

This man was up to something. A forty-percent cut was steep. He would barely keep his men paid after we took our cut. Hell, I don't know if he would even be able to keep his business afloat if we took nearly half his profits at the end of the day. Yet, he didn't seem worried about that. Something wasn't right.

Feeling a soft push from Angel, I reluctantly let go of her, looking at her with a raised brow. "One minute with Igor, that was a part of the deal." She seemed a little too excited about this.

I watched as Angel tied her hair up in a messy ponytail before reaching into my back pocket and fishing out my switchblade. "You won't mind if I borrow this would you, *anh*?" She asked with a saccharine smile that would send chills to anyone on the receiving end of it.

The twisted look in her eyes made the darker flecks of her coffee brown eyes sharpen with a precision of deadliness. She was a deadly predator with her prey in hand, and I couldn't be happier for her. A natural born killer, even if she did deny it.

"What's mine is yours, *lisichka*. No need for borrowing." Not like I was fond of that knife, just another in my pocket that was easily replaceable.

I watched her with excited eyes, hiding my proud smirk as I watched her approach the quivering Igor. The deadly look in her eyes, and the way she carried herself was such a turn on. Beautiful and deadly; her strength well hidden under an innocent exterior.

Chapter 18

Angel

I COULD HAVE BEEN merciful and let him go, but something just ticked in me. Questions filled my mind as I approached Igor with the knife twirling between my fingers. What if I wasn't Nikolai's wife? What if I hadn't stopped him? What if I didn't stand up for myself? How far would he have taken things? How far would he use his influence or power?

As I approached Igor, his father meekly stepped aside to allow me access to the cowering fool. "I thought you wanted a moment with me." The devious smirk on my face struck fear into his eyes. "Don't worry, I don't bite." Without warning, I pulled my hand back and backhanded him, hard.

Igor stumbled a step back upon impact, his head whipping off to the side. "Though you're going to wish that's all I would do to you." Reaching out, I grabbed his wrist and pulled him towards me, kneeing him in the gut then using my foot to stomp the back of his knee, forcing him to the ground.

Then, I slammed his hand down onto the coffee table and stabbed the knife into his wrist. His short scream filled the room for a moment before he pleaded with his father to make me stop and to make me pay. Of course, no one dared to twitch a muscle in Igor's direction.

Sighing disappointedly, I gave him a hard kick where no man should ever be struck. Maybe I should have asked for longer than sixty seconds because time went by too fast, and I still had things I wanted to do to him. I wanted him to grovel at my feet until I was satisfied. How unfortunate, for me, not him.

I didn't even bother with pulling the knife out of his wrist, leaving him pinned there while I made my way back to Nikolai's side. Huffing, I leaned back into Nikolai's embrace, tensing for a split second when I felt something hard press against my behind.

Did he get turned on from watching me just now?

Slowly, I pressed myself against him, rolling my hips teasingly and smirking a little when I heard him suck in a sharp breath.

"Leave, our business here is done. Stepan or one of my other brothers will reach out to you tomorrow to work out the details of your protection." Nikolai was still mad. I could still feel his tense muscles as well as his suffocating rage.

"Thank you for reconsidering, you won't regret it, and I'll assure that my son will be punished for his actions. Have a good night." Ivan was quick to scurry out of the room, leaving his guards to free Igor and drag his sorry ass out.

The moment the doors to his office shut, Nikolai spun me around and cupped my face gently, "I'm starting to regret not going forward with my threats." Then, his eyes went down to my arm where the indentations of Igor's fingers were starting to fade into bruises. Nikolai brushed the area softly with his fingers before leaning down and kissing my forehead. "Do they hurt?"

"Not too much, it's easy to ignore them. But I don't like him, Ivan I mean. I also feel like I've seen him before." I felt uneasy around the man, not fearful but wary.

"I don't like him either. I mean, business is business, but at the same time, you and I both know that his profits are going to be pocket change for us." Stepan's words and attention were directed at Nikolai who looked at his brother for a thoughtful moment.

"Something isn't right with him, and I want to know what it is. I have a feeling they are up to more than they told us." Nikolai agreed with a deep sigh. "I usually wouldn't bother with small fry like them, but if what they are doing starts affecting our business, I want to stop it before it spreads too far."

"Angel, you said he looks familiar?" Stepan asked, turning his attention to me.

"Yeah, I've seen him in triad territory before I think. He kind of looks like a lot of other people too though, but still." There was a nagging feeling clawing its way up to the surface that told me it was him. I believe I've seen him loitering around triad territory and not some other older looking Russian man.

"He might have gone to the triad first for a request of protection?" Stepan suggested a plausible idea.

Humming softly, I shook my head, "No, that's not something the triad deals in, everyone knows that. We don't ever offer protection like that unless it's some kind of favor to someone who is deep in our pockets."

Pausing for a moment, I chewed at my bottom lip softly, running through some brief possibilities in my mind. "Unless he offered more than money in return, but we are already at the top of the drug game in our area. I really can't think of a reason as to why he would want to or be in business with the triad. I'm going to ask around though, to see if there was something that wasn't reported to me."

I couldn't see a reason for Ivan to be in business with the triad for the reasons listed. Was there something going on I was unaware about? It was highly possible, and I hated the possibility of it. There was already a lot going on I was unaware about, and it got out of my hands faster than I would like.

"What I really don't understand is his willingness even though we're practically robbing him of his profits. I didn't expect him to agree to that forty-percent cut because honestly, that's steep. Factoring into account that he has to divvy up the rest of that six-percent, there's no way that's enough for him to keep men employed under him, and I doubt he can afford to cut his manpower right now." Stepan pointed out what I thought, and no doubt what Nikolai thought as well. "Then the fact that he was willing to give up his son like that. I mean, yeah, there are shitty fathers, but still, for a little over half the profit and less men from us?"

"No, there is something going on, which is why I'm even entertaining a deal with him. We can easily get our men behind his lines with the deal and get eyes on everything. I know a rat when I see and smell one. In the meanwhile, I want you to tell Arseny to dig up what he can about Ivan." Nikolai had this air of power around him when he spoke, something I've noticed over the past few days whenever words were exchanged between him and another.

"We'll look into Ivan some more, dig up all we can about him. You and Angel go home for the night, I'll wrap things up here." Stepan told Nikolai, patting his brother on the shoulder.

"Wait, what about my friends? Shit, they don't know where I went." They were probably trying to tear up the club right now looking for me. I didn't have my phone on me either because I had left it with one of the boys to hold since they had pockets.

"Someone will fetch them and take them home safely, don't worry." Stepan assured me with a soft chuckle. "I'll see to it myself personally, don't worry. You two just go home for the night."

"Come here!" Nikolai's playful growl made me squeal as I ducked away from his grab.

"No! I told you I was sorry!" I shouted while running up the stairs, not daring to look back at my husband whose footsteps weren't far behind.

"You and I both know that is bullshit, so quit running or it will be the belt tonight." His threat only spurred me on more.

If I could get to the room before him then maybe I could lock him out. Maybe after one night he'll forget about punishing me. It was very wishful thinking because the practical side of me knew this would only make the punishment worse.

The sight of the bedroom door gave me a sense of false hope that I would get away scot-free. Unfortunately, it was short lived. I barely registered the feeling of the back of my neck being grabbed before I found myself pressed against the wall, and the feeling of panic ensuing as I felt Nikolai's sturdy body pinning me to the hard surface. "Kolya, turn me around, please." I sounded pathetic with how urgent and panicked my voice came out.

Instantly, my body was turned around and the impending anxiety attack retreated. "You're safe with me, *lisichka*." He assured me sweetly as he softly held my neck in his hand.

"Says the person who's about to beat my ass." I remarked snidely with a roll of my eyes.

I knew I could trust him wholeheartedly. One look in his eyes and I could see a certain warmth towards me. If I had any control over my mind then I would will the trauma away in an instant, but my scars ran too deep for me to forgo them easily. Hell, I couldn't even work myself up to tell him the full truth like the strong woman I had built myself into. Instead, I gasped like a fish out of water when he pushed.

"There will come pleasure with the pain, *lisichka*. I am going to punish you, then I am going to pleasure and cherish you like the angel you are. Although, with all the sinful noises that you're going to make, I'm not sure how much an angel you will be when I'm done with you tonight." His voice slowly dipped lower and lower as he spoke, sending shivers down my spine. I could spend forever in his arms with him whispering sweet nothings into my ear and orgasm from his voice alone. Damn I must be more aroused than I thought if that's where my brain went.

"Do you trust me enough for tonight, Angel? Trust that I won't bring any harm to you? That I won't overstep?" There was a slight tip to his voice as if pleading with me.

A softness to his hungry eyes told me I could trust him. He was in control, like always. "I will always trust you, *anh*. Take me. I am yours tonight and forever. The only thing I will ask of you for tonight is don't turn my body away from you when we're in bed." I wasn't sure if I could handle another panic attack or make any promises that I would stay tame, and I didn't want to ruin tonight.

There was a look of understanding in his eyes as he nodded softly before capturing my lips in a passionate kiss that made my legs give out from the intense pleasure that washed over my body. Out of instinct, I wrapped my arms around his neck to keep myself from falling, gripping at his shoulder with one hand and tangling the other one in his fine locks that had just enough length for me to grip at firmly.

"I got you," he said breathlessly against my lips after parting for a quick breath. Keeping one hand on my neck and his lips locked with mine, he slipped his other hand down the length of my back, eliciting a small moan from me as I leaned into his body. His hand gripped at my bottom as he gave my leg a soft nudge up with his knee.

With a small jump, and some help from Nikolai, I wrapped my legs around his waist, anchoring myself to him. "Drop me and I will stab you." My empty and playful threat got a small laugh from him.

"I'll let that one go tonight." He mumbled against my lips before carrying me to the bedroom, kicking the door shut with his feet before untangling me from him and tossing me on the bed like a ragdoll. "Stay." He commanded before walking back to the door and locking it.

When he turned towards me with those dangerous eyes of his, I knew I would be in for one hell of a night. Biting my bottom lip, I watched him with needy eyes as he loosened his tie with each stalking step. God I couldn't wait to get my hands on his chiseled body. The one I've been seeing for the briefest moments when he'd come out of the shower or when he'd be changing. He was mine to have and to hold, but I have yet been able to do that. Seeing those perfectly carved muscles of his, but being unable to lay even the faintest of touches on him was torture the past few days.

His jacket was thrown off somewhere in the room in a blink of an eye before his shirt became untucked and the top buttons of his shirt came undone, giving him a sexy and messy look, especially with how he pushed his sleeves up to his elbow. This man of mine was every girl's wet dream. Just the sight of him right now made me soak my panties with anticipation.

Another shiver of pleasure racked my body when I caught his dark and lustful eyes again. The sheer and raw lust heating up the room was almost enough to push me over the edge. God I was a desperate bitch in heat for him, and I loved every second of it despite the nagging voice in the back of my mind. I wanted nothing more than to reach out and rip the rest of his clothes off like a savage to free his glorious cock.

"Enjoying yourself, darling?" He asked with a smug smirk as he stood before me at the edge of bed between my open legs, ones I wasn't even aware I had parted.

"Yes, sir." I shuddered as I reached out for him, only to have him stop me shy with a firm grasp on my wrist. "Sir?" Needy and confused eyes looked up at him as I tried to pace my breathing so it wasn't going along with my racing heart.

"Remember? Punishment before pleasure. Now get up and strip." His domineering voice made my pussy clench and throb with need as my breath got caught in my throat.

Reluctantly, I slid off the bed, keeping my eyes trained on him, watching him slowly work his belt open and off. The soft clinking of his buckle made me swallow hard when he palmed the metal end. He made no indication of discarding the belt, meaning I would feel the sting of it soon.

Soon, the two of us had swapped positions, him sitting on the bed while I stood before him. With nervous fingers, I reached behind myself, unzipping the dress and letting it slide off my shoulders and down my body. The dress pooled around my feet with a faint *thump*. Slowly, I stepped out of the dress, pulling my arms up to cover my breasts out of habit and instinct as I stood there before him in nothing but a lacy white thong.

Reaching up, he pried my arms away and pulled me closer. "Never hide your perfect body from me, Angel. You are so perfect. And you are all mine. Mine." His possessive growl made my knees weak along with how he eyed me like a starved lion seeing meat for the first time in forever. His hand shot up and fisted my hair, bringing me down into a hard and hungry kiss filled with nothing but pure animalistic lust.

With a deep growl, he pulled my head away and dragged me over his lap, bending me over his knee. "You are going to get forty lashes, and you are going to count them. If you don't count the lash, then it doesn't count. Understand, *lisichka*?" His deep voice was next to my ear after he tilted my head back at a strained angle.

There was no escaping. I could either accept my fate or make it worse with retaliation. "Yes, sir." I whimpered nervously. My heart raced, and not in a good way. Maybe I should put a stop to this. I could feel my anxiety running up to me, ready to slam into me like a bull charging at a red flag. I thought maybe I could do this because I was so aroused, and because it was with Nikolai. But I think I bit off more than I could possibly handle.

Opening my mouth, I was about to put a stop to it all, but the sudden crack of his belt against my bottom made me give out a sharp yelp of pain. Any reservations I had were cut away from the sting of the leather. I couldn't focus on anything else but the pain and the throbbing between my legs.

The second and third came in rapid succession of the first, not giving me enough time to process and react to it as I was too busy counting, "One! Two! Three! Oh god!" It stung so bad, and every hit only aggravated the pain of the first. Yet, I couldn't bring myself to throw in the towel. I kept chasing the pain, my twisted self wanting more even though my logical side told me to put a stop to this madness.

My eyes burned with tears that I couldn't control and stop from spilling over. The hot trail of tears streaming down my cheeks made me unconsciously thank my past self for putting on waterproof mascara, otherwise I'd probably look like a huge mess right about now. The faint *pit pat* of my tears hitting the hardwood floor barely registered through the pounding in my ears. Hell, I could barely register my own voice as I continued to count out the lashes.

The numbers left my mouth uncontrollably, not missing a single one with the threat of getting more than needed if I missed one. "Twenty-three." I was a whimpering and yelping mess. My hands gripped tightly at his pants as he continued to deliver blow after blow, leaving no part of my bubbly ass untouched by the leather.

Nikolai barely paused to give me a reprieve, but a part of me was thankful he didn't pause much to rub my ass with his big hand because that only seemed to prolong the pain by stretching out the anticipation of the next hit. I wanted to get it done and over with, even if it would break me to take it all at once.

"You are doing amazing, *lisichka*. Just a little more." His soothing praise made me swell with pride and happiness that made enduring the last few hits more bearable.

"Forty! Fuck, it hurts so much." I cried as my ass burned like hell. How the hell was I supposed to sit after this? My ass was on fire, but my cunt was dripping wet. I could feel the heat all the way down my inner thighs, and I wouldn't be surprised if my slickness had spilled over my swollen pussy lips.

Though painful, it was strangely cathartic. Being punished like some child at this stage in my life should make me feel anger, resentment, embarrassment, but I felt none of those. Well, maybe some embarrassment, but this feeling of release, this freedom. I felt high, and safe. Every crack of the belt broke away at this wall I had put up, easing me more and more into Nikolai's hands.

Releasing my hair, he stroked my hair lovingly as he leaned down and kissed away the tears that stained my cheeks. "Shh, you did amazing, *lisichka*, amazing. You took those so well. Didn't miss a single one, I am so proud of you." The clatter of his belt hitting the floor made me clench instinctively, nearly snapping me out of my daze. I could feel myself sinking back into the pleasureful haze of pain as he rubbed my burning cheeks but stopped short when I felt his hand snaking up my back.

"No...!" I had forgotten why I was going to stop him earlier until now. Reaching back, I grabbed his hand before he could make it past the bottom of my rib cage. "Please, don't." I didn't want him to touch my imperfections, afraid it would repulse him. Afraid I would be triggered into an episode if I felt even the slightest of touch to the sensitive area. I could only hope the darkness of the room with his shadow over me and my hair had kept them well hidden so far.

A flash of understanding crossed his eyes as he let his hand slacken from my grip. Gently, he pulled me up and positioned me so I was nestled comfortably in his lap. Leaning down, he let his forehead rest against mine. His lips softly brushed against mine for a moment as his soft eyes settled deeply into mine. "I won't go any further tonight, and not any other night until I know what your limits are. We will talk more about that after tonight and figure out a permanent safe word, alright? For now, I won't give more than what I think you can take. If I do cross a line then stop me with three taps to the shoulder and verbally tell me what's wrong, alright?"

"Mhmm. Yes, sir." I hummed softly with a soft nod and smile, shivering a bit as the small wave of delight rushed through me. I was worried I'd ruined our moment or upset him tonight with my little outburst. So, the tender touch and words were unexpected but much needed and appreciated.

Smiling softly, he kissed me deeply. Then, when he pulled away, I couldn't help but shiver. "On the bed, and spread your legs. I want to taste you." His eyes darken with hunger within seconds as he smirked at me, giving my sore bottom a smack.

"But—"

Another smack promptly cut me off. "No buts, I want to taste my slice of heaven." He had a determined look in his eyes, meaning he would get his face between my legs one way or another.

Licking my bottom lip nervously, I crawled off his lap and laid down on the bed, wincing and shivering at the feeling of the covers rubbing against my raw ass. "You don't have to, you know." The only guy I'd ever been with wasn't keen on returning the favor, making it seem like no guy ever did like to go down on a woman.

"I want to. I need to. You have any idea how intoxicating you smell? It's clouding my senses so much that it's driving me to madness. There's no way in hell I'm not feasting on you. So, just lay back and enjoy it." The starved look in his eyes made me shiver with anticipation and excitement as I laid back fully.

The feeling of his rough fingertips trailing up my leg made my pussy throb as goosebumps washed over my body. He was so gentle compared to earlier with how he touched me as if I was a porcelain doll. The way he ghosted his lips and gently kissed as if I'd dissolve in his palms if he put too much pressure.

Softly, I moaned as I reached down and weaved my fingers through his hair, wanting to be sure this was real and not some dream. Shuddering, I gripped his hair a bit when he kissed and nipped at my inner thighs. He was so close to my pussy, only a breath away, and I needed him so badly. I wanted to feel his soft and hot tongue on my aching pussy. No, I needed to feel him. It wasn't a feeling of want when it came to Nikolai anymore; it was a need. I needed to feel his hands on me, the taste of his lips, the praise of his words, and most importantly, the feeling of his cock stuffing me.

"Aah!" My body tensed and arched at the feeling of his tongue licking up my slit, parting my folds to fully expose my sweet core. Instinctively, my hips bucked at him, wanting to feel more pleasure from his tongue. I don't know if he took his sweet time or teased me or both, but my patience ran thin with how he explored every inch of my sex but never touched my clit or entered me directly.

Just as I was about to snap and beg, he ran his tongue slowly against my love button, making me moan deeply and curl my toes from the sudden immense pleasure. "Fuck..." I purred. The way he moved his tongue was amazing. Was it always supposed to feel this good? Whenever my ex went down on me in the past, it always felt half ass and subpar at most, but this. Oh god, the moment he picked up his pace and latched onto me fully, he was a starved man feasting on a godly meal.

"Fuck you taste so amazing, *lisichka*. I could spend forever between your thighs." The vibrations of his words against my sensitive sex made me tremble with pleasure. "Don't hold back on me." His tongue immediately went back to lashing at my clit, easing the pressure with some soft sucks that dragged out my pleasure to where I teetered at the edge.

"Kolya!" I couldn't help but gasp and give out a smothered moan when I felt his tongue dip down to my entrance, teasing the opening before shoving his tongue in deeply. "Oh fuck!" No one has ever done that before, and I started to feel sorry for myself that no one had. "Oh, fuck keep going like that, sir, please. Please, I'm so close." My grip on his hair tightened as I pushed his face closer to me, wanting to get the high he had me chasing.

"Come, *lisichka*, come for me." He drove his tongue back into me with vigor, his arms wrapped around my legs and hips to keep me anchored as he continued his motions. This time, he started to use his nose to brush against my clit while his tongue worked at my soft walls.

"Oh, fuck...!" The knot in my stomach eased as waves of pleasure washed over me. My body tensed and arched off the bed slightly. "More, please, more." The tension in my stomach hadn't fully snapped, and I needed a big release. "Please, sir, please." The desperation in my voice was so pathetic, but I didn't care. I'd get down on my knees and kiss his feet at this point if it meant I would get my big orgasm.

"Since you begged so nicely." He chuckled softly after slipping his tongue out.

Without warning, he entered two fingers into me, nearly making me scream from the sudden intrusion. He didn't start slow, instantly finger-fucking me without abandon as he busied his mouth with my clit. The pleasure he brought upon me was maddening. Each sweep of tongue, every little suck, paired with his fingers assaulting my sweet spot; it was too much all at once.

My moans started to pick up in pitch along with the thrashing of my body, coming to a silent scream as my body stilled from my orgasm crashing into my body. "Fuck! Kolya! Fuck!" Everything faded for a moment as my body processed what just happened. Nikolai didn't stop his assault on me as my body shook from the aftershocks of my orgasm. "*Anh*! You're going to make me—fuck!" The second orgasm built up nearly instantly and snapped before I could get a grasp of control on it.

The covers below were already slightly soaked from my first orgasm, now they would be drenched from the way my juices gushed and squirted out of me. "Fuck! I'm sorry, I should have warned you." I groaned as my high started to die down. I didn't think he would bring me to the brink of pleasure with just his fingers and mouth. I was afraid I had ruined the mood and prepared myself for some rejection.

Much to my surprise, I found myself pinned under his weight as his lips crashed into mine with a growl. His tongue swept into my mouth, and the sweet, tangy, and musky taste of myself mixed with his own taste filled my mouth, making me moan in response.

Breaking the kiss, he wrapped his hand around my neck, holding my face using his thumb and index finger. "Never apologize for your pleasures. That was fucking perfect, more than I could ever ask for." He grunted against my lips, looking at me with unadulterated lust and adoration.

God, I must have done something right to have this amazing man as my husband.

Chapter 19

Nikolai

*M*Y *A*NGEL. *M*Y *PERFECT* little wife.

Her squirting orgasm came as a surprise, but a good surprise I eagerly lapped up like a thirsty dog. I would never get enough of her sweet nectar. The taste of her from my fingers in the car earlier already hooked me, but having a forbidden taste from the source was so much more intense. My sinful delight, my drug, my high, all mine. Mine. No other man is ever going to get a chance to have a taste at this, and I basked in the idea pridefully.

Angel was all mine now, for better or for worse, til death do us part. No matter how damaged she was on the inside, she was still perfect to me. The hesitation would take time to tackle, but I was more than willing to be patient with her. Even if it took forever, I would be patient hand in hand with her.

Groaning softly, I parted my lips from hers to trail kisses along her jawline, down to her succulent neck. Her scent was just as intoxicating as her taste. I could spend forever with her in my arms and be surrounded by her warmth. The taste of her skin seared into my tongue as I ran it along the length of her neck to the junction of her neck and shoulder. Unable to help myself, I kissed the area roughly, leaving the first of many marks on her. To mark her as mine.

Her little whimpers and mewls spurred me on more as I let my tongue lead me to the soft flesh of her shoulders where I sunk my teeth into her, causing her to let out a pained moan as she gripped at my hair.

The sweet sounds that left those luscious lips of hers sent waves of pleasure down my body, straight to my painfully hard cock that twitched to get inside of her sweet pussy. I had been ready to ram myself into her so many times tonight, especially after watching her go off on Igor. If Stepan wasn't there, and if I hadn't promised myself and her that our first time would be in our bed, then I would have taken her right then and there on the couch in my office or over my desk—those situations would eventually happen though.

Growling softly, I leaned back up fully onto my knees to quickly shed my clothes fully from my heated body. I didn't want anything between us when I took my Angel for the first time. I wanted to feel her soft skin pressed against my bare body while I'd be buried deep inside her.

A smirk tugged at my lips when I heard her gasp. Her hungry eyes had drank my body in, stopping at my proud member that yearned achingly to be surrounded in her warmth. Those lustful eyes darkened after she gingerly ran her fingers down the contour of my V-line before wrapping her small hand around my girthy member. I sucked in a sharp breath at the sudden contact and pressure from her squeeze.

Narrowing my darkened eyes at her softly, I watched her carefully. A shiver threatened to spill over my body the moment our intense gazes locked and I caught the playful smirk that curved at the corners of her lips while she slowly stroked me twice before retreating her hand, raking her nails up my length then my abs.

Leaning down, I caged her between my arms and kissed her deeply with a soft chuckling growl. My lips never broke contact with her silky-smooth skin as I peppered open mouthed kisses down to her breasts.

Chuckling softly, I looked up at her deviously as I grazed my teeth at the swell of her breasts, watching as her breath hitched with a wary look in her eyes. "Nikolai, I swear, if you bite my—ah!" It wasn't a hard bite, just enough to make her squeal and shut up. There wouldn't be a mark, maybe some redness that would go away in a few hours, but nothing like what I left on her shoulder.

"I will do what I please, *lisichka*. Don't forget who you belong to." I reminded her with a smirk before running my tongue against her hard nipple, making her moan and arch her back.

With gentleness out the window, I captured her hard bud between my teeth, pulling with just enough pressure to make her whimper. I loved making her squirm under me, such a lovely feeling and sight. To reduce my Angel to nothing but a whimpering mess made the sadistic side of me rear its head. As I covered her nipple with my mouth, my other hand went to her other breast, cupping her roughly and squeezing until I got a whimpering moan that made my hardened member twitch.

I rolled her hard pebble between my thumb and forefinger, twisting, pinching, and pulling roughly without a care. If she kept up with those beautiful whimpering moans of hers, then I wouldn't push any further than needed, for now.

"Sir, please, I can't take it anymore, I need you inside of me, now, please." Her needy plea didn't fall on deaf ears. On any other night I might have held out longer, teased her to insanity until all she could do was beg for my cock to fill her like a bitch in heat.

"What? You need this?" I rolled my hips into hers, rubbing the length of my girthy shaft against her wet slit with a groan. That was a better idea in my head, but the feeling of her hot sex against my aching length would make it impossible for me to hold out any longer.

"Yes, please, sir, please, please." So desperate, and the way those wanton eyes of hers were begging me. Her eyes were so dark with how blown her pupils were, and they made her look all the more lovely.

Luckily for her, I wasn't keen on torturing her much on our first night. So, after rubbing myself along her opening to slicken myself up, I managed to get about half of myself into her with a single, slow thrust before she clamped down on me too much. "Shit! *Lisichka*, you have to relax." I hissed through gritted teeth as I felt my resolve crumbling like a dirt wall. The feeling of her nails clawing at my back didn't help either.

Leaning down, I slid my hand up to grab her neck and lift her head up a little to kiss her forehead. "Baby, relax." I whispered against her forehead, slowly trailing kisses down to the corner of her lips.

"I'm trying, you're so big." She whimpered, still digging her nails into me as she struggled to adjust.

I could feel her walls throbbing around my length, relaxing for just a moment before tightening again whenever she tensed up. I would make an embarrassment of myself if she kept this up.

Placing my lips over hers, I kissed her deeply, hoping it would be enough of a distraction for her. Forcing my tongue into her mouth, I coaxed her tongue out to play with mine until we were both making out heavily. Only then did I feel the vice grip around my aching cock ease.

Slowly, and carefully, I started to pull out until only the tip remained before easing back into her. "Did you come already?" The fluttering and tightening of her walls along with that blissful face of hers made it easy to discern.

"Couldn't help it, felt too good." She moaned with a smile before glancing down. "Fuck, you're not all the way in yet?" The slight shock to her eyes made me chuckle as I held onto her hip with one hand, the other still wrapped around her throat as I shifted my weight onto my legs.

With a few more slow thrusts, I worked more of myself into her tight cave with soft grunts while struggling to hold onto my resolve. "Almost there, *lisichka*." God, I felt like a stupid teenager again getting pussy for the first time the moment my full length became wrapped in her tightness.

Fuck! So tight and good!

This tight cunt of hers was all mine now, and I loved that fact.

"Fuck, you're going to ruin me." She managed through a strangled moan as she looked up at me with adoring eyes. "And I think I'm even more crazy for loving that idea."

"I am going to ruin you so bad that no other man will come close to giving you a fraction of what I can. Not that any man will ever get a chance because you belong to me, and I have no intentions of ever letting you go." I whispered deeply into her ear before taking the edge of it between my teeth and tugging, making her shiver under me.

Giving her a chaste kiss, I leaned back up and held her firm by her hip with my other hand as I started to thrust in and out of her at a decent pace so she could fully adjust to me. The way her face scrunched up and twisted in discomfort urged me to not fuck her like there's no tomorrow yet for her sake. I could be a twisted fuck after tonight.

Slowly, she pulled her legs up around my waist and locked them at her ankles in order to easily thrust her hips up to meet my thrusts. "More, please." Her sweet voice was saturated with lustful need.

Leaning down, I kissed her roughly as I tightened my hand around her neck, choking her lightly as I picked up my pace. It didn't take a full minute for the room to start filling with the sounds of our bodies slapping against each other with how hard I started to pound into her. The sounds of her moans and my grunts nearly drowned out the sounds of our bodies as we started to get lost in our pleasures.

The way her soft walls felt gripping me drove me to my breaking point sooner than later. Then seeing her happy fucked out face as I choked her while fucking her fast and hard made my balls curl, ready to release my seed into her. The thought of filling her tight cunt made the task of holding my release nearly unbearable. "Fuck I am going to fill this sweet cunt of yours up, *lisichka*." This was her only chance to tell me in or out.

"Do it, come in me, please. Fuck I'm so close, please." Not even a second after she uttered those words did her face twist with pleasure, her mouth dropping open into a sweet 'O' as her body clenched around me.

The sight was all I needed for my final thread of control to snap. It would have taken a damn miracle to hold me back at this point. "Shit." With a deep groan, my thrusts slowed and became sloppy as my release squeezed at my balls.

Releasing her throat, I planted my forearm next to her head. Leaning down, I settled my forehead against hers as the two of us breathed heavily. Seeing her in such bliss was aweing. Just when I thought she couldn't get more beautiful, the world proves me wrong.

The world also threw reality back into my face when my high died down. I was always careful whenever I slept with someone. Even if Angel was my wife now, and I wanted nothing more than to have nothing between us. We should have talked about protection before letting our desires get the best of us. "Do you need me to get you the morning after pill or anything?" The idea of children with Angel was great, but the timing right now wasn't. Just because we were married didn't mean we could get sloppy.

"No, I'm on birth control, so don't worry. And I'm clean too if you're worried about any of that. Not that I've slept with anyone since that bastard." She answered between her deep breaths. "I'm going to assume you're clean too, if not then I'm dragging your ass into my work tomorrow so you can get a shot in your ass. Don't care if you need it or not, I will stab your ass." She chuckled softly before leaning up and kissing me.

"Don't worry, I haven't stuck my dick into crazy for a long time, and even when I did, I was careful and used protection." One pregnancy scare was enough to set my stupid ass straight to pull a condom on every time I would stick myself into someone. That and not wanting to face my father's wrath if I ever caught something because I was stupid. Poor Lev found out the hard way, and that was all I needed to witness.

"Should I be worried about any crazy ex's?" Angel laughed softly as she dropped her legs from my waist.

"I'd be more worried about them than you. I'd probably get a phone call to clean up their body from Benjamin than a call from him saying you were injured or went missing." An honest truth in my opinion.

Angel's not like any other woman I've met in my life. She wasn't afraid to pull a gun and shoot or pull a knife out and stab someone. Hell, I'd truly be worried about my life if I ever crossed her, because she probably could successfully assassinate me in my sleep. That's what I liked about her though, she was truly a strong and independent woman unafraid to do what's necessary.

Breathlessly, she let out a chuckle and sigh. "Oh please, as if I'd waste my time and energy on something like that. Besides, I don't get my hands dirty like that. I love to torture, but killing, well, death's a mercy to me, and I rather them suffer to pay for their wrongs."

"Someone's a little sadist." I mused with a chuckle before moving my hips again.

"What are you doing?" She looked at me with a raised brow as she tried to squirm out from under me, only to have me pin her down by her shoulders.

"Did you think I was a once and done?"

The look on her face was too adorable because no doubt in my mind, she knew she was fucked.

Chapter 20

Angel

"DID YOU EAT BREAKFAST yet?"

Shit.

Cheekily, I held the coffee mug tightly in my hands as I smiled at him. "Good morning, Kolya, my dearly beloved husband, my—hey!" I didn't even get to finish trying to charm my way out before he snatched my mug away and gave me a stern look.

"That's five. You're a nurse, you should know better than to just fuel yourself with coffee on an empty stomach." He chided me, calm and collected like always. Smug ass bastard.

"You can't punish me for that. You're getting yourself a cup, I haven't seen you eat anything, you literally just got here." I retorted with a pout, getting off the stool from the kitchen island and going up to him to attempt to get my coffee mug back.

"Ten now. I can punish you for it because you're not taking care of yourself properly. Now, go get some breakfast then you can get your coffee back. And I already ate before working out." He said matter of factly, holding the coffee mug out of reach of me easily because he was built like a fucking tree.

"Hmph. Bastard." I muttered under my breath, crossing my arms and turning around to go to the fridge. I didn't even make it a step though because he grabbed my hair and pulled me back, forcing me to look up at him.

"Hm? What was that, *lisichka*? I don't think I heard you." The dark look in his eyes made me shiver with pleasure.

"N-nothing." Maybe I can weasel my way out of this one. "Ah!" My head was yanked back more by my hair, making me more aroused as I tried to hold my gaze with him.

"I don't like liars, *lisichka*. And I sure as hell don't tolerate them. So, one last chance. Repeat what you just said." God damn it, his tone meant I was in trouble.

I was backed into a corner. I would get in trouble either way. If I continued to lie to him, trouble. If I told him what I said, trouble.

Ugh, fuck me.

"I said you were a bastard." I muttered, averting my eyes from him.

"That's not what you were saying last night." He whispered teasingly in my ear, giving it a small nip before looking at me with a smug smirk. "That's another ten." Chuckling, he let go of my hair before getting his cup of coffee. "You must have a penchant for punishment. The morning's barely started and you have racked up twenty within ten minutes of being around me. Guess I took it too easy on you last night if you're still being a little brat."

He enjoyed this too much, and the temptation to smack that smug look off his face itched at my hands. "Hmph." Chewing my tongue to keep it at bay, I opened the fridge and pulled out some yogurt and fruit. He didn't say what I had to eat, and technically this could count as a breakfast meal.

"I thought you had work today." He said, taking a seat on the stool next to mine at the island.

"It's my half shift today, so I'm just getting some business done before going in." I replied while going back to my spot.

I didn't care about him having full access to what happened on my laptop screen, not like there was anything for me to hide from him. "Hey Kolya, do you want it? The Triad territory. I know it might be a lot to take on in a short amount of time, but it would expand your empire greatly. There's lots of ports, warehouses, and you'll have a nice prison place out in the desert for holding and or torture."

"I'm fine maintaining what we have, but to have more control of Nespin wouldn't be something I would oppose to. Why? Are you taking what your friends said from before into consideration?" It would be ideal to hand things over to Nikolai and try to peacefully merge things while I still had some control.

The last thing I wanted was for everything to go into the shit hole and have the territory up for a power grab. We'd most likely win in a turf war, but I'd rather avoid a war if necessary. Mass casualties weren't fun to deal with, and innocents would be caught up in a turf war. I've already seen my fair share growing up when my father expanded, and I would rather not add another to my memory bank.

"I'm starting to lose my hold, and if I let Lady Qing continue then it's going to be bat shit hell. I don't know how she's doing it yet, but she's still thriving even though I'm cutting off her streams of profit. I've shut down so many of her warehouses and shipments, enough to where she shouldn't even be getting half a penny. Yet, her posse grows every day, and what few loyal men I have are being cut off one by one. If I merge the territory fully under you then we can run her out effectively, which is what I want to do. It'll be a win for you in a sense that you get more turf to expand your businesses to. I'm not going to force it on you, you know what's best for the Bratva and what's needed, but I'm just putting it out there for you to think about. I'll support you in whatever you want to do, but I just want to know what you would rather do, so that I can know how to prepare for the future."

The plans were simple in my mind. If Nikolai wanted the merge, then I would assert my full power as temporary head to do that. If he didn't, then I would go with my original plan of tearing the whole empire down to where not even the foundations remained. The only problem was my father. I had to figure out how to ensure his safety before I do anything too drastic that would tip off my stepmother that I was the one behind her failings.

Picking up my phone, I sent a quick message to Bao, letting him know to send the pictures I had been looking at on my laptop to the others for later on and to schedule an email to the police so they could have their piece of the cake.

The operation to tear down the Qing Triad had been in the midst for a while now, but we had been taking it very slow and cautiously. We didn't want to get too involved, wanting to keep our hands hidden. So, we had been digging up dirt and sending the information to trusted law enforcement agents to handle the dirty work for us if it seemed simple enough.

"What are your plans, darling? If I agree, then there's still the truce in place that prevents a merge like that. Both sides agreed to keep our territories as is. Even if you were to exact your power and merge the territory into Bratva territory, then that would break the truce on our end which could mean war as well. If I don't agree, then what my little fox?" Nikolai posed a good point, and it was one I had thought about carefully before even popping the question to him.

"The truce is contingent to the marriage. No marriage, no truce." Glancing over at him, I could see his eyebrows furrowing together as he looked at me knowingly.

"So, you're going to divorce me?" He didn't sound too happy, nor did he look happy. "You know I won't let that happen right?"

Scoffing, I looked at him with disbelief as my eyes rolled. "You won't let it happen? Excuse you." I challenged him with a glare as I turned around in my seat to face him. "You have no say in whether I divorce you or not, not that I was going that direction mind you. There is a way to nullify the marriage, and actually I was going to bring up the issue to you a little later on because it is a real legal issue. You didn't marry me. The name on the documents, all of what was signed that night, that's not my legal name." A false identity was a sure way to get legal things nulled and voided. "I didn't say anything that night when I noticed their mistake just in case—"

For the first time, he raised his voice at me. He snapped at me, "In case you needed an out? When were you going to tell me this? Were you always planning an escape?" Okay, now he seemed really upset, not that I blamed him.

After a few nights of passionate sex, it was clear to both of us that we both felt more for each other than we were willing to admit. So, for something like this to pop out was like a stab to the gut. I would be upset if I was in his shoes, and rightfully so.

"Yes, but I tossed that idea out of my mind the moment it was you I was going to marry, and after seeing that you weren't some horrible bastard. I kept that secret because I knew it was going to come in handy in the future, not in the sense of nulling the marriage because I don't want you, because I do. I just wanted a means to keep you out of anything messy if it came to it. Also, I knew the treaty would be a problem, one that I would need to be rid of, which is the main reason why I kept the fact that the name penned was not me. I'm not going to divorce you or leave you, not unless you give me reason to run far from you." It seemed messy and overly complicated, but this is the business of mafia life.

"I promise you Nikolai, when this shit is over, and you still want me, then we can get our marriage legally set straight." The chemistry between us was undeniable. From what I've been told, it wasn't easy to find someone who set that passion within you on fire like this.

We weren't two horny teenagers needing to fuck each other out of our systems, and the past nights had been a testimony to that. We were never going to get enough of each other. The look of desire, and the fire in his eyes whenever he set those gorgeous azure blue orbs of his on me was the same as the first night I pulled him out of the car. Even now as we sat here, having our first argument, he still held that same fire along with the hurt.

"Damn right we are." He said with a scowl before turning away from me and giving me the cold shoulder.

"*Anh*, I'm sorry, but I didn't know how or when to even bring it up to you." Granted, there would probably never be a good time to bring something like this up. Deep down, I knew it wasn't going to get a good response no matter how or when I did it. "I have no intentions of hurting you or using that fact as a means of escape. You might find that hard to believe right now, but it's the truth."

"Hm." At least he wasn't giving me the silent treatment.

Sliding off my seat, I got behind him and wrapped my arms around him. "Let's put this behind us, yeah?" Even though he was upset at me, his body betrayed him. The way his skin crawled with my touch. The subtle shiver. His muscles tensed wherever my hands touched, and most important of all, his arousal evident. "I'll make it up to you." I whispered sultrily in his ear as I palmed his hardness through his pants.

In a flash, he turned around and grabbed me by my neck and shoved me onto the island countertop, glaring down at me with blown pupils that darkened his blue eyes hotly. "You're going to spend forever making it up to me, and I am going to make sure of it. And don't think I won't punish you for it either because I will, and it's going to be one you will remember for the rest of your life." His voice was full of conviction, and no doubt he would make good on those promises. I expected no less from him, and I looked forward to seeing what he had in store.

His lips set my body on fire as he kissed me angrily and deeply, wanting to indulge but not at the same time. His tongue aggressively invaded my mouth and fought mine as his hands yanked my pants down and off.

Growling softly, he pressed himself against me, grinding his hardness into my aching cunt. "You're so wet already." He whispered against my lips as his fingers stroked the length of my pussy.

My body flinched at the sudden sting on my aching sex, and it took me a second to realize why. Nikolai had brought his hand down on it. He fucking spanked my pussy! And it wasn't just once! Every time he brought his hand down on me, my body jolted from the painful pleasure that made a fire cascade over my body, stiffening my nipples under my shirt.

Then, he stopped, pulling me away briefly to turn me around. "Bend over, *lisichka*." The feeling of his hand on my back sent chills of panic down my spine.

Looking back at him with scared eyes, I reached back and grabbed his arm. "Please, no. I can't." My voice wavered as I looked at him pleadingly.

"What's the safe word?" His body softened for a moment as his eyes searched my face for an answer.

"Fire." I quickly replied in a firm voice.

Something the two of us did right after our first night was figure out a safe word after discussing our limits. Nikolai was adamant on having the serious discussion before we engaged in anything rough again, so I was more than eager to discuss with him sooner than later.

"Do you want to use your safe word?" Another thing I've come to appreciate about Nikolai when it came to our sexual activities was how he'd always look out for my safety and put it above all else. I've never had to use my safe word yet, but he was always keen on paying me enough attention to ease back at the first sign of discomfort.

Softly and quickly, I shook my head, "No." My voice barely came out as a squeak, but one syllable was all he needed to continue.

"Then bend over. Just a little, darling. Can you do that for me? Just bend over a little and grab the edge of the counter." There was a gentleness to his stern voice that eased my nerves a little. With a shaky breath, I nodded my head and bent forward a little and gripped the edges of the countertop.

"Good girl." The praise made me let out a breathy moan as I leaned into his hand when I felt it on my bare bottom. Then, the feeling of his hand weaving into my hair made me tense again for a moment. Glancing back at him, I could see him studying me closely with his sky-blue eyes that were shaded from his blown pupils.

"Keep going, sir. I can take it." I hope. I already teetered on the edge of wanting to fall into the abyss of lust or shutting down completely. Nikolai wouldn't harm me, he wasn't like *him*, but that bad taste still clawed at me like a demon trying to drag me down into Hell.

Bracing myself, I sucked in a sharp breath when I felt the first hit jolt my body forward. There was no pause before the second and third came down on me, barely giving me any time to brace myself again. I tried to hold back my sounds of pain and pleasure, not wanting to give him any kind of reaction, but I failed after the fifth hit. The squeal squeezed out of my throat, and the whimpers followed after with every hit until tears fell from my eyes. I didn't know how many spanks he delivered, having lost count after fifteen. The fact I still ached from last night's punishment didn't help either.

The feeling of my body being turned around and placed on the counter again barely registered in my pain riddled mind. The feeling of his hand around my throat again being the only thing keeping me rooted to reality. The faint sound of his zipper coming undone barely registered in my hazy mind before the slight pain of him entering fully into me ripped a moan from my throat. He didn't wait for me to fully adjust before moving his hips erratically, making me moan loudly at the sudden pleasure and pain that ravaged my body. "Kolya!" I could feel my orgasm ready to snap already.

"No." The anger in his voice made me shiver under him as I gripped at his arm that pinned me down by my neck. "You are not allowed to come." He only made things worse when he slid his hand under my shirt and ran his hand up my body to my breasts, cupping it roughly and pinching my hard nipple between his digits to where it became painful.

He showed me no mercy, his hips slamming into me hard and fast. The feeling of his thighs hitting my sore ass jolted more pain into my body with each thrust, reminding me this was a punishment and not for my pleasure.

"Kolya, please, I'm sorry, please don't do this to me, please." I knew his intentions. This was a punishment for my deception, but whether it was the full brunt of it was unbeknownst to me. "Sir, please."

"No." He was firm and determined. Just one look in his eyes and I knew he would make me regret it greatly if I dared defy him.

His hips were relentless as he let out his anger using my body. It was so unbearable, holding back my orgasm like this. The painful knot in my stomach became worse when he propped my legs up on the edge of the countertop, enabling him to drive himself deeper into me. "You best burn this in your mind, *lisichka*. Remember this the next time you think of doing anything like that, if you even dare think about a next time." He snarled, making me whimper pathetically.

The rough pad of his thumb brushed against my cheek, wiping away at the tears that started to spill from my eyes.

"I'm sorry, I'll never do it again, I swear." My emotions were spilling over, and I couldn't hold any of it back. I was angry, at myself, at him, at the world. Angry at myself for hiding things from him, for being a soft-hearted person and allowing my stepmother to manipulate me into her schemes, and for being such a messed up person. I was mad at Nikolai for not hating me, for being the better person and forgiving me so easily like this. I wasn't even mad at him for punishing me like this; I deserved it. Then I was just angry at the world for everything, for being shitty, for how my life had been forced down this road where I had to go back on my own promises to myself.

"Sir, I can't, it's too much." I whimpered needily, digging my nails into his forearm as I felt my shreds of sanity disappearing with my control.

"Just a little longer baby, I'm close. Just keep holding it for me, *lisichka*. You can do it." He whispered sweetly against my lips before kissing me softly.

His hand released my breast and slid down my body between my legs, his fingers brushing around until he found his prize. My body jolted from the shock of pleasure that came from having my clit rubbed as he fucked me like a madman. "Let go, *lisichka*. Let go."

Everything snapped at his command. My scream of pleasure filled the area briefly before being cut short from the intense pleasure of my orgasm which made my mind go blank. I didn't know when I came back to reality, but I found myself within Nikolai's comforting embrace when I did. "Shh, shh, it's okay, I've got you, just let it go, *lisischka*. Let it out." I was confused as to why he was soothing me. I was fine. It was just an intense orgasm.

Then the sounds of sobbing hit my ears. I wondered where the sound came from for a second before realizing it came from me. I sobbed uncontrollably and clung onto Nikolai for dear life. Everything I had bottled up behind the dam now rushed out.

Being remorseful and afraid of losing everything took its toll on me finally. I had been so afraid of losing Nikolai just now with my secret. I don't know why I reacted so badly to it because we hadn't even known each other for half a month. Maybe it was because I was so fucked up I clung onto the first man who treated me decently and look at me with want. Hell, if that's what I wanted then a dog would have been a better companion. I don't know what was wrong with me anymore. All I knew was I was a dumpster fire of a mess.

"I'm sorry." My voice was muffled by his shirt and chest as I kept my face buried into him.

"I know you are, and I forgive you. I already forgave you before punishing you." His chest rumbled with his deep words when he spoke. "You're not hiding anything else from me are you? Like a secret husband or kids? An evil twin? A dump site for all your victims?" He joked with a soft chuckle as he pulled me away from him, holding my face with his hands and wiping my tears away with his thumbs.

Unable to control it, I smiled back at him and laughed softly. "No, none of that. There's stuff about my past, but I'm just not ready to bring that back up yet. But nothing as important as that whole thing with my mistaken identity on the papers." Nothing I had left should have a big impact. "Sorry for getting your shirt wet and snotty."

He didn't seem too bothered by the fact I just sobbed all over him. Then again, he chose to hold me. I figured if he was bothered by it then he wouldn't have pulled me against him like that. "Comes with the territory. Doesn't matter, I have a lot of shirts. What are you even doing anyways?" He asked with a nod towards my laptop.

"Oh, just surveillance photos of the warehouse we're going to tackle tomorrow night." I spoke as if it was a typical Friday night activity and not something dangerous.

"By tackle you mean?" He pressed for more clarification.

"It's just something me, Greg, Bao, and Hanna do to chip away at my stepmother's profits. We occasionally raid her warehouses and send the information we find there to the authorities, after we have our fun." Nothing like fucking with my stepmother to make my day. Too bad I won't be around this time to see her distress like always.

"And when were you going to tell me about your late-night Batman activities?" And there's the tone of 'you're in trouble young lady' I anticipated.

"Hey, you have your business meetings, I have my business meetings." I had triad business and he had bratva business, so I saw no difference between our activities. "You're not going to stop me, and if you try, I will make you regret it. I know, it's dangerous, I shouldn't be doing this, blah blah blah. But, I mean, I can say the same about the shit you do, so don't give me that bullshit if you're planning to." There are some things he won't compromise on, and there are things I won't. My activities regarding my personal vendetta against my stepmother was a huge one I would never let him control along with my career.

"At least take Benjamin or Tim with you, preferably both, but at least one of them." He gave in reluctantly with a sigh of defeat.

"Seriously? That easy? Huh, I expected more from you." Not like I wanted to complain, but I had the whole argument planned out in my mind.

"Well, arguing with you about it will get us both nowhere. The only way I'd be able to prevent you from doing anything is chaining you to the bed and locking the room, which we both know won't end well because you'd probably stab me in my sleep as payback. Besides, it's not like you're some pampered princess. Will I worry about you? Of course, I always will no matter where you are or what you are doing. But I'm not going to attempt to put a stop to your life. That wouldn't be fair for me to continue running the Bratva and making you stop running your end of the Triad or whatever it is that you are doing. Just promise me that you'll come back home, alive." Nikolai didn't seem happy with the fact, but at least he wanted to work with what we got.

Our marriage wasn't normal from the very start, and I never expect it to become something out of a magazine. We were mafia, we weren't going to come home from our 9 to 5 job to nice home cooked meals and sleep soundly in our beds without a single worry. And I was fine with it because normal is overrated.

I'm thankful Nikolai wasn't an ass and tried to control my life and force me into some housewife role or treated me like some possession to be locked away at the estate. The only control he ever asserted over me took place in the bedroom, which I welcomed and craved. Other than that, my career and major life choices were fully mine to make.

"Thank you." Smiling, I wrapped my arms around his torso and hugged him tightly. "I promise I'll be as careful as I can. I always am, but I promise. And I promise I will do my best to come back home to you alive and kicking." I wasn't going to come back home unharmed, but I'd be alive at the very least.

"And I'll take Benjamin with me." Guess he'll just be the getaway driver because my crew and I had our system down to a tee. Tossing a new person in this close to a raid would be disastrous.

Chapter 21

Angel

SMILING HAPPILY TO MYSELF, I carefully loaded the magazine into the new Glock Nikolai gave me as a stay safe present.

Nothing like a new gun to make the missus happy.

I probably sound like a psychopath being happy and giddy about my husband gifting me a gun. Even though I never killed—unless absolutely necessary—a gun was always a good thing to have in the mafia business.

"Damn, wish I had a man to gift me nice shit like that." Hanna grumbled with a pout as she loaded her handguns. "Seriously, fuck chocolate and roses, I want guns and bullets. Or a nice bat."

"I honestly don't get why you like using a bat so much, it's so impractical." I remarked with a chuckle as I loaded my spare magazines into my leg's holsters. "I mean, you have to carry the big thing around with you, and you have to get up close and personal to use it which puts you in the danger zone."

"It's fun to beat people up with it. Honestly, guns are nice, but they do things too quickly. I mean, put a hole in someone and you gotta find a new spot to blast, while with a bat or my fist then I can hit the same area as much as I want." Hanna justified her reasoning with a small shrug of her shoulders. "Either way, I'm ready."

"B-Boy is ready too." Bao's voice came over our earpiece.

"Bao, how many times do I have to tell you, you are not nick-naming yourself B-Boy, that is just bleh." Hanna replied, sticking her tongue out at the end for effect.

"Oh come on, it's a classic." Bao argued with a playful whine.

"It's also stupid. Now shut up and glue your eyes to the monitor." Greg chimed in. "I'm ready at the back with my crew."

"Hanna and I are ready over here along with everyone else." I replied, looking at the three other men who were a part of our crew.

"Alright, it's all clear. No workers, just a few guards. Gimme a second to count... Okay, seven on the upper floor, and eleven on the main floor. Careful, they're armed with assault rifles and pistols, and no doubt knives and daggers. There are a lot of flammable things in there, so be extra careful. Floor plans indicate a basement, but there must be no cameras down there because I can't detect anything with my sweep." Bao relayed the information to us from the safety of the equipment van.

"Copy. We'll clear the guards then take the basement. Remember, no killing unless necessary. Dead men don't talk. Is that clear?" I wanted information, and someone in there was bound to know something about Lady Qing and her plans. Even if it was just a grain, it was better than none.

"Yes, loud and clear." Everyone replied.

"Alright. Go!" I commanded, kicking in the front door with Hanna.

Chaos ensued the moment the barrier was breached, the guards wasted no time shouting at us and letting the bullets go. We were forced to duck behind the stack of crates to avoid becoming swiss cheese as we waited for an opening to fire back.

"Everyone cover your eyes." I warned before throwing a flash bomb at the guards. "Go!" I commanded after the bomb went off, vaulting myself over the crate and rushing forward.

The sounds of gunshots filled the air again with the sounds of bodies dropping and complaints of pain as we fired back.

A pained grunt coughed out of my throat from the impact to my cheek. "Oof!" Okay, that would leave a pretty mark. Unfortunately, a butt of a gun always wins against a face.

I quickly recovered and caught myself from stumbling back a few steps. I couldn't give the guard in front of me more openings.

Reaching out, I grabbed the barrel of his gun and used it to pull him towards me, kneeing him in the gut and bringing my elbow down on his arm to pry the rifle away from him. After tossing the rifle a distance, I backhanded him with my gun and watched as he fell to the ground. Then, just for good measure, I placed a single shot to both his knees.

THUNK!

Looking behind me, I watched another guard fall to the ground in a daze. "Hanna, what the..."

"I found a crowbar." She stated matter of factly as she gave the dazed guard a swing to the face, cracking something in the area of impact. Then, she turned her attention to another guard who had his back to her. Poor man had no idea what hit him, literally. He was out cold on the floor with a busted head the moment the crowbar connected.

THUD!

The body narrowly missed me by inches. "Sorry! He fell!" Greg shouted from the second floor. Whelp, that was another person we weren't going to get information out of. Not with how his brains were splattered on the concrete floor.

Movement out of the corner of my eyes made me turn my head. A downed guard crawled on his elbows towards a gun. "Nah ah," I quickly ran over and stomped on his wrist, feeling it give under my weight as the man screamed in pain. "Don't even think—" A sudden tackle cut me off, a pained grunt leaving me when I landed on the ground. My head snapped to the side following the impact of a punch.

Instinctively, I threw my arms up to block the incoming blows. Once I saw an opening between his punches, I reached out and grabbed at his face, digging my finger into his eye before sliding my other hand down to pull my dagger out. Swiftly, I swiped the tip of the dagger across his face, causing him to lean back.

Without hesitation, I brought the dagger down into his shoulder, using it to help throw him off of me when I bucked my hips up to dislodge him from myself. I threw him off to the side and pulled my dagger out before stabbing the blade into the side of his knee.

Spinning around, my eyes locked onto my next target. With a small grunt of effort, I threw my dagger at a guard who aimed his gun at one of my men. The dagger embedded itself into his chest, a dead hit. The guard's body fell to the floor with a thud.

The fight ended faster than I hoped, which was a good thing in my books. No casualties on our side, major injuries, but no casualties. Thank God. Once we rounded the survivors up, we bound them up and set them well outside the warehouse for now.

After leaving my men to guard our captives, I went back inside with Hanna and Greg. "Hanna and I will check the basement. Greg, you stay up here with the others and keep an eye on these idiots until the van comes around." I said while reloading my gun with one of my spare magazines. "Bao, where's the entrance to the basement?"

"About thirteen-feet from you to the right, looks like a crate might be on top of the hatch." Bao replied.

Carefully, I went over to the area with Hanna and started to clear the crates away until I saw a handle and hatch. Grasping the handle, I looked at Hanna who nodded at me to indicate she was ready. Pulling the hatch open, I ran in behind Hanna, gun at the ready. Scowling deeply, I hissed angrily under my breath, "Shit, we're too late. It's empty." The basement was lined with cages like an animal shelter. Heck, the cages at the shelter were nicer and more secure than these beat up looking ones.

I hoped we wouldn't find something like this today, but that was me being too hopeful. Just like the last two raids, we stood before empty cages that should be filled with human beings. "We'll get to them next time." Hanna placed a hand on my shoulder, squeezing it softly.

My grip on my gun tightened until my knuckles turned white while I gritted my teeth. "That's what we said the last two times. I am just starting to get really pissed off about coming in a step behind like this. I can brush the first time off as luck, maybe the second, but for us to come up empty a third time. Well, I don't believe it. Something is going on, and I don't like it one bit." Was it possible I had a leak? How else would we come up empty three times in a row? But if I did have a leak then why is the warehouse even stocked still? It wouldn't make any sense to just move the bodies and not the crate of drugs.

What the hell is going on?

Chapter 22

Angel

"Isn't—"

"Jesus fucking Christ! Don't scare me like that!" I practically jumped out of my pants at Nikolai's sudden appearance in the bathroom. Taking a few deep breaths, I placed my hand over my racing heart to calm myself. "Quit laughing, it's not funny! You nearly gave me a heart attack."

"I'm sorry, you were too cute and funny. For someone who's supposed to be trained into their surroundings all the time, that was too easy and cute. I wasn't even hiding my steps either." His laughter had died down to a chuckle as I pouted and glared at him.

"I know, I can hear your thundering steps from the damn kitchen all the time." I shot back with a roll of my eyes. Taking another deep breath, I turned my attention back to the mirror as I used the washcloth to clean the blood off my face. "Have you been home long?"

"No, just got home and Benjamin informed me that you were up here." Nikolai answered while taking the washcloth from me. "Here, let me." I wasn't going to fight him if he wanted to clean me up.

Relaxing, I let him pick me up and set me on the countertop, watching as he rinsed the cloth before gently wiping at my face and neck. "You know, isn't it supposed to be the other way around? Me coming home bloodied and beaten and you cleaning me up?"

"Oh we'll have plenty of those moments no doubt." I laughed softly as I pictured the scene perfectly in my mind. No doubt the two of us were going to be cleaning and patching each other up as time went on. "Thanks for doing this, you don't have to."

Chuckling softly with an adoring smile, he leaned in and placed a quick kiss on my forehead before going back to cleaning me. "My wife comes home covered in blood and grime, of course I'm going to take care of her. And I'm not doing it because I have to, it's because I want to. So, get used to it." No one would ever think a brute like him could be so gentle and caring. I wonder if anyone would believe me if I told them about this.

"You really want to get used to me coming home in this state?" I joked with a chuckle, earning a small flick on the nose from him. "You're not going to lecture me?"

"About what? Going out there and doing what you need to do? Do I like seeing you coming home like this? Absolutely not, but we both know that in this line of business, if you are involved then you're going to get your hands dirty and beaten. You came back home with no major injuries, so I can rest easy." He wasn't happy about any of this. I could hear the edge in his voice, the wariness of it along with the apprehension.

"*Anh*." Reaching up, I placed my hand over his, holding him at my cheek, "I promise, when things settle, I won't be coming home like this. I plan on going back to being as uninvolved as possible. So, this is just temporary." I wouldn't rest easy until I put Lady Qing down with my own bare hands. Afterwards, I have no intentions on being so hands-on in the business, mine or Nikolai's. "I don't like it, but it's just what I have to do right now."

Sighing heavily, Nikolai pulled his hand away to set the cloth down so he could use both of his hands to cup my face, his thumb softly brushing my bottom lip as he looked deeply into my eyes with worried ones. "Let me help then, you don't have to shoulder the burden yourself anymore. I know you can handle yourself, but it'll put me at ease if I had your back out there."

Unable to help it, I giggled softly with a smile. "Who would have thought that my big bad bratva husband is such a softie at heart." It was endearing, and it made my heart melt, as cliche as it sounded.

"I hate that you bring this out of me, but in a way it's good to know I still have some shred of humanity in me." There was a stormy conflict in his eyes with his words. "Though, it's also damning."

Gently cupping his face, I kept his eyes on mine as I spoke, "No, it's not, *anh*. I know in this line of work it's better to be a heartless bastard, but having emotions is a good thing for this world. Emotions don't make you weak, they make you stronger. When you feel for something, the desire to preserve it will drive you to greater lengths than you could ever imagine. Yes, your enemies will use your emotions against you, but those same emotions will drive you to better yourself for your own sake and those you care about."

Breathing deeply, I wet my lips with the tip of my tongue before letting out a soft chuckle and continuing, "Maybe I'm just soft, but I also know that nothing good ever comes out of shutting your emotions out entirely. It's a lonely and sad life to deny your emotions to where you shut yourself off from everyone who cares about you. You only have one life, might as well live it how you want. And I don't want to hear some bullshit about your standing as the head and how it will be weak and shit because it doesn't."

Pausing to collect my thoughts, I looked deeply into his eyes briefly as my thumbs stroked his cheeks. "Being a leader is so much more than just techniques and methods, you need that emotional aspect, to make yourself a little vulnerable. Good leaders are supposed to inspire themselves and their followers. It's all about the actual experience and not some stupid processes. There's no guidebook that outlines things step by step when it comes to leadership because it's not that simple. It's not some stupid routine."

I had no idea where the fuck I went with things, and I'm pretty sure what bullshit I spewed made no sense. "Please don't drag this on more because philosophy is not my strong suit, and I've reached my inspirational quota for the year." I don't know how I passed the damn class in college, but I did somehow with my pants on fire.

The two of us fell into a moment of laughter as we leaned into each other. "I try so hard to break away at what my father beat into me, and sometimes I wonder if it's the right thing to do or if I am just retaliating to spite the damn bastard in death." He admitted with a heavy sigh.

"What you are doing is right. Your men follow you and remain loyal to you because they respect you, not fear you. So, even if you think otherwise, you are doing more right than wrong as a leader." Did it make any sense? I have no idea, my brain tapped out for the night, and my words sounded like utter nonsense to me. Well, as long as it helped him, that's all that mattered.

"Well, I couldn't have fucked up that bad if the world gave me you." He chuckled against my lips before kissing me deeply. "You know, you look hot in this outfit." His hand worked at the straps of my holster as he spoke with a smirk.

"I'm just wearing a typical tactical outfit, nothing hot about that." Everything was all black too. It wasn't like I wore something scandalous.

"You just have this aura of power in this outfit, more than usual. Reminds me of just how deadly and formidable you can be. And what really gets me going is the fact that this powerful woman is all mine." He growled proudly before pressing his lips against mine in a possessive kiss. He captured my bottom lip between his teeth, tugging it as he pulled away. "Let's get you cleaned up properly, then I can show you who you belong to at the end of the day."

"Yes, sir." I purred with a smile.

"After your punishment of course." The smug bastard.

"Oh come on, I just came home all beaten up, are you really going to bend me over your knee and beat me some more?" I asked with a pout, doing my best to give him some puppy dog eyes.

Chuckling, he slipped his hands under my shirt to rest them on my bare waist. "*Lisichka*, that's never going to work on me. Also, I am not going to beat you, I am going to spank you, punish you, there's a huge difference. I thought about letting it spill into tomorrow night until the fact that you disobeyed me regarding Benjamin coming with you. So, now I can't let you off the hook, otherwise I'd be losing my touch."

"Fuck. He told you? Damn, I must be losing my touch if he got free." In my defense, I had intended on taking him so he could be the driver, but after a stressful shift, I didn't want to deal with the possibility of Benjamin jumping in because it was his job to protect me.

"Of course he told me about your little stunt of sedating him and leaving him hogtied in the back of his own vehicle." And there was the stern, dominating tone of his.

"Snitch." I grumbled, crossing my arms and turning my pouting face away from Nikolai.

His strong fingers gripped my cheeks, forcing my head back to him. "I'm his boss, of course he's going to tell me about any shit you pull. He may be your bodyguard, and you technically his boss, but I'm the one he reports to at the end of the day." He paused for a second, darting his tongue out to sweep it across his lips before continuing, "Now, like I said, we're going to get you cleaned up nicely, then I'll dish out your punishment before taking all that is mine."

"Yes, sir." I sighed softly, letting him help me off the counter and back on my feet. Resigning to defeat was the only option unless I wanted to make things harder for myself. It was either give in and get pleasure or fight and be left hanging. It was clear to Nikolai I enjoyed getting punished, or at the very least my body did by how wet and aroused I would get every time he took me over his knee. If I behaved then he'd let me orgasm, if not then it would just be a night filled with frustration.

Just as he was about to pull my shirt off, his phone went off. He showed no sign of answering it, letting it ring out, but then it went off a second time right after. "I have to get this. I trust you can get yourself cleaned up without much trouble, *lisichka*. I expect you to be naked on the bed when you're done."

"Yes, sir." I muttered, fidgeting with my fingers as I thought about later. I was nervous, but not for the right reason.

Nikolai gave me a quick kiss before leaving the bathroom, shutting the door behind him. Alone in the bathroom, I quickly stripped myself and hopped in the shower, letting the hot water cascade over me. I've been lucky with the lights off and the over dark nights, but there was no way I'd be able to avoid things for much longer.

"Ouch!" The snap of my hair tie stung at my wrist more than I had expected. "Come on, you have to tell him eventually... Just rip the bandaid off..." Okay, maybe pep talking to myself in the shower wasn't as helpful as I thought because it only made me more anxious. It also made me feel like a madwoman finally losing her damn mind.

The soft click of the door opening took my attention. "*Lisichka*, I have to head out, something requires my attention. It's going to run late unfortunately, so guess you're lucky tonight." Nikolai's voice echoed through the bathroom.

"Oh, okay. Be safe out there, and make sure you come back to me alive." I half shouted after him.

Love you.

No, that's just crazy. I cared for him, deeply, but to go as far to say it was love? It felt too strange, too soon. Besides, it almost made us feel normal, which we weren't.

"Alright, good night, *lisichka*. I promise I'll come back." I couldn't help but feel a tinge of disappointment when I heard the door shut. The solution to my problem presented itself, but it was just another excuse to prolong the inevitable at this point too. I couldn't keep something like this from him, but I couldn't face *that* demon again, not yet.

What if he couldn't look at me the same way after knowing? I don't know if I could handle that kind of rejection from him. I didn't want to lose Nikolai, not after falling for him this fast and hard. But, if it happened sooner than later, wouldn't it be less painful? The more I got involved with him, the more deeply rooted with him I would become. But, maybe he won't react to how my paranoia presented things to me. Nikolai wasn't a shallow person from what I've seen, and he wasn't immature to the point where he'd react poorly... I hope.

Chapter 23
Nikolai

THE BURNING STING OF alcohol on open injuries never bothered me since I was a child. After being subjected to what I deemed as torture back then by the hands of my father, I had been conditioned by him to not react to pain or let pain bother me. The vile man used to purposely inflict open injuries to me to dump bottles of rubbing alcohol and hydrogen peroxide on them until I would stop screaming and crying. Then he would proceed to beat me for reacting in the first place.

"Hope whoever was on the receiving end looks worse than your knuckles." Angel joked with a dry chuckle, not looking up as she kept her focus on tending to my busted knuckles.

I thought I could sneak by my slumbering beauty when I came back late from my business outing, but either I was louder than I thought or she wasn't deep asleep. I barely managed to wash my hands in the bathroom sink before Angel was by my side and took over.

"What even happened anyways? I thought you were just going to check out a warehouse like you usually do to make sure things were going okay." This time she did look at me for a split second, letting me know with her stern eyes she wanted an answer.

"Well, it wasn't a routine check. One of the men who I've sent to help Ivan tipped me off about unusual activity at one of Ivan's warehouses. I was supposed to meet up with Ivan at the place and we'd go in together, under the guise of me wanting to see exactly how he ran things and such. He bailed on me last minute, whether it was planned or not is yet to be determined, but you and I both know that coincidences like that don't just happen. We were ambushed when we got there, and so far Ivan's saying it's his worker going rogue and that he had no idea about anything. Things still turned into a shitshow of bullets and punches, but we managed to capture some for holding and questioning. At least his men couldn't aim for shit, they were just a bunch of amateurs." I ended with an exhausted sigh.

Thinking back a few hours ago to the ambush ticked me off. I felt like I had been tricked from the very start, and no one tricks me. I had questioned my informant, and he swore he didn't mislead me. After a few blows to his face and body, it was clear he didn't turn on me. So, either he was fed false information, or I had missed something. Maybe the attack covered for something, or it could have been a distraction. My men and I didn't get a chance to do a sweep through the place because of the ambush, and we didn't stick around after either because we had to get medical attention.

At least we managed to round up some of the men who survived, and they're being kept at a secure location until I get a chance to question them. Funny thing was Ivan didn't seem to notice the missing men, or if he did then he didn't mention it. For someone who was tight on money, I would think he'd want to keep what he had instead of trying to hire new talent because rates are going higher and higher everyday unless he managed to snag a complete idiot who was high or drunk off their ass.

"No casualties right?" Angel asked, glancing up at me again briefly before turning her attention back to the bandage wrappings she used to mummify my hand with.

"No." Thank God.

"Might not be the best time to bring up Ivan, but Bao did find some stuff that might be useful. He managed to get his hands on some shipping manifests, and some things aren't adding up. He also traced Ivan's activities back to Russia as well, but he's having a bit of a harder time getting his hands on information from that end of things;

because of the system that is used over there." Angel informed me as she finished with one of my hands.

Sighing heavily, I ran the bandaged hand through my messy hair. "I have some contacts in Russia that I can call favors from, and I can contact our branch there too. Whatever he's hiding, we're going to find it eventually." The damn snake has to slither back to his nest eventually, and that's when we'll see what skeletons he hid.

Speaking of skeletons, "*Lisichka*, how much do you know about your father's health and how it came to be?"

"Well, he is old, and old age brings on sickness. Arthritis developed, then his mental health slowly started to creep on him, he got frail, then not enough nutrition eventually led to his malnourished state, and eventually he ended up in a coma because his health had declined so much due to the stress." It sounded like a fair answer, and no one would think twice about something like this.

Unfortunately, our lives weren't so simple. "I don't think it was old age that got to your father." Not after what was revealed to me.

"*Anh*, what are you getting at? If you're trying to suggest foul play then I did look into that, but I've seen my father's medical records. I also can't find any kind of proof, even with all the lab tests to rule out poisons and shit. I want to think otherwise as well, but the medical side of me tells me otherwise. There is no proof, just old age, stress, and the conditions that come with it. I was very much in denial about his health, but I've learned to make my peace with it." Her tone told me otherwise. She hadn't accepted it, not fully. I could hear the reluctance in her voice. A part of her still doubted.

I intended to bring this up to her earlier before I got too busy, and I wanted to wait until tomorrow since it was late into the night now. But, since we got onto the subject, I saw no point in withholding.

So, taking her hand, I led her to my office, settling in my chair behind the desk with her comfortably seated in my lap.

"I've asked some of my people who work in the hospital to keep a close eye on your father, and they've noticed some discrepancies," I said before opening a drawer at my desk, pulling out a manilla envelope. "One of the doctors who works for me took over your father's care, and she found some interesting things when she combed through his chart."

Angel opened the envelope and pulled out its contents, quickly skimming through them. "These are his chart notes, and I've seen them before." Now she gave me a confused look like I was some delusional idiot. "This is such a big HIPPA violation, I hope you know that." She informed me with a chuckle and roll of her eyes.

"Look at them again, carefully." I watched as she went over the stack of papers again, this time taking her time with each page. It only took a few pages for the realization to hit her after flip-flopping between some of the sheets. "You were given a false chart, one that made it seem like nature took its course with your father. Did you ever find the timing of his condition to be odd?"

"Yeah, but... If my stepmother was behind all of this, then why the timing? It doesn't make any sense." She was upset and confused, and rightfully so. She had been duped this entire time.

"Your father was ready to divorce her from what we could dig up. Maybe she was becoming desperate. You and I both know what desperate people can do." Divorce often led people to take drastic measures more often than not.

"No. She would have gotten half of his shit if they divorced, and he did talk to me about the idea of it, and she knew as well. She would have gained more in a divorce than if my father was gone. I don't understand it though, because she knew that if my father were to become incapacitated then the title of head would fall to me." Angel's eyebrows furrowed together as she bore holes into the papers, deep in thought.

Reaching out, I took the papers from her and set them down on the desk before taking her hand in mine and rubbing the back of it with my thumb. "Well, maybe your father has the answers."

"Unless you've gained magical abilities to jump into someone's head, we're not going to get anything from him anytime soon or possibly ever." Now she looked at me like I had two heads.

Chuckling softly, I shook my head and opened the drawer again, this time pulling out a small fabric sack and dumping its contents onto the desk. "Your stepmother has been drugging your father to keep him in a coma. My men have been able to pickpocket these from the people administering medication to your father. They ran checks on what was administered against what was ordered, and these vials were never found on the order list."

I had no idea what half of those bottles were, but I trusted my men when they told me they were drugs used to induce a comatose state and keep a person in a suspended state. Also, a quick Google search confirmed what they said as well.

No doubt Angel would know and recognize the drugs given her profession. It would seem I was right too because the look of realization and rage stormed within her dark eyes when she examined the various vials. *"Con đĩ đó. Tôi sẽ giết nó!"* Damn, she must be really upset to switch her tongue like that, a habit of hers I had picked up over the past few weeks.

"I am going to assume that was a threat?" I could never figure out which language she is using half the time, let alone what she is saying.

Angel could speak four languages: English, Vietnamese, Cantonese, and Mandarin. I couldn't discern between the two Chinese dialects, but I had gotten keen to know when she spoke Vietnamese. Apparently that was her native tongue from what she told me. Her mother was a Vietnamese woman, and her Chinese father grew up learning the language for business reasons. Since she was home with her mother, it came natural for her to learn and pick up Vietnamese. The other languages came later when her father pushed for her to partake in the triad business briefly. She could only speak the languages though, not read or write in them from what she told me.

"That bitch. I'm going to kill her." She seethed, gripping at the vial in her hand. "I want the doctor too. I have many bones to pick with him."

Is it wrong for me to be turned on right now? Seeing her fired up like this, ready to go wreak havoc, always made my member twitch in my pants. "Whatever you want, *lisichka*, I will make it happen."

"I want the doctor." Her sadistic eyes gained a dark edge to them while the corner of her lips tugged into a smirk. As much as she denied it, she had a sadistic side to her. Ironic given she was a nurse hell bent on doing good and easing the suffering of others. Yet, when it came to her enemies, she often liked to play with them too much. Although, true to her word, she would never outright kill, but everything else was fair game to her.

"Don't worry, I'll have the good doctor all tied up for you, *lisichka*." Kidnapping someone was child's play, and I could easily get away with it because of the hold and sway I had on the law enforcement and officials here in Nespin. I could kill nearly half the population and not spend a second in jail.

Giggling twistedly, she turned her body in my lap until she straddled me. "You're the best," she said with a dark grin, grabbing my face and kissing me deeply. The twisted fire within me flared to life when her lips touched mine. I shouldn't be excited over the fact I just offered a man for her to torture, nor should I get excited at the thought of her enjoyment with torturing the poor man. God we were going straight to Hell for how fucked up and twisted we are.

"Tol'ko dlya tebya moya lyubov'."
Only for you my love.

Although it felt too soon to let her in that far, I knew it in my twisted heart. I won't ever let her go.

"Hm you know, I love it when you speak Russian, but I really hope you're not cursing me or something." She sighed softly with a smile on her face as her finger traced my lips.

"Never, only ever sweet things about you, darling. I wish I could say the same about you when you speak Vietnamese, but I know half the time it's you giving me lip." The attitude she had with her words made it clear she wasn't saying sweet nothings to me. I found it a little too amusing and cute to punish her for it, for now.

"Oh come on, I say sweet things... Sometimes..." She admitted while averting her eyes from me.

"Am I going to have to start counting whenever I hear attitude from you?" It was a playful threat. I already had many reasons to punish her, not as if she didn't give me enough reasons herself. Some might find it annoying, redundant, but I enjoyed her brattiness more than I cared to admit.

"No, sir." She pouted with a slight roll of her eyes. "I'll be good." That was a lie, and we both knew it. I wouldn't have it any other way though, the bite back from her was what kept my blood rushing with excitement.

Her sweet taste invaded my mouth when she pressed her lips against mine, taking it upon herself to force her tongue into my mouth. "Someone's feeling a little bold." I chuckled against her lips after a brief break to breathe. "*Ty takoy vkusnyy. YA nikogda ne nasytlyus' toboy.*" I growled softly before grabbing her face and bringing her back into a bruising kiss.

My hands slowly ran up her bare legs that were exposed from her silk nightgown. Gripping her thighs, I yanked her closer and pressed her firmly against me. The only thing between my throbbing member and her pussy right now were her panties and my pants, but even with the barriers between us, I could feel her needy heat as she ground her hips against me.

I don't think the burning passion for her will ever die down no matter how many times we fucked. I thought this desire for her would fizzle after our first night, but I still found myself craving and thinking about her every second of every damn day. If anything, I wanted her more after our first night together. She was my drug, and the first night the first hit. Now I desperately chased her for another high every chance I got with her.

It didn't matter if I had her over my knee with my hand cracking at her bubbly ass or had my thick length buried so deep in her she lost her mind; every little thing with her was the best. I could fuck her for hours on end or I could simply have her in my lap while I did work, both granted me the same pleasure and satisfaction.

Growling softly, I bit her bottom lip until it swelled before pulling away completely. "Get up. Turn around and bend over the desk." I commanded, giving her plush ass a firm smack to urge her off. I couldn't wait to mark up her pretty ass again with my belt. The thought and act of it always brought out the more primal side of me;

the fact it was me who was marking up her pretty body to give her nice reminders as to who she belonged to.

Reluctantly, she climbed off my lap and turned around to face my sturdy wooden desk. Slowly, she bent over slightly, gripping at the edge of the desk as she stood firmly with the bottom of her nightgown bunched up around her waist and her ass out. I wanted her to fully bend over the desk so she laid flat against it, but I wasn't going to push for it and have her shut down on me.

One thing I've learned about Angel so far was she hated having her back to me, reason still unknown. Most of the time when I had to punish her, I had her over my knee or against the wall—even those moments were icy.

If I walked into the same area she occupied, she'd instantly turn to hide her back from me if she faced away. Even when we showered together, she kept her back hidden from my eyes by always being the last in and last out, and always kept her front facing me the whole time. I've been patient with her so far regarding it, barely ever asking or pushing the issue, but when I would she would either avoid it or shut down.

I wanted to push her, but I feared about crossing a line with her too soon and being unable to recover from it. I had enough sense to know when to push her limits. I may spank her ass red or give her welts that would last over hours, but I never gave her beyond what she could handle. Just enough to get the point across. The point was to punish her, not traumatize her.

Getting up from my chair, I stood behind her and quickly worked my belt off, palming the buckle and folding it in half. Reaching out, I groped and rubbed at her bare ass framed by her black thong. "You know, I have to say, you did good today, *lisichka*. Or at the very least better than yesterday." I could still see some of the marks from last night which brought a proud smirk to my face and made my hardness strain against its confines. "Only twenty-five today. You know what you need to do, right *lisichka*?" I gave her a small pat, making her suck in a small breath.

"Yes, sir. Count each one." Good to see she learned her lesson from that one time she decided to test me.

With a snap of my wrist, the sound of the leather biting her skin brought a shiver of pleasure straight down my spine to my dick. I made her punishment a quick one this time seeing her discomfort about bending over onto the desk. She pushed herself out of her comfort zone, so I didn't want her to linger for long to where it became too much for her. Even though I made it quick, I made sure each lash counted—no such thing as quick *and* easy. Each lash left a nice line against her reddening skin after having contact with the worn leather. The sight of the skin paling before blushing back up brought a twisted smile to my face as I marked up nearly every inch of her plush bottom.

A wave of satisfaction washed over me at the final lash. With one big stride, I stood right behind her. Softly, I placed my hand on her hot bottom, rubbing the reddened cheeks while praising her, "*Ty tak khorosho postupila, lyubov'. YA tak gorzhus' toboy.*"

My belt clattered onto the floor after I let it slip from my grasp. Bringing the freed hand up, I trailed a finger down her arm and took her hand to spin her around to face me.

Smiling proudly, I released her hand to bring my hand up to cup her face and wipe away her tears with my thumb. "You look so sweet right now." The sight of her tear-stricken face aroused me so much knowing it was all because of my doing. "So perfect."

With a soft groan, I captured her lips in a deep kiss, pulling her with me as I backed up into my chair and sat down. Angel landed in my lap with a small grunt as I positioned her legs to straddle me. "Ride me, *lisichka*. Show me how much you need me in you right now."

My hands quickly traveled down the sides of her body to the hem of her nightgown, bunching it in my large hands and pulling it over her head and off of her, discarding it on the floor next to us. Leaning in, I tilted her head back by grabbing a fistful of her hair, making her moan softly when I pulled rather harshly.

Her body shivered when I ran the tip of my nose and lips down her neck to her breasts where I left open mouthed kisses across her chests and mounds.

"Ow!" Her little yelp made me chuckle and glance up at her while I kept my teeth sunk into her soft flesh. It didn't truly hurt, otherwise she wouldn't be pressing herself closer to me or moaning wantonly.

Her chest and breasts were covered with scattered love bites when I had my fill the other day; the various purple and red markings made the primal urge to pin her down and fill her bubbled to the surface. "I don't see you bouncing on my cock, *lisichka*. Do I need to take you over my knee already?" I threatened with a smirk as I took one of her hardened nipples between my teeth, biting just enough to where she whimpered as she frantically worked at undoing my pants to pull my hardened member out.

Chuckling softly, I took her nipple fully into my mouth, rolling my tongue across the hard bud and flicking at it with the tip. My fingers played with the other nipple as I kneaded her soft breast in my hand. I always found it cute how self-conscious she was about her breasts being on the smaller side, but I couldn't get enough of them. They were a nice fit in my big palms, just enough to fill them perfectly. No matter, I'd spend forever showing her how much I loved every inch of her perfectly imperfect body until she learned to love herself fully for how she is.

"*Yebat'! Tak chertovski plotno i khorosho.*" I groaned sharply at the sudden tightness around my manhood when she slammed herself all the way to the hilt in one swift movement. My hands instantly grabbed at her hips, keeping her firmly planted against me as I wanted to savor this moment before letting her bounce to her delight. "God I am never going to get enough of your tight cunt."

Her soft walls always brought a sense of bliss to me whenever they surrounded me no matter how many times I took her. Her tight cunt felt so perfect to me, and my need for her never wavered. She felt unlike any other woman I've had, and I've had my fair share of screwing around to sate my needs before her. Everyone else before her paled in comparison. I never craved anyone before Angel no matter how good they were.

I felt like a dog on a leash for Angel, an obedient little dog following at its master's heels eagerly for its next treat. Ironic since I'd be the one to hold the leash between us. I could laugh if this situation was different. I held the belt, yet I got whipped by this woman. And I couldn't give a damn about it.

A small needy whimper made my attention snap back fully to the little vixen seated on my cock. She moved her hips against me, her walls squeezing at me. "Sir, let me move, please, I need to feel you more, please, let me ride you like a good little slut, please." She whimpered needily, picking up the pace of her hips grinding against me because it was the only form of gratification I granted her with how my firm grip kept her locked against me.

"I love how needy you become after a punishment. Is that why you're such a brat sometimes, *lisichka*? You like getting that sweet ass of yours spanked don't you?"

I don't even have to dip my fingers between her legs anymore to know she was wet and needy after taking my belt or a spanking with my bare hands. She would always be aroused and soaking wet after a spanking, no matter how much she cried out in pain—she loved it. I've seen the look in her eyes enough times now to see she thoroughly enjoyed the pain I inflicted on her.

I'll never forget the look of her blown pupils from her reflection in the mirror the first time I punished her in the bathroom over the sink. I wasn't sure if she realized it or not, but she had this look of bliss on her pain riddled face whenever I would punish her.

I thought I imagined things at first, but after I punished her a few times in front of the bathroom mirror and the dresser, it was clear she enjoyed taking what I gave as much as I enjoyed dishing it out to her. It was more than a sexual aspect for us though. I don't punish her to get myself off, nor do I punish her to arouse her. Both of us engaged in it because it brought us closer to each other on an emotional level. The immense trust exchanged between us wasn't something either of us would ever take for granted. It made me cherish our relationship immensely.

When she failed to answer me, my hand snapped firmly against her supple ass, making her yelp in response. "I expect an answer, *lisich-*

ka." The dip in my voice should make it clear to her a punishment would be in order if she didn't comply.

"Y-yes." Her cheeks flushed with embarrassment as her eyes averted from mine. Her movements became timid as she tried to make herself small from my gaze.

SMACK!

"Ah!" Her moan made me grope at her hot cheeks as I rolled my hips into her more. "What was that for?"

Clicking my tongue softly, I gave her a harder smack while I looked at her sternly. "Do I need to teach you a lesson in manners again, *lisichka?*" If I gave her an inch then she would run a mile with it. I learned the hard way when I let her slip once without counting it against her, and she pranced around with it. She promptly regretted it though after I gave her welts that lasted nearly two days.

"No, sir. I'm sorry, sir." She replied properly, earning a small pat on her backside along with a proud smile from me.

"Good girl." The small smile on her face from my praise made my own smile soften as I lifted her up until only my tip remained before dropping her back down with a groan as I felt my balls tighten under me. "*Pokatay menya, detka. Osedlay moy chlen, kak budto ot etogo zavisit tvoya zhizn'.*" My hands gave her bottom cheeks another firm smack before resting on her waist as she started to move on her own. "Mhmm fuck, that's it darling."

Moaning softly, Angel rested her hands on my shoulders to help steady herself as she started to move faster, making the office fill with the sounds of our bodies clashing against each other. "Fuck, I love your big cock so much, sir. Never going to get enough of it." She moaned happily with a smile on her face. She started to bring herself down harder on me even without my help, loudly moaning every time she took my length fully into her.

Unable to help myself, I dug my fingers into her hips while bucking my hips up to meet hers. I wouldn't last much longer if she kept this up. "I want to hear my name from those sweet lips of yours when you come, *lisichka*, alright?" I could tell she was close to her limit by how her walls were starting to twitch and clench around me more frequently. Also, the way she picked up her pace and brought herself down onto me more as her moans picked up in pitch was another good indication she was about to go over her edge.

"Yes, sir." She moaned out her reply as her soft face started to twist with pleasure.

Deciding to help her, I reached a hand down and slipped my thumb between her slit, quickly finding her engorged pearl and rubbing at it with the pad of my finger. The slickness from her arousal made my thumb easily slide back and forth against her clit, and I was careful to apply just enough pressure so I wouldn't rub her raw and cut things short. "Come on baby, come for me like the good little slut you are." I encouraged her with a growl, watching as her movements became more erratic with her tensing body. "That's it, come on."

"Oh fuck!" She gasped, her movements getting sloppy and jerky. "Kolya!" Then the sweet release. One final bounce and she remained seated against me as she threw her head back, her lips parting sweetly as her face relaxed with bliss.

When I felt her clamp down on me, I blew my load with a deep groan. My hips thrusted into her while my hand pulled her down flushed against me. "My sweet Angel, so fucking good." A sharp breath caught at my throat when I felt her nails dig into my shoulder and break the skin. "Angel." It felt like my balls were trying to squeeze everything out as they curled into my body.

Releasing her hip, I reached up and grabbed the back of her neck, bringing her into a passionate kiss as the two of us rode out our releases. "You are so perfect." I groaned softly against her lips before nipping at her bottom one.

"A perfect wreck is more like it." She giggled, sticking her tongue out at me.

SLAP!

"You need to learn to start taking compliments, *lisichka*." She really did need to give herself more credit where it's due. Angel was an amazing woman, and everyone but her could see that. I wish she could see it herself, so she could cut herself some slack. She always pushed herself too hard and took on more than she could handle, and I hated how she did so in order to prove herself.

"Why does it feel like my list of things you punish me for just gets longer and longer?" She sighed playfully with a roll of her eyes.

Smirking, I leaned in and gave her a quick kiss before stroking her hair. "Because you give me too many reasons. *Moy malen'kiy otrod'ye.*" My little brat, and I wouldn't have it any other way. I never thought I'd enjoy such brattiness from someone considering how I always demanded obedience and submission because of my controlling nature. Yet, it was refreshing and wanted from Angel. I don't know if it was the reason for the punishment, or the fact she needed a firm hand to discipline her. Whichever the reason was, I didn't care at this point.

"I swear, I'm going to have to start recording you to ask your brothers what you're saying if you won't tell me." Angel chuckled breathily as she let her body rest into me, snuggling her head into the crook of my neck.

"You sure you want my brothers to know what I'm saying to you, *lisichka*?" I teased with a smirk and chuckle as I wrapped an arm around her to keep her anchored against me. Maybe the possible embarrassment would be enough to override her curiosity. I couldn't care less if she asked though, it would just be entertainment for me to watch or hear about the outcome.

"You have a point... But you won't tell me what you're saying and it irks me!" She pouted, smacking my arm lightly. "Meanie."

"Of course I'm mean, or did you forget who you're married to, *lisichka*?" I gave her bottom a playful smack to prove my point, smirking proudly to myself when she sucked in a deep breath and jolted from the impact. "You know, I am never going to grow tired of spanking this ass of yours red and marking it up with my belt or hands." The fact she enjoyed it too made the sadism in me purr with pleasure.

The fact I enjoyed inflicting pain on my lovely wife was ironic given how I swore I'd never raise my hand against a woman. I swore to my mother I'd never hurt a woman or make one cry after seeing the abuse she suffered at my father's cruel hands. Yet, I found myself having a rather sadistic taste as I matured, much to my disgust.

I didn't want to turn into my father or anything like him. He was a deplorable being, not even worthy of being called a human being in my eyes. He was so hell bent on turning me into a ruthless leader like him that I swore I'd never stoop to his level out of spite and for my own sake of being a better person. When I realized I had a taste for inflicting pain on others, it terrified me because all I saw was myself becoming what I hated, what I swore I'd never be.

I could still hear my father's taunting laugh when he'd mock me, but he would never get the satisfaction of seeing me becoming what he wanted because I had control. My father was too much of a loose cannon, letting the power get to his mind and letting it lead instead of his heart and mind. I would never let my mind be clouded by power. No matter how much power I'd gain and hold in my hands, I'd never lose sight of myself nor my promises.

My sadistic tastes were a part of me no matter how much I tried to deny them though. It took me a long while before embracing that side of me after discovering the world of BDSM. To see I wasn't some twisted psychopath who got off on inflicting pain on others opened my eyes. It wasn't long until discovering the community that I was taught how to properly channel my inner sadistic needs.

One of the main reasons why I never bothered trying to settle down with a woman was because of my sadism. It might not be extreme, but I knew being forced over to take a belt until sitting became impossible wasn't on most people's lists. Hell, even the women I did hook up with never could satisfy that need of mine, even if they were into it.

The craving could never be satisfied until Angel came along. Maybe the chemistry between us made sex and punishment satisfying. I've never once felt pent up still after dishing out a good spanking to Angel and fucking her past her limit—but never more than she could handle. As much of a kick as I got from spanking her and being rough with her in our private moments, I would never harm her though. The mere thought of bringing actual pain to her or harming her by raising my hand against her in a violent manner made my blood boil.

"Penny for your thoughts?" Her soft and soothing voice lulled me out of my head.

Humming softly, I placed a kiss atop her head. "Just thinking about how crazy it is that I've ended up here with you."

"Fate works in mysterious ways. I never would have thought that the man I pulled out of a car crash would be the head of the bratva here, let alone my future husband who I craved for like a starved beast." She agreed with a giggle.

Bzzt... Bzzt... Bzzt...

The sound of a phone going off cut my train of thought short. Looking over at the desk, I reached for the phone that lit up. "Here." It was Angel's phone, so I held it out for her.

Taking her phone from me, she quickly opened it and scrolled through the messages before looking up at me with curious eyes and a hopeful smile. "You busy the rest of the night or anything? The others want to hit the food stands and chill." Her eyes were pleading with me to agree.

Looking at the time on her phone, it was close to 10 PM. "You go enjoy your time with your friends, don't let me crowd you all." She was stuck with me most of the time if she wasn't at work. She hadn't been on a big business assignment since the warehouse raid she did weeks ago. From what I know, she'd only been messaging everyone and corresponding from home and not going out to actually meet any of them.

"They want me to bring you, and I want you to come along too. We haven't really been out since the club, so it'll be nice for us too. I mean, nothing better than a late night snack and stroll at Stand Street. So, please?" She pouted with pleading eyes. "I mean, if you're busy then I understand or if you want to rest after everything so far." She quickly backed tracked with a soft frown.

Shaking my head softly, I chuckled and placed a kiss on her forehead, "Let me change and wash up. I don't think anyone will appreciate me showing up in bloodied clothes." It wasn't too bad, but I had enough splotches of blood on me it made it obvious I had gotten into it with someone.

"Still can't believe you have never been here before, it's like the best place for a quick bite or a late night snack." Angel said as we entered a dead end street lined on both sides with food carts and seating areas.

The area was in a weird limbo place between both of our territories, and one of the main reasons why I never ventured here was because it touched triad territory. If I hung around an area like this too much then attention would be gained along with trouble that would probably end up with bullets flying back and forth. Even as we entered just now we turned some unwanted heads.

My reputation was too great to hide from.

Before I became Pakhan, my name was already known throughout the city as my father's second in command and top enforcer. People were terrified at the sound of my name. The sight of me made people cower and run because rumors about how violent and cruel my methods were spread through the streets like wildfire and burned itself into the city.

"A man like me can't go wherever I please. I never had any time either. Then when I finally got time on my hands, fast food or street food was the last thing on my mind." My father never let us have the luxury of having outside food, deeming it a waste of money, so everything was homemade from my mother. When I finally had the freedom, I just saw no point in busying myself with meager chores when I had other responsibilities and activities to put my mind and time towards.

Huffing with a slight pout, she grumbled a bit. "Well, get used to being more normal and typical because like hell am I going to let my husband be hauled up in his office nearly 24/7. I mean, when was the last time you went on a hike or spent time at the park? Grabbed something from the local pub or a hole in the wall place? Went out for drinks or to a club to actually enjoy it? I've only ever seen you engross yourself in work and business so far, and I get that those things need a lot of your time and energy, but you still need some time for yourself as well. And some time for us."

"I mean, we haven't gone out on a date or anything remotely close to it since that night with dinner and your club. I'm not saying I want a date night every night, but something at least twice a month would be nice." There was a small and sad smile to her face as she looked up at me. "I know our relationship isn't exactly normal, but that doesn't mean we should not do nice and typical couple things."

If it weren't for the fact she was a deadly woman, I would say she was too innocent and good to be my wife; a life like hers shouldn't mingle into my twisted world. But she had a good point. I should put more effort into typical relationship activities or even time for myself. I could easily counter half the things she threw out at me just now, but I knew it'd be a pointless argument.

"Oh! There they are!" Angel grinned happily the moment she spotted her friends and they waved at each other. Her little feet instantly picked up and dragged me over to the small group who greeted us with warm smiles. It didn't take long after a few hugs before the whole group, mainly Angel and her friend Hanna and Bao, started bouncing from cart to cart, quickly filling their hands and arms with small trays of food.

"Quit stuffing your face so much if you keep worrying about your fat ass so much." Bao half shouted out at Angel and Hanna who were both too busy stuffing their faces while they made their way down the line of the food carts.

"Oh shut the fuck up, you're just jealous that I have a nice juicy ass unlike your flat board." Hanna retorted in a sassy manner, sticking her tongue out at Bao.

"Remember this the next time you decide to complain to any of us about your jeans not fitting anymore because your ass won't fit in it." For the quiet one, he sure could bite.

I haven't interacted or been around Angel's little group much, but from the many snippets, and descriptions, from her, Bao was the quiet one who always worked in the background as their techy. Her half-brother Greg was a detective at the Nespin Police Department and the most mature and reserved of the four of them. Hanna was basically a female version of Lev, which I agree with a hundred-percent; both of them had a penchant for violence and chaos, and both being much too trigger happy for everyone's sake.

"This place is nice. Angel said that you guys used to do these little get-togethers more often in the past." I mentioned to Greg as I picked at my little tray of salmon poke. The two of us hung back behind everyone, just observing everything and watching the three energetic young adults.

"Yeah, almost every other week kind of spiel. It was a nice way for us to just catch up on life and talk about plans briefly. We've just been way too busy with life and business to be able to get together like this. I don't know if she's told you yet, but things have been going down the shit hole recently." Greg replied with a sad smile and sigh of annoyance at the end.

Angel tried not to bother me much about triad business, claiming that she didn't want to put unnecessary things on my plate even if I argued with her otherwise. She never went into a lot of details, always keeping things very short and simple. "She mentioned that you guys were finding more holes and tunnels than you initially thought?"

Sighing with a shake of his head, Greg looked ahead at his sister with a sad smile, "Yeah, and she's been taking it hard on herself for being so careless for not noticing all of it. We keep coming up with empty hands with our research, just dead end after dead end. Then there's our father too. She's worried about Lady Qing going through with her threat of killing him if Angel steps out of line, which is why we've been struggling more than usual with grabbing at leads and following them. We have to be extra cautious, and that's tying our hands more than we like."

I knew they were having some difficulties lately from what Angel told me when I'd make her talk to release some of the stress. I didn't think they were being backed into a tight corner this soon or hard though. "Well, she can rest easy about your guys' father. I've got my men in the hospital watching over him and taking over his care."

"Thank you, you didn't have to do that, but we appreciate it greatly." Greg gave me a grateful smile before picking at his own food and drink for a moment. "She's lucky to have you. Never thought I'd say that given your career and standing, but you two are a great match for each other. I don't think I've ever seen her this grounded before. Hell, I never thought I'd see her talk to any other guy with the capacity of dating after what happened with her last one."

Now that caught my interest. "What happened with her ex?" It was one of those subjects neither of us have really touched on. I guess the both of us just silently accepted the fact we had lives before each other and never really questioned each other about our past relationships.

"Bad shit that makes my blood boil." Greg's jaw tensed as he gritted his teeth, his expression hardening as he took deep breaths.

"What happened?" Was Greg just being an overprotective brother and overreacting? Or was his rage warranted even after all this time?

"It's not my place to tell, that's something you're going to have to ask Ange about." Greg was still upset, and clearly I wasn't going to get an answer from him about her history with her ex.

"Alright, fair enough. But can I ask you something?" Well, maybe I can get an answer to another thing that's been on my mind.

"Don't know if I got an answer, but shoot." Greg replied with a small shrug of his shoulders.

"I don't know if she's like this with you and the others, but is there a reason why she doesn't like having her back to people and having her back touched? She always gets so jumpy whenever she has to turn her back to me or anyone else around the house, and I know it may sound weird, but she never shows me her back or lets me touch it. If I come into the room and she's shirtless or anything then she instantly turns her front side to me the moment she has inkling of my presence. I've tried to ask her about it, but she gets anxious and avoids it or shuts down." I wasn't losing my patience with her in regard to the matter, but

I started to worry more and more about her. I wanted to understand her reasoning and be there to support her.

Sighing heavily, Greg gave his sister another sad look, this time more heavy than the last. "Unfortunately, that goes back to her ex, which isn't my story to tell. It's probably not the answer you want to hear, but it's one of those personal things that she has to tell you herself. Although, I'm surprised you don't know about her ex. It was all in the news when it happened. Did it not come up when you dug around into her background? Which I'd be surprised if you didn't given that we dug into yours."

I didn't take any offense to the fact they dug into me, but I had nothing dirty that would show up besides being the head of the Volkov Bratva if they dug deep enough—I wouldn't consider that a spec of dirt though. I was a legitimate business owner in the eyes of the law and government, and everyone involved in the bratva had legitimate fronts as well.

Even if I did trust Angel to an extent, I did my research on her the night I brought her home after our rushed wedding. Much to everyone's surprise, nothing came up. Maybe that should have been the first flag for us when we couldn't find anything about her, but we didn't think much of it back then because the marriage was a done deal. Thinking back now, it was sloppy and careless beyond reason.

"Maybe you can answer this question instead then." I waited until Greg gave me his full attention again before popping the question.

"What's Angel's real name?"

Chapter 24

Nikolai

THE ALL TOO FAMILIAR brown packet sat before me on the coffee table, my eyes boring holes into it from my spot at the armchair.

The tense silence in the air was thick as my brothers and I eyed the folder, neither of us knowing what to do with it. The five of us were convening for our typical weekly meeting to keep each other caught up with happenings in the week regarding the family business and our own personal businesses.

Since I found out Angel's real name, I had my people dig up all they could about her—the real her. Everything and anything about Angel Vu packaged in one neat little folder which sat there tauntingly on the table. This was nothing unusual for us, but the fact it was about Angel, who we've all grown close and personal in a short time, felt somewhat wrong.

A part of me wanted to burn the file, the part of me who trusted my wife, but the doubtful and cautious side of me told me to rip through her life to know just exactly who I married. Yet, I felt like if I did open the file then we couldn't go back. It would feel like I betrayed her, betraying her trust in me. She hadn't given me a reason to doubt her, and I wanted her to tell me things at her own pace. So, if I did this, it meant I didn't trust her. All the dirt and grit would be revealed. It felt wrong to expose her behind her back like this.

"So, that's your wife in there then, your real wife err your not real wife? Fake wife? Was to be wife?" Arseny broke the tense silence in the living area where all five us were occupying the seating spots and staring at the information folder.

"Arseny shut up." Alexei hissed, smacking his twin on the arm. "This is serious. I mean, I know we do our research into people and everything, but this feels wrong."

"Oh, now you grow a conscience." Lev retorted with a snort. "She's been duping us the whole time, I say we have a right to know the real her." Lev wasn't too happy about the fact Angel never came forward with her real name, and now he doubted everything about her.

"It's only a name, it's not like she's a bad person. She's been honest with us about everything else so far. I don't know, it just feels wrong because she's part of the family and we've grown close." Alexei argued with a frown.

Alexei was the softest amongst us, and if anything he might be the only one to have a heart along with Arseny. The twins were lucky they were spared most of my father's harsh hand and indoctrination into the family business, so they were the least jaded.

"Oh please, take your little boy crush and shove it where it matters." Lev bit back harshly with a scowl.

Alexei shot up from his spot on the couch positioned across from Lev's spot, arm cocked back and ready to swing. If it wasn't for Arseny and Stepan holding him back then he might have gotten a solid swing at Lev's face. "I do not have a crush on her! That's just disrespectful to our brother! Angel's been nothing but good to all of us! Sure, she might have not been forthcoming about her name but that's it, the rest of it is the honest truth, and her. She's an amazing and strong person who is nothing but good, so watch what you say about her before I stitch your mouth shut."

Out of everyone in the family, Angel got along the most with Alexei, which I figured to be the case because they both worked in the medical field and in similar jobs. Also, Alexei had grown attached to Angel, seeing her as the sister we lost.

Standing up from his seat, Lev took a towering step towards Alexei, looking down at our little brother who was shorter than him by a few inches. "Oh please, it's clear as day how you look at her with those lovey dovey puppy dog eyes. You wear your damn heart and emotions like a neon jacket, so don't lie or deny any of it. Did you ever stop to think that maybe she's been faking the whole time? Everything being a fucking lie? Oh wait, you probably don't because your gullible ass is all snuggled up to hers."

Lev's voice still had its harsh edge to it as he continued to snark back. "You wished it would have been you to marry her instead of Kolya, the perfect little nurse to the perfect little doctor. Heck, I'm willing to bet that you knew about her name being fake and that you and her probably came up with some plan to get hitched after her marriage to Kolya gets annulled once she's done using him."

"Lev!" Stepan scolded with a glare as he buckled down on his hold on Alexei who started to struggle more to get free.

"Enough!" It was rare for me to raise my voice, especially with my brothers, but this got too out of hand. What Lev said was way out of bounds, angry or not, there were lines that don't get crossed.

Letting out a heavy breath to keep my rage at bay, I downed the rest of my whiskey before setting the glass down on the table and getting up.

Clenching my jaw, I closed the distance between Lev and I by two long strides. Pulling my arm back, I elbowed him hard in the chest, shoving him back down onto the couch. "Do not speak of my wife like that, and don't you ever talk to any of our brothers like that, ever. Whether you like it or not, Angel is loyal to us, to me, and is still my wife, who I still chose to be with given the new circumstances. We're all family here, brothers by blood, so don't you ever accuse any of us, especially Alexei, of something like that. I should let him get a swing at you and bust your face up for what you said to him and what you insinuated about my wife. I understand that you are upset, we all are, but that is no excuse to say half the things you did. Now, simmer down before you say something more to piss me off."

Of course, Lev and his rashness ran himself straight first into a trainwreck. "Then what? You'll put my ass down like dad? You know, for someone who swore they'd never be like him, you're starting to sound and look like a spitting image of him!" Lev raised his angry voice as he stood up and got in my face. Everyone knew very explicitly how much I hated being compared to my father, and it was just one of those subjects to never be touched or at the very least to be treated around carefully like thin ice. With the way Lev went about it was the same as stabbing a sleeping bear awake.

Usually I could easily forgive and turn my head away from Lev's angry words. He always had a temper and trouble with his emotions, often running his mouth a mile before his brain. But this time I couldn't excuse him. He already went too far with insinuating things about Angel and jabbing at Alexei, but to cut open a deep wound and dig his hands into it as well pushed me beyond my limit with him.

I didn't care for the fact Lev was bulkier than me, my rage having pushed it aside when I laid my hands on him. My hands grabbed him by his shirt, shoving him down to the ground and getting on top of him before landing a solid punch to his face, busting his lip, and making his head snap to the side.

The other three were quickly on me, the twins on my arms and Stepan at my back, trying to pull me off of Lev. "Kolya, stop!" Stepan pleaded as he put more of his strength into trying to pull me away. "You know he's just spewing shit, just get off of him and go cool off."

Oh it was too late for that now.

"What the fuck is going on!?"

Chapter 25

Angel

ALL I WANTED TO do after sixteen hours of hell was to grab a bottle of wine and waste my little brain cells on TikTok before the wine would kick in and knock my ass out. But no, I came home to my husband trying to beat his own brother up. I already got enough of this shit with drunk idiots in the ED, I did not want to deal with it at home. I was almost tempted to pretend I didn't hear or see anything, but it was too late now.

Sighing heavily with a small groan, I looked at everyone with an 'are you serious' look. "Why the hell is Nikolai on the floor with Lev? I am way too tired and exhausted for this shit right now, so what the fuck is going on?"

"Well?" I urged impatiently as I hooked my hands onto my hips when no one dared to move an inch or utter a single sound.

"This doesn't concern you, Angel. Go wait in the bedroom." I could hear the strain in Nikolai's voice, as if he held himself back. I could barely see his face from where I stood, but I could see his tense body and tightly clenched fists. He wasn't done, and no doubt if he wasn't being held back then he wouldn't stop until his knuckles bled.

"Oh that's rich coming from you and given the subject of this whole issue. This whole shit is about her, so no, she should very much stay." Lev spat with a twisted smirk, making me wary of him when I caught sight of it.

"Someone tell me what the fuck is going on." I demanded sternly, refusing to budge from my spot.

"Angel, right now isn't the best time. We'll explain things to you after we get this mess sorted out. Please, go somewhere safe for now." Stepan looked back at me with pleading eyes and a soft smile. "Please. We just need to get these two simmered down and then we can all talk, but I don't want you around here when it gets messy."

"Go to the bedroom." Nikolai repeated, glancing back at me with a hard gaze, making me shiver slightly.

"No." Was I going to regret my defiance later? Yes, a hundred-percent yes, but I'll take punishment later when it comes. "Either I am staying and you all chill the fuck out and tell me what is going on or I am going to go change and go out."

"Like hell you are, just do as you're told for once and go and wait in the bedroom, Angel." Nikolai's patience with me ran thin, and the reasonable side of my brain told me to listen to avoid less trouble later and to avoid whatever crap show I just walked in on. On the other hand, the other stupid brain with two functioning brain cells kept me rooted in my spot, challenging the raging bull. "Angel, I am not going to repeat myself one more time. Go wait in the bedroom, now."

Scoffing, Lev dug his grave deeper. "Oh, or what Kolya? Threatening her now? What are you going to do if she doesn't listen huh? Make her listen? Drag her around like a sack of shit? Beat a lesson into her? Do all the things that dad used to do to mom?" I guess Lev had a death wish tonight.

"Lev!" I shouted at him in disbelief. Even I knew better than to goad Nikolai on, especially using *that* sore subject.

With a roar, Nikolai quickly headbutted Stepan, breaking his nose with a crack and causing Stepan to reel back and hold his face. The twins were next, they were both promptly thrown off his arms with some effort. Nikolai got in two quick punches at Lev before I threw myself at him.

"*Anh*! Stop! Lev was way out of line but this is insane!" Did Lev deserve a few swings to the face? Probably, but it still didn't make it right. But what the hell brought all of this on? I knew Lev was a hothead and liked to make too much trouble than he could handle, but this was way too far. Surely he knew better than to poke at a raging bear.

"Kolya, please, stop. He's your brother, even if he deserves it, don't." I pleaded as I clung onto his cocked back arm for dear life as if it would make any difference. Nikolai could easily throw me off without any effort if he wanted, which is what he proceeded to do. He easily shook me off like I was some annoying little bug.

I didn't know what came over me, my body moved before I could think the moment I saw Nikolai pull his arm back more to swing at Lev again. Lev was probably the biggest asshole in the world. He and I barely got along as it is, but he didn't deserve to be beaten by his own brother. I knew I shouldn't get between them, but I acted on impulse when I threw myself over Lev, shielding his body with mine and bracing myself for the impact of Nikolai's punch.

"The fuck are you doing? Are you insane?" Lev scolded me with wide eyes as he stared at me in disbelief.

"I don't know." I laughed pathetically as I gripped at the fibers of the rug. "I don't know." Maybe I was certifiably insane, but I couldn't let this little tiff of theirs continue like this.

Suddenly, my body was yanked up and away from Lev and spun around to face a seething Nikolai. "The fuck were you thinking, Angel?! Don't you ever put yourself between me and a target like that. I could have hurt you." He scolded me as both his hands gripped at my shoulders.

"Well, I couldn't let you hit Lev again! I don't care if he kicked your demons in the balls, but you shouldn't have gone off on him like that. Just what the hell even brought it all on? Unless Lev really lost his damn mind and wanted to die tonight." I replied with a harsh glare at Nikolai with an upward tilt of my chin and a small puff of my chest.

"You can punish me all you want later, I don't give a fuck, but I am not going to let you keep doing something you're going to regret later and beat yourself up about." I said through gritted teeth as I clenched my fists together.

Shrugging Nikolai's hold off, I stepped aside and looked at the coffee table where a file sat. Letting my curiosity kill me, I snatched it up and opened it. "What's a file of me doing here?" My real file. Not going to lie, a part of me felt torn about seeing this file sitting there.

How long have they had this? How did they find out my real name? I hadn't even told Nikolai my real name yet. How far did they read into this?

"That's what we were talking about before Lev dug a hole to hell." Arseny admitted shamefully, averting his eyes from me to the floor.

"What? About my file? What about it? There's nothing in here that I haven't told you guys about. Why is it even here after all this time? Were you trying to dig up dirt on me or something?" I have been pretty open with all of them, always answering their questions; I haven't hidden anything from them besides my real last name and one moment in my life. The one *I* didn't even want to look back on myself.

"It was stupid of me, but I did it out of habit when I found out about your real name." Nikolai admitted shamefully while staring ahead.

"Tsk." Scowling, I threw the file down on the table, letting the contents scatter across the surface. "Well, not that I have anything to hide, nor would I have lied to any of you about anything if you asked. But since you're all so curious then go ahead, have fun reading about what schools I went to and how I got suspended in grade school for clocking a boy in the face." I wasn't worried about anything in the file because there was nothing to worry about.

Well, at least I thought I had nothing to worry about until I saw the edge of a picture peeking out of the scattered piles of paper. The urge to snatch the picture up along with anything pertaining to it chewed away at me, but it would only prove their point that I hid something. But I wasn't ready for any of them to know about *that* yet.

"Fuck this. I'm going out." I hissed under my breath, the need to drink and dance the night away drove my attention away from snatching the file up to burn it. "And don't you dare try to stop me." I directed my glare at Nikolai who watched me out of the corner of his eyes.

Quickly and silently, I darted out of the living room and upstairs to the bedroom, discarding all my work gear in a pile on the floor, making a note to myself to bother with it tomorrow morning while I would be nursing a hangover.

After a quick wash, I did a quick face of makeup. Then, I threw on a little black dress with some silver heels before rushing downstairs with a small purse in hand and snagging the keys to Nikolai's Aston Martin DBS on the way to the garage filled with luxury cars that would be any car person's wet dream. I wasn't one to care about cars too much, but I have to admit his Aston was one sexy thing. Also, it was my favorite amongst his cars, and at this point, with how often I drove it, it might as well have been mine.

It didn't take me long—speeding really takes off time—to pick Hanna up after calling her. Then, the two of us were at White Out in mere minutes, and we—me—were wasted in seconds.

"The audacity of that man, I swear. 'Go to the bedroom' like who the fuck does he think he is ordering me around like that. Like fuck does it concern me if he's throwing his ass down with his brother like that over my stupid file and dignity or some shit." My words were blurring in my buzzed mind; the words were just flying out of my loose lips uncontrollably.

"Honey, I think you need to—"

With a soft scowl, I slapped Hanna's hand away when she tried to take my drink away from me. "I'm fine. I don't need to do anything but drink, relax, and dance a lot."

This time, Benjamin spoke up, who I totally forgot was even here after so many shots. "I don't think that's a good idea, Nikolai isn't—"

"I don't give a fuck about Nikolai right now, he's not in control of me god damn it. I'll do whatever the fuck I want whenever I want." There is a moment and time for everything, and him trying to pull what he did with me earlier upset me greatly. "Who does he think he is, dismissing me like that? I am his fucking wife, not some damn booty call."

I was livid. Livid and drunk—a very bad combination.

Whelp. Fuck it.

Chapter 26

Nikolai

"Yo, SHE JUST TOOK your car." Arseny noted as his eyes followed something—probably my car—out the window.

"Not the best time, Arseny." Alexei huffed.

Taking a deep breath, I pulled my phone out and sent a message to Benjamin to keep Angel safe and make sure she got back home in one piece whenever she was done with her little fit. "Hope you're happy Lev." I hadn't bothered to budge from my spot from where I had some words with Angel, still keeping my back to everyone and my eyes fixated on the display cabinet before me. "I'm going for a swim, you all know where the door is, either out or to your rooms."

I hadn't fully calmed down, only enough to where I didn't want to pummel Lev's face in. But I was afraid if I looked at him right now then my rage would come back and the five of us would just end up like before. I'd deal with the aftermath later once everyone had calmed down, or at least until I wasn't feeling a tad murderous towards my own brother.

"Kolya, I think you should stay." Stepan's nasally voice piped up, reminding me of the fact I had busted his nose just minutes ago.

"No, I don't think that would be wise. I am sorry about your nose, have Alexei fix it before you lose all hope in the looks department." I snarked with a quick smirk and a dry chuckle.

"Don't worry about it, chicks dig the roughed up look. But I mean it, you should stay... There's something you should see." From playful to serious, whatever Stepan wanted my attention for had to be worth it for him to push for my presence to remain.

"I know all that's in that file, I know my own wife enough. I don't need to read it all from some stupid sheets of paper." I trusted her enough to know she wouldn't have hidden anything from me. She had been forthcoming about everything so far. Well, everything except the matter about her issue with her back.

"But have you seen the photos of her attack? The ones that weren't released to the press?" Stepan asked with a downturned voice.

"What?" Confused, I turned around warily, "What attack?"

"Guess you don't know your perfect little wife well enough then." Lev quipped, making my hand twitch with an itch to sock him again. "Give me that." Lev grumbled, tearing some papers and photos from Alexei's hand aggressively.

Slowly, Lev's angry twisted face softened to one of regret...? It was hard to tell because it was only for a split second before his expression became angry again as he threw down what he had in his hands and stormed out of the house, slamming the front door when he did exit.

"Derzhu pari, on chuvstvuyet sebya ublyudkom seychas." Alexei scowled with a scoff. "Serves him right."

"Yeah, bet he does feel like a bastard. Just hope he doesn't get into too much trouble because of it." Arseny sighed with a soft shake of his head.

"I'll deal with him once he's had a moment to self-reflect, hopefully that happens before someone ends up with a bullet through them." Stepan said as he slowly gathered the papers back up into neat piles. "Did she not tell you about what happened to her about a year and a half ago?" Stepan asked, looking at me with pitiful eyes as he held out a copy of a news article.

I knew I shouldn't, this was her secret to keep until she was ready, but my need to know trumped the thought. Reaching out, I took the papers from Stepan and held them for a moment, not letting my gaze fall down to the bold words of the headline. I could turn back. I haven't read it yet. I could easily hand it back to Stepan or put it down on the table. Yet, I didn't.

23 YEAR OLD FEMALE FOUND STABBED AND ALIVE

The crude picture made my upper lip peel back into a harsh scowl. Unfortunately, the headline picture of Angel laying in a blood soaked bed was tame compared to the evidence photos of the unsolved case. I don't know why I kept flipping through the case file, each page and picture did nothing but fueled the rage I felt towards the man who dared do this to my Angel. She didn't deserve for this to have happened to her. Hell, no one deserved to have this happen to them.

"Kolya, you should probably go after Angel yourself. I'm pretty sure she was triggered by the sight of the picture earlier and that's why she decided to go out. She's not in the right state of mind, she might do something risky or dangerous." Alexei said with a worried look on his face.

Groaning, I pinch the bridge of my nose, "Fucking hell, how did this night go from shit to shittier. Just... Spend the night, we'll try this damn meeting again tomorrow once everyone's got their head on straight." Me included.

Sighing, I sent my driver a quick message before grabbing my jacket from the back of the armchair and throwing it on. "Alexei, patch Stepan and Lev up whenever he comes back." Lev was definitely going to need some tending to.

The drive into the city district felt longer than typical, even if we were breaking the speed limit by a good twenty or so miles. I hated it because it gave me more time to stew with my thoughts when all I wanted to do right now was find my little wife, cradle her in my arms, and spoil her with all the affection in the world. I just wanted to hold her, protect her, and kill the son of a bitch who dared scar her.

My thoughts came to a halt when my phone went off. When the caller ID showed to be Angel, I quickly picked up. *"Lisichka—"*

Hanna's voice cut me off. "Uhh no, but you do need to come pick your woman up before she starts stripping on stage. Don't know what happened between you two, but she went at the drinks. Hard. Wasted in record time—hey get down from there! God damn it, just hurry up and get your ass down here."

"Where are you? Where's Benjamin?" From the deafening background music, I would wager they were at a club, but that didn't exactly narrow it down considering how there were nearly seventy clubs in the huge city.

"We're at White Out, and you see, uhhh Angel got Benjamin kicked out of the club after smashing his phone. She was kinda not happy about him rejecting her advances. Soooo Benjamin is having at it with club security last I checked. Shit! I gotta go before Angel flashes the whole damn club. Just hurry up!" The call ended without another word.

God damn it! She hadn't even been gone for a full hour! Well, at least I knew the owner of White Out, so one quick call to him and I had Angel and Hanna pulled from the floor to safety along with letting Benjamin have access again. It wasn't long after my phone call that I arrived at the club and retrieved the girls along with a disgruntled Benjamin.

Once we were in the parking area, I looked at Benjamin, "Benjamin, go home, I got it from here." Then, I looked at my driver, "Take Hanna home, then you can be off."

The three of them went their separate ways, leaving me with my drunk wife. With a sigh, I dug through her purse for the car keys. Keys in hand, I led the two of us towards my car—the Aston Martin she took.

"You know, you remind me a lot of my husband. Oh man, he'd be so pissed if he knew where I was right now. You won't tell him right?" Angel could barely walk as she clung onto my arm for dear life.

"I am your husband." I sighed heavily with a shake of my head.

God my headache got worse by the minute. Tonight was not the night for her to be pulling this kind of crap, but I couldn't fault her for it. My bottles of top shelf vodka had been calling my name ever since I simmered down enough to not rip Lev's head off. If I weren't so worried about Angel to the point of going out to fetch her myself—per my brother's advice—then I would be at least ten shots deep.

"You may look like my husband but you ain't, no sir eeee." She giggled with a drunk grin. Angel only made it three stumbling steps in before I had to pick her up in my arms and carry her the rest of the way to the car. "Hey, this isn't how you pick women up!" She protested, smacking my chest lightly. "Put me down or else I'll shoot you in the knees." She threatened. As annoying as this was, I couldn't help but find some amusement to this. I wonder if she'll even remember any of this tomorrow when she wakes up or if she's so far gone that none of it will register.

Glad to see she was still feisty in this state, not that it would do her much good with the poor coordination. "*Lisichka*, as good of a shot you are, you wouldn't be able to hit a wall right now if it was in front of you." I retorted with a chuckle.

"I am not your little fox mister, and I am a great shot." She argued back with a pouting glare. "Where are you taking me?"

"Home." I answered bluntly as I set her down to open the car door before getting her in and putting her belt on. "Now, behave."

Crossing her arms with a pout, she stuck her tongue out at me. "No, you can't make me." If she wasn't drunk then I'd be tempted to throw her in the back seat and make her regret those words, but I wasn't one to engage with an inebriated woman.

Thankfully, the drive home was peaceful, mainly because she passed out the moment I hit the freeway. As I drove, I couldn't help but glance at her from time to time, the corners of my lips falling down with gravity as the pictures flashed through my mind.

It was one thing to survive a bullet or brush off getting shot at, but what happened to her was so personal it wasn't something that could be shrugged off. I'd probably be traumatized if I went through exactly what she did, and there wasn't much I would consider traumatizing to given my fucked up life.

Once we got home, I carefully carried my slumbering wife up to our room and settled her in bed before stripping her. After her shoes were off, I quickly worked her dress off, but before I could get to her bra, I found myself being pulled down onto the bed with a giggle. Then, a pair of lips were on mine, and the taste of alcohol flooded my senses. Deft hands started to feel up my body, working my shirt out of my pants as her touch trailed upwards to the collar of my shirt. *"Lis—"*

A finger to my lips stopped my words, "Shh, let me have a bite of you love. I want you so badly right now." From the glazed over look in her lust filled eyes and the dopey look on her smiling face, it was clear she was still under the influence.

The fact she wasn't sober was enough kept my urges at bay. The thought of doing something we might regret in the morning was enough to keep the blood from rushing down to my cock as Angel kissed at my neck while her fingers worked at the buttons of my shirt. "No, *lisichka*, you're not in your right mind. I am not going to sleep with you when you're like this." Also, I couldn't trust her or myself while she was in this state. I could easily hurt her in the height of our pleasures and she wouldn't know any better to stop it.

"I'm perfectly fine, I know what I want, and my thoughts are clear. I'm completely fine now, promise." The fact some of her words still slurred slightly was another clear indication she was not back to baseline.

"Please, I'm so horny right now, I need your cock in me so badly." She pouted, grabbing at the waistband of my pants and tugging.

"Don't you want me too?" Her other hand grabbed mine and brought it up to her breast, pressing my open hand against it and using her own to make me cup her.

Jerking my hand away, I could feel a pang of hurt cross my chest at the sight of rejection on her face. "Angel, baby, not like this. You're not sober. I am not going to touch you while you're in an altered state." I told her softly, hoping it would get through to her.

Desperation. Hurt. Her blown pupils constricted as her lust faded. "Do you not want me anymore? Are you disgusted with me after seeing the file? After hearing about how much of a whore I was to let myself be used by a man like him? You don't want me anymore because I'm just broken and used trash, huh?"

"Darling, no, never. I don't care about what's in that file, nothing in it changes how I see you or my feelings for you." It was the truth. If anything, I only felt more for this strong woman who I am more than proud to call my wife.

"Then why don't you want me right now? I'm not even that drunk, I'm barely tipsy or buzzed." Sure, she might be in a better state than when I picked her up, but she wasn't in the clear.

Sighing softly, I pulled her down against me in a tight hug, stroking her hair soothingly. "You're still under the influence. I am not going to do something that both of us might regret in the morning. I don't want to take advantage of you in this state, even if you do want it, your inhibitions are loose." Placing a gentle kiss on her forehead, I pulled her off and got off the bed. "Stay, I'm going to get a cloth to clean your face."

"I can do it myself." No she couldn't. She nearly fell out of the bed when she tried to get out of it. I had to catch her and force her back in it.

After making sure she would stay put, I left to the adjoining bathroom and got a few warm washcloths, saturating one of them with her makeup remover, before returning to the bed and cleaning her face while she protested. I did let her try, but she ended up smearing everything and making a bigger mess. "You don't have to do this." She pouted defeatedly as she let me wipe her face in peace.

"I know. I want to. You're my wife, so I am always going to take care of you whether you like it or not." That much I could promise her. Even if she were to change her mind and nullify this marriage in the end, I would still watch over her at the end of the day. If she wasn't set for life already then I would have ensured that as well, even if she didn't want it.

"Do you ever regret agreeing that night?" The sad look in her eyes made me want to grab her face and kiss her until she was happy.

"No, never." I replied without an ounce of hesitation. "As we've said before, this marriage is unconventional, but I will never regret my decision that night, ever. If anything I'm thankful for it because it forced my hand into doing what I was hesitant about. I wanted to seek you out after that first night I laid eyes on you, but I didn't. What little conscience I had left in my mind made me leave you be. You were just an innocent little nurse, you didn't deserve to be involved in the ugly bratva life that I lead. If I had things my way and were twisted enough then I would have snatched you off the streets and kept you locked up in my bedroom until the end of time."

"Is it crazy to say I wouldn't have opposed to that." She giggled with a grin.

"You are definitely not sober if you're saying that." I chuckled softly as I finished cleaning her face.

There was no way in hell she would ever let me do that to her without fighting me tooth and nail. She was too independent and strong in her own right, so there would be no way she would ever let herself be degraded like that. And that's what I loved about her. She knew her worth and wasn't afraid to express it—when she wasn't in a self-doubting state. She didn't need anyone but herself, which was a good thing and a bad thing, but I found that part of her admirable.

"Well, what if I was tired of everything and wanted someone to take care of me, hm?" She challenged me with a smirk as she crawled up to me. "Maybe I want a big brute to take me." The tip of her finger trailed down my chest as she kept her playfully dazed eyes locked onto mine.

"Not like this." I shot her down again, my hand grabbing at hers to put it back at her side. "Trust me, I am doing this for both our sakes." I told her with a soft sigh, placing a kiss on her forehead and getting off the bed to toss the used washcloths in the hamper. Going over to the dresser, I pulled out a gray tee shirt before going back to Angel.

After taking her bra off, I bunched the shirt in my hands before telling her, "Arms up." With a pout, she did as I told, letting me slip the shirt onto her body easily. "*Lisichka*, don't look at me like that." The sad pout of rejection remained on her face as she sat there on her knees. Sighing heavily, I pulled the covers back, pulled her under, and settled the both of us in for the night.

"Good night, *lisichka*."

Chapter 27

Angel

My. Fucking. Head.

The bed dipped slightly as Nikolai sat down next to me. *"Lisichka."* Even Nikolai's typical deep and soothing voice sounded like hammers to my skull because of this hangover.

"No, leave me alone to wallow in my self-pity and embarrassment." The memories of last night hit me like a freight train after I had woken up and laid there staring at the ceiling for a good while.

Can't believe I didn't even recognize my own husband because I was so wasted. Then the fact that I tried—and failed—to seduce him had me reeling with embarrassment.

I can't believe I threw myself at him like that, and got rejected!

Granted, in hindsight, it was sweet of him to not take advantage of me. Then the fact he took care of me and prepared me for bed was sweet enough to take some of the edge off my embarrassment.

Last night was a fuck fest I now started to regret. Maybe I should have listened to him and gone to our room instead of sticking around, but if I did, then how much worse could things have gotten? Pretty sure Nikolai would have continued to pummel Lev into a necessary hospital trip.

Speaking of Lev, "Is Lev okay?"

A pathetic and dry chuckle was heard from Nikolai. "Drink some water and your meds first, then we can talk." He bargained, nudging the arm I had thrown over my eyes to keep the light out.

Groaning, I sat up slowly while holding my heavy head. A black hole to swallow me up sounded grand right about now.

Sighing, I took the glass of water and the pills from Nikolai with a small 'thanks' before downing everything and laying back down in the bed, bundling myself up with the covers. I could barely face Nikolai right now as last night kept playing on repeat in my brain.

"Lev's fine, just a busted lip, black eye, and a broken nose." He sounded like a psychopath with how nonchalant he sounded. "Alexei patched him up. You probably wouldn't even be asking about him if you knew all he said last night." Nikolai got pissed again, which made me wonder what was exchanged before I showed up.

"*Anh*, I don't care if he called me all the ugliest shit on God's green earth, unless he put a bullet through my dad's brain, he shouldn't have deserved to be beaten by his own brother." Maybe I was too nice. Maybe it was hungover Angel talking too.

"I mean, I don't have the full story, not sure if I want to at this point, but I still think you went too far, even if Lev dug at a rotten grave and fell in. I mean, we all know how Lev is, even I know he's an asshole with anger issues who needs to get laid." Maybe I forgave people too easily—with a few exceptions.

His eyes narrowed as his face scrunched up with a scowl. "He insinuated that you and Alexei were going to end up together once you were through with me and annulled the marriage." Nikolai's irritation showed through his tone, and I don't fault him for it.

"Okay, and? You know he was probably just spewing utter bullshit. I already told you, I am not annulling the marriage unless you want to, but I really hope you don't. Also, me and Alexei? Really? I mean, Alexei is great and we get along the best out of all your brothers, but there's no chemistry between us. At best we're just two best friends who never found each other until now, but I see him more like a brother than a friend. He reminds me a bit of Greg with how protective he can get and how he's always there." I might spend more time with Alexei than I do with Nikolai, but my heart only calls to one person.

"Do you regret this marriage?" His blue eyes were broken with uncertainty and insecurity, a look that made my heart ache.

With all the sincerity I could muster, I smiled and looked at him deeply. "I didn't exactly have a choice when she threatened my father's life, but no, I don't regret it, and I never will. But only because it's you." It was the honest truth.

Again, if my stepmother forced a marriage between me and anyone else who wasn't Nikolai then I'd be long gone with my father, or my husband would have unfortunately disappeared under mysterious circumstances and never to be found.

"*Anh*, I probably sound like a stupid and pathetic idiot, but I felt some kind of spark the night of the crash. I chalked it up to my hormones reacting to an insanely sexy beast of a man, but clearly that's been fucked out of my system by now. You're an amazing man, and there's no denying the chemistry between us now. I always believed in fate and miracles, that things happen for a reason, and I like to think that the crash was a way of the world throwing you at my face."

If it weren't for the crash, I never would have crossed paths with Nikolai. Him and I ran in different circles, mostly, so the chances of us bumping into each other outside of otherworldly intervention would have been slim to none. So, in a way, the crash introduction was necessary for both of us.

Smiling a small, sad smile, I sighed softly. "The only regret I have is not trying to seek you out because of my own self-esteem. I kept thinking about how there's no way a man like you would give me a second look, that I'm not worth it because I'm so broken. And how I would never be that blonde bombshell arm candy. That's all before the fact that I wanted nothing to do with the mafia life, especially since I was actively avoiding it."

Not a night went by where I didn't open the nightstand drawer and picked up the card, debating on whether I should send a message and bother him boldly for a date. I always chickened out at the last moment, thinking about how our worlds would be better off without each other in it. Oh how wrong I was.

"Hey." His stern voice made my eyes drift up to his face, "Don't you ever say or think any less of yourself."

His fingers threaded through my loose locks, splaying them out on the pillow under me. "You are perfect in my eyes, from those sharp yet delicate eyes, those lovely lips, the subtle curves, the tone of your body that screams dangerous woman. You hold yourself with such elegance and power in the right situations, where just one look at you and people can tell that you are not someone to be trifled with. I don't care about arm candy, never have, never will, but you will always be a whole damn dessert table that'll overly satisfy my cravings."

Leaning down, he kissed me deeply, holding my face with a needy grip as if he's afraid I'll slip away. "I don't care if you're broken either, not like I am a saint with a clean background. We all have our demons and skeletons in the closet, and I've long accepted mine. So, who would I be to judge you for having your own baggage when I have a house full of it?"

"Good point. You would be quite the asshole if you judged me while being a wreck and a half yourself." I chuckled softly in response. "But, question: what if it wasn't me? Would you still have agreed to be married off to whoever?"

There wasn't an ounce of hesitation or reluctance in his terse response. "No. I went into that meeting with my brothers with no intention of agreeing to the marriage. I was in the mindset that we would leave with the promise of war or an altered agreement between both sides. The plans went up in flames the moment I saw that it was you, and I took it as a sign from the universe to take you since you were being presented to me on a golden platter. If it was anyone else, I wouldn't have agreed, nor would I have forced any of my brothers into the marriage."

Frowning softly with worry, I traced a finger down his cheek. "Is there something else? You have that distant look in your eyes." I noticed a pattern with Nikolai: whenever he held something back, his eyes took on an empty and distant look, and usually, a brush-off or a cold shoulder followed shortly after.

"Just... I never thought I'd engage in such an archaic act after what happened to my sister." Nostalgia, sadness, anger, the emotions softened and hardened his eyes within seconds.

"Your sister... What happened to her?" I knew his sister had passed from the land of the living, but he never once mentioned her after that night in the car. I've never brought the subject of his mother or sister back up, sensing it was a sore spot for him that was better off left untouched until he was ready.

Nikolai had spoken about his mother from time to time without any prying from me. She was a lovely person from all he's told me, a lovely but poor woman who was stuck in an abusive and loveless marriage to a monster of a person who was his father. Despite her situation, she loved her children with all her heart, always doting on them and teaching them to be proper and right men, to not be like their father. I would have loved to meet her if she were still here, and no doubt I would have loved her and been eternally grateful to her for raising such an amazing son; Nikolai assured me the feeling would've been mutual if she were still here, that she would have doted on me like her own daughter.

But never would he touch the subject of his sister. He would always shut the door before we even approached it.

"Natasha, she came before the twins, the true apple to my mother's eyes because she was tired of being outnumbered. I remember the day she laid eyes on my sister for the first time, there was such happiness, but it was fleeting. I didn't understand it back then, why my mother suddenly shed tears and looked so disheartened and sad when it was supposed to be a happy moment. I realized it when I got older, that the reason my mother reacted the way she did was because she realized the hell that she had brought an angel to. She had damned her own beautiful daughter by having her. My mother tried her best to shield my sister from the ugly world we were forced into and from my father, but she could never truly keep my sister away from it all." His voice wavered as his breathing became irregular.

Reaching out, I let the tips of my fingers stroke the back of his forearm in a comforting gesture. His body trembled with some deep breaths under my touch, and for a moment I worried he might shut me out again until he simmered back down.

"My father married her off to form an alliance. We never saw her again until her body was discovered months after the wedding. My father knew the vile son of bitch that he arranged my sister to, he knew what kind of sick and twisted things the man was prone to, yet he didn't care, not that it surprised me considering how he treated his own children. We all tried to stop it, finding whatever loophole we could, even going as far as hiding my sister, but he found her in the end and dragged her into that church crying and screaming." Nikolai's voice wavered with his heavy breaths, and he had to pause for a moment to do some deep breathing.

Moments later, he continued. "Natasha's husband kept her locked away from the world, and we couldn't get into any kind of contact with her no matter how hard we tried. Months later, my cousin contacted me when the police in Moscow found the body of a female. I had to fly over there to identify her, and I could barely recognize the person who was on the coroner's table when I first laid eyes on her."

There was another pause as he sat there breathing deeply, calming his raging body. "It broke me to know how much she suffered before her death. My sister was the sweetest thing in the world, never did anything wrong in her life. So, to see her suffer like that, all because of our father, I snapped, especially after I found out about the evil things that had been done to her."

Chortling, he smiled darkly. "It was the first time I attacked my father and went on a rampage that wiped out Ovechkin Bratva off the map."

Then, with a rise and fall of his chest, his face saddened again. "My sister would still be alive right now, enjoying her life to the fullest, if it weren't for that damned arranged marriage. I swore then that I would never force any of my brothers into such a situation where they could end up in a damned relationship, I didn't want to take that kind of choice from them, the choice to choose their own life partners. Same went for me, and I feel like a selfish prick for taking your hand that night, but I couldn't let you slip away a second time."

"Kolya... I'm so sorry." I couldn't begin to imagine the kind of pain he must have gone through. The thought of losing Greg or Hanna or Bao already pained me, so I could only imagine it was a hundred times worse for Nikolai since he was so close to his siblings and placed such importance on them. "You got the bastard?"

"Yes, and I kept him locked in a basement for a whole week just to inflict a fraction of what he did to my sister onto him before beating him to death with my bare hands. I only wish I had the patience to drag his torture out longer." There was this twisted look to his eyes, one a criminal would have after committing a crime and getting their rush. It was a look of a killer, a true killer.

"Mhmm, too bad you hadn't met me yet, I probably would have talked you into letting it drag on." I drew the line at killing, but torture was fair game. Death was a mercy in my eyes. Why should someone get an easy way out for the crimes they committed? They needed to suffer in this life for their sins.

I was a horrible person, twisted beyond salvation. The only thing keeping me from having a room at the mental hospital was the fact I had control over my twisted tendencies. I repressed my urges for the right time, and maybe the reason why I stuck around the triad was because it gave me a huge supply of victims—all who were very deserving of the torment I inflicted on them. It should never be okay to hurt another human being, justified or not, but I always hated that. Justice, especially by the law, was never sweet enough. Rotting away in prison was a luxury; perpetrators needed to suffer just like their victims—an eye for an eye.

It was good to see an insane enough person to want me for everything, even if it did seem too good to be true. "I swear, the moment this circus is over, I'm throwing you over my shoulder and hauling you down to the courthouse to get us married again, for real this time. I am never letting you go, ever." The anger that rolled off of him in waves died down as his eyes studied my face.

Laughing softly, and groaning regrettably right after, I let my hand drift down and settle on his thigh. "We are not having a quick courthouse wedding if we're going to get married for real. I want an actual wedding, the stupid little ceremony, the aisle, the white dress, the reception, all of it. It sounds stupid and childish, but I want all of that with you." Sure, did I dream about the stupid fairytale wedding growing up? Yes, but I threw that dream out the window after getting stabbed in the back, literally and figuratively.

Smiling, Nikolai reached out and cupped my face, stroking my bottom lip with his thumb. "We can have whatever wedding you want, *lisichka*. As long as you're happy, then that's all that matters. God knows we can both afford to throw whatever kind of wedding we want." There really would be no limit given our seemingly unlimited bank account.

"Come here." I lazily reached up and grabbed at the front of his shirt, pulling him down into a soft kiss. "So lucky you weren't some slob of a mob boss." I laughed softly with a groan. I really gotta stop doing that until this headache calmed down.

"And if I was?" Nikolai asked with a raised brow and a curious, yet knowing, smirk.

"You'd be swimming with the sharks." I replied, sticking my tongue out at him with a cheeky smile. "Think I'm going to nap a little to try and sleep off this hangover some."

"I'll just be in my office if you need me then." Nikolai placed a kiss on my forehead before leaving me to slumber away.

Unfortunately, as tired as I was, sleep didn't take me instantly. Even though things felt fine between us, there was a slight tension. Nikolai didn't bring up the subject of the file or its contents, but I could see the push and pull in his eyes. A part of me was thankful he didn't bring it up, but I also wanted him to so that I could finally set the record straight with him. Even if he did know about what happened, I still felt like I owed him a personal explanation, for it to come from me and not some words on pressed wood.

"Arseny, I swear to fucking God, if you do not put that vodka bottle away in the next second, I will crack it over your head." Just the sight of the alcohol bottle made me want to hurl.

My hangover was mostly gone after sleeping nearly half the day away, but the thought of alcohol right now repulsed me. So, to see Arseny pouring himself some shots in the living room as we were waiting for Nikolai to join us for the family meeting triggered me a little.

Deviously, Arseny grinned and waved the open bottle at me, making me gag a little when I caught a whiff of its contents. "What's wrong? Did you have a little too much to drink last night?" Cheeky little asshole.

"Arseny, leave her alone." Alexei spoke up, snatching the bottle of vodka away from his twin and setting it elsewhere out of my sight. Thank God.

Everyone, except Nikolai, filled the living room. "Do I have to be here?" I groaned, rubbing my temples as the dull ache of my hangover lingered. It was their weekly family meeting, and usually I didn't partake because it was over by the time I got off work.

I've only partaken in two of their gatherings so far, and it was the typical what's happening, what's going on, what are your plans, yada yada. Nikolai always gave me a run-down of what they discussed at the end of the night, so I've never really missed anything important.

"Well, you don't *have* to be here, but we did find some things pertaining to your stepmother that you might want to hear." Alexei informed me as he sat down next to me on the couch, holding out another glass of water for me.

Groaning, I pushed his hand away, not wanting to drown myself with more water. Sighing, Alexei pushed the glass back at me before throwing his little threat at me. "Unless you rather I hook you up to a banana bag, drink." Yeah, no. Last time he tried to stick an I.V. in someone it took him three tries too many—it was an easy stick too.

"I swear, all you Volkov men are so demanding." I grumbled, taking the glass of water from him and downing it with a groan.

"It's part of our charm." Arseny grinned with a wink, making me roll my eyes at him.

Nikolai took his sweet time with his phone call, leaving the five of us to stew in our seats. Although, I felt like a boiling pot under all their gazes. I tried to ignore it at first, thinking maybe I just saw things, but glance after glance, I could see I wasn't mistaken. "Quit looking at me like that."

"Hm? Like what? We're not—"

My harsh glare made Alexei shut his mouth and avert his gaze from me. "Like I'm a victim. Those pitiful eyes." I hated how weak they made me feel, always reminding me of my vulnerability.

Alexei quickly kicked into doctor mode. "You're not a victim, you're a survivor, and what you went through is..." Alexei's sentence trailed off as he struggled to search for the right word.

"I know the spiel, you don't have to give it to me. I still hate all of it though. It's not like getting shot by a bullet or getting stabbed in a fight, none of that shit ever bothered me... But what happened... I don't want to talk about it." Even if they probably knew what happened, I didn't want to personally divulge it myself because I don't think I could.

The last person I expected to hear anything from spoke up. "Because none of that shit is personal, that's the difference." Lev grumbled.

Lev had been strange ever since last night, as in he has been nice to me. Lev and I tolerated each other, we weren't best friends by any means, but we remained civil with each other if we had to be in the same room. He's wary of me, which I didn't fault him for. Even if I gave him no reason to doubt me, it was his personality according to the others, so I let it be.

After last night though, he's been nice, almost warm towards me, but I was wary about his angle because did he act this way because he pitied me? Felt bad for what happened? Or was he actually regretful and wanted a good relationship with me?

"As if it's going to make any difference to you." I retorted with a roll of my eyes.

"Listen, I'm sorry if I've been an asshole to you, if I'd known why—"

I didn't let him finish speaking, interrupting him. "It shouldn't matter if I had a shitty background or not for you to start treating me decently. I get it, you're a cautious person, you just want to look out for your brothers and protect them, but have I given you reason to doubt me so far?" I know he's tailed me and stalked me from afar a few times, and I could care less about it if it appeased his wariness. Not like I have anything to hide. "Just quit being a douchebag and we'll call it even and start over."

"At least let me apologize for all the shitty things I've said about you." Lev had this guilty look to him, which amused me, but considering it was Lev, it felt more strange than amusing.

"Fine, apology accepted, now go back to being a raging asshole." I grumbled, pulling out my phone to occupy my time.

"I am not a raging asshole." Lev bit back with a playfully harsh glare, chucking a pillow at me.

Holding my hand out, I swatted the pillow away before grabbing one next to me and throwing it at him only to have him dodge it. "You are. You're practically the male version of Hanna with a healthy dose of testosterone to further fuel your rage." Probably the only reason how I've managed to not lose my shit on Lev so far is because I'm used to dealing with Hanna, and the two were basically the same.

"Shockingly the two of them haven't torn the city apart yet." Stepan said, not looking up from his phone.

"I'm surprised you agreed to hire her and let those two work together. Don't get me wrong, I'm happy that Hanna got an official job on the books and shit and that you're willing to give her a chance, but to partner her and Lev up is a PR nightmare waiting to happen." No, I didn't pull any strings to get Hanna a job with the family's services company, I just mentioned they were looking and she went through the hiring process like usual. But I'm pretty sure Stepan looked past her spotty resume because she was my friend and rolled the dice on her.

"Hey, she was qualified, therefore hired." Stepan replied with a shrug of his shoulders, brushing it off like nothing. "And the two are star workers, shockingly."

"Hey, Hanna is fun to work with, she ain't afraid to get down and dirty." Well, glad to see Lev liked someone acquainted with me. Although it was kind of strange to see how well the two of them got along. Pretty sure if left unchecked, those two would go on a rampage for shit and giggles.

"Sorry, the call took longer than expected, but I got some new information regarding Ivan's activities." Nikolai's voice and presence changed the whole atmosphere of the room the moment he walked in. "Seems like our little business partner is double dipping with the triad."

"So that information was good?" I looked over at Nikolai as he leaned against the fireplace mantle with a glass of whiskey in hand. The only response I got from him was a firm nod.

"Damn, I was hoping those fuckers were lying." I muttered, pinching the bridge of my nose. The men I had captured on my raid a while back said Lady Qing was in cahoots with some old white man, and further prodding revealed it to be Ivan. Although, I haven't been able to dig up much on my end regarding what they were involved in together, so whatever those two were planning was either off the books or being disguised really well.

"Ivan's been letting your stepmother use his ports to get her shipments, probably because you've cut off most of her routes with your little plan of tearing down her reign. In turn, it looks like your stepmother has been letting him sell on triad territory along with supplying him." Nikolai informed us as he swirled the golden liquid in his glass, letting the soft clinking of the ice cube ring through the room.

Something wasn't right. The part about the ports sounded highly plausible, but letting another sell on triad territory was fishy. Why would she let someone do that and lose out in profit after monopolizing the drug game in the territory? It wasn't as if Ivan was some hotshot with a miracle drug no one else had on hand, nor was he a huge player.

She could easily pay him for the ports. Hell, she could more than easily take them from him considering the triad's forces were triple that of Ivan's. It would have made more sense for her to take his turf in a small war and take over all he owned. So, why work with him? She wasn't exactly a team player kind of person.

"*Lisichka*?" I knew that prodding tone of his by now. He wanted me to spill my mind.

"Just... My gut is telling me that there's a lot more going on than that. I know my stepmother enough to know that she wouldn't just work with Ivan like that. I'll see if my men have any updates and tell Bao to dig into things more with his sister, but something isn't right." What was she planning? What does Ivan have to do with anything?

Letting out a heavy sigh, I ran a hand through my hair. "Anything about the shipments that Bao flagged?" Maybe it had to do something with the unknowns of our whole equation.

Letting out a deep breath, Nikolai pushed off the mantle and went over to the armchair, settling down before speaking, "Your stepmother's shipments, but looks like they were also some other goods like weapons and art."

Running a hand down his face, he breathed deeply for a moment before continuing. "But that's only from our end, still working with my cousin on Ivan's shipments coming out of Russia. So far he hasn't found anything strange with the shipments, but that's what's strange is the fact that Ivan seems too clean." If he were anyone else then being clean would be a good thing, but a clean mobster was always suspicious because it meant they were good at hiding.

Chewing my bottom lip, I zoned out the rest of the meeting, too engrossed in my own thoughts to hear about the brothers playing catch up. If my stepmother worked with Ivan then things were going to get dicey. It was one thing to attack within my own domain, but I can't freely touch Ivan's shit without major blowback. But also, why Ivan? There were other gangs that would make more sense if she wanted ports for her shipments.

A small nudge to my side snapped me out of my head. "*Lisichka*, let's go?" Nikolai's voice sounded a little distant when I zoned back in.

"Go where?" Did I miss something important? Did we have something planned? Was it a surprise date? No, I don't think that's possible since he wasn't urging me upstairs to change out of his shirt.

"I picked up the good doctor for you like you wanted, little rat was trying to dip when we caught him." Now this brought my mood up, almost enough to make me forget my hangover. "Go change and we'll go question him."

Chapter 28

Angel

A QUICK CHANGE AND a car ride later, we arrived at some run down area at the very edge of town. I've never been to the area, only heard about it from Nikolai. His family paid the authorities and city a pretty penny to overlook activities in the abandoned area filled with worn warehouses. Nikolai told me that his family converted the place into a storage unit and a place to hold people. Everything took place underground in the basement bunker built by his father.

"Please, I don't know why you are holding me here, I am innocent!" The faint voice of our victim could be clearly heard through the viewing area of the interrogation room. Dr. Hosti was an older man in his sixty's and has been my family's doctor for as long as I could remember. He was one of my father's friends as well, which is why I found the fact about him working for my stepmother to be a hard pill to swallow.

"That's what all the guilty criminals say." My voice was flat with anger when I entered the room with Nikolai.

"Oh thank goodness, Angel, I knew someone would come for me. Tell these brutes that they've made some kind of mistake." It pissed me off how easily he could fake it to my very face even after being caught.

"My husband doesn't make mistakes." The urge to stab him through the eye twitched at my fingers. The knives were right there, sitting pretty on a table less than three foot from me along with other little devices I had requested.

"Husband? I didn't think your mother was going to go through with her plan. Listen, I tried to—"

Tired of hearing his pathetic words, I quickly grabbed a small knife off the table and held it up to the underside of his chin. "The only words I want to hear coming out of your mouth next is the reason why you decide to work with that bitch. Anything else, and you'll start losing fingers by the bone. So, talk." Of all the people to betray my father, Dr. Hosti was the last on my mind because of his relationship with my father.

Letting out a shaky voice, he tried to lean away from the blade as he spoke, "I had no choice. Your mother—"

"Stepmother." I corrected him with a scowl as I continued to press the blade against him.

His Adam's apple slowly moved with his nervous gulp. "Stepmother." He looked at me with fearful and apologetic eyes when he corrected himself.

Taking in a nervous and shaky breath, he continued, "She forced my compliance, she was going to take my wife and daughter and put them in the auction if I didn't do what she wanted. I didn't want to do what I did to your father, I really didn't, but I can't let something like *that* happen to my wife, and especially my daughter." He shook in his seat, his terrified eyes bouncing between me and the knife.

"Auction? What auction? And you could have came to me, told my father about that witch's plans." This was the first time I heard of this auction, and I could only hope his answer wouldn't be what I thought.

"I wanted to, but she had them stashed somewhere, and I couldn't risk it. Please, you have to understand. I can't risk their lives like that, you have to understand, please. I wouldn't have been able to live with myself if I knew I damned their lives." He rambled, thrashing a bit in his seat against his bindings.

"Does she still have them? And you still haven't told me about this auction." Even if what he did was wrong, I couldn't fully hold it against him if he was backed into a corner like that.

"Please, I'll tell you what you want to know, just put the knife down, please." He begged, still looking at me with those shaky eyes of his as I glared at him.

Gritting my teeth, I dug the tip of the knife into his jaw, just slightly. "And how do I know you won't lie just to escape somewhat unscathed? You're a little too cooperative right now, and I don't like that." People would do anything to save their own skin, and right now I wouldn't be surprised if he started to spew lies to try and work on my good side.

"I have no point in lying to you now. My family is safe, I'll tell you what you want to know, just promise me you'll let me go after this, please. Please, I just want to disappear with my family after all this time, please." He whimpered while trying to jerk his head away from me.

"Start talking. I want it all, from the beginning." I don't move the knife, keeping it planted at his jaw to remind him of the threat before him.

Dr. Hosti was quick to move his lips, "Your stepmother needed your father out of the way when he found out about her involvement with human trafficking. He was about to cut her out of everything, so she approached me and demanded that I put him out of commission until she figured out a permanent plan. I refused at first, but then she kidnapped my wife and daughter and threatened to put them into her auction. She's kept them hostage this whole time, I only managed to get them to safety recently, which is why I was running when I was picked up."

I didn't detect any lies from him. What he said was highly plausible, and the part about my father would have been true because he had a rule about no forced prostitution or anything with human trafficking. It was one of the biggest rules he had, and if he found anyone breaking that rule then he would break all their bones and leave them for dead. I also knew my stepmother took up human trafficking as a main way to get her gains, and it only grew once my father was in his coma.

"What is this auction you speak of? I've never heard of it." Was this the missing piece that's been hiding from me? I knew she trafficked people, had brothels that stood as fronts for the abhorrent business, but an auction?

"It's something she keeps under tight wraps and out of the triad books at all cost. She keeps the people she deems high quality or those of high profile that she kidnaps, and twice a month she holds this auction event to sell them off to the highest bidders. She auctions off other things like stolen artwork and such, but the people are what brings the sick fucks to the event. They go there to buy what's considered the best of the goods, and to witness other unsavory events that happen down there like the cat fights or the live torture. Words can't even begin to describe the monstrosity that happens down there." Well, unless he got his rocks off of telling elaborate lies and stories, it was the truth. At this point, I was inclined towards the latter because that was one fucked up story to lie and weave.

"Where does this auction happen? How does one get in?" This was it. If I could get the information needed then I could take her down. If she went through all that effort to keep everything from the triad then it would be crippling once I yanked it from under her.

"The Catacombs, and it's invitation only besides her, the guards she employs, and her suppliers." The look of defeat in his eyes as his body became more laxed was telling enough that he spilled the truth.

"My father decommissioned The Catacombs long ago and cut off access to it." The place was practically destroyed if I remember correctly. I recalled sitting in the car with my father, watching the place go up in flames from a safe distance.

Shakily, the doctor replied, "She restored it in secret. That's where she holds everyone and everything for the auction." Hearing this pissed me off.

How the hell had she been doing all of it right under our noses?! Maybe I underestimated her by far if she managed to restore an underground facility and run a successful black market auction out of it. And here I thought taking her down would be as simple as ABC.

Well fuck me.

"What do you know about the participants? The guests? What about her suppliers?" Seems like Dr. Hosti was the only source for information I had right now, so might as well milk him for all he's got.

"Politicians, business mongols, other mafia leaders. Too many to name, but if they're a big player with a background then chances are that they participate. As for her suppliers, there are very few, only three that I know of: Lilian Wu, Ramon Cortez, and recently Ivan Petrov. Those three constantly supply her with means for her auction for a cut of the profits and some business on triad territory." The names came as no surprise to me, but the fact there were so many people working with my stepmother only aggravated me more.

Gritting my teeth, I twirled the knife in my hand after standing up straight. Then, with a deep exhale, I stabbed it through his hand out of anger, making him fill the air with his pained scream. Sighing deeply, I pulled the knife out and held it back under his chin after leaning back down so my face was leveled with his.

"If I find out any of the information you gave me is bad, then I'm coming back to break a bone for each bad piece." Just because he spilled what I needed didn't mean he was free to go, yet.

"You can't keep me here! What about my family!?" He started to panic and thrash around in his seat again, causing the knife to dig further into him.

"I can keep you here, and I will. How long depends on how quickly the information you gave me pans out. As for whether you'll leave here unscathed or alive depends on that information as well. I won't touch your family, I'm not inhuman." Also, I quite liked his wife and daughter, they were the sweetest people alive. More importantly, they were innocent victims in this shit show.

"You'll kill me?" There was terror in his eyes again as he looked at me brokenly.

"No, I'd break your bones, cut a few tendons, anything and every-thing in the books besides end your life. I mean, you've known me for twenty-four years doc, you know that I'm no killer." The small handful of lives I have taken were justifiable or accidents. I've never intentionally killed anyone for the sake of it, nor have I ever had the inclination to. Of course, there was one exception, possibly.

"I mean, I'm no killer, but I can't say the same for my husband." Nikolai had no qualms about snuffing out a life. I've seen it first-hand.

"B-but you wouldn't let him kill me, right? I gave you what I know. I promise it's all good and legit!" It's hard to trust a desperate man, but I have no doubts his information was good. Still, I couldn't let him go without hard evidence that his information was solid. I still have a reputation to uphold.

With a cruel smirk, I pulled back and tossed the knife back onto the table. "That is yet to be determined, doc. You will remain here under lock and key until further notice. No harm will come to you, for now. And you have my word that no harm will come to your wife or daughter, they will be safe and unharmed." His protests faded into the background as I took my leave with Nikolai.

"Well, that was uneventful." Nikolai muttered as the two of us made our way out of the compound.

"Sadly. I was hoping for more of a fight from him. Oh well." I was a little disappointed that I didn't get to have a little fun with prying the information out of him.

Sighing, I wrapped my arms around one of his, leaning against him a bit as we continued to walk, "We're going to need to talk to our little business partner sooner than later, don't you think so, *anh*?"

"I'm starting to regret going into business with him more and more every time his name comes up." Nikolai groaned with a slight roll of his eyes. "I don't particularly like protecting snakes. The only thing they do is bite you when you aren't looking."

Even the best get played sometimes, it was an inevitable evil of the business. Sometimes the chances panned out, sometimes they were train wrecks.

Best we could do right now is prevent the impending train wreck with Ivan.

Chapter 29
Nikolai

"KOLYENKA? IT'S 3 AM, come back to bed." I couldn't help turning my head towards the sweet and tired voice of Angel who stood at the doorway of my office.

Looking over at my phone, I could see she was right. "*Govno.* Sorry, I guess I lost track of time." Again. The past few days have been a headache and a half. It always was around collection time.

Sighing softly with an apologetic smile, I looked up at her before replying, "Just go back to bed, *lisichka*. I'll be there in a bit." Hopefully a bit won't stretch past an hour, but I didn't want to leave things hanging before calling it a night.

Guess Angel wasn't having any of it tonight though. The soft pitter patter of her feet floated across the room until she was between me and my desk, her hand nearly slamming the laptop shut as she leaned against the desk. "Bed. Now." She demanded with a pout, making me chuckle.

"Is that how you ask for something, *lisichka*? I am not opposed to giving your backside another beating tonight." I wouldn't make good on that threat for tonight though, seeing how tired she was right now added with the fact she had a shift in a few hours.

Whining, she tiredly stomped her foot before slipping into my lap and throwing her arms around my neck. "Kolyenka, come back to bed now, please."

She was being a brat, and she knew it. "*Lisichka*, I am only giving you one more chance to fix that attitude before I bend you over my knee." No doubt she was still sore from earlier, so maybe I'll be a little generous. "And where did you even learn that? Kolyenka."

Her tired face instantly woke up at my question. Her confused, and slightly panicked eyes, shooting up into mine. "It's nothing bad is it? I swear, I'll kill Lev if it is, he said it's supposed to be a cutesy thing with your name. I mean, it wasn't his exact words, but he said it's a nice nickname of sorts with your name."

Chuckling, I shook my head as I tucked her hair behind her ear. "No, it's nothing bad, it's just another diminutive of my name, specifically a more intimate one. You sure it was Lev that told you? And you trusted him?" Things between Lev and Angel have been better ever since that day. They weren't best friends by any means, but they were getting along much better.

"Well, I asked Alexei for cute pet names I could call you in Russian, and Lev overheard and butted in. Alexei didn't oppose it, so I decided it was safe. Unless those two just wanted to fuck with me, which I can see from Lev, but not Alexei." She elaborated in a small voice.

"You could have asked me, you know." I chuckled softly as I leaned back in my chair with my arms loosely wrapped around her small body.

"But then that would ruin the surprise." She giggled, sticking her tongue out at me.

Smiling softly, I leaned in for a kiss, only to be stopped by her finger to my lips. "Nah ah, bed first." Smirking, she slid out of my lap and pulled at my hands. "Come on, bed, please." At least she actually sounded nice about it this time.

Deciding to let her win this time, I got up and let her drag me back to our bed where she pulled me down with a kiss and giggle. "I don't think I'll ever get tired of kissing you." She whispered sweetly with a smile. Her fingers lightly danced down the side of my face as she looked at me with those soft and adoring eyes of hers. "Take my robe off."

"As much as I want to ravage you again, it's late and you have a shift in a few hours. You're not going to get any sleep if we go for a few more rounds." It never ended after one round with us, not with my little needy vixen. It didn't help that I could never get enough of her no matter how many times I screwed her stupid.

Confused, I watched Angel shift under me shakily until she was on her frontside. "Please." She trembled like a leaf under me, her breaths coming out broken and shaky.

"You don't have to do this if you aren't ready, Angel." The two of us had this unspoken rule to not touch *that* subject ever since that night. I didn't push her, and I respected her space more by being more mindful to not touch her upper back.

Just as I was about to pull my hand away, she stopped me by placing her hand against mine and firmly pressing it to her trembling body. "No, I'm tired of this wall between us. It's not fair to you. I don't think I'll ever be ready to uncover this rock, but I can't keep this wall between us."

"I want—no need. I need you to help me break down that wall. I trust you." The only time her eyes have stilled and didn't have a look of reluctance were when she uttered those words. "Please."

Gripping at the back of her silk robe, I bunched the thin material in my hand as I searched her eyes for any signs of hesitation or regret. It didn't need to be said aloud. Both of us knew and accepted the fact there would be no return if we pushed forward. "*Lisichka*. Angel." I gave her one last chance to turn back.

The trembling in her body stopped for a moment as her eyes hardened with surety. "I trust you. I am yours, and I trust you."

No going back.

Roughly, I pulled her robe down her body, baring her full back to me for the first time. Her body jerked under me as she tried to turn back over, probably a reflex she'd developed since the event. "No." My hand grabbed at her shoulder and pinned her firmly to the bed.

Breathing deeply and shakily, she gripped at the sheets and tugged at them for a moment before speaking. "Six times."

It was a little sudden, and it took me a moment to realize she meant her scars after my eyes glanced carefully down her back and took count of the discoloration of her once smooth back.

A shaky breath in and out, she tilted her head back and looked at me with sad and weary eyes. "That's how many times he stabbed me with a kitchen knife that broke at the tip with the fourth hit. Six times total. His messed up version of Russian Roulette he told me. I couldn't fight him off, and I hate myself for it."

Her hand reached out and grabbed one of mine, settling it on her upper back with a shudder. "It was our anniversary dinner at his place. He drugged my drink, and by the time I felt off and tried to escape, it was too late. I was so close to the door, but he pushed me to the ground on my stomach and held me there before forcing himself onto me and stabbing me when he was done using my body for his sick pleasure."

Sobbing softly, she fisted the sheets as she squirmed a bit. "I should have been more careful. I hate how the memories don't fade like the scars."

Leaning down, I gently kissed each scar longingly, wanting the feeling to linger when my lips would be removed. "I don't ever want to hear that you hate yourself for this. It was out of your control, darling, you have to accept that. None of it was ever your fault. You didn't choose to be drugged, to be helpless, to let him stab you, none of it. You couldn't have predicted any of it either. So, I don't ever want to hear you blaming yourself for any of it ever again, understood?" When I find the bastard, he'll wish he never touched a hair on her.

"Y-yes." She whimpered under me, still trembling and struggling to get free of my grip.

Gripping her hair, I pulled her head back and traced the shell of her ear with the tip of my tongue. "The only thing you're going to be able to think about whenever you get bent over is how amazing you feel coming undone around my cock. No more snapping at that little wristband of yours." I'll give her something much better to channel her attention to.

Easing some of my weight onto her, I kept her body pinned under mine as I parted her legs with my knee. "You're so wet already, *lisichka*." The dampness soaking through her panties was hard to go unnoticed, and the wet spot that formed on my sweatpants as I continued to press my knee against her arousal was damning evidence.

"Stay with me, *lisichka*." I could see her eyes fading out, a telltale sign she would slip into an anxious state. Leaning back, I forced her up onto her hands and knees by her hair. Her whimpers filled the room when my hand came down on her marked ass.

Letting go of her hair, I shifted my hold down to the nape of her neck. With a firm yank, I turned her body around to face the end of the bed, still keeping her on all fours. "Look at yourself Angel, and don't you dare take your eyes off. I want you to see how your body reacts as I replace those horrible memories with better ones." I whispered deeply in her ear, keeping my eyes trained on her shivering reflection off the mirror of the dresser across the bed.

"Don't." I gave her nape a firm squeeze while jerking her when I saw the switch in her eyes. "You're not there, you're here, in our bed, safe with me."

Pulling her robe away fully with my free hand, I tossed it over the side of the bed before using the same hand to run down the length of her back, making her whimper and shudder under me. "Koly—ah!" The slow approach never worked with her. My hand on her nape squeezed when I felt her struggle under me as I kept my teeth sunk into her back over one of the scars.

Keeping a firm hold on my squirming vixen, I applied more pressure with my teeth until I felt warm liquid flow into my mouth, bathing my tongue in the familiar metallic taste of blood.

"Ah!" Her body writhed away from me, or at least tried to, when I moved onto the next scar and slowly sank my teeth into the discolored patch until I broke her smooth skin and tasted her blood again.

Ghosting my lips over her skin, I move back up to her ear. "The next time you look at your back, all you are going to be reminded of is this night filled with pleasure." A strained groan escaped me when I pressed myself against her and rolled my hips into her to grind my covered hardness against her heat. "I am going to replace every scar with my own so all you will be reminded of is me."

A sharp breath sucked through my gritted teeth when Angel returned my ministrations with her own, firmly rubbing her ass against me while moaning softly. "Is that what you want, *lisichka*? For me to replace those marks with my own?" There was no denying the wanton look in her eyes as she eagerly nodded in response to me.

"Use your words." A firm smack ripped a yelp from Angel as she jerked her body from the sudden impact.

Leaning back up, I wiped her blood off my lips with the back of my hand while watching her reflection intently with my sharp eyes.

There was a fight in her eyes as she stared at our reflections in the mirror. For a second, it seemed like she might end it all when I saw her chew her bottom lip. I wouldn't stop pushing her out of her comfort zone and beyond unless I heard the safe word fall from her lips. I trusted her to stop me if it got beyond what she could handle. She could fight me all she wanted, struggle, kick, scratch, bite, none of those actions would stop me unless *that* word—her safe word—was uttered.

Her body tensed for a second before her hand reached back and grabbed at my wrist, clawing at it as she tried to kick me off using her legs. "Kolya, I—"

With a firm shove, I pin her down to the bed by her neck. "What's the safe word?" For my sake, I needed to know she was still clear enough in the mind to know and use it.

"Fire." She replied, still struggling against my unmoving body.

"Fire? Yes or no?" My grip remained firm and unchanged, but I was ready to release her within a blink of an eye.

"No." She replied meekly as her hands gripped at the sheets after releasing my wrist.

"You understand that I am not going to stop unless I hear that word, Angel? I don't care if you fight me on this, I expect you to, but know that I am not going to stop unless I hear 'fire,' is that clear?" We've never gotten to the point where she had to use it, and I hope we never do. But tonight would push a lot of her barriers and limits.

"Yes, sir." Her body relaxed under me for just the briefest of moments until I started to touch her back again which caused her to jerk under me. "Wait, let's—"

"No." Using my hips and weight, I pin her legs under me to keep her from kicking. "I am going to mark your body up, replace those scars with my own. Fight all you want, but it's going to happen."

And you're going to love every second of it.

I wanted to tell her that but held my tongue. The way her eyes fluttered with pain and pleasure when I bit into her those first two times told me enough.

"No!" She went back into fight mode, jerking her elbow back at me and caught the side of my face enough to where I loosened my hold on her enough for her to slip from under me.

I could feel her pulse pounding under my fingers when I wrapped my hand around her slender neck and pulled her body up against mine. "We're way past the point of negotiation, *lisichka*." Her body shivered in my hands as I growled in her ear.

"Keep looking in the mirror." I reminded her before shoving her back down onto the bed, grabbing her nape to keep her from scrambling away from me.

Keeping her pinned with my knee on her back, I quickly pulled my shirt off and took my pants off, tossing both articles of clothing off the side of the bed before easing my weight back onto her and using my hips to pin hers down. "*Segodnya tebe ne sbezhat'.*" She was in the palms of a beast now, and I've got my claws in too deep for her to run.

The impact of her hand hitting my side made me chuckle out of amusement. Her hits didn't hurt from this angle. She wouldn't be able to put any force into it to make it hurt. Leaning back, I let her scramble away while I got off the bed to pick up the sash from her robe. "*Lisichka*, come here."

Angel stood defiantly at the opposite side of the bed from me, her head shaking as her apprehensive eyes glanced up at me. "There's nowhere for you to run my little vixen." I couldn't help the devious smirk that curved at my lips as I slowly rounded the bed and watched her scramble across the bed.

I didn't let her fully clear it though, and my reach was more than enough to snag her even if she tried to put some distance between us. "Come here." Angel squealed with a smile and nervous giggle when I dragged her to the end of the bed by her ankle. I grab her wrists and bind them together with the silk sash then secured them to the metal bar at the end of the bed frame.

"Let me go! Untie me!" She demanded, tossing a glare and scowl at me as she jerked her bound wrists.

Watching her with amused eyes, I slowly climbed back onto the bed while watching her tug and struggle against the makeshift restraint. Even while she struggled, her eyes never left me as she watched me carefully through the mirror. "Your legs will be next if you don't behave." My eyes quickly glanced over to the nightstand where I kept the rope, and she would know from the glance I would make good on my threat.

"I can't—ah!" A quick snap of my wrist and her lace panties were ripped from her body.

I could feel and see her panic rising again as I fisted her hair and forced her onto her elbows while keeping her ass high in the air. A firm smack to her behind jolted her out of the budding panic. Gripping her hips, I entered her to the hilt without warning and groaned at the feeling of having her warmth surrounding my aching cock.

Her body shuddered under me as I kept her firmly planted against me, not letting her move away one bit. "Kolya, please, I don't think I can handle this." She whimpered shakily under me.

"Your body can, and you will." She squeezed around me so tightly. Her hips rocked back and forth to gain any kind of friction she could. "This." My hips slammed into her once then I paused, "Is all you're ever going to think about from now on whenever you get bent over. Feel how deep I am inside of your tight cunt, *lisichka*. Don't deny it either, you nearly came from me entering you just earlier. Admit it, you love getting bent over and fucked like a bitch in heat deep down."

"I won't admit—fuck!"

I don't give her a chance to spew her half ass defense, cutting her off with a harsh thrust that jolts her body forward. "Your body is telling me otherwise, *lisichka*. Don't lie to me." Gripping her hip with my free hand, I kept her backside up as I rammed myself in and out of her roughly at a hard pace.

The cocky smirk tugged at my lips unconsciously as I watched her slowly lose herself. "Already?" I could feel her tightening around me as her body shook from her orgasm. Her loud moan and the roll of her eyes were a dead give away too.

Her glazed over eyes filled with pleasure looked at my reflection while she whimpered needily. "I didn't—ow!"

The slap on her ass was a little harder than usual, but it got her to stop her nonsense. "You can lie with that pretty mouth all you want, but your body tells me all I need to know." It only took a few more thrusts before I found that sweet spot of hers that got her gripping at the silk sash and arching her body.

"Kolya, I don't—ah!"

Another harsh slap reddens with the imprint of my hand on her creamy cheek as I continued to slam my hips into her. Another yelping moan escapes her when I lean down and bite at another scar of hers. There was still some fight left in her eyes as I continued to drill into her harshly.

It slowly slipped though.

The more pleasure I ravaged her body with, the more the conflict chipped away from her lust blown eyes.

Sliding my hand from her hip down to between her legs, I quickly found her clit and started to pinch at it with my fingers. "I can't, fuck!" Another shuddering moan shook at her body as she reached another climax.

"Keep your eyes on me, don't you dare think about that bastard or that night." I growled in her ear. "Focus on how good it feels to get pounded from behind, not the dread from before. Think about the pleasure, not the pain." I whispered softly, easing my hold from her hair to run my hand down her back. "Think about my touch, not his. He can't hurt you anymore." I start easing off with my hips, giving her slow, deep thrusts rather than hard ones that jerked at her body.

"He's still out there. What if he comes back? You have any idea how paranoid I get thinking about him coming back to finish the job? That's why I have so much trouble moving on. He still taunts me.

Whenever I think I'm getting ahead, he comes back." She whimpers, her tears slipping from the corner of her eyes.

Cupping her face, I wipe her tears with my thumb before kissing her cheek. "I won't let him touch you. You have me now. The next time he comes around will be his last. No one torments my wife and gets away alive." It was a promise. I wasn't going to rest until I settled the demon that haunted Angel.

"Now, no more of that." Leaning back up onto my knees, I hold her hips firmly with both my hands and bring her back onto me to meet my thrusts as I start to put more force behind them again.

"Kolya, I'm too sensitive like this." Her tight walls were constantly griping at me with every thrust.

"Good." I smirked with a hard thrust. "Makes my job of fucking you stupid that much easier." Her hands pulled at her restraints when I picked up my pace, making her moan loudly as I rolled my hips into her more to get that sweet little spot of hers. "That's it, ride it out baby." Her body jerked under me with another orgasm as she strained out a moan.

Pressing a hand against her back, I press her frontside down into the mattress to get a better angle at her. "Breathe baby, you're safe, so just take me like my good little slut that you are."

Her eyes nearly melted at my words with how soft her gaze went. All the resolve that hardened at her irises disappeared with a few soft and dirty words. "God I hate how hot you sound right now. How the hell can you be so soft and vulgar like this, it's not fair." She whined with a moan.

Chuckling, I dug my fingers into her hips to make sure I've a firm hold on her before thrusting into her with reckless abandon. My pace doesn't falter one bit at her constant pleading for me to slow down. If anything, it spurred me to drive into her harder the more she begged me to slow down or stop.

"That's it *lisichka*, you're such a good girl." With how much my fingers were digging into her, there was no way she wouldn't have bruises after this session. "*Takaya khoroshaya malen'kaya shlyushka.*" I whispered deeply into her ear with a chuckle at her quivering body.

"Not fair. Ugh, should've just kept my mouth shut about liking how you talk." The metal bar creaked under the pressure of her tugging as her body shook with another release. "Ugh, I swear, you could curse me out in Russian and I'd still find it hot."

Not that I would ever do that, but it amused me to see the huge effect I had on her.

"God, Kolya, I'm going to lose my mind if you don't stop. Fuck, I don't think I can take it anymore, please." She cried with a whimpering sob.

I couldn't help but smile arrogantly at her words. "You think I am going to stop after hearing you admit that, *lisichka*?"

I chuckled darkly as I ran my hands up her body to cup a quick feel of her breasts before sliding them back down to her hips. "I am not going to stop until I've had my fill, until all I see in that reflection is your glazed over eyes and broken face filled with nothing but pure bliss."

I also didn't want this to end quite yet. I can't count how many nights I spent thinking about the day she'd finally let me take her on her hands and knees like this, to pin her down beneath me in a vulnerable position.

Time was a concept that flew out the window as I continued to ravage her body for God knows how long. Angel quickly came undone beneath me the more I pounded into her and forced her orgasms from her shaking body.

"Please, please, please." What she begged for wasn't clear, and I don't think either of us knew at this point. Was she begging for more? For me to slow down? Stop? Faster? Harder? She got so lost to the pleasure being inflicted on her. Her words started to fade into incoherent moans the more she ran her mouth until she was but a true moaning mess.

I couldn't get over the feeling of her walls coaxing my own release out with each orgasm I ripped from her tiny body. My resolve slowly chipped away with each of her orgasm, the tight pulsating grip of her cunt becoming too much after a while.

She was spent by the time I came inside of her with a deep groan, her a body shaking mess under me as her poor used body all but a crumpled mess after her arms and knees finally gave out.

With one quick pull, the knot of her restraint came undone, and her hands fell limply onto the bed. Carefully, I gathered her up into my arms, holding her trembling body tight and close as I sat at the head of the bed with her in my lap.

"Breathe, come back to me Angel, come back to me. You did amazing baby, so great. Come back to me." My rubbed at her arm soothingly as I peppered her forehead with soft kisses.

"Kolyenka?" Her voice barely came out as a soft squeak as she looked up at me with her tired eyes that were still glazed over with remnants of her pleasure filled state.

Smiling softly down at her, I cupped her face, "Shh, I am here *lisichka*, I'm here. I've got you. You're safe." I assured her sweetly.

Glancing out of the corner of my eyes, I grabbed the bottle of water she always kept filled at her nightstand. "Here, drink. I'll get you something to eat once you have come down some more." I wasn't going to leave her in the middle of her sub-drop. Carefully, I tilted the lip of the open bottle against her lips, urging her to drink small sips at a time.

Minutes later, when I was sure she came down from the bulk of her sub-drop, I started to shift her out of my lap but stopped at her outburst.

"No!" Her arms locked around my neck, clinging to me tightly.

Holding her tightly, I rubbed small circles with my thumb on her back while shushing her soothingly. "You need to get some food in you, *lisichka*." I didn't want her to pass out on me.

"Drawer." She mumbled against my neck, as her body started to relax again.

Sure enough, there was a stash of chocolate in the top drawer of her nightstand. Grabbing a small piece, I slipped it into her mouth after unwrapping it.

The next few minutes were filled with a calm silence as we basked in each other's presences, and the occasional feeding from me until she had consumed a good handful of sweets.

"Kolyenka." My eyes drifted from her body to hers, humming softly for her to continue. "*YA tebya lyubly*."
"What?"

Chapter 30

Angel

HIS WIDE EYES COULD mean so many different things, and my spaced out brain couldn't begin to make out what his reaction could possibly be. "What did you just say, Angel?" Either he didn't hear me or he actually asked me to repeat it.

"*YA tebya lyubly.*" I repeated the three words carefully and slowly just as I had said it the first time around.

"Uhh am I saying it right? Or the right thing?" Oh god, I hope it was the right thing. There was no way all four of his brothers would gang up on me and have me say the wrong thing, right? I wouldn't put it past Leo and Arseny to pull one on me, but not Stepan and Alexei.

The panic in me subsided when Nikolai's face lit up with a big grin as he looked at me lovingly. "I just wanted to make sure I heard you right." He chuckled softly before leaning down into a deep and passionate kiss.

"*YA tozhe tebya lyublyu.*" He whispered heavily after our lips parted. "I love you too, Angel. *YA tozhe tebya lyublyu.* Your words were a little stiff, but that's okay, it doesn't matter." He was elated, and I couldn't help but let it spill over to me.

Those three little words always scared me, especially since the last time I uttered them I got stabbed in the back, literally. I knew there were feelings that festered for Nikolai, but I didn't want to jump the gun just because we were married. I wanted to be sure before I made myself vulnerable to him by giving him my bleeding heart on a platter.

I couldn't deny it any longer though, especially after tonight.

Carefully, he pulled me under the covers with him. "As much as I want to throw you down and make love to you right now to celebrate, you need rest, *lisichka*." He whispered against my forehead before kissing it.

I wanted to protest, but I knew I was at my limit tonight. I needed to recharge fully after the trip and drop. I was too exhausted, and I could already feel the heaviness of sleep dragging me down into the darkness of slumber. "Good night, *anh*." I mumbled happily with a smile as I snuggled myself into him.

"Good night, *lisichka*." His voice a distant echo by the time his words filled my ears as I drifted off.

I woke up around midday after going back to sleep once I had called out of work, because no way was I able to drag myself out of bed after a night like that. I was still exhausted and aching after sleeping the many hours I did. I only faintly remembered mumbling a quick 'bye' to Nikolai when he had to leave this morning for business reasons, but even that felt like some strange dream.

My body was still so heavy I barely managed to drag myself to the bathroom for a quick rinse and back to bed. I was way too tired for anything but to sleep again after I haphazardly pulled on a pair of shorts and short sleeved shirt after the shower. Food could wait. Nikolai could scold me later for it, but I wouldn't be able to eat a bite in this exhausted state.

So, with a tired groan, I slowly wiggled my way over to Nikolai's side of the bed, burying my face into his pillow to surround myself with his scent. Then, just as sleep's sweet embrace started to take me, I was startled with a shot of adrenaline when I heard some clattering in the house.

Is Nikolai home?

A quick check of my phone answered my question. Nikolai religiously informed me about when he would be coming home if he knew I was home so his presence never came as a surprise. He also did so because sometimes he wanted to come home to me ready in bed for him, which I indulged him with most of the time.

But if Nikolai wasn't home, then what was going on? There wasn't any mention of remodeling or moving things. No shipments either. No way that came from equipment because it sounded like papers and dense boxes being moved.

Chewing my bottom lip, I quickly shot a text message to the family group chat, asking if any of them were present at the house. It wasn't unusual for any of them to hang around the house since this was their second home. Unfortunately, all of them replied that they weren't.

Honestly, it might be nothing. Maybe I was being a little too paranoid... On the other hand, when has my gut ever been wrong?

Ugh, fuck it.

Getting out of bed with another groan, I opened Nikolai's nightstand safe and grabbed one of the Glocks, loading it with a full magazine before throwing on one of my robes. Then, I headed towards the source of the noise. I kept my small body firmly pressed against the wall as I slowly stalked towards Nikolai's office where the noise came from.

Was he home? No, he replied to the group text he wasn't, and he wasn't one for pranks. So, who the hell was in his office? The place was always locked if he was gone, and no one was allowed in there besides Nikolai himself, his brothers, and I. Not even the house cleaner was allowed in to clean the place.

"Come on, I thought you said you were the best cracker." A hushed voice said. A male from the sounds of it.

"I am!" A second male voice replied frustratedly.

"Then why the fuck does it keep popping up error?" The first male hissed.

"Do we really need to get access to his computer? We have the books." The second male spoke up again.

"Kolya? Honey, is that you in there?" I called out as I slowly pushed the ajar door open more.

With the gun hidden behind me, I leaned against the doorway with a fake surprised face. "Oh, sorry, I thought Nikolai was back. What are you guys doing in his office?" I kept my voice light and clueless, hoping to play them to avoid setting the two men off. At least there were only two. Only problem? They weren't strangers.

The man behind the computer grinned at me sheepishly, and the nervous tick of his lips didn't go unnoticed by me either. "Oh, Mrs. Volkov. I'm sorry if we disturbed you. Mr. Volkov sent us to retrieve some documents from his office, but he kind of forgot to give us the details for his access code. Do you think you could help us out Mrs. Volkov?"

So, that's how they want to play it huh?

Faking a smile, I responded in an innocent voice, "Sorry, Nikolai doesn't divulge any of that to me either. Family business and all ya know? Why don't you just call him? He's out of his meeting by now."

I couldn't make a move yet when I couldn't fully assess them. Being bodyguards for the family, I knew they had at least one handgun on them. So, I had to assume they were armed, but I don't know if they were packing any other surprises.

I had a clear shot of both of them. One stood by the desk while the other sat behind the computer screen, but the computer guy was offset enough to where I could get a clean headshot. I would have to shoot one of them down because I wouldn't win against two guns if both of them pulled their piece on me. The big question: who. I was intent on keeping one of them alive enough for questioning, but who would be my snitch?

The man standing quickly patted at his pockets then threw his hands to the side with a sigh. "Damn, I think I left my phone on the charger. You got yours Tony?" Tony—the one sitting at the computer—quickly shook his head in response. "Do you think you could call him for us, Mrs. Volkov?"

Bullshit.

I could see the faint outline of something akin to a phone in the guard's pocket. But I could use this to my advantage. "Yeah, I just need to get my phone from my room, wait here, I'll be right back." I kept up the innocent act which they seemed to buy. It would seem these two weren't as close to the family like Benjamin and Tim, otherwise they would have been able to see through my act.

Although, speaking of Benjamin and Tim, where the hell were they? Those two stuck to me like flies to a glue trap.

Turning my heel, I walked swiftly towards one of the accent tables that lined the hallway. Well, if things went my way then both of them would be alive. Unfortunate for them, but at least I would keep my hands relatively clean if things went smoothly. So, while clutching the Glock in my right hand, I reached under the table with my left and quickly located the gun strapped under the wooden furniture.

Good thing Nikolai was prepared and smart enough to stash handguns around the house.

After checking to make sure it was loaded and ready, I went back to the office earnestly. The wooden door flew back on its hinges with a swift kick, startling the two guards who were still in the same position when I left.

"Don't even think about it." I warned them sternly when I saw their hands go for their weapons. "I can shoot faster than you can draw." I already had a gun pointed at each one of them.

Waving my gun at Tony, I signaled for him to get up. "There's some rope in the first drawer. Tie your little friend up with it then disarm him, slide all of his weapons over to me. If there is so much as a twitch outside of what I say then it'll be a bullet between your eyes. Am I clear?" The conviction in my voice should tell them I wasn't playing around.

Nervously, the one standing chuckled weakly as he held his hands in the air along with his partner. "Mrs. Volkov, let's be rational. You can put the guns down before any of us gets hurt. Listen, I don't know what you're thinking, but we are here on Mr. Volkov's orders. So, please, put the guns down. We don't want any stray—"

BANG!

It was a warning shot. A small graze to the standing man's cheek. The slight tilt of my hand straightened after I fired the gun to aim it back at the center of the man's head. "There won't be any stray bullets. You two obviously don't know who I am and what I am capable of. Now, either comply, or you can say 'hi' to the devil for me when you meet him."

With shaky hands, Tony quickly opened the drawer to Nikolai's desk. "And Tony, if you dare try to go for the gun in the drawer then you'll be a good demonstration for your buddy as to how deadly accurate my aim can be." I warned him with a flat smile.

Times like this made me think maybe the life of organized crime isn't so bad. I mean, I feel like a boss ass bitch right now with two men at my mercy because I have guns pointed at them. Eh, maybe if I had more of a desire to be in a position of power, but I knew this feeling would be fleeting at best. I may have my moments, but that was the extent of it.

My eyes trained on Tony as he carried out my instructions, tying his partner up and sliding all his weapons over to my feet. "On the couch rope bunny." I demanded with a nudge of my head, watching as the bound man resigned himself to the couch. Then, my attention went back to Tony, "Bend over the desk with your hands flat on it." I waited until he did as he was told before slowly going over to him.

Uncocking one of the guns, I tucked it into the waistband of my pants before using that free hand to fish out a pair of black leather handcuffs from the drawer. "Hm, guess you're out of luck today, they aren't the fuzzy ones." I was rubbing it in their faces now, and I loved every second of it.

They're the ones who thought it'd be wise to break into Nikolai's office and steal, at least I'm pretty sure that's what they were doing in the office. So, I might as well humiliate them and have my fun before my dear husband gets home and rips them a new one.

After I got the cuffs on Tony, I dragged him over to the couch and undid a small length of rope from the other man's bindings to use it to secure the cuffs together, effectively securing Tony to his partner. "I never do the tying, so I don't know how to do safety knots. Sorry not sorry."

Note to self: not a rope master.

Sitting down at the couch across from them, I kept the single gun trained on them as I pulled out my phone with my other hand to call Nikolai. "Darling? Is everything okay?" I could hear the concern in his voice when he spoke.

Chuckling softly, I shook my head before replying, "Everything is fine *anh*, but you should probably book it home to deal with the rats I found before I put more holes into the house." Twitching my trigger finger, I smirked and snickered softly when I watched the two men jump at the action. "We're in your office."

"Alright, I'll be home in fifteen. Lev should be arriving shortly, he was already on his way there. Stay safe, darling." The line cut out after his last bit, and I tucked my phone away into the pocket of my robe.

"Well gentlemen, do you want it quick and painless? Or long and painful? I mean, you're probably going to die after everything, but how you go is completely up to you. Just so you know, if you decide to play the tough guy then you'll probably have to deal with me in the interrogation room. And let's just say that my methods are... Different. I'm not a punch first ask questions later kind of gal. I have my methods to inflict pain without bruising up your handsome faces, but I've heard some say they prefer a brutal beating to my methods." They could spill their guts now and save everyone the trouble of dragging them to the bunker.

"Man, I told you she was a crazy bitch." Tony grumbled while struggling with his restraints.

"You also told me no one would be home, but guess you're wrong about a lot of things today asshole." The other man replied with a huff.

"She's usually at work at this time!" Tony snapped back, jerking his shoulder against his partner. "We shouldn't have let her walk away that first time." He continued to grumble before glaring at me. "How did you know what we were up to?"

"Well, I don't know exactly what you're up to, but I know it can't be anything good if you're in Nikolai's office without him. No one is allowed access to the office besides him, his brothers, and I. So, you two are really not supposed to be here. Although, if I was his clueless wife then your little ploy would have worked, but I am not. It was a good effort on your end though." I did feel a little offended because they thought I could be easily played like that. Did they really underestimated me that much?

The slamming of a door echoed to the upstairs seconds later. "Angel! Where are you!? Are you here!?" It took me a second to discern the slightly frantic voice.

"I'm in the office Lev!" I called out, not taking my eyes or budging the gun even a millimeter.

Heavy footsteps thudded their way up the stairs towards us, and soon a very pissed off Lev stood at the doorway. "*Bozhe, ya na sekundu zabespokoilsya.*" He let out a heavy breath he held in his chest. "When I saw Benjamin and Tim out front after Nikolai told me to get my ass over here..."

"Aww, you were worried about me, how sweet." I teased playfully with a grin in his direction. "I might have been screwed if these two knew what they were doing or if they had it more planned or something. They weren't expecting me to be home it seems like, so I caught them by surprise. Helps that they thought I was just the sweet and stupid wife. I honestly thought it was a ploy for them to get me to turn my back so they'd put a bullet through me."

"Stanley, Tony, what the fuck is going on?" Lev demanded with a scowl as he approached them like a predator stalking up to its injured prey. His hands unbutton the sleeves of his shirt with each step. Then he pushed the sleeves up above his elbows.

"They didn't hurt you did they?" Lev asked me after turning his head in my direction.

"No. Are Benjamin and Tim okay?" I would hate to think of something bad to happen to those two. Even if it was part of their job description, they still had lives of their own. I've also grown somewhat fond of the two after it was clear I couldn't shake them no matter how much I tried. They were also good company on occasion when I had no one else around to entertain my mind.

"Yeah, they'll be fine. Alexei is on his way with another doctor to tend to their injuries. These two newbies blindsided them with a few others. Seems like we'll have to pick through our guards to weed out the bad apples after we're done with these two." Lev replied before punching Tony in the stomach, making him double over and cough. "What were you after in here?" He questioned the man, grabbing him by the hair and forcing his head back.

"You don't want to wait for Kolya to come back before we start turning them into punching bags and pin cushions?" Nikolai probably wouldn't care too much as long as we got the needed answers, but I also knew he liked to personally deal with problems close to home. Well, not like we'd kill them by the time he gets here, hopefully. I could vouch for myself, but Lev was a different story.

"We're not going to say anything, so might as well kill us." Stanley spoke up in a shaky voice. Clearly he was scared by how his leg twitched and how his eyes darted around the room like a ping pong ball.

"Killing you would be too easy. I mean, I could do it right now with one well-placed bullet, but where's the fun in that? But there are two of you, and we just need one for answers." Slowly, I bounce the loaded gun back and forth between Tony and Stanley, an attempt to shake them up. If we could find who was the weaker one between the two then we'd save a lot of time and energy. "Also, killing you would be giving you what you want." Both the men were eyeing the gun nervously, twitching and jumping whenever the gun aimed at them.

"God damnit, just shoot us you crazy bitch!" Tony shouted impatiently.

A pained grunt left Tony when Lev punched him, "Don't be talking to her like that. Did your mother not teach you manners?" Lev scowled, throwing Tony's head at Stanley's, causing a soft thudding of heads to sound through the room.

As fun as it was to watch them squirm helplessly in terror, I couldn't continue forever, unfortunately. "You." My gun landed squarely on Tony who froze up at the end of the muzzle. "Talk. Every minute you waste will be a bullet in a toe. Any lie will be a bullet in the toe. And yes, omission counts as lying too."

To make my demand clear, and to scare the poor man some, I aimed the gun at his feet and fired a shot next to his shoe. "I'll move onto your little buddy's toes after all ten of yours are done for, and I've got enough rounds in both guns to go for all twenty little piggies."

"Wait! Why do you have to shoot mine if you're going to question him? He's not going to care about my toes!" Stanley shouted in a panic as he struggled to get away from Tony, but there wasn't much length to the rope between them to put much distance.

"Well, then I guess you better start convincing your buddy to talk or talk yourself before his toes are gone." Shifting my aim, I fired another shot into the floor, this time next to Stanley's foot. "You're both lucky I am feeling nice today, otherwise I'd forgo the gun and use anything stab-able for your shitty feet, and that can range anywhere from knives to the pens on the desk, depending on how generous I am feeling." Bullets destroyed too much in their path, which meant less landscape to work with.

Well, if I ever got tired of nursing, I could always become a not so legal interrogator. But on second thought, I liked helping people too much. Torture gets so boring after a small while. Ironically, I didn't like seeing people suffer. Very ironic given my threats just now, but this was part of the job of being Nikolai's bride I had placed upon myself. He was a formidable man, and I wanted to show the world I was just as formidable to be standing hand and hand next to him.

Silence filled the room, neither man moving their lips like I wanted.

Shame.

BANG!

It took a second for everything to sink in after I fired the bullet into Tony's foot. "Motherfucker! She actually shot me!" Tony screamed, jerking his bleeding foot any which way.

Placing a hand over my heart, I feigned hurt with a fake expression of disbelief. "What? Did you think I was kidding? I am offended that you would think I wasn't serious." Seldom were my threats empty in situations like this, and Tony learned things the hard way. Hopefully Stanley will see this example and learn from it before it's his turn.

Smirking, I held up the wrist with my watch on it and waved it tauntingly at Tony. "Tick tock Tony, you got fifteen more seconds before it's another full minute, and you know what that means."

The seconds ticked by in my head as I continued to stare down Tony who tried to keep a brave face with me. The tough guy bravado his quivering body tried to maintain was almost laughable. Once the next minute was up, I took aim again. He still had his shoes on, so I could only assume the spot right next to the first bleeding hole would be his second toe.

Another bang rang out after I pulled the trigger, and another scream from Tony followed suit. Then another stagnant pause before a third shot filled the room. Tony wasn't going to talk, I had already figured as much. He was merely target practice and a means to spook my intended target.

Five minutes passed by in a blink of an eye—and a bloody foot later. "Down one foot already Tony. I gotta give you props for not letting the shock get to you yet." Then, my eyes fell over to my intended prey. "You see how fast five minutes go by Stanley? Soon it'll be you before you know it. I mean, look," I paused briefly to pull the trigger, letting out another shot, "Only four more toes to go before you now."

Tony wasn't the weaker one of the two, no, it was Stanley. I had to shake Stanley up enough to get his lips loose. Tony could take the beating, he was the tough guy of the two, which was why I picked on him. Sometimes fear and anticipation worked a lot better than pain when it came to prying information out of people. Seeing what happened to Tony and knowing he would be next should be enough to spur Stanley—at least that was my hope.

BANG!

"Three." A twisted smirk pulled at my lips after firing another shot. Dragging it out would hopefully build that fear and anxiety.

The sound of scuffling shoes against hardwood came to a halt at the door. "Angel!" Nikolai's shoulders relaxed the moment he laid eyes on me. The gun in his hand lowered as he entered the room, running a hand down the lower part of his face. "I thought you got shot." The flash of concern and fear flashed in his blue eyes when he looked at me.

"Don't worry, I'm untouched." I assured him with a soft smile before turning my attention back to Tony and giving his remaining foot another shot. "Two. Almost your turn, Stanley." I couldn't help myself from giving an unhinged chuckle for effect, nearly chuckling with purpose when I saw how Stanley shook in his seat. "One." I couldn't help the dark rasp of my voice as I pulled the trigger again.

"They wanted locations!" Stanley shouted over the sounds of Tony's screams.

"Shut up! Just shut up!" Tony screamed, kicking at Stanley with his bloody foot. "Don't tell them jack shit!"

"I'm not having my toes blown off one by one over a span of ten minutes by the crazy bratva bride!" Stanley thrashed wildly, tucking his legs up under him to hide his feet from me. "I'll tell you what you want to know! Just don't shoot my toes!"

With a hardened face, he turned his attention to the bound men. "Talk, or my wife shooting your precious toes will be the least of your worries." Nikolai had a threatening aura to him as he shed his jacket and pushed his sleeves up past his forearms.

Stanley quickly squealed despite his partner's protests. Protests that were muffled by a ball gag, courtesy of Lev after he dug through the drawer. It would have been a wad of paper, but I guess Lev found more equipment while pulling out scrap pieces of paper to ball up. "He paid us a lot of money to break into your office and steal the locations of all your warehouses, safe houses, business, just every location tied to your name. He wanted bank accounts too, but we couldn't get into your computer!"

"Who? Who is he? Who paid you? Who hired you? And why?" Nikolai pressed as he stalked up to the shrinking Stanley.

"The one you sent us to protect, the warehouses at Gorth Bay. He paid us triple to work for him. He didn't tell us why he wanted the documents, just told us what to steal. That's all I know, I swear!" Stanley stammered nervously, pressing himself further into the couch as if he could just sink into the cushions and disappear.

With a clenched fist, Nikolai punched Stanley in the face, breaking his nose with a crack. "Ivan. He dares to steal my own men from me? Damn *ublyudok* is going to regret ever crossing paths with me." Nikolai seethed with anger, the silent kind that meant a storm was coming. Grabbing the bleeding man by the collar of his shirt, Nikolai lifted him up to his face, "What does he do around his warehouses? His ports?"

"H-he stores his goods there along with that one crazy Asian lady, your wife's mother, he stores her goods there too, mainly counterfeit goods, drugs, and warm bodies." Stanley's pathetic whimpers were starting to get annoying the more Nikolai glowered at him.

"Stepmother, but what do you mean warm bodies?" I questioned with my own glare as I pointed the gun at him as a reminder that I was still a threat as well.

"Girls, kids, men, women. They come from shipments overseas and from the Asian lady's previous warehouses. She was talking to Ivan about how a pest was messing up her trade which is why she moved the humans to Ivan's warehouses. I don't know what their deal is, but Ivan gives the lady some of his girls to sell too. We take them to this location in the desert every now and then." Stanley answered my question quickly and nervously.

Damn. The doctor was right then. Hell, it's worse than what the doctor told us. Although, I'm sure he wasn't privy to how they obtained the humans.

Fuck.

Disarming the gun, I set it on the table before getting up. "I need to get in touch with the others and let them know about this. I don't need anything else from these two rats." The adrenaline was already dying down, and the scent of iron started to make my empty stomach feel rather queasy.

I was done here.

Nikolai could handle the rest just fine on his own. Besides, they were his men, so I didn't want to overstep much into his business.

"*Lisichka*, are you okay? You don't look well." The concern etched in Nikolai's charming eyes made it hard to deny even though his face remained stoic.

"Yeah. I wasn't hurt or anything, really. I think I'm just still tired from last night, plus I haven't eaten anything. I'll be okay, promise." I did feel like crap now since my adrenaline rush died down. Stress on an empty stomach wasn't a good thing, but I could easily fix one of those two problems quickly.

"Lev, go with Angel and make sure she stays safe until the whole place is swept and secured and our men are sifted through." I thought about arguing with Nikolai, but the way his eyes hardened at me made me shove those words into the trash.

I hated being treated like this, but I knew it was one of those things where it was better safe than sorry. Nikolai knew fully well I was just as capable as him, but he's also made it abundantly clear on many occasions how he would never put my safety and wellbeing at risk because of how precious I was to him. It was sweet he cared for me deeply like that, even if it annoyed me at times.

Much to my surprise, Lev didn't argue like I had expected him too because no one wants to be stuck on babysitting duty. But one glance at the look Nikolai gave his brother was enough to send shivers down my spine. It was a look that meant business and to not question his words, otherwise there would be consequences. To say it was his serious look would be a grossly inaccurate description because it was beyond serious.

The moment the door shut, I let out a breath I didn't even know I held. I hadn't realized how stuffy the room was until I was clear of it. The breath of fresh air dizzied my vision for a split second. "Let's go to the kitchen. I think I might pass out if I don't get food in me right now." I forced out a weak chuckle as I lifted my heavy feet down the hallway towards the stairs with Lev.

When we got to the stairs, I had to stop when I felt my vision drop. The stairs I had gone up and down a thousand times by now seemed like they'd doubled in size. "Are you sure you're okay?" I didn't need to look at Lev to know he was concerned from how he sounded.

"Y-yeah, I just..." Shit, was I that famished? The area started to spin the longer I stood.

Then, I felt myself hit something solid and flat. "Hey, I got you." When did I start to fall? My vision went out of whack, and I found myself leaning over Lev's back when I refocused. "Don't pass out on me now, otherwise Kolya will have my head." Lev joked with a chuckle as he started to move down the stairs with me on his back.

"Think I still have some leftover sushi bake that can be heated up." Like hell would I cook something in this state. Plus, I don't think I could wait for the chef to whip something up if I requested something. I needed to get food in me a lot sooner than later. "Should be enough for you too if you want some."

"Let's get you fed first then you can worry about me." Lev's body shook with his chuckle, making me giggle a little because it felt a little ticklish. "On a different note. Why the fuck is there a ball gag in Nikolai's drawer?"

Unable to help it, I let out a small laugh. "What do you think Lev? I doubt your mind is a virgin." I'd run to a convent and lock myself in it if Lev was a damn virgin in any sense.

Lev groaned in response as he set me down on the island stool. Whether the groan was one of disgust or regret was undiscernible to me. "Never mind, forget I asked. I can't get the images out of my mind now." Definitely a regretful groan.

Snickering, I propped my elbow up and leaned my chin into my hand. "What? The images of Nikolai tied up?" Now I was just being evil, but I lived for the chaos.

"*Iisus chertov Khristos*, I did *not* need that image in my mind. God, I don't think I can look at him after this without those images." Lev groaned, rubbing a hand through his face and glaring at me out of the corner of his eyes.

My laughter rang for a few seconds as I watched the horror twist on Lev's face. "Don't worry, I'm on the receiving end of things." I couldn't help but laugh some more at Lev's flushed face as he buried his face behind the open fridge door.

"You're a horrible person." He grumbled as he pulled out the leftover food I made last night.

"Oh, I know, you didn't have to state the obvious." I snickered with a devious smile.

Once I got some food in my system, I started to feel a little better, barely. I probably needed some more rest to feel completely like myself, but I would be more than fine right now for a quick phone call to everyone. Thankfully everyone was free.

"Hey, you're on speakerphone, so behave. Lev's here also." I warned everyone once the three way call connected.

"Aww, so no talking about how you wanted to know ways to get Nikolai to fuck you harder?" Hanna snickered deviously. No doubt she had a matching smirk on the other end of the line.

"Did not need to hear that shit!" Lev complained with a groan.

"Hanna, I swear to god... Ugh, never mind, I'll deal with you next time. Just, we have a big problem." I was not in the mood to entertain Hanna's antics right now, not with only half my brain working.

Unfortunately, the severity of my words didn't fully sink into Hanna. "You mean *you* have a big problem, the big problem being Nikolai's big—"

I didn't even let Hanna finish that sentence. "I am being serious! Lady Qing has been trafficking humans at a bigger scale than we've known." I snapped, a little more aggressive than I intended.

"Oh shit." Hanna's jovial tone took a serious turn.

"What do you mean?" Greg pressed.

Sighing heavily, I pinched the bridge of my nose before speaking. "Long story short, Nikolai and I found out about her restoring The Catacombs in secret. Apparently the place is fully functional again, and she's been holding black market auction events every two weeks along with other events during the time the auction takes place. She's been keeping her prisoners there and in Ivan's warehouses and possibly others. All I know for now is that she's working with Ivan Petrov, Lilian Wu, and Ramon Cortez."

"Shit." Hanna's voice chimed in again.

"Yeah. Shit indeed. Separately, they're just small-time gangs." I started, groaning a bit when I felt my headache worsen out of nowhere.

"Together they're going to be a bitch to take down. Fuck." Greg sighed heavily on his end.

"Yeah, it's going to be a bitch and a half." I agreed with a sigh of my own.

"What do you need from us? What can we do to help?" Bao asked, bringing the issues to the forefront of my mind more.

Groaning, I took a moment to think before responding. "Get me the blueprints for The Catacombs, the most recent. Then, as much as I want to rush into the place, we have to bide our time to do surveillance, plant bugs, research, all the works. We also need to filter through all our men to make sure we don't have any leaks or rats. I do not want either of them getting even the slightest whiff or inkling of an idea of what we're up to. All this stays between us four and the Volkovs, is that clear?"

I waited to hear agreements from all three of them before continuing, "In the meanwhile, we have to get ahead of those shipments. Expand our net to the other players as well. I want to minimize the amount of victims as much as possible. Try to keep a distance though, send things to the police anonymously so that they can bust them. We need to keep their eyes off of us. No one will think twice about the police busting their operations."

"It might even play to your favor too. If you heavily involve law enforcement like that then it might cause discord within the gangs as well. They might start doubting their own men." Lev pointed out, reminding me of his presence next to me.

"Lev has a good point with that." Hanna agreed, making Lev chuckle.

"I always have good points." Lev bragged with a cocky smirk.

"Says the one who always charges in without much planning on assignments." Hanna retorted with a scoff.

"Hey, I already told you, if it's just a single target who's a flight risk then it's better to act first then ask questions later." Lev replied with a scoff of his own.

Breathing in deeply, I rubbed my temples with my thumb and index finger before speaking, "Hey, you two can bicker over dinner some other time. Back to the point at hand. Like I said, keep as much distance as possible. Greg, Hanna, I'll leave you two to vet our men. Nikolai has some traitors already, and I really want to make sure our men are tight before we let them in on anything because if Lady Qing or any of the other three get wind of any of this then it's going to turn to shit real quick. Bao, get busy with that computer of yours."

Slumping over the counter, I propped my elbows up and settled my head between my hands. With my head cradled in between my hands, I let out a groan of pain. The throbbing pain clawing at my head got worse by the second.

Fuck this headache is not going away!

"I'll touch base with you all later tonight probably to talk more about this. I need to go right now." My thoughts were getting muddled, and I would start getting snappier by the second.

The three of them bid farewell before hanging up on the call.

"Angel?"

THUD!

Chapter 31

Nikolai

"No, thanks Dima, this is more than enough... Yes, you have my word that he will suffer and that whoever we save will have a safe return if they so wish... Yes... I'll keep you posted... Yes... Alright, thank you, bye."

With a long sigh, I toss my phone onto my desk. Using my hands, I rubbed my temples in an attempt to ease away the budding headache that came on from the information my cousin just provided me.

Seems like I underestimated Ivan. He'd been trafficking humans right under my nose while my men unknowingly protected the places where the humans were housed. Well, most of them were oblivious to the darker trade that happened—literally—right under their noses. Those who worked with Ivan would all be dealt with once I figure out who betrayed me. And let's just say the river has been fed good the past two weeks with how many bodies were dumped into it. I had no place for traitors, and their deaths would serve as a stern reminder for everyone who worked under me to never cross me.

Ivan would be dealt with accordingly once I got my hands on him. If it were up to me then I would kill the snake outright, especially after finding out all about what he was involved in. Some might see me as the devil, and given the things I've done, I wouldn't argue with them. I may be a devil, but I was a devil with morals, very gray morals, but they still existed.

Ever since I took up the mantle of Pakhan, I abolished any and all activities related to human trafficking within our businesses. Women, children, the elderly, and anyone innocent were to never be touched or harmed in any way, shape, or form. I never cared for arms deals, drugs, prostitution, murders for hire within limits, but human trafficking and all that went hand in hand with it appalled me to no end. Anyone who partook in such activities would never be in business with me. If I knew Ivan smuggled and sold humans then I wouldn't have ever shook on anything with him.

"Kolyenka?"

And there's my only solace in this hell.

"Angel." The only person I'd ever smile upon seeing their face. Hell, the only person I would ever smile unconsciously with just a mere thought.

"Everything okay? You have been up here longer than expected." Sometimes I feel like she was actually an angel in moments like these where she showed genuine curiosity and concern for me.

Sighing softly with a nod, I stood up from my desk. "Yeah, just got off the phone with my cousin from Russia. I'll go over that information in a bit with everyone else." Walking over to her, I took her in my arms, kissing her forehead and holding her for a moment to take in her soothing scent.

"How are you feeling? Did you get enough rest?" Even though it had been two weeks since her fainting incident, I still worried about her greatly. I nearly had a heart attack when Lev shouted for me that day and I ran down to see Angel passed out in his arms. Both Alexei and the doctor said it was because she was highly stressed and needed a lot of rest to recover fully, but she still hasn't been her full self ever since.

Smiling softly, she loosely wrapped her arms around my waist and rested her head against my chest. "I'm fine, don't worry. Once this whole shit show with my stepmother and Ivan are over then I'll be less tired and stressed, probably. The others will be easier to deal with once we cut off the bigger players." She tried to give me a reassuring look, but I saw right through it.

Her exhaustion was clear as day to me upon a quick glance. As breathtakingly beautiful as she was, her eyes have gotten darker and more sunken, the lines on her face more noticeable than before, her movements held a weight to them as if she struggled to move her own limbs every time. No doubt I look like that on a daily basis, but to see how much all of this affected her weighed on me as well.

With my arm around her waist, the two of us headed downstairs to the living room where all my brothers, Angel's two friends, and Greg filled. The polished coffee table nowhere to be seen being buried under all the papers, pictures, and laptops.

"How was the phone call with Dima? Everything okay back in Moscow?" The idle chatter in the room died down with Stepan's question. Everyone's eyes trained on me as I sat down in the armchair, pulling Angel onto the armrest and keeping my arm around her waist.

"Yeah, things are running smoothly in Moscow still. It's running smoother now thanks to Bao discovering those shipments. It flew under the radar over there, corrupted port officials that were being paid off by Ivan, and some of the workers were those who worked for him when he had a name over there. Dima's going to shut it all down tonight though, so we'll need to be quick to act before word can get back to Ivan that his little shipments are permanently shut down. Once we cut off his source of inventory then he's either going to retaliate or run. Either way, we need to act before he can." Like hell I would let him slip away so he could restart operations elsewhere.

"Is there a way for you to tell your cousin to wait five more days? The next auction event is this weekend, and I think it's best if we wait to strike them there because they'll all be there. The sicko I nabbed yesterday is a regular attendee and says that it's very rare for the head honchos to not be there to witness the atrocities." Greg scoffed with a disgusted scowl on his face at his last words.

"Please tell me he dropped the soap." Hanna snickered with a devious and curious smirk.

"No, he's locked up in a basement for now. He'll get his dues once we shut down Lady Qing's event and get some cuffs around the slimeballs who attend the thing." Greg paused for a second to run a hand through his dark hair and take a sip of his drink. "From what he told me, it's an exclusive event, members and exclusive invites only. You can only enter with a member's card once Lady Qing accepts you. I got the sleezebag's card, so if we want then we can send someone in ahead to scout the area, be our eyes on the inside."

Sighing loudly, Angel shook her head. "We can't do that, she knows all our faces."

"She might know us, but I doubt she knows all of Nikolai's guards." Greg's hopeful eyes fell to me, and I knew what he asked for.

It was risky to send any of my men in there like that with no backup, but if we got a scope of things before charging the place then it would give us the advantage. "It's risky, but I'll think about it. I don't want to risk the life of my men like that because if I send someone in, they'll be by themselves with no backup. Although, I do agree that it would be a great advantage to get eyes on the inside. We may have the building's schematics and blueprints, but knowing the layout only goes so far if we don't have a clue as to the enemy's numbers and positions." It was a risk, but a damn good one if we could pull it off.

"We can bring that back up later when you have thought about it more. I know it's not easy to pick a lamb to send into the wolf's den." Bao spoke up before pulling out some sheets of papers from the various piles.

After spreading the sheets on top of everything, he started to talk. "These are the blueprints I managed to get, and a quick fly by of my drone confirms that these are accurate. We can assume that there will be guards posted at the three entry and exit ways. I'm going to assume two each to err on the side of caution. I'm also assuming that she'll have guards around the perimeter as well. The only problem with everything is that we won't have any cover for a sneak attack. The place is built underground, with only the entrances above. The rest is all desert, flat barren land. You kinda see the problem? Unless all of your men know how to fly killer drones, we ain't getting close without setting off some kind of alarm."

"Then we'll just do a very coordinated drive by. If you can hack their network and shut down their system long enough for us to wipe everyone then we can break in smoothly. If they can't get into contact with the others then everyone will remain clueless on the inside. We'll just take out everyone above ground while communications are down then storm in on all sides." Angel had a good plan, albeit simple and straightforward, but it might be the way to go.

The only problem with my wife's plan was that we'd still be going in blind, and we wouldn't have full control of the situation. We might surprise them briefly to cut down some of the guards inside the compound, but once they'd get their bearings then we'd be gunned down. Ideally I would want to sneak more men inside so we'd be able to attack on both ends, but if this event was as tight knit as Greg says, then that's not possible.

Digging through another stack of papers, Arseny pulled out a rather hefty stack of files. "Oh, and here's a list of *all* the known members. Whether they are regular attendees or not is unknown, but this is the list that I dug up along with rather *juicy* details of the not so legal kind."

Taking the stack, I quickly flipped through them, barely skimming through a quarter of them before I got the general idea. The men and women who partook in the event were caked with mud and dirt, filth that we had solid evidence of now.

"One of the requirements to being able to be a member and partake in the events is that you have to give something up on your side to show that you belong in the sick and twisted world that happens within The Catacombs. The guy said it was insurance, a will of good faith or some shit. With that dirty evidence in hand, it guarantees that the member won't squeak about the event or anything related." Greg said, nodding at the files in my hands. "Basically prove that you're filth and give it to them to hang over your head."

"Took me forever to hack the damn network of theirs to get my hands on that, so don't lose it." Bao sternly said with a hardened glare, his finger jabbing at the files in my hands.

Chuckling, I shook my head softly as I tossed the files back onto the table. As much as I wanted to burn the thing to ashes, it would come in handy. "No, this kind of information would ruin a person completely if it ever fell into the wrong hands. Unfortunately for these bastards, those wrong hands are mine." Each and every single one of those people in those files were going to pay for their sins.

"I knew half of those people were sickos, but I didn't think they were that far down the pipeline." Angel seethed beside me with a scowl of disgust.

"Don't worry, we'll deal with them after we deal with Ivan and Lady Qing." I assured Angel with a dark smirk. We were going to be set for multiple life times after I'm done going through that stack of files.

Reaching over, I picked up the blueprint of the place, drinking in every little detail Bao had marked out. "Bao, can you hack the video feeds?" There were quite a few stationed around the place. If we could get a visual through the cameras then we could map the area out better.

"If you can get me close enough, yeah, but the problem is getting me close enough. Close enough as in fifty yards or less. Which brings us back to the problem of the thing being a fucking flat desert for miles. An idle van out of nowhere is going to raise questions. I'd be shot down before I could hack anything, and I rather like my body whole." Bao pointed out while pushing his glasses back up the bridge of his nose.

"If we get you close enough, without putting your body up as a meat shield, then you can do it? Yes?" I had an inkling of an idea as my eyes scanned the aerial surveillance photos that were scattered on the table.

"Yes. If I can hack the freaking government then I can definitely hack Lady Qing's shit. It'd be child's play." Bao sounded almost offended when he replied with a cocky grin.

Reaching out, I grabbed some of the aerial photos. "These cargo boxes, what do you know about them?" I questioned, tapping at the items in question.

"From what I know and gathered, they get brought in typically a few days before the event. They transport everything that is to be auctioned or used in the event. They are also used as disposal of things afterwards." Bao answered after taking a closer look at the photos.

I wanted to confirm something before I got too far with my brewing plan. "So they remain until after the event takes place?"

"From what I know and gathered, yes." Bao looked at me warily as he answered in a wavering voice.

"Why are you interested in the cargo, *anh?*" Angel questioned with a furrowed brow.

"What if we set Bao up in one of those cargo boxes? Judging from the images, it would be within the range that Bao would need to operate. If we can figure out when the transports take place then we could hijack one of them, place the equipment that Bao would need in it, leave the cargo box at the site of the event, then on the day of we just sneak Bao into the cargo box after we take out the guards." It sounded like a long shot, but that would set Angel's friend up to do the damage he needed.

"That sounds like a plausible idea. It would save us from sending anyone in and risking them being made and killed. We'd be able to properly work out a plan of attack that minimizes damage to our side. Do we know when the next shipment is going to be made? If we can figure out the next one, we can intercept them enroute, take the contents of the cargo for ourselves if it's worth it, and replace it with our equipment. Might also be a good idea to replace the drivers just so we can get an idea of the route to the place." Stepan's plan sounded good, like most of his plans.

My eyes shifted to the corners to glance at Angel when she spoke. "What do you think our chances are of getting a shipment on the day of? Or would that be too suspicious?"

Bao muttered under his breath for a second while tapping at his chin in thought as his eyes scanned a log of sorts on the table. "Might be risky... But last minute deliveries can be a possible thing."

"Let me see..." Bao quickly dug through some of the papers, pulling out various logs and laying them out for us to look as he highlighted certain entries. "I think we could pull it off. I can hack their system and adjust one of the deliveries to be set for the day of."

"Seems like we have a solid way in. Now, what about when we're inside? It's going to be a shit show once we're discovered, and as much as I would like to put a bullet through everyone in there, that's too much of a mess." Stepan pointed out our next problem.

Bao had a mostly confident answer, thankfully. "I can keep jamming their communications from the safety of the cargo box. We might need to take a minute once we get there to get situated, but what I'm hoping is that I have enough time to record a loop to hack into the surveillance area, that way we can move around undetected until someone can take out the guards in the surveillance room, hopefully. But once I have the camera feeds up on my end then I can direct you guys towards or away from the enemy."

"We'll have teams set up at each entry point." Arseny spoke up, pulling the blueprints back up to the top. "This one," his finger pointed at an entryway marked 'B' with a red circle around it, "Right here is the closest to the surveillance room. We'll have to send that team in first to eliminate the eyes of the compound, and I say we stick some of our own men in there too so that Bao doesn't have to be torn in so many directions with monitoring and informing us."

"I can stay in the room with some of our men to monitor the cameras. We'll each have a designated team to observe and inform, that way there's no confusion." It surprised me to hear Alexei injecting himself into the plan. There was no expectation of him to participate in this operation, at least not directly.

Looking over at Alexei who sat across the room from me, I raised a brow at him questionably. "You know you don't have to—"

"I know." He tersely interrupted. "I know... But I want a part of this, and we're going to need all the men we can get. I'll be fine in the surveillance room."

Alexei knew at this point he had nothing to prove to us or the family, but sometimes I felt as if he pushed himself to try and make himself valid. It was pointless, no matter how many times I told him otherwise. Even if our father didn't dig his claws into the twins compared to the others, it concerned me to see the extent of our father's effects on them.

"You don't have to prove yourself or anything, you know that right?" Alexei helped more than enough as our doctor, and if I was a hard-ass then I would command him to stay in that lane. But I wasn't my father. I didn't want to force anyone into a role they didn't want.

"I know, but I want to take part. I want to help." Alexei reiterated, this time more confidently as his eyes bore into mine.

Sighing, I nodded my head, dropping the subject. There was no point in arguing with him. If I forced him to remain behind the scenes then he would be pissed at me, and it would just cause unnecessary tension within the family.

I remained silent for a moment to think. My eyes scanned over the blueprint again to see if I missed any details the other times I studied it. "We'll have four teams. Team Alpha, Beta, Charlie, Delta. Team Alpha will be stationed at entrance A, Beta at B, Charlie at C, and Delta will remain above ground. Angel and I will head Team Alpha. Alexei and Stepan will be lead in Team Beta. Lev and Hanna will take charge of Team Charlie. Delta will consist of Arseny and Greg whose main job is to hold the surface and protect Bao."

I paused for a minute to ensure that everyone kept up with me before continuing, "We'll each be stationed accordingly at each entrance. Once Beta team secures the surveillance room then I want Alexei to remain with two other men while Stepan will take some men to the holding area to secure and protect it. Any objections to what has been put forth so far?"

I waited until all of them gave me some form of agreement when there were no objections. "Team Alpha and Charlie will attack the main floor in a pincer movement towards the back wall where there is no escape for our enemies. We take out any guards we see, but no killing the participants and attendees."

"Why? They deserve to die for being deplorable vermin." Hanna spat with a scowl, the disgust clearly laced in her voice.

"Because that's too much to cover up. If it was one or two prominent figures then we could cover it up, possibly, but not that many. Besides, I have other ways to deal with them. We're going to extort them for all they've got before letting the law handle them unless they're of use for us." I haven't looked through all the files of the attendees, but I saw some very prominent figures from my quick skim. As sickening as it was, having some of them in our pockets would be very beneficial for us in the long run.

"Seriously? You would want to keep scum like that in our pockets? Is it really worth it?" Lev was not happy to hear what I proposed, not that I blamed him.

"Only some, if they are really worth it, and it's only until they've outlived their use to us. I saw the police commissioner in the files, if we have him under our thumb then we basically have the entire law enforcement under us." It would make our less legal activities easier to conduct if law enforcement turned a blind eye to us completely.

"It's a necessary evil Lev. I don't like it either, but that's the nature of our business." Stepan agreed with me with a heavy sigh and slump of his shoulders. "But, maybe it could be a temporary thing. It might be a lot of work and effort, but what if we eventually replaced them with those on our payroll? If we install a new police commissioner of our choosing, then that would be just as good as having one under our thumb."

Smirking, I glanced over at Stepan with a firm nod, "Exactly where my thoughts were leading."

"Ugh, I hate it, but if it's like that then I guess I can keep myself from putting a bullet through them, for now." Lev grumbled with a roll of his eyes.

Clearing my throat, I leaned forward with my elbows on my knees, propping my chin up on my interlocked hands. "We'll only head in once Bao and Arseny confirm the number, location, and position of *all* the guards. I want to keep casualties on our side to the very minimum, is that clear? We apprehend all the guards and mafia members and deal with them after the fact, got it?"

I looked at each and every person in the room for their agreement before continuing, "Bao will be in charge of leading Team Alpha through the compound. Alexei, you will be in charge of Stepan and his team once he splits from you, and I will trust you to assign one of the other men to direct Team Charlie while the other remains on lookout."

The blueprints showed long winding hallways lined with rooms leading to the main area, so we were going to need eyes while we made our way to the main event center. We were going to be busy clearing the rooms in our wake, so we were going to need those manning the cameras to be on the lookout for guards rounding the corners or coming onto our path.

"We'll all come in with the cargo with Bao's equipment and fifteen men. The rest can come in once we clear the area." If the cargo crate was the size depicted in the pictures by Bao then there would be no way we could fit fifty plus men, Bao's equipment, and all of us in one. The rest of our crew would have to file in after we secure the topside.

"Anyone have anything to add? Objections?" I was a fair leader, not a dictator. I wanted to know if any of the others saw anything wrong with the plan after I laid it all out.

"Seems solid and straightforward to me." Greg tossed his opinion in with a shrug of his shoulders.

Everyone else slowly followed with their own nods or verbal agreement. "Angel, I'm going to need a list of your men to compile a team with my own." I could spare fifty of my own men, but this was a joint effort. Also, if I somehow lost all fifty men then that would be a small blow to my forces. Finding good and reliable help these days wasn't easy.

"Will do." Angel agreed with a soft nod.

Chapter 32

Angel

I WAS PREPARED TO hash it out with Nikolai because I thought he wouldn't include me in the plan. So, it was a good surprise to hear him including me without me having to butt in and fight for a position. For sure I thought he would forgo me because it would be too dangerous or some shit along those lines.

There have been times where I've had to remind him I was tougher than I look. He thought he did good by me to keep me out of some of his business, which half the time I didn't care for as long as it didn't affect us much. But there were times when I was curious or wanted to be caught up with certain situations, and he wouldn't indulge me. I've had to remind him at times his problems were technically mine as well because I was tied to him by marriage. Which he usually rebutted with "It's not your problem if I don't make it so."

Despite my nagging, he never involved me much in his business much. He didn't want to expose me to his enemies. Though most people knew he was married at this point, a good majority don't know the face of his wife. We didn't exactly post wedding day pictures all over social media. Those who did manage to find out about me would be led to dead ends considering the name on our marriage certificate wasn't my real name. Granted, I doubt his true enemies would stop at a small mishap.

As much as I hated him not including me in his business, I knew it was probably for the better considering how I want out of the mafia life. I still had no intentions on taking over the triad once we shut down Lady Qing, and I probably would never take up the mantle of head unless my father pleaded with me to. The only involvement I wanted was with Nikolai's bratva, but just the bare minimum, kind of.

I didn't want to be the clueless or glorified mob wife. I still wanted to be kept in the loop. Maybe I was being nosey as well. I liked being the back seat observer with the bucket of popcorn.

On the other hand, I also wanted to be somewhat involved to help Nikolai behind the scenes. Did I want to be taken to meetings and shit? Probably not all the time, but I wanted to know all the juicy details and have my two cents put into the pot.

Yeah, I probably sounded very contradictory with saying I wanted out of the mafia life while also saying I don't. Even if I were to cut all ties and be oblivious and blissfully ignorant to Nikolai's shady business, it would all come back to bite me in the ass one day. Hell, I was roped into an arranged marriage when I wasn't even involved in much of the triad. Unfortunately, in this line of business, just being associated in any way, shape, or form was enough to be damned.

I would always have to watch my back wherever I went. Being my father's daughter was enough to put a target on my back to his enemies who wanted to harm him or use me as leverage. The target only grew enormously the moment I tied myself to Nikolai. He wasn't much of a liability to me as I was to him. If any of his enemies got their hands on me somehow then they could get Nikolai in a bind.

If my life was going to be damned then I might as well take part in it.

"You're awfully quiet." Nikolai stated the obvious in a low voice.

The meeting was well over now, and the two of us had retired to our bed for the night. The rest of the meeting consisted of us working out any kinks in the plan we could see, and Nikolai catching us up on Ivan's situation. Apparently, the slimeball bit off *way* more than he could chew back in Russia and was forced to flee to America where he was now trying to restart his ashen empire. Though, it seemed he still had his hands dipped in Russia with what little loyal remaining men he had.

Even if he didn't have a presence in Russia anymore, he was still a thorn in their side. His main cookhouse was in Moscow still, and that's where he got most of his victims for trafficking as well. Dmitri, Nikolai's cousin and the head of their bratva branch in Russia, had been looking for more solid evidence to steamroll over Ivan's operations in Russia. Ivan's ties were strong enough that if Dmitri acted without solid facts and evidence then it could mean a small war for the Volkov Bratva branch in Moscow.

Sighing heavily, I leaned up on my elbow and used my other hand to push myself off his chest where I had been laying. "Just thinking too much about this whole thing, that's all. I just can't believe that it's finally all going to be over in a few days. I can finally be rid of a headache. The pessimistic side of me is thinking it's all too good to be true. Maybe it's just because I've dealt with her for so long that something happening this fast and soon just seems unrealistic."

Sighing softly with a smile, I leaned into Nikolai's hand when he cupped my face and traced my lips with his thumb. "You and I both know fully well that it's not something too good to be true. It's happening, and it will happen, and it will be over. You will have your peace, and I'll be right there next to you all the way."

Unable to help the smile on my face, I let the feeling of excitement and happiness control the curling of my lips as I placed my hand over his, stroking the back of it with my thumb. "Still crazy to think that you're my husband. You're more than I could ever ask for." If anyone ever told me I would be the big bad bratva boss's wife before this, I would have laughed myself to death or sent the person for a psych eval to make sure they weren't demented.

"Darling, you deserve so much more than me, an actual good man who isn't a criminal. But you're stuck with me for life now because I'll never let you go. The saying of if you love someone then let them go is bullshit. I am never, ever, ever letting you go my little vixen. You belong to me. Now and always. Til death do us part." Nikolai's voice dipped lower and lower with his words while his body twisted and towered over me, caging me in with his arms and legs.

Giggling with a playfully devious smirk, I reached up and lightly trailed a finger down the side of his face. "Really now? I belong to you?" This was so going to bite me in the ass—well more like a slap in the ass. "I don't belong to anyone. I don't belong to you."

Big mistake.

I knew I dangled a piece of steak in front of a rabid wolf, or at least I liked to think I did.

Nikolai's hand wrapped around my neck, squeezing at the sides, making my senses buzz. His face lowered until he hovered a mere inch from me. "If you wanted a fucking then all you had to do was ask, *lisichka*. Instead, you decide to be a brat. So, now, you're going to be punished." His low voice paired with his sexy smirk and the dangerous and dominating look in his eyes nearly made me come that instant.

I fucked up. Bad.

My vision blanked for a split second when the oxygen rushed back into me from the lack of pressure on my neck when he released me. During my short daze, Nikolai flipped me over onto my frontside and kept me pinned down with a hand on my upper back. Then, without warning, he buried himself deeply after bunching my nightie up and pushing my thong aside. No prep or foreplay needed because I was already soaking wet from him choking me while looking at me so deeply.

The sudden surge of pain and pleasure caused a silent scream to tense at my body. "Fuck! I'm—ah mhmph!" He didn't even give me a chance to try and backpedal. His hand fisted at my hair and shoved my face into the pillow while his hips slammed into me with no remorse.

His voice cut through the haze of pleasureful torture he inflicted on me. "What? You're sorry? Don't give me that bullshit because we both know you're not. You're only sorry 'cause you realized you fucked up. You're not truly sorry for your words." I couldn't help but shudder at the feeling of his hot breath hitting my ear as his words echoed into me.

I couldn't argue back because his words were true. So, with muffled whimpers, I threw my hands back to try and push him off only to have him trap both my wrists with his burly hand and pin them to my back.

Then, my head was yanked back by my hair. A sharp intake of breath scratched at my throat as the precious air filled my lungs. "Better keep your voice down, *lisichka*. Otherwise you better start coming up with some damn good excuses as to why you were screaming through the night." His deep chuckle shook me to my very bones as I bit at my bottom lip to keep my sinful noises back.

The pressure from my head eased when my hair was free from his grasp. Then a muffled yelp caught in my mouth when I felt a hard impact on my behind, followed by three more in quick succession. "No coming until I say you can, understood?"

When I didn't answer, another hard smack landed on my burning ass. "Understood, *lisichka*?" The rasp to his voice meant he wasn't playing around—not like he ever did.

Struggling to keep my moans back, I nodded my head. But that wasn't good enough because his hand cracked down on me again. "Y-yes, sir." I whimpered, nearly giving out a moan when my voice came out.

"Fuck!" I squealed into the pillow when I felt his hand slip between my legs, his fingers quickly finding my clit—pinching it hard—while his hips piston in and out of me like an unrelenting machine.

This wasn't fair!

My orgasm tightened at my abdomen painfully as I held out. The thought of defying him played in my mind, but I didn't dare tempt the sleeping demon right now. If I disobeyed him then this punishment would turn a hundred times worse, and I didn't want to think about enduring that right now.

He wasn't taking it easy on me either, which I guess was the point of it being a punishment—but still. Every time I came close to zoning out, he'd snap me back to reality with some extra stimulus; harsh slaps to my ass, rough hair pulling, painful nipple pinching, anything to give my body a painful jolt to keep me present. He even chided me, reminding me this was a punishment so therefore no escape.

"Please." I don't know how long or how many times I've begged and pleaded with Nikolai at this point, nor did I know when the tears started spilling down my cheeks.

"No." And I had no idea how persistently he's denied me over. And over. And. Over.

"Please." I sobbed needily.

"No." I could hear the little tick in his voice which meant he was enjoying this greatly.

Fuck this went nowhere!

I knew for a damn fact he wouldn't ever cave, and if he really wanted to then he could keep this up for a very long time—all night if he was really determined.

"Please, sir, I'm sorry, please let me come, please, I'm sorry." I sobbed and trembled helplessly under him. My hands were starting to tingle from his grip on my wrists. It started to hurt so much, but I didn't hate it. It was twisted, but being denied like this aroused me to no end, which made holding back harder and harder every passing second.

"What are you sorry for?" I could clearly hear his grunts and heavy breathing behind me as he continued to pound into me. It may not sound like it, but he was going strong still. I made the mistake of testing his resolve one too many times to know his limit.

"For saying I don't belong to you, sir." I would reach my breaking point soon, whether I wanted to or not. There was only so much control I could have over my body. "I won't ever say that again, ever, I promise."

His movements started to slow—but never stopped—as he leaned down and chuckled softly in my ear. "Who do you belong to, *lisichka*?" The arrogant but victorious smirk on his face was clear as day when I turned my head to look at him with hooded eyes.

"You, sir, I belong to you. Only you." The possessive and dominating look in his eyes made me shiver and shrink beneath him as I kept his gaze.

A wave of relief and utter pleasure crashed into my body when his eyes softened right before he kissed me deeply. "You better not ever forget that. You are mine, for now and ever. Mine." He growled possessively, taking my bottom lip captive between his teeth as he groaned deeply. "Come. Now. Scream for the whole world to hear who you belong to."

Fuck it.

Fuck it if his brothers heard me. I could care less right now, as long as I could come—that's all I cared about this instant. Consequences be damned.

"Kolyenka!" It felt like the pleasure shattered every inch of my body as my orgasm ached at my muscles. "Kolyenka! Fuck..! Kolyenka! Kolyenka!" His name wouldn't stop rolling off my tongue and spilling out of my lips like a mantra as I lost my sanity to the immense lust and pleasure.

I could feel him reach his release too, right before my mind went blank from the pleasure. The feeling of his warmth spilling into me from his throbbing cock was the last thing I remembered. "Fuck. Angel." His voice sounded so distant to where I had to question whether or not I hallucinated it. "Mine. You are all mine. You belong to me, and only me."

"Yours... Only yours..." I sputtered pathetically through my ragged breaths.

Everything became a blur after that. My mind barely registered him settling down next to me and pulling me into his strong arms. His soothing words flew right over my head by a fucking mile because of how out of it I was. The only reason why I jolted back to my senses fully was because of the cold feeling of water trickling into my mouth and down my throat as I swallowed instinctively.

Laying there in his arms, I let my senses come back to me fully. Nikolai's slow circles on my shoulder slowly came to a stop as he drifted to sleep, leaving me to my lonesome thoughts before slumber caught up with me.

It all felt like a dream I would wake up from. I felt as if I would wake up alone in my apartment with my sheets around me instead of being in Nikolai's arms. That if I went out of my room then I would see Hanna making us some coffee or that she needed to be patched up after an assignment, not to a kitchen out of a magazine with my husband holding my caffeine hostage until I ate breakfast like a responsible adult.

People like me didn't deserve fairytale lives. The happy, poor on their luck girl with a heart of gold deserved the prince charming, not the twisted triad's daughter who loved to torture people more than she cared to admit.

Chapter 33

Angel

WELL, THE NEXT MORNING was definitely a little awkward, no thanks to Lev. "Well, I can see why Kolya had a gag in his drawer. You scream like a banshee." God I wanted to punch his snickering smirk off his damn face. Sadly, I had to settle for throwing my bagel at him—which he dodged.

"I don't even want to know how or why you know our older brother has a gag in his drawer." Stepan sighed with a shake of his head as he sipped at his coffee.

"Wait, how do you know he has a gag in his drawer?" Maybe a family breakfast wasn't a good idea. Arseny fed into Lev too much, and since it was against me, I didn't like it.

"Remember when we caught those two rats? Well, we—"

Before Lev could finish, Nikolai interrupted him. "Do I need to bring up junior prom night?" That seemed to have shut Lev up real quick. Nikolai didn't even need to shoot his brother one of those warning looks or even glance in his direction to press the severity of his words.

"What happened junior prom night?" Arseny was genuinely curious, and so was I.

"Nothing. Nothing happened. Forget anything said for the past ten minutes. Breakfast is good by the way, delicious. Tell Anna that her cooking is amazing as always." It amused me to see Lev deflect the topic. I was definitely going to have to try and pry this out of Nikolai later.

Seeing Nikolai with his brothers was always a refreshing sight. Moments like these where roles didn't matter—where they could all be themselves. They were just five big ol' idiots. There was no business talk, no bratva talk, just a grand time.

Times like these made me forget that the five of them were bratva brutes. One look at them in these picturesque moments and no one would think they're violent criminals with their hands drenched in blood.

Although, that's the funny thing about images I guess. A quick glance at me and no one would ever think this run of the mill ED nurse was the sadistic daughter of a triad head. If word ever got out about the things I've done, no one would believe me to be the perpetrator.

Oh, a body was found with forty-six stab wounds? Obviously it was done by a sick and twisted individual, not good ol' Angel—no, never. This sweet nurse with not a blemish on her record could never commit such a heinous act.

Not that I would ever get caught—because most of the law was in our pocket—but having a seemingly innocent image was a good cover to have myself be overlooked initially.

Remaining the silent spectator, I quietly ate my breakfast while continuing to watch the brothers banter with each other and have a good time. I couldn't help myself but wonder if this was how a family was supposed to be. Happy, content, united. Obviously my family was all kinds of fucked up. Greg being the only good sibling I had, but we weren't as close compared to Nikolai and his brothers.

I wonder if our children would get along like this.

The image of seeing our children playing in the backyard, enjoying a game or a tv show in the family room, and being all together for meal time at the dining table brought a big smile to my face. Hopefully we'd have that one day once we deem business to be smooth sailing.

"What are you smiling about over there? You look like you took some happy pills." Arseny joked with a chuckle, snapping me out of my little day dream.

Looking up, I could see that the table went quiet as all five of them had their beady little blue eyes trained on me. "Hm? Nothing, just remembering something good." I lied with a smile. No way in hell would tell them I just imagined our house filled with little mini mes and Nikolais. I'd get teased to no end for a good month.

Thankfully, Nikolai prevented any further prodding from his brothers. But I knew it was far from over with the look he gave me. Nikolai would bring this back up later tonight, and there was no escaping it. "Do you have any plans today, *lisichka*?"

"Besides my appointment, no. Why? We didn't have anything planned today, right?" I was usually pretty good about remembering any dates, outings, and events. But given how much of a ditz I've been the past two-ish weeks, I wouldn't be surprised if something didn't get filed away properly in my brain.

"No." His head lightly shook with his chuckle, "We didn't. Just wondering for later possibly. Don't worry about it." It was his typical smile that always made my heart flutter, but there was something different about it this time—and I wasn't sure how I felt about it. Usually the little uptick to his smile meant he would be doing some shady business, the ones where he came home in ruined clothes or with blood on his hands—or both.

A part of me wished he'd let me know what his plans were, so I won't get a bad surprise when he'd come home. Granted he hasn't come home in terrible shape; the worst I've seen were minor knife cuts and grazes from bullets.

There was no stopping him though. He had his family business to run, and I wouldn't try to convince him otherwise. This wasn't one of those 'oh I can change him' relationships and shit. Honestly though, when have those ever worked out?

Besides, I didn't want to change anything about Nikolai, even if I were an innocent party in the marriage. Having my own protective bratva boss was damn awesome. Someone wronged me? They'd be dealt with. I want someone gone? Done. Sure, not everyone wants a killer as their husband, but I honestly didn't mind.

Then again, I was pretty fucked up. So, I don't think anyone should ever follow my life.

Everyone wants the hero, but the hero would never make the sacrifices needed. I only realized it once I grew up. The hero is nice, but I don't want nice. I want the fucked up villain who would fuck shit up for me if I asked them to. I want the man who wouldn't be afraid to get his hands filthy to keep mine clean.

If I asked Nikolai to shoot someone, he'd say who and pull the trigger with no hesitation. If I asked for a victim, then he'd procure one. That's what I liked about our relationship. Nikolai didn't care about my twisted tendencies—hell he indulges them. He doesn't try to stop me if I do decide to shoot someone in the knees or if I decide to go on a raid and burn down a building. Hell, he'd provide me with the ammunition and means.

I really adored this husband of mine. "Well, stay safe out there. Just remember to come home to me alive." It's the least I could ask of him. I could deal with minor injuries—hell I'd take missing limbs—as long as he was alive.

"Don't worry, we'll bring him back alive and in one piece." Stepan assured me with a confident smile. "Ain't ready to be a dad yet, so he's gotta give me some nieces and nephews to spoil." His soft laugh stirred the others into one too as he patted his older brother on the shoulder.

"Go get laid yourself." Nikolai sneered, shoving his brother back a little before getting up from his seat. Looking at me with a positive smile, he leaned over and placed a kiss to the top of my head, "I'll be back to you, promise." With that, he left along with his brothers, leaving me alone with Benjamin who stood at the entryway of the dining room.

I had planned on staying home until my appointment time came closer, but I decided against lazing around when I thought about my father. It had been a while since I've gotten to spend quality time with him. My life's gotten a little too hectic lately to spend much time with my father after work or outside of it.

When I arrived at my father's private room in the hospital, I was a little surprised to find Greg there. He knew about what Nikolai discovered along with the plan to wean our father off the drugs, and he had to be fine with it. Not like Greg had much of a say in our father's medical care. While I valued his opinion because he saw things from a nonmedical person's perspective, I still had the final say.

Even after the medical proxy papers were—illegally—fixed, I couldn't put Greg on it because it would put him directly in Lady Qing's path. Greg kept under the radar for a reason, so if his name suddenly appeared on papers connected to our father then Lady Qing would dig into him and tear his life apart.

"Still nothing?" Greg asked with a heavy sigh as he stood there by our father's bedside with his hands in his pockets.

"It's not an instantaneous thing, or fast thing... Or a guaranteed thing either..." I held out too much hope to accept the fact our father would never wake up again.

"You gotta stop beating yourself up about this. I can see how it's eating you up still." Greg sighed heavily with concern, his eyes furrowing together with his eyebrows.

"I should have just stuck to my initial gut feeling about her being more involved in *ba's* condition and been more persistent." I should've been stubborn like a bull and plowed head first into the walls that popped up when Greg and I dug into Lady Qing for evidence of foul play against my father. Everything thread we grasped led back to nothing concrete or nothing at all. Maybe if I had been more persistent then I could've found something and reversed things for our father sooner.

"Ange, we did what we could, and nothing panned out. Even the best cops get cold cases." Greg's attempts to ease my inner turmoil fell onto deaf ears.

Sighing softly, he shook his head and stared off for a few seconds before speaking up again, "What are you going to do if he-"

"He's going to wake up." I wasn't even going to let him finish that question. I knew I should be seeing all the possibilities, be reasonable and rational. It's what I told all my patients whenever it came down to them needing to make difficult decisions. Yet, I couldn't find it in myself to think objectively when it came to our father.

"Angel... I know this is hard for you, but you need to step back and think like a nurse right now. I don't want you getting hurt more than needed if the worst comes true. You've already been through enough shit." Greg said with a sigh, throwing his arm around my shoulder and pulling me against him in a brief side hug.

"I'll think like a nurse when I'm on the clock." I snarked with a soft scowl, not wanting to admit my older brother was right, like always.

Sighing in defeat, Greg shook his head softly at me before giving my shoulder a squeeze. "I'm heading out of town for a day or so for a case. So, I was just popping by to see him for a bit before leaving." There was some hesitation to his voice as he looked at our father with sad eyes.

Greg probably hoped for the same thing I did. Hope that we would come in one day and our father would be awake and alert in his bed, not comatose.

Any day now though.

"Any news on our rogue men?" Maybe a change of subject will help lighten my mood. Well, hopefully it would.

"One is dead, one is still in the wind, and the other is tied up and being ripped into as we speak." Greg reported to me flatly as he shoved his hands into the pockets of his pants. "The rest are good though, we made sure of it. The three that swapped sides only did so out of greed from the looks of it."

I knew having moles and leaks were a danger when working with people. I just didn't think I would have to deal with them this soon. Well, at least the three who went rogue didn't do it because I was a shitty leader. Granted it still sucked to have it happen, but my stepmother was currently richer than me by far.

"Is the one we have captured spilling anything useful?" I started to grow tired of being a step or two behind my stepmother. Hopefully with my leaks out of the picture, I would get that footing I needed.

"Hanna hasn't reported anything to me yet, but we'll keep you posted, like always. Just, don't think about it too much right now, you have a lot going on today." Greg assured me with a soft smile, nudging my shoulder softly with his.

Sighing, I ran a hand through my long locks and looked at my father with sad and regretful eyes for a moment before looking out the window.

Greg's question broke the brief silence and prevented me from going down a dark rabbit hole. "Where's Nikolai? I thought he'd be with you."

"I actually have no fucking clue." I grumbled in response. I was feeling pissy and icky with everything after talking with Greg.

For the first time in our marriage, I really had no idea about his plans or location. And with this foul mood, I didn't like that fact one bit.

My mood soured more when *she* showed up out of nowhere with an unsavory accomplice. "What are you doing here?" Might have been a stupid question, but I saw no reason for her visit with Ivan in tow.

"Your husband has yet to teach you manners, I see." My stepmother snarked back as she came to a stop a little ways from me with her arms crossed. "Maybe he's as incompetent as everyone says if he can't control a simple girl like you."

Luckily for her, I wasn't one to make a public scene. Otherwise, I would have slapped her across the face for insulting Nikolai. "Yet he's more successful and powerful than you, so I guess that makes you very incapable of handling anything and helpless. Keep talking bad about my husband and you'll find your tongue at the bottom of the ocean."

I'll settle for being a mouthy bitch instead. "You still think you've won with carting me off to the bratva? Well, news flash, not everyone is an insignificant little piece of shit floating around in the sewer like you. Some people actually know how to be decent with others and play well with them."

Perhaps she thought arranging me to Nikolai would be the end of me given his past reputation, but she was dead wrong. I wasn't six-feet underground or locked away in some dreadful basement. I flourished with Nikolai, because of Nikolai.

"Enjoy it while it lasts. Your kingdom was doomed before you knew it." The cocky smirk on Lady Qing's face was too much for my comfort.

It could have been a ploy to get under my skin, but it looked and felt too real. Victory was in her grasp, and she rubbed it in my face.

Had she won? No, she couldn't have. Was I clueless about something huge under way? Did she have something planned or done already? What did she mean with her words?

I can't let her win. I refuse to let her win.

Chapter 34

Nikolai

T ENSE SILENCE FILLED THE van as my brothers and I sat there observing an apartment complex that came apart from the seams. One quick look and no one would think the place was habitable because it looked so abandoned. I was skeptical when the location was given to me, but seeing flickers of light and bodily movements confirmed there were bodies occupying the crumbling place.

"Pretty stupid to stick around after committing a crime, but also pretty stupid that he hasn't been located until now. Bastard really makes hiding in plain sight a real thing." Lev scowled as he checked his magazine for the umpteenth time.

He started to get a little antsy along with the rest of us. I couldn't blame him. If I was reckless then I would have charged into the damn complex guns blazing. But I was better than that. Charging in blindly would be suicide.

"Don't know how the hell he runs a successful crack den out of this dump. But damn, oh how the mighty have fallen. Successful chemist to a low life crack maker and dealer. Honestly, if he wasn't a piece of shit then I'd say we could try to recruit him. Too bad his sins are too unforgivable." Arseny's sarcasm made me snort softly as I reached for my shoulder holster. My fingers itched with anticipation as I brushed them against the smooth, cold metal of my gun.

Taking in a deep breath, I let my anger ebb as I pulled my gun out. "Remember, we take the bastard alive." A reminder to myself more than for my brothers. No matter how much I wanted to put a bullet through the eyes of the bastard who harmed my wife, his fate rested in Angel's hands.

"Unfortunately." Lev grumbled with a roll of his eyes. "We gonna bust his door down now?"

"Everyone know their positions?" Confirmation never hurt, and there was no such thing as overly cautious when it came to my brothers.

Once I got a verbal confirmation from everyone, the five of us filed out of the van once the patrolmen rounded out of sight. Pressed against the side of the building next to the door, I gestured at Arseny and Stepan to split and take care of the guards around the perimeter. Then, when they darted off, I looked at Lev with a nod and glanced at the door.

Lev got into position to kick down the door, waiting for my signal to act. I waited until I felt the familiar squeeze on my shoulder from Alexei—letting me know he was ready—before holding up three fingers and counting down.

The moment my fingers sank down into my fist, a loud thud and bang disrupted whatever operation went on in the lobby of the complex. The stunned silence didn't last a millisecond before gunfire started to go off from both sides, with us being the instigators. The first shot came from me the moment Lev breached the door, and my bullet met the head of some poor sap who dared to raise his gun at me.

All hell broke loose after the first shot.

People started screaming and scattering as we exchanged fire with, who I assumed to be, the guards.

One quick look and it was clear this base level of the complex was the production area with all the little knick knacks they had set up in the area. The cooks wasted no time scrambling out of the line of fire, cowering behind crates and various equipment.

Shot after shot our guns went off, every bullet from our side hitting its mark dead on. Can't say the same for the other side; they were lousy shots. Good for us that their aim was worse than a child's. Also, we weren't worried much because we had bulletproof vests on. So, unless they got really lucky or went for a headshot, we weren't going to die in this amateur gun fight. We'd live with a few scrapes and grazes.

"Runner!" Alexei shouted, pointing his head at the back exit that opened to let in a stream of light from the outside.

"Don't shoot! That's our target! I got him! You two clear and secure the building!" A foot chase would do well to run the buzzing adrenaline pumping through my body.

Tucking my gun away in its holster, I took off after my target. He had a head start, but it didn't matter since I was faster. I gained on his scraggly ass with a few large strides, his body tumbling to the ground when I tackled him with a grunt. At least the idiot made it easy by running in a straight line through the empty alleyway.

"Hey, hey, hey, I'll give you the money I owe, I got it, I got it." One look at his glazed eyes and I could tell he wasn't fully here. "Come on just—wait, you're not Richard."

It'd be so easy to kill him right now. I could pull my gun out again and put a bullet between his eyes. Or I could kill him with my bare hands, strangle the life out of him, or beat him to death and get bloody. I had enough anger and adrenaline to beat him to hell. I wanted to inflict a fraction of Angel's suffering onto him.

Scowling, I kept my murderous rage at bay. I had to remind myself he wasn't mine to kill. Angel would be his judge, jury, and executioner if she so wished. "You're going to wish I was." I grumbled as I hauled him to his feet and dragged him back to the abandoned apartment complex begrudgingly.

Dragging him behind me made me wonder how I didn't crush him under me with my tackle. The lanky asshole was barely half my size.

It also made me wonder what the heck Angel was thinking with this... Scum bag. The struggling twig in my grip didn't deserve to be classified as a man.

"If ya ain't Richard then who the fuck are you? The fuck you want? Wait, do I owe you some supply? Listen, if you're after something I owe, I got it, I swear." Good, he was too high to have an idea as to who I was and what was in store for him.

"Want me to put a bullet in his mouth?" Lev asked with a cock of his gun. His annoyance written clearly on his face as all of us were subjected to a desperate criminal's musings.

Fortunately, Alexei came prepared. "Hey! What are you doing!?" The man started to struggle in my grip when Alexei approached him with the needle. "What is—ow! That hurt! The fuck did you... Stick me..." The body went limp in my grasp before we made it fully to the van.

"Are we going to need the cleanup crew?" Alexei asked, looking at the bodies that were scattered in the street and building.

Shaking my head, I don't bother sparing a second glance at the area. "No. No one is going to care about these low lives, especially in this area. And if anyone dares to retaliate, then we'll show them how bad of a decision it is to fuck with us." This area of town was worse than the slums. The chances of any crime happening here escalating to something serious was basically none.

Looking at Lev, I asked, "The building cleared?" I wasn't worried about witnesses either in this area of town. Most of them are too cracked out of their mind to be reliable. Besides, even if they were somehow credible, they wouldn't get far with making a case against us. Not with the cops in our pockets.

"Yeah, not much to clear. Got us some pocket change. Stepan and Arseny are setting the charges right now. And before you ask, yes every single living being is cleared for the next half mile basically." Lev reported to me as I tied the passed out scumbag with some duct tape and tossed him into the back of the van.

"I'll drop you guys off and let you get our *guest* settled at one of the warehouses while I head back to the house. Just text me which warehouse when you guys decide on one. Don't rough him up too much, we all know who gets first shot." Again, if it were up to me then the idiot in the back wouldn't be alive still.

The three of us waited by the van for Stepan and Arseny to finish setting the explosives before driving a small distance and setting them off, watching the flames engulf the collapsing building for a good minute before driving off.

"So, do you think she's going to take this well? I mean, it's not like she asked you for it, nor did you run the idea by her." Stepan questioned when we were on the road.

Sighing softly, I ran a hand down my face. "Hopefully she takes it well..." Well, it could only go uphill or downhill once I told her what I did.

"Not everyone needs death therapy Kolya. I mean, have you thought about whether she would want this or not? I mean, this could go well like you think, or it could dig at wounds she'd already healed from. Not everyone needs to kill their problems, *bratok*." Stepan had a good point, and in hindsight, this seemed like a good idea.

But now that I have the bastard in the trunk. Well, what if she didn't appreciate this gesture? Sure, my wife was a twisted little thing in her own right, but what if this was too much? She'd never expressed any opinions on what she'd do if she encountered her past.

In my eagerness, I didn't think far to think about how she'd even react to seeing the demon that's been haunting her. The answer at the time seemed simple enough to me: kill the fucker. But that was me. That's what I would do. But I didn't go far enough to wonder where Angel's mind would go.

"Did you think that maybe she doesn't need any of this for closure? Maybe she's moved past it?" Okay, now I wanted to punch Stepan in the face for bringing up the obvious questions I should have asked myself before coming up with this manhunt and kidnapping. "Kolya, I would just brace yourself."

"Oh come on, I'd be fucking delighted if my partner brought me the monster from my nightmares to kill." As nice as it was to have Lev in my corner, I don't think it was a good thing in this instance.

"I'm sorry, I missed the part where we were back in the ice age and are cavemen." Arseny's sarcastic remark stirred a small chuckle from most of us. "Seriously, for the head honcho, your brain goes out the window when it comes to Angel. You can't just bring her a prized kill like some cat bringing a dead bird to its owner."

Scoffing with a roll of my eyes, I responded with a bit of snark, "Okay, that is a horrible analogy." But was it any different than what I was doing? I was essentially presenting a potential kill for her.

"Horrible but accurate. Although, I guess it's the thought that counts, right? Or would that not apply in this situation?" Alexei's tone turned awkward towards the end as he sounded like he regretted what he said.

"I don't think any of us are allowed to have wives with how stupid we are." Stepan groans with a shake of his head. "You want to make your lady happy? How about a nice necklace or diamond ring? Nah that's not enough, here's your ex who I just kidnapped." The sarcasm was heavy and hard to ignore. "God we're too fucked up for relationships."

"Oh like you're one to talk Stepan, you're seeing someone on a regular basis." Arseny remarked with a smirk that I could see from a quick glance in the rearview mirror.

"Doesn't mean we're an item." Stepan argued weakly, his voice wavering.

"So if she were to, oh I don't know, shack up with another man, or God forbid Lev, then you wouldn't mind one bit?" Arseny was being too much of an ass for his own good right now.

"Don't make me pull this van to the side of the road." I threatened, silencing everyone.

Okay, so maybe our ideas of displaying our affection is a little skewed, but that's what makes us unique... Right? I might also be refusing to admit we're *that* fucked up.

Chapter 35

Angel

OH MY FUCKING GOD. Nikolai is going to kill me.

"Benjamin! Put the fucking phone down! You are not telling Nikolai about this!"

The scene of me jumping onto Benjamin's back and climbing him like a monkey up a tree to snatch his phone out of his hand would probably be a funny scene to those who didn't know the severity of it. Also, they'd probably think we were two crazy people arguing in front of the hospital.

"If I don't tell Nikolai then it's going to be my balls on a silver platter!" Benjamin hissed while trying to throw me off his back.

Putting on my best smile of confidence, I chuckled nervously, "Don't worry, just let me take care of it. Both our asses will be fine. I'm his wife. You're one of his best men and friend. He's not going to kill us..."

I hope. I hope he won't kill us.

"I might be one of his best friends, but that is not going to be a valid enough reason for me not to report this shit." He continued to argue with me, finally able to get ahold of me and throw me off to hold me in front of him at arm's length.

Once his phone was in reach, I swiped it. "Ah hah!" With a victorious grin, I held my prize—Benjamin's phone—in my hand.

"Give me back my phone." He demanded gruffly with hardened eyes.

"No." There was no way he would make a grab for it considering how I shoved it deep into my bra, giving me a comical lump that stood out against my small chest. "I'll take care of it, don't worry." I tried my best to give him a reassuring smile, but I probably looked like an awkward fish.

"The last time you told me not to worry I ended up tied in the back of my trunk. Nikolai still hasn't let me live that down. So, give me my phone back so I can report back to him." He demanded, holding out a hand to me with a hard but pleading look.

"Don't worry, he won't notice anything, don't worry. I got this." I hope. I hope I got this. In all reality, I probably don't. I'm fucking screwed six ways to Sunday, and not the good kind.

Ben's eyes darted around to scan the area before speaking in a low voice. "Of course he's going to fucking notice his favorite car missing! What'd you mean he won't notice!? It's a fucking car not an apple from the fruit bowl!" I mean, Benjamin had a good point.

Chuckling nervously, I scratched the back of my head as I racked my brain for ideas. "I just have to replace the car." I said with a dismissive wave of my hand. "And I'll just keep 'taking the car' and not give him a chance to drive it until I get a replacement that's an exact replica." Boom. Problem solved.

Sighing, Benjamin shook his head and rubbed his temples with his thumb and forefinger. "As good of an idea as that sounds. That's fucking impossible. This isn't some Toyota Camry that we can swing at one of twenty-thousand dealerships to get. You can't keep taking the damn car for god knows how long, he's gonna drive it eventually when you're not using it. There's no way you're gonna be able to get another Aston Martin here in the next three hours unless you have a teleportation machine that we don't know about or a magic genie with wishes." Benjamin groaned exasperatedly.

Okay, problem not solved. I couldn't argue with him because his points were valid and true. There was no way I'd be able to get an Aston Martin replacement so soon—not when there wasn't one for a gazillion of miles. A quick Google search also shot the idea down because the nearest Aston Martin was five states over and not even the right model.

"Okay, so just back to plan A. I'll handle it." Somehow. "Let's just get back home, and I'll figure something out." For my sake and Benjamin's sake, I needed to figure something out. Well, I'd probably be safe at the end of the day, but I didn't want Benjamin's ass on the chopping block because I prevented him from doing his job. Nikolai wouldn't care much about my interference, just that Benjamin didn't do his job.

"I am telling Nikolai the moment he sets foot through that door." Unfortunately, Benjamin seemed determined with his intended course of action.

I would have to take care of Benjamin somehow once we got home from the hospital. "Not if I knock you out and throw you in the shed." I muttered under my breath.

"What?" Benjamin raised an eyebrow at me.

Smiling innocently at him, I waved my hand dismissively at him, "Nothing, just thinking out loud."

Quickly, I pulled my phone out and called Bao to come take whatever was left of the wreckage away to analyze it all to see if there were any leads to a possible culprit. Benjamin wasn't happy about it, but there was nothing he could do without his means of communication stuffed in my bra.

Once Bao and his little crew came to clean up the mess, Benjamin and I drove home in silence in his car. But all hopes of Benjamin keeping his trap shut went out the door the moment we entered the house.

"Quit waiting at the door like some eager dog!" I hissed under my breath. It was laughable at how I tried to drag Benjamin away by his arm when he situated himself at the front door like some dog awaiting its master's return. I probably looked like some small child trying to drag their parent away right now given the size difference between us.

"No. I'm getting ahead of this before I get too deep into shit." Benjamin deadpanned, not bothering with me one bit as if I was nothing more than an annoying fly unworthy of attention.

"Benjamin pleeeeeease, I'll explain it to him, I promiiiiiise. I'll even let him know I took your phone and prevented you from telling him. Just please let me do it pleeeeeease!" I desperately begged at this point, almost to where I would be willing to get down on my knees for extra added effect. It was kind of pathetic, but I didn't care right now.

"*Lisichka*?"

Without an ounce of hesitation, I took a cheap blow to Benjamin, sending him to the ground in pain with a swift punch to his family jewels. "Sorry!" I apologized with a half genuine smile before facing Nikolai with a sheepish grin. "*Anh*, honey, baby, you're back."

Great, smooth one Angel, real smooth. Now he's definitely going to know something is up.

His face immediately flattened at my words. "What did you do?" He sighed heavily, running a hand down his face, probably wondering what kind of damage control he had to do. "And why did you cockshot Benjamin?"

"Nothing, nothing, just glad you're back." Although, the look he gave me told me he wasn't buying my bullshit. "Uh so, quick question: how much did you love your Aston Martin? Like love love to where if even a scratch gets on it you'll be heartbroken? Or like yeah I love it and it's my favorite but eh?"

Letting out a long sigh, he settled a hand on his hips. "Am I going to need a fucking drink?" He asked with another heavy sigh as he rubbed his temples with his other hand.

"Uhh... Noooo..? Maybe?" I drew out my answer while rolling back and forth on the balls of my feet.

"Nikolai, she—omphf! Sonofabitch!" Benjamin groaned in pain when I cut him off with another kick to his crotch.

"If I go into the garage, will the car be there?" Nikolai looked as if he was ready to answer that question himself with how he turned his body towards the hallway. But the silence from Benjamin and me also gave him the answer.

"*Lisichka*, I am only going to give you one chance to tell me what happened. Don't beat around the bush." I knew by the tone of his voice that a second chance meant my ass getting belted later tonight with no mercy.

Nervously, I chuckled, fiddling with my fingers as I struggled with the words. "Umm... It's uhhh... So uhh funny story, it kinda... Blew up... Like ka-boom blew up..." Hopefully Nikolai wasn't some die-hard for his cars.

"What do you mean blew up? Honey, a seven-hundred-thousand dollar car doesn't just blow up." He started to look like he regretted not getting a drink, and he probably should regret that decision given the news.

"Like I said, funny story." The glaring look from Nikolai cut my nervous chuckle short, "I was just getting out of my doctor's appointment, and then boom."

It really was that simple. Benjamin and I left the house a little while after Nikolai and his brothers left, got some lunch, visited my father, then went to my doctor's appointment. Bao hasn't gotten the details back to me yet, but I know it was some kind of bomb, because the car literally blew up just as I left the hospital with Benjamin flanking me. It was a huge pain in the ass to make sure the authorities weren't called in and the whole thing was covered up from the media.

"Are you okay? You weren't close to the blast were you?" The concern replaced his disbelief as he grabbed me with both hands and gave me a quick once over.

"I'm fine. Benjamin and I were a good distance from the blast, not even a speck of dust on us." Luckily both of us escaped unscathed by some grace of God or whatever was out there.

"Why didn't I hear about this until now? Where's the car now? Is anyone looking into this?" His eyes bounced between Benjamin—who was still on the floor—and me.

Chuckling sheepishly, I gave him a cheeky, lopsided smile. "Because I didn't want to freak you out, so I didn't let Benjamin call you by taking his phone... But uhh I called Bao and my men, they're going to pick it apart and see exactly what kind of bomb it was and what not. We did damage control already so don't worry. Just, sorry about the car..." Well, at least he didn't seem too hung up about the car, thankfully.

Sighing as if he was relieved, he ran a hand through his tousled hair. "*Lisichka*, I don't give a damn about the car, I can just get a new one. I can't get a new wife or friend though. Just, I'd rather hear from one of you if something happened and not from the hospital or the damn news or some cops."

"Benjamin's not going to be in trouble? I mean, I took his phone and refused to let him contact you or tell you." Job or not, I butted in when I probably wasn't supposed to.

"I think the two hits he took from you is enough punishment, just quit interfering with his job *lisichka*, please." Nikolai sighed tiredly.

Letting out a heavy breath, he hugged me tightly, stroking my hair and kissing the top of my head. "When will we hear back from Bao?" He asked in a tired voice.

"Soon, he and his sister are picking it apart as we speak. But enough about what happened with me. You're okay right?" He looked fairly okay, just some scrapes by the looks of it, nothing major that required immediate attention.

Chuckling softly, he pulled away a little to kiss my forehead. "Yes, it's going to take a lot more than some amateur gunmen to take me down." But one stray bullet or a lucky shot was all it could take to kill Nikolai, amateur or not. "Let me get cleaned up real quick, then I have something to show you."

Rolling my eyes, I lightly smacked his hard chest. "Well now I feel like shit for getting your car blown up if you're giving me something." Did I forget something? Definitely wasn't an anniversary, not a holiday either. So, why the gift?

"Don't worry, this is... A belated marriage present." As if that would make me feel any better because not like I gave or got him anything. But now I would have to think of something. Maybe I'll replace his car. Seven-hundred thousand was a shit ton of money, but I had the funds for it. Or at the very least I had the means—illegally—to obtain those six figures.

"But your doctor's appointment went well? Nothing wrong? Did they figure out why you've been so fatigued lately?" He looked down at me with worried eyes while waiting for my response.

Giving him the best—fake—reassuring smile possible, I looked up at him, "Just the stress. Also, just because I got put on this new birth control, so it's my body is trying to adjust to it."

I couldn't tell him the truth.

Not yet. Not when I hadn't processed it fully myself.

Chapter 36

Angel

"Is this all really necessary?" I asked for the thousandth time, resisting the urge to peel the blindfold to get a forbidden peak. "Are you showing me your kill chamber or something?" I joked with a chuckle after hearing the faint echoes of his footsteps against metal.

His chest rumbled with his chuckle, making my ears ache with pleasure upon hearing it. "You've already seen my kill chamber. Quit asking, I'm not going to tell you anything, so be patient."

I had no idea what this surprise could possibly be. All I knew was we drove a bit of a distance, definitely out of the city because I could hear the bustling noise die down as we drove. But that's all I could surmise. I couldn't take any other guesses besides us being somewhere with a lot of metal because his footfalls sounded like they were against metal grates. So, maybe a warehouse? But the air felt too stuffy to be a warehouse.

I couldn't feel around for a better idea either because Nikolai refused to let me explore, keeping me tight in his arms as he carried me off to—hopefully not—my doom. I doubt he'd wait all this time to get rid of me, so I was hopeful he wasn't bringing me to my death.

The sound of locks clicking and a heavy door opening followed Nikolai's voice when he said something in Russian. I could feel the air slamming against me when the door opened, followed by familiar voices.

"Hundred bucks Nikolai gets slapped." Lev—I think—snickered before a slapping sound was heard.

"You're on." I think it was Arseny, or Alexei, but I would be more than willing to bet it was Arseny given that they accepted the bet. But also, Arseny's voice was more jovial compared to his twin's more serious tone.

"Why do they think I'm going to slap you?" Should I be worried about this surprise now? Was this some sick joke?

"Well... I went into this thing with good intentions, but I might have been an asshole and didn't think about things from your perspective in my excitement." Nikolai sounded uncomfortable as he set me down on my feet.

"Nikolai, what did you do?" Did he kill someone who mattered to me? No, he would have told me if he decided to.

Is he selling me out?

Slowly, the pressure around my eyes lessened when the blindfold was removed to reveal Nikolai's nervous smile. Taking in a deep breath, he leaned in and kissed my forehead softly. "I'll take whatever you throw at me later, but just know that I'll be right behind you." He whispered against me before turning me around by my shoulders, keeping his hands there afterwards.

My eyes widened in shock at the sight before me.

Fight, flight, freeze, or fawn. That's our body's natural responses to any perceived threat. And right now, my brain cycled through all four of them as my body tensed up. But I wasn't sure why my body tensed up. Was it to fight? Run? Freeze? Definitely not fawn. My legs were itching to bolt, but my arms wanted to swing. But I couldn't move because my chest felt like a truck sat on it.

Then, the voice of my nightmares spat its poisonous venom at me, "Was wondering where the fuck you went to, you triad trash. See you put yourself to use being a bratva bitch."

His words made something within me snap. The scream of anguish from the trauma hitting me full force didn't even sound like me—it sounded like some feral animal. I don't know exactly how, but I went from one end of the room to being on top of a toppled monster who remained bound to the metal chair. I guess this is what people meant by being blinded by rage because it felt like my body moved on its own, acting upon the pent up anger that exploded in an instant. It was as if my mind was in a red haze.

I wanted to end him so badly—kill him right on the spot. My hands were wrapped tightly around his scraggly neck; my nails dug into his flesh to where I drew blood. I could feel his body struggling to breathe under me as he thrashed helplessly. It would be so easy to keep this vice grip on him until his life left his eyes. It wouldn't be a quick death—suffocation was never quick. Yet, the thought of ending his life like this brought no satisfaction to me.

Just as his eyes started to roll back, I pulled my hands back, watching as he took in deep breaths through his coughing fit.

I don't know what came over me—maybe the flood of emotions—but my body started to shake with laughter as tears streamed down my crazed face.

Maybe I've finally lost it. Whatever shred of sanity I had left—I lost it.

Out of the corner of my eyes, I spot my weapon with a twisted smirk. "Let's play a game darling, you always did love your games." Keeping my crazed eyes locked onto my victim, I got up and went over to the table of weapons. "I'll even indulge you and play your favorite." Instantly, my hand went for the revolver. "I'll even add your little twist to it, like you did me. Only I won't miss. The last hit will have a hundred-percent chance of death."

Tearing my eyes away from the man on the floor, I started to load the revolver. "Six bullets. I could take it easy on you and empty out five of the chambers, but where's the fun in that. Five blanks, one live one." Giving the barrel a quick spin, I snapped it shut in place before going back over and picking the chair back up along with the tied man.

"You're bluffing. You don't kill." His confident answer was shaky with his voice.

Situating myself in front of him, I stood between his open legs that were stuck in that position due to his legs being tied to the legs of the chair. "That was the me before you roofied me, violated me, and plunged a fucking kitchen knife into me six times and left me for dead." I seethed through gritted teeth as I pressed the cold barrel against the underside of his chin. "Oh, and quick tip, not that you'll ever get to use it: make sure your target is actually dead before leaving."

BANG!

The sick giggle that left me when he flinched at the first pull of the trigger surprised me. I truly did sound like a lunatic. "Shame. Oh well, five more to go." I gave out a fake sigh of disappointment as I dragged the gun down his body to his heart. "Your name isn't Harriet. It was just an alias. So, what's your real name? I want to know the real bastard that masqueraded as my pathetic ex."

No matter how hard I had tried with all the resources I had, he always eluded me. But now that I had him under my thumb, err gun, I wanted answers—the truth about everything.

"Why the hell would I give you any satisfaction? You're going to kill me anyways. I know what my odds are." He spat back venomously with a hateful glare.

The sound of something flat hitting and sliding across the floor made my ears twitch. My eyes darted down to my left foot when I felt something nudge it. "Michael Gillow. thirty. Single. PhD in biochemical engineering. A rather bright man who disappeared off the face of the earth three years ago." Nikolai read off the first few lines of the open file that laid at my foot with a picture of Harriet—who apparently was actually Michael.

BANG!

Another blank. Another flinch. Another twisted giggle. "You crazy bitch! Just kill me already!" Michael struggled against his restraints, trying to wiggle away from the gun as I lowered it to his crotch. "You're a psycho!"

Smiling twistedly, I brought the gun up to his temple and tapped it a few times. "Yet you were so keen to stick your tiny dick in this craziness, so what does that say about your mental health? Hm?"

BANG!

"Halfway there, three bullets left Mikey." I chuckled deeply as I let the gun fall back between his legs.

"Your sick cunt wasn't even worth the fuck, but knowing I took away that precious first moment of yours to give you a glimpse of what your men did to my sister was enough to spur me on." He started to lose his edge. Even if he tried to keep a strong front, I could see the subtle tremble of his body as his eyes started to nervously dart around the room.

His words managed to break through my madness. "What?" Now, I was genuinely confused. "What are you talking about?"

"Of course you wouldn't remember her, just another girl amongst a bunch. My sister, Michelle, brunette, short like you." Whatever fear I shot into him with the blanks went away as he glared at me with angry eyes. "She was only fifteen when your heinous men came to the house and took her for your little whorehouses to work off my parents debts." He wasn't lying, not with the kind of resolve in his eyes.

"The Qing Triad doesn't deal in such activities, not for the past thirty years." Now I was pissed. Was I a part of a revenge plan? Did he attack me due to some kind of mistaken identity shit? "And we don't touch children, ever."

"Don't fucking lie you whore! You and your men parade children around for favors all the time, have them meet clients in those run down apartments, the ones above the restaurants." Great, was I going to discover another layer of shit? "Your damn mother was there too. She was the one who snatched Michelle. Said she was going to make great money."

Ah, there it was. Unfortunately.

"I'm gonna kill that bitch." I hissed under my breath before pulling the trigger again, letting out a fourth blank. "My mother is dead. That lady is my stepmother, a demon on earth. Me and my men would never touch anything to do with humans. My father banned everything to do with services that included people except for consensual prostitution, but trafficking and brothels and anything else was banned upon his leadership."

Needing a release for my anger, I pulled the trigger again after aiming at his midsection—unloading another blank. "My witch of a stepmother never got that memo and has been doing that shit behind our backs for a few years. What I say now won't change what happened to your sister, but if I had known back then, then I would have prevented it and offered your sister and family protection. I'm sorry I couldn't have prevented what happened to your sister. But that didn't give you the right to take it out on me. Is that why you went after me? Revenge?"

Only one bullet left, and I aimed right at his heart. "Answer me." I demanded, pressing the barrel into his chest until he squirmed under it.

"Yes. I wanted you to suffer like she did in her final moments. I wanted your family to suffer like mine did—like I did. But you're still fucking alive, you psychotic bitch. You weren't supposed to survive. I stabbed you six times! Just like they did her. I even left the fucking knife in your chest like some dart on a board just like they did her! You're supposed to be dead just like her. Your family was supposed to be mourning over your damn coffin." The boiling rage that rolled off of him was almost suffocating—even from a small distance.

BANG!

The last bullet fired, instilling a heavy silence in the confined area. "Guess we both got our lives fucked up by my damn stepmother." He may have wielded the knife, but she was the one who gave it to him along with the encouragement. "You know the reason why I don't kill, Michael?"

I felt empty as I looked at him with dead eyes. All the adrenaline and rage I had felt moments earlier was all gone—just like that. I should be murderous towards him, give him his dues, get my revenge, redeem myself and whatnot. But I couldn't. Not after hearing his reason behind things. Well, don't get me wrong, I was still resentful towards him, but I wasn't feeling murderous right now.

"Wha? I... How?" Michael looked around all confused before his eyes landed on me and the empty revolver I threw to the ground by his feet.

"You're right. I don't kill. Besides, even if I were to kill you, it wouldn't be with a damn bullet. That would take away my fun." I couldn't help but crack a crazed smile and small laugh as I watched his face twist from terror, confusion, defeat, and back to anger.

"They were all blanks. There was never a live one in there." I wanted to watch him suffer with each pull of the trigger. I wanted to see the fear and terror form in his eyes as the bullets counted down, knowing the next could be his maker.

"But, answer me: do you know why I don't kill?" I repeated my question as I leaned down, placing my arms on top of his that were tied to the armrests. "Answer me darling."

"You don't like death, you never did, that's why you always try to save everyone who came through those emergency room doors." It wasn't a lie. I did tell him that when we were dating after a particularly rough shift. But that wasn't the real reason behind why I never killed if I could help it.

Taking a deep breath, I dug my nails into his forearms until I drew blood. "True, but the real reason why I don't kill is because I see death as a mercy. There is no suffering with death. I don't give a shit what the devil dishes out when those fuckers go down to hell, but I believe that they should suffer in the land of the living as well. Killing ends things too quickly. Here one second, then gone the next. There is no dues for their crimes."

Again, call me a twisted bitch, I'd already accepted it a long time ago. But that was my stance on killing. It wasn't that I viewed it as a heinous act; I just hated how the perpetrator would never suffer.

"God you're a twisted bitch. How the hell are you a nurse if you're such a psychopath!? You're not any better than those monsters out there." His head flew at me, making me pull away to avoid the headbutt.

"Tsk, tsk, tsk. That's just rude. If I were a psychopath or a monster like the sick men under my stepmother's employment then you'd be half way dead by now. Fortunately for you, I have this thing called empathy and sympathy. I am not going to kill you." He didn't deserve the torture I had in mind, not after knowing his reason behind attacking me.

I planned on making him suffer though. I was vengeful enough to inflict some pain on him.

With a deep breath, I walked back over to the table and picked up the KA-BAR knife, twirling it in my hand as I walked back over to him. Leaning down, I cut the ropes that bound his ankles to the chair before cutting the ones on his wrist.

Rubbing his red wrists, he looked up at me with a confused expression. "What? You're just going to let me go?" He was wary, as he should be.

Giving him a saccharine smile, I reached down and took his hand, holding it softly and stroking the back of it briefly before gripping it and pulling him downward onto the floor with a grunt. Quickly, I climbed atop of him, pressing my knee into his back and leaning my full weight onto him to keep him pinned under me.

The anger that had subsided came back full force, only this time it wasn't explosive like earlier. "Yes, and no. Though I understand your revenge, it was all wrong. Then your stupid taunts. You couldn't fucking leave me alone, just had to make me relive that shit every month with your stupid little notes about being around the damn corner. My body and mind is scarred because of you. My lungs never fully recovered from all the scar tissue, so I can't ever breathe at full capacity ever again. I couldn't let anyone touch my back without flipping out and getting some kind of flashback for the longest time. I couldn't even let my own fucking husband touch me because of you."

Ripping the back of his shirt up, I brought the knife down between his ribs after aiming very carefully. "An eye for a fucking eye." After pulling the knife out, I stabbed him five more times in a calculated manner to how he stabbed me. On the last hit, I left the knife embedded in him.

Breathing heavily, I got off of him, went over to the door, and opened it. "Go on, you can leave now." I said with a twisted smile and nod of my head towards the hallway.

"Wait, what—" Lev was cut off by Alexei's hand on his shoulder.

No doubt Alexei knew. I didn't hit any major arteries or his heart, but six stabs to his lungs at such a depth was a death sentence in itself unless he got medical attention right away.

The chances of him surviving long were slim, but not nil. If someone were to take pity and give him medical attention or if he somehow got lucky and survived enough to get to a hospital then he'd live. If he succumbed to his injuries then oh well. Not like I killed him outright. I couldn't help it if he succumbs to his injuries or not.

"Tik tok Mikey, you have a chance of surviving if you hurry." I taunted with a smirk as I walked back over to Nikolai, wrapping my arms around one of his and leaning against him. "I would also get moving before my dear husband decides to take matters into his own hands for your insults towards me earlier. Unlike you, he doesn't put up with people calling me names." I could see the murderous storm that darkened Nikolai's typically vibrant eyes as he stayed rooted to his spot.

With a pained groan, Michael got up and quickly stumbled out of the room, leaving a trail of blood behind him.

"You're really going to let him walk out of here?" Nikolai did not sound happy when he leaned down to ask me in a low voice.

"His chances of surviving are near none. Unless there's an ambulance waiting outside, he'll probably drop at the front door or way before then. He's going to drown in his own blood more than likely." I was shockingly calm, and it kind of scared me considering how I just went psychobitch not too long ago. Although, maybe I just needed to release the pent of trauma to fully reset myself.

"Remind me to not play Russian roulette with you." Nikolai chuckled, wrapping his arms around me and holding me tightly.

Frowning, I pushed myself away from Nikolai. "Don't push your luck mister, I am still half tempted to slap you right now for blindsiding me like that." Having him pop the can of worms and throw it in my face was the last thing I wanted today after everything.

I thought getting his Aston blown up was bad, but this was a hundred times worse in my opinion.

"Someone's in the doghouse tonight." Arseny teased with a snicker.

Chapter 37

Nikolai

"Lisi—"

"No!" My hands were slapped away before they even came close to touching her. "Do not touch me right now. I am still pissed at you. Don't fucking talk to me. Don't even look at me."

Well, at least Angel wasn't giving me the silent treatment anymore, but not sure if this was much of an improvement. "Ang—"

Never has she raised her voice at me until now. "No! I do not want to hear a single word that comes out of your mouth right now. I don't care if you were trying to be considerate with giving him to me on a silver platter. I didn't ask for it. But the fact that you didn't even run the idea by me or give me a heads up is what upsets me the most because I had no idea what the fuck I was walking into. Do you have any idea how humiliating it would have been if I had shut down? Just froze in place and pissed myself or something? I didn't even know what the fuck to do until he spoke, then I just snapped, but before then I was about to have a fucking full blown panic attack and flashback."

She seethed with murderous rage. Absolutely loathing me. The anger in her glaring eyes made those soft, warm, brown eyes of hers harden to sharp copper that cut into me deeply. But I couldn't do anything but take it because I deserved it.

I wasn't even hurt by her words. It was the fact I had upset her this much to where she made herself vulnerable and cried emotionally around me that twisted at my gut as if someone stuck a burning knife into it.

I already felt like an asshole earlier when I saw her initial reaction to Michael. She looked like she was about to break apart before she flew into a sudden rage and went after him. Seeing her freeze up initially made me want to pull her out of the room and drag her home, especially when I saw the panic set into her wide eyes.

Apologizing so far hasn't worked. It only seemed to agitate Angel more whenever I did apologize. She'd given me the cold shoulder and silent treatment ever since we left the bunker, only recently breaking her vow of silence now.

With a heavy heart, I watched her disappear into the closet for a long minute before reemerging in full tactical gear. "I'm going out. Don't wait up." She didn't even spare me a fraction of a glance when she sped by me briskly.

"*Blyat*!" I cursed under my breath, taking after my trudging wife. "Angel, please, you're not in the right mindset to be going out like this." Last thing I wanted was a phone call from one of her friends that she'd been shot or severely injured because her mind was clouded. The guilt only laid on thicker due to the fact her mind was muddled because of me.

"My mind is perfectly clear. Unless you rather me shoot your kneecaps, you'll shut up and leave me alone until I'm ready to talk to you again." She didn't even bother looking at me when she spoke, too focused on digging through the small armory room and stocking herself up.

"I would turn it back on you and say how'd you like it if you were trying to forget your dad and I just toss him in front of you one day going 'surprise honey' with no forewarning, but your little simpleton brain would probably be like 'oh I would have appreciated it a lot and just killed him' and shit." Now she was just rambling, a habit of hers I've noticed whenever she was emotionally riled up.

Still, her jab hurt a little. What kept my tongue at bay was the fact she was right. There was no way I could imagine or feel what she went through even if the situation was reversed like her scenario. Of course,

I felt like a huge prick right now because I should have used my brain and put her first.

Scowling deeply, she continued to ramble. "Fucking men. Honestly, ya'll don't ever fucking use your damn pea brains when they're actually fucking needed. Not even going to bother arguing with you because it'll be fucking pointless 'cause you won't get the fucking point." The harsh slam of the magazine clip was probably a clear sign for me to back off and leave her be before it ends up being emptied into me.

Hanging back a good distance, I watched her prepare in a hurry and take off in my Bugatti. A part of me wanted to grab her by the arm, stop her and make her talk it out, but the logical side of me won by a margin. Nothing shy of a shouting match possibly could have come from having a talk now. The argument was unavoidable, but the hostility was something we could control.

Also, I knew better than to talk to someone armed to the teeth, especially my pissed off wife.

With a heavy sigh, I dragged myself to my office on the first floor, hoping to drown myself with some work to get my mind to cool off before Angel came home. We had some important shipments coming in soon, so I really did need to make sure everything was as perfect as can be.

After a while, I felt a presence at the doorway but didn't bother paying them any attention.

"So, how pissed off was she to speed off like that?" Stepan asked, snapping my attention away from my laptop.

"Well, she wanted to pop one in my kneecaps. Do the math." I sighed with a soft groan at the headache that formed. "But, I can't blame her." I really couldn't. If I were Angel, I'd do worse to me.

Running a hand through my face, I leaned back in my chair and looked at Stepan fully as he leaned against the door frame with his arms crossed. "No, you really can't blame her. No offense, but for a smart leader like yourself, that was one stupid ass fucking decision. I mean, I can understand your good intentions behind it, and maybe it's because I'm outside the relationship that I can see how bad of a 'present' that was. Or maybe it's because I'm the only one out of the four of us that has a functioning brain."

Well, I couldn't argue with him there because he was the smartest out of all of us, or at the very least the one with the functioning brain. Pretty sure the rest of us only had half a functioning brain on a good day.

"Either way, one of my men got back to me about the location of our stolen shipment of weapons. You game?" Stepan's subtle way of begging me to go and take the lead because lord knows he hates leading raids.

Forcing a small smile on my face, I chuckle under my breath. "Yeah, like hell am I going to let you have all the fun." Hopefully it'll take my mind off of the issue with Angel, because I sure as hell had no idea how to approach it without making a damn fool of myself.

Sighing heavily, I push myself out of my chair almost reluctantly. "Meet you out front in a bit." No way in hell would I go in sweats and a t-shirt—unless I had a death wish that is.

It didn't take me long to change into my tactical gear and stock myself up with knives, guns, and extra magazines. On the way out, I grabbed the black duffle bag filled with assault rifles from the safe of the arsenal room before hopping into the SUV with Stepan.

Pulling out his tablet, Stepan showed me the layout of the warehouse and shipyard we were going to raid in a couple of minutes. "That's one heavily guarded warehouse." It wasn't a big one either, so thirty guards seemed rather excessive.

Looking closely at the tablet, I couldn't help but tense my jaw as I took note of the amount of guards. "That bugs me because honestly, the shipment they stole wasn't even much in value or quantity. So, why throw such caution at it? Also, the other thing that bugs me is the location of the warehouse." I voiced my thoughts out loud as I continued studying the information.

No way in hell this was a coincidence. Gritting my teeth, I let out a short huff before speaking again. "I want the place torn apart from twenty-feet underground to the fucking rooftop. They're hiding something. No way in hell is someone stupid or desperate enough to guard a small shipment of weapons with thirty armed guards." Then the fact the warehouse was within both triad territory and Ivan's made it damn clear there would be more than meets the eyes.

"I managed to round up fifteen of our men and Lev. I plan on taking two for the rooftops, so that leaves you with Lev and thirteen others. I'll deal with the guards on the rooftop with the two snipers I'm taking." Stepan told me his plan as he looked through his duffle bag, digging out a magazine clip and filling it.

"Looks like there's two entrances, one to the north and the south. I'll take eight of the men and cover the north entrance while Lev can take the rest and cover the south. I'll relay all of this when we meet up in a bit." I wasn't worried about the fact we had less men than the enemy. We were all trained to militaristic levels, most—nearly all—of the men who worked for us were ex-special ops soldiers. We weren't run of the mill thugs with guns and knives.

It didn't take us long to reach our destination where everyone waited. True to my word, I relayed the plan to everyone before splitting the teams up.

Slipping the earpiece into my ear, I waited for everyone to come online. "I want at least one alive for questioning, but the more the merrier." I spoke through the communications system.

No doubt Ivan had his hands dipped in this mess, and I wanted answers he wasn't going to give. Well, hopefully his men were more than willing to squeal like the swine they are. I would deal with Ivan later once I can get a better idea of what his play was.

"Everyone in position?" I asked, waiting for everyone to give me the clear before giving the command to breach.

Rounding a corner, my arms shot out, grabbing one of the perimeter guards in a chokehold. "Two options: I kill you, or you answer our questions. Tap my arm if you want to go with option two, if not then I'll slit your throat right now."

When the guy made no indication of going with the latter option, I didn't hesitate to pull my knife out and slice him from ear to ear, being sure to dig the knife deep to sever his arteries completely.

Letting the gurgling body drop to the ground, I continued forward, only stopping once I got to the door to wait for everyone. "I'm at the door." I whispered through the communicator, waiting for a response from Lev and my men before kicking the door down and filing into the building.

Some poor sap who stood behind the door when I kicked it flew into some crates and was knocked out cold. At least that was one person we could question later. The guy who got a headshot from me probably won't be talking any time soon—or ever.

Looking over at the man next to me, I nod at the unconscious guard. "Tie him up." The man gave me a nod and went over to the unconscious man while I pushed forward with the others.

Ducking behind a crate, I avoided a shot from the guard ahead of me who continued to unload his clip at me. I waited until I heard the telltale *click click* of an empty clip then lunged from behind the crate, tackling the man to the ground and punching him square in the face. Grabbing him by his head, I slammed it into the ground, knocking him out. Then, I pulled out the zip ties from my pocket and secured the man's wrists and ankles before hiding him in a crate and continuing.

The initial fact there were thirty guards somewhat unsettled me, but after seeing how easily it was to take them down, I could see why they needed so many. All the guards were idiots with weapons, only a few knew how to aim and shoot correctly. Guess Ivan couldn't afford good help.

Even though my men and I were half of the hired guards, we took them out with ease and no casualties on our side. Thankfully we managed to capture a few for questioning, and those guys were being moved to one of our bunkers for holding until tomorrow.

"Anything?!" I shouted after prying open another crate to reveal bricks of cocaine.

"Drugs and more drugs over here!" One of my men shouted from a corner of the warehouse.

"I found our stolen shipment! Everything is still intact!" Lev shouted from his spot.

"What do you want to do boss? Want to take everything back with us?" The man standing next to me asked as he looked through the crate with me.

"No. We'll only take our stolen shipment back and any other weapons we find, everything else gets dumped into the ocean." I didn't care for the drugs, and it would take too much effort and resources to test all the supply here to make sure it's safe for distribution. Last thing I wanted to do was kill off our clientele with poorly cut coke.

"Hey boss, you might want to see this." Another called me over, waving his hand for me to come his direction.

Going over to him, I looked at what he pointed at. "Everyone! Find the entrance to the basement!" I could see the wires for the second thermostat winding down below the floor, indicating a sublevel.

What the hell are you hiding Ivan?

Chapter 38

Nikolai

IT WAS LATE BY the time I came home with Lev and Stepan. All of us were exhausted after finding the basement and freeing the females who were being held prisoner under there. That wasn't the exhausting part though. The ambush that jumped us was what took away the last of our energy for the night.

"Hilda, please make sure the ladies are comfortable and fed in the housings outback. I will deal with them in the morning." My house-keeper had been waiting for me at the entrance just as I had instructed in the phone call on the way home.

"Of course sir." She replied respectfully with a slight bow of her head. "Miss Volkov is home, and I am slightly worried about her. She has been shut in the bathroom after coming home bloodied from head to toe." Hilda's subtle way of telling me to go check on my wife and work out whatever beef we have between us. "I swear, both of you are too stubborn for your own good." She sighed with a shake of her head.

If it was anyone else then I'd say something, but Hilda was a close family friend who has helped us out ever since we moved to the states. She was also old enough to be my grandma, so it felt too disrespectful to talk back to an elder.

Sighing heavily, I could feel the weight of everything slowly creep its way back onto me as I ascended the stairs to our room. It was quiet besides the sound of the shower running from our adjoined bathroom.

I couldn't help but wonder how long she'd been in there as I slowly approached the door and let my hand linger around the doorknob.

I was about to leave her to finish, but my mind quickly changed when I heard a faint sob cut through the sound of pelting water. She could be mad at me all she wanted, but I wasn't about to let her sit and cry alone in the shower. I created this mess, so I would damn well clean it up.

So, without knocking, I opened the unlocked the bathroom door. I don't know if she chose to ignore me or didn't notice me, but she didn't make any indication to acknowledge my presence.

I didn't want to spend a second longer from her, so I didn't bother stripping. Without a word, I entered the shower and looked down at Angel who still sat under the rain shower heads while hugging her knees to her chest. Her head barely lopped over to the side to look up at me for a split second before going back to staring down at the floor. "Just leave me alone." I could barely hear her whimpering voice over the sound of the rushing water.

"I cannot leave you alone, and I am not going to." I reply with a sigh, bending down to grab her by her arms and drag her up into my own. "Listen, I am sorry for not thinking about how stupid bringing Michael to you was. I was running too high on the idea that you'd feel a lot better if you wrung the life out of him or dealt him the same hand, even the score. I didn't think it'd upset you this much. I am sorry for being a complete ass, really, I am."

Honestly, I should have used my brain, the one that's been so successful at keeping my family's bratva running smooth and high. The prospect of making Angel happy ate up whatever logic floated around in my head.

"Why am I such a mess? I hate being this stupid and weak. I don't want to be upset with you to the point that I am, but I feel like things are just spinning out of control, especially after tonight." Her actions reflected her inner turmoil by how her body twisted into and away from me, as if she wanted me to hold her but at the same time wanted to shove me away.

Tightening my arms around her, I held her squirming body close and upright to prevent her from wiggling away. I wasn't going to let her go, she would have to deal with me because that's what a good husband was supposed to do, right? Bug the shit out of their wife and be there for them even in their shittiest moments? I'm pretty sure if I let her shove me away now then she'd just close herself off more then get pissed with me later.

On the other hand, I have no idea how to even be a decent husband, let alone a good one. What do I even say to her right now without sounding like an ass? I know there's no right thing to say really, but there sure as hell a shit ton of wrong things to say.

Sighing softly, I rubbed her arm soothingly. "You've just got a lot going on right now, *lisichka*. You've every right to be upset with me, and if you need to take things out on me then go for it, I can take it."

Leaning down, I placed a loving kiss on her forehead. "And don't you ever say that you are weak and stupid because you are not, and you won't ever be." What else was there to say? If I let my mouth run then I'd dig my own grave.

"I'm sitting in the shower bawling my eyes out." She deadpanned.

"We all reach a breaking point, and we all express that differently. So what if yours is crying it out in the shower? There are worse vices for you to take up as a means to release your pent up emotions." I had a bad habit of drinking too much then wrecking my knuckles on a punching bag—or on the faces of unlucky idiots.

"I know we haven't been together long, but do you regret this marriage? Do you regret me?" There was her insecurity rearing its head again.

Breathing deeply, I snaked my hand around her neck, squeezing softly while tilting her head up to look at me. "No matter how many times you ask, and no matter how long we've been married, my answer to that question will never change no matter what. You better burn my answer into your brain, *lisichka*. I will never. *Never*! Regret marrying you. You are the only slice of heaven that I will ever experience in this lifetime and the next, because God knows I'm going straight to hell before my eyes even shut in death. I don't care if you're a mentally unstable bitch with twenty-three personalities, I will never leave you nor will I ever stop loving you."

Our psychotic personalities fed off of each other at this point. A modern day Bonnie and Clyde, perfect partners in crime. I wouldn't want to lay waste to my enemies with anyone else by my side but Angel. I loved indulging her dark desire for torture, always tossing her victims left and right.

It sounded so fucked up, but watching her work apart a human psyche and seeing how elated it made her drove me wild. Even if she denied her enjoyment, I could see the way her eyes lit up with a crazed glint whenever she'd dig her claws into the poor soul I would offer as a sacrifice to her.

Also, the crazy, hot sex afterwards was a very clear indicator she enjoyed torture more than she was willing to let on.

Speaking of sex after torture. "All things aside, did you enjoy making him squirm before plunging that knife into him?" Probably not the best time to try and get my dick wet, but a man's gotta try. Besides, with the adrenaline dissipating into other problems, a good fuck always solved it very well.

That's probably another reason why this strange relationship of ours worked out. Besides the obvious chemistry and affection for each other, we both indulged each other to calm our inner demons at the end of the day. I've lost count of how many nights we've ripped each other's clothes off after an assignment, riding out our adrenaline highs until we crashed.

It didn't matter if the other was tired or in bed when the other would get home. There have been many times when I've been startled awake by Angel's aggressive kisses or overall aggression to get me up and going. My little hellion would stop at nothing until I pounded into her with no mercy and pushed her beyond her limits.

Of course, there were some nights where things didn't go such ways, tonight being one of them. "I'm way too exhausted to fuck right now, *anh*. If I wasn't such an emotional mess earlier then I would have fucked you in front of him before and after having you kill him." She didn't even bother to force a chuckle out or hit me playfully.

As much as I wanted to shove her against the shower wall and have my way with her, I knew when to stop. Looking down at her, I could see the exhaustion painted on her face. If I tried to push any luck I have, I'd most likely end up alone in bed tonight, or a knife to my arm if I really piss her off too much.

Besides, I really shouldn't be toeing the line with her after my little stunt today.

"Let me wash up and we can just cuddle in bed with some back rubs? And I promise it'll be just that, nothing beyond." It was adorable how easily I could get her to melt with such a simple act.

At least she trusted me enough to bear her back to me now. Even after that first night, things were a little touch and go for a moment whenever I would flip her around or touch her back. But she lowered her walls eventually after I forced my hand on the matter and basically conditioned the hell out of her.

"Only cuddles and rubs. I really am exhausted." She sounded drained, only further pushing the idea of any fooling around deeper into the recess of my mind.

Nodding with a hum, I kissed her forehead. "What happened tonight?" Even if I did fuck up with throwing her emotions onto a rollercoaster from hell, no way it should have affected her this much. Also, she did mention something about it earlier when I entered the shower.

Sighing heavily, Angel slowly wrapped her arms around my waist loosely and let herself lean into my body. "Shit hit the fan, that's all. Found out we had a mole too late, lost two of my men, lost the shipment, and a lot of us got badly hurt. It was just a big shit show the moment we set foot in the damn place."

Breathing deeply, she stood there in silence for a while, letting the water wash over us as we held each other. "Well, I'll wait for you in bed, I already washed myself before you so rudely interrupted my sob session." She forced a small smile on her face as she pushed away from me and slipped out of the shower.

Unable to help it, I let my eyes linger on her delicately strong body as she towel herself off on the other side of the glass. I will never grow tired of seeing my lovely wife's body. Even if she liked to argue with me otherwise, she was beautiful and perfect in my eyes. All her insecurities about her body are what I loved about her. I loved her silky black hair, her sharp but delicate features of her face, even her small breasts never bothered me one bit no matter how many times she tried to argue.

She was imperfectly perfect to me. She was my perfect little wife, and I wouldn't trade her for anyone else in the whole universe. God I was stupid to not pursue her, and that was my only regret so far when it came to us.

Her soft and melodic giggle got me out of my mind. "Quit drooling over there and hurry up, I need my heater of a husband in bed." With a light snicker, she left the bathroom.

Not wanting to keep her waiting, and not being able to be patient myself, I quickly washed myself and rushed to the bedroom after running the towel down my body and throwing on some boxers, a pair of gray sweatpants, and a black t-shirt.

I needed her in my arms. *Now.*

I was such a needy man for her, but I couldn't help it. Having her body pressed against mine while we remained tangled in each other's arms was the only thing I looked forward to at the end of every night. The fact my other half waited for me was my motivation to be successful, to make sure every aspect of my illegal business would always go as planned because I'd be damned if I took a bullet to the head and left her with an empty bed. Or worse yet, in another man's arms.

The thought of her being with anyone else boiled my blood. It took every ounce of my control to not snap the neck of every man she ever glanced at whenever we'd be out together. Even if she never looked at them *that* way, it still pissed me off.

No other man should have the grace of laying eyes on her either. She belonged to me and only me. Everyone else needed to keep their eyes glued to the floor whenever she walked into the room.

I would never take over her life—as if she'd let me—but I hated when she'd go out to the clubs or bars with her friends because of other men who would leer at her with hungry eyes. She may deny it, always downplaying it saying no man would ever look at her because she wasn't worth it, but she truly underestimated herself. Even with my arm around her possessively when I'd be with her, some men still dared to eye her like their next conquest.

"You're staring again." Angel giggled softly.

I didn't realize I had zoned out until Angel's voice brought me back.

Playing it off with a smile, I climbed next to her in bed, instantly wrapping my arms around her small body and pulling it flush against mine. "I can't help it, you are too beautiful to not admire." Smooth. Real smooth.

With a roll of her eyes, Angel lightly smacked my chest before snuggling into me. "I'm too broken to be beautiful, but I appreciate it."

"What did I say about talking bad about yourself, *lisichka*?" Now I just needed to condition that habit out of her. She really did need to give herself more credit and stop putting herself down. "You will always be my beautiful wife, Angel. My beautiful, cute, and sexy wife." I whispered against her lips with a deep chuckle before closing the distance between us completely with a passionate kiss.

Moaning into the kiss, Angel let herself melt into me the more I kissed her. Remaining lip locked with her, I carefully bunched her sleep shirt up around her waist to slip my hand onto her bare ass.

Chuckling, I broke the kiss and looked down at her with a teasing smirk. "You said no funny business yet you're here with no underwear on." I accused with a playful tone.

"Just shut up and kiss me. It was for tomorrow morning if I felt like it." She replied in a sassy manner paired with a roll of her eyes.

I leaned back down, but I didn't let my lips meet her pursed ones. The small pout that followed made me chuckle as I brought a hand up around her neck, holding her firm to keep her from leaning in to close the distance. "Is that how you ask for a kiss, *lisichka*?"

"Oh come on, you stir up my past trauma and make me go through an emotional rollercoaster." She argued with a soft glare, struggling a bit against my grip to try and steal the kiss I withheld.

With a soft tut of disapproval, I tightened my hands around her neck, smirking more when she let out a sigh of pleasure. "Doesn't give you an excuse to be a brat and demand things and forget all your manners."

"Asshole." She muttered, sucking in a sharp breath when I gave her ass a quick—and hard—smack with my other hand. Yelping, she glared at me softly. "You can't do that!"

Two slaps fell down on her pink cheek, making her squirm under me. "Do I need to remind you who's in charge between us, *lisichka*? I can do whatever the fuck I want." She made it very hard to keep things from going too far.

I could easily slip into her right now, rail her until she forgot her own name, but I respected her wishes from earlier. Still, her being a little brat right now made me very hard with the idea of punishing her more.

"Whatever game you're playing at, *lisichka*, you better stop before your exhaustion is the last thing you'll worry about." This was the only warning I would give her, and the look in her eyes meant she understood.

A second later, she averted her eyes from me before speaking up in a small but sincere voice, "I'm sorry, sir. I just want your kisses and your touch. Please, can I have more kisses sir, please? I didn't mean to act out, I'm sorry."

Loosening my grip a little, I moved my lips up to her forehead, placing a soft and lingering kiss. "You've had a rough day, I wasn't going to hold it against you much since I was the cause of most of it."

Just this once I would let it slide since it was my fault. I wasn't going to punish her for something I caused. "There won't be a next time though, so don't think you can act out after a rough day without being bent over my knee for it. Understood?"

Her head moved against my lips in a nod, "Yes, sir."

After giving her forehead another kiss, I tilted her face up to kiss her properly with a soft groan as I slipped my tongue into her mouth. "Be good and let me take care of you tonight alright, *lisichka*?" I spoke against her lips.

"Okay, sir." She replied breathlessly.

Pushing her fully onto her back, I lowered myself down between her legs while pushing them wide open. "You're soaking wet." I teased with a soft chuckle when I noticed how much her folds were glistening with her juices.

Slowly, I circled her clit with my middle finger, getting a few soft moans from her as she relaxed a bit. Carefully, I slid my finger down to her entrance, circling it a few times as I leaned in and latched my mouth around her clit.

I continued to tease her entrance with my finger as I ran the length of my tongue against her little love button, making her gasp sharply and tangle her fingers into my hair. She was always so fun to tease with how sensitive she was.

Moaning deeply, she arched her back as I sank my finger into her, "Ooooh fuuuck." I could feel her velvet walls clench around my finger when I finally entered her, slowly fingering her while I gently worked at her clit with my tongue.

"Don't hold back baby, come all you need and want for tonight." Tonight was all about her pleasure. I wasn't about to make her beg for her releases like usual, for tonight at least.

"*Spasibo, ser.*" She sighed happily with a soft smile.

"You sound so fucking sexy, *lisichka.*" Hearing her speak Russian—no matter how stiff she sounded most of the time—was such a turn on. It started out with her just learning a few words and terms to tease me, get me riled, but after a while the effect it had on me grew to where it just aroused me greatly—especially when she'd beg me to fuck her.

"You better teach our kids Russian, they'll sound so cute." She giggled softly, looking down at me with loving eyes as she stroked my hair softly.

"As long as you teach them one of yours as well." I bargained with a chuckle before dipping my head back down to her sweet pie and digging in fully this time.

With one arm wrapped around her leg and thrown across her hip to keep her squirming body pinned, I worked a second finger into her tight cunt as I licked and sucked at her clit.

"Oh God, coming, fuck!" Her head was thrown back as her orgasm coated my fingers and tongue. Her body arched as her hips pressed against me, grinding on my face as I dragged her orgasm out.

It wasn't long until her hips started to jerk away from me, forcing me to tighten my grip to keep her firmly planted against me as I worked her body into another orgasm that made her squeal and whimper.

"Kolyenka, fuck you're going to overstimulate me. Oh God!" Her body fought against me; her hands pushed at my head while her hips tried—and failed—to pull away from me.

I wanted to reply to her, to tell her I wouldn't stop until she became a muttering mess, until the sheets were soaked all the way through, and until her juices dripped from my face. But I didn't because it meant stopping my tongue from lashing against her throbbing clit.

God I was so tempted to tie her down right now to have her at my complete mercy. Maybe tomorrow night. If I tied her down now then I'd go back on our agreement of no funny business tonight.

"Fuck!" She cried out as the first gush of fluids flowed out of her, coating my chin and dripping down onto the sheets. "Fuckfuckfuck, Kolyenka fuck, oh God!" Her hands released my head and slammed down onto the sheets next to her, fisting at them as her body writhed under me from my continuous onslaught.

"Oh fuck!" She moaned loudly when I dug my fingers deeper and harder into her sweet spot, drawing out another orgasm that made her juices gush out of her.

Fuck I would never get enough of her. As cliche as it sounded, I could spend forever between her thighs, feasting on her sweet little pie until the end of time. She tasted divine, so addicting. Fuck.

I continued to stay buried between her thighs for God knows how long, bringing her to orgasm after orgasm after orgasm and making her fill our room up with her cries of pleasure. "Kolyenka, no more, please. I'm spent." She whimpered between her ragged breaths. It was only then when I started to ease up, giving her one last orgasm before coming to a complete stop.

Chuckling softly, I placed a quick kiss on her inner thigh before crawling up and kissing her softly. "You are so beautiful." I couldn't help but admire her flushed face as she looked at me with her adoring eyes.

Propping myself up next to her, I pulled her up a little before grabbing her water bottle and holding it up to her lips. "Drink." At least she was always compliant in her post orgasmic bliss. She was also usually pretty silent, clingy, and cuddly afterwards, all which I didn't mind.

Actually, I found it rather endearing how clingy she became after sex or anything somewhat intense. Always holding onto me and lingering around me as if I was her lifeline; it was nice. Usually I hated clingy people, but it wasn't as if she was constantly clingy—it was just after sex and such activities.

As much as I loved her independent nature and personality, sometimes I did wish she'd let me care for her more often outside of the bedroom. I didn't want her to worry about anything in her life. A part of me wanted her to stay home and safe behind the estate gates, but I knew that would never fly with her in a million life times.

"Thank you," her soft lips pressed against my cheek, "Didn't think I needed that, so thank you." She sunk down fully onto the bed, snuggling into me as she curled herself up into a tight little ball with a big, happy, loving smile on her face. "God I love you so much."

Smiling softly, I kissed her forehead before getting off the bed to change the sheets and crawl back into bed with her afterwards.

With her secured tightly in my arms, I let my fingers trail lazily up and down her back, easing the tension out of her. "Sleep, darling, you deserve it." I whispered softly.

"I don't deserve anything, but alright." She replied sarcastically, rolling her eyes at me with a giggle too.

Sighing with my own eye roll, I gave her ass a quick spank, leaving a reddened imprint of my hand. "You deserve the world, so stop selling yourself short. Or else." My voice dipped with my warning, making her shrink a bit in my arms.

"Sorry." She muttered against my chest as she buried her face into it, breathing deeply as she gripped the front of my shirt tightly in her small hands.

It still puzzled me at how little her self-esteem was in contrast to her confident and flamboyant personality. I've seen her with her men and on the floor at her work place; she walked around with her head held up high, and she walked with a purpose. She was one helluva leader under pressure.

The mask she had on was enough to fool everyone around her. It even fooled me for a short while until I tore away at her layers. I honestly didn't think her self-esteem issues were as bad as they were until we grew close and deep with each other and she exposed herself to me intimately.

"Good night, *lisichka. YA tebya lyublyu.*" I whispered sweetly with a loving kiss.

"I love you too. *YA tozhe tebya lyublyu.*" Angel giggled back with a big smile.

I don't know about Angel, but I slept well into the morning, only stirring awake when I felt the missing warmth in my arms. Well, and the sound of Angel clamoring around in the bathroom woke me as well.

"*Lisichka?*" My concern grew greatly when I walked into the bathroom and saw her hunched over the toilet. "Are you sure the doctor said everything was fine yesterday?" I doubt vomiting and looking like death constituted as fine.

Kneeling down next to her, I rubbed her back and held her hair back as she remained strewn over the toilet seat, groaning while her face remained sickly green. "Yeah, just the new birth control is fucking with me more than I hoped. I'll talk to my doctor after breakfast about changing it. Sorry you had to see me like this." She sounded so weak and drained, and I felt hurt I couldn't help her with any of it.

"If we weren't going to try for kids later on then I'd offer to put myself on the snipping table. I hate seeing you like this and being helpless to you." If her medication fucked with her this much then I'd rather just get snipped and be done with it all, so she wouldn't have to keep suffering to keep herself protected.

"Well aren't you husband of the year." She chuckled weakly in a sarcastic manner. "God you are so getting snipped after we're done though, I ain't gonna risk shit." She added with a weak smile.

"Just say when." If it meant less suffering for her then that's all that mattered to me.

"How many kids do you want?" She asked with a soft groan at the end as she pushed herself off the toilet, leaning into me and holding me with loose arms.

"At least two, maybe three max. I definitely don't want anything beyond four for both our sake and sanity. I honestly have no idea how my mother put up with the whole lot of us and I definitely do not want to be dealing with that many kids at my age." Not like I was young like Angel, and by the time we'd have kids I'd be older. Last thing I wanted to do in my mid-forties and fifties was chase around some energetic children; I literally won't have the energy for it.

I couldn't imagine putting up with six children; I had to praise my mother for being able to do so. I already wanted to rip Lev's head off whenever he'd get into a tuff with one of us. I can't imagine having all six kids having a go at each other and trying to sort out that mess. How my mother didn't chuck half of us out a window was beyond my comprehension.

Back to the situation at hand though, "Do you want or need me to get you anything? Any medication or food?" We could talk about children when we weren't on the bathroom floor.

"Maybe just some food to settle my stomach. Can you have Anna make a light breakfast? I'll be down in a second, just need to wash up." She tried to assure me with a smile, but I could tell she wasn't for it right now.

"I'll wait for you outside, I don't want to leave you up here alone like this." Last thing I wanted was to find her passed out on the bathroom floor.

With a smile, she hugged me tightly for a few seconds before urging me out of the bathroom.

Thankfully, the two of us made it down and through breakfast just fine, and Angel did start to look a little better after she got some food in her. But I couldn't help but fret over her still because she was still sluggish and sickly pale. Before I could bring up the issue again—and try to talk her into seeing the doctor again—her phone went off with some grim news.

Chapter 39

Angel

I DON'T LIKE PLAYING Death. Having a person's life in my own hands was too much responsibility that I didn't want to have on my conscience. That's another big reason why I don't kill unless necessary. My guilty mind wouldn't be able to handle it all in the end.

"Angel." Even Nikolai's comforting hand on my shoulder felt like a ton of bricks dragging me down because it was a stark reminder of the situation presented to me. I couldn't find any comfort in his touch right now; it kept me from escaping the realm of reality.

The doctor's voice sounded like a distant echo in the wind even though he was a mere foot from me. But my mind drifted too far out, wanting to shut down and hope for some magical reset button to be pressed. "I know this is a very difficult decision, and I am truly sorry that I have to put such a burden on you."

Just when I thought I started to recover from the trauma with my ex, a bomb explodes in my face.

"Angel, would you like me to go through the typical protocol with you? Or what would you like?" The doctor's question barely registered in my mind as I busied myself with focusing on my vegetative father before me.

"I would like to be left alone, please. I know how the conversation goes." I've been in many of these situations to know all to be said and laid out. I just never thought I'd be on the receiving end of one, ever. I didn't want to hear everything from the doctor, to have a stern reminder.

"I understand. You know where and how to reach me once you've made your decision, Angel." It wasn't typical for the provider to just leave so easily, but the provider knew me well after working with me for a long while. "I am sorry. I really wish things would have turned out differently."

"You have nothing to be sorry for. You did what you could. You're not God, you can't perform miracles, none of us can." At the end of the day, we're only human. No matter how much anger and sadness I felt, I couldn't take it out on the poor doctor who had no control over the situation.

I couldn't hold it against the doctor for not being able to save my father, not when he did try his very best. Nature and the human body couldn't be controlled. By the books, everything was done to a tee, but there was only so much we could do by our hands. It wasn't the doctor's fault my father tanked out of nowhere after we had weaned him off the drugs.

"Do you want to have a moment alone, love?"

Nikolai's question brought a wave of panic. My eyes bounced between him and my still father as I struggled with what I wanted in the moment. Did I want to be alone? Have a few precious moments with my father, try to fully process everything and prepare myself for the inevitable. But I didn't want to truly be alone.

It was one of those confusing yes/no moments I hated. I didn't want to have Nikolai stick around just to see me break down when he could be using his time elsewhere. On the other hand, I wanted him to be there to support me as my husband, especially since Greg couldn't be here right now.

I don't know if he was a mind reader or good at reading me or maybe he sensed the turmoil within me, but he came up with a great solution. "I'll leave you for a few, get you something to drink, give you a moment with your father and all, then I'll be back and stay if you want me to. Alright, darling?" His voice was low when he spoke with his lips softly pressed against my temple, his arm still around my shoulder while his hand gingerly squeezed.

Unable to find the strength to reply properly, all I could manage was a small nod of my head, leaning into him a little before sitting myself down at the edge of my father's hospital bed.

I couldn't bring myself to say anything to my father, only managing to sob silently as I held his limp hand. It wasn't going to be long until he would be laying in a wooden box six-feet under, and I would be the one who put him there.

"I am so sorry *ba*. I swear, I'll make this all right." My stepmother wasn't going to have the last word. I'll ruin everything for her, make her wish I'd grant her the same sweet mercy of death that would take my father.

This was fucking bullshit.

I knew life wasn't fair, that not everything sailed smoothly, but still. Things were supposed to look up after he was weaned off the medications which kept him in a coma. He wasn't supposed to tank. He wasn't supposed to be on life support. I wasn't supposed to have to decide whether or not the plug should be pulled.

In the perfect life he'd be awake, recover fully, enjoy his retirement with his grandkids.

But life wasn't perfect.

Maybe karma was finally catching up to me.

"Darling?"

I was so swallowed up in my sorrow I didn't notice him fully until I felt his touch on my cheek, his thumb wiping away at the tears that were staining my cheek.

"It's not fair." My voice was broken as I struggled to hold my tears back. "He should be fine, old and fine and awake, not comatose and brain dead in a bed."

Was my father a saint? No, but he tried his best to be a good man, and he was a good man—for a mafia leader. Either way, he didn't deserve to be poisoned like this and pass away without a fighting chance. It wasn't fair. I wouldn't be so strung up if he had passed away from natural causes or was shot by some enemy, but to have his fate met by the hands of my stepmother through a dirty tactic of poisoning was something I couldn't accept.

Sighing, I wrapped my arms around Nikolai's waist and buried my face into the bend of his neck. "I can't do it. I know what's needed, but I can't do it. It feels so wrong when it's not." The decision was a logical one. A quick scribble on a line, and it'd all be over. I've only signed my name on an infinite amount of documents at this point, so what's one more? It should be as simple and mundane like always—a quick flick of my wrist.

"It's your father, baby, nothing about it is easy or simple. Just because something is needed doesn't mean that it'll be easy. I understand it's not easy, and I don't envy you one bit." Well, at least he's not being an asshole about this whole thing. "Just take your time to come to terms with everything."

"I don't think I'll ever come to terms with it. I mean, I'm basically killing my dad, or at the very least giving permission to. And if I stall on it then everyone will be on my ass, and my father would just be suffering in silence." It was a lose-lose situation for me. Keeping my dad alive meant prolonging his suffering and my delusions which would only worsen with time. Not to mention everyone would be one my ass for being an evil bitch for keeping a vegetative person alive for no reason other than my own selfish reasons.

On the other hand, if I pulled the plug, everyone would question why I'd make such a decision, how I should have waited for hope he would recover. But, I knew there was no way he would recover. No one comes back from being brain dead. If he did come back by some God given miracle then he would never fully recover or ever be the same.

Sighing heavily, I ran a hand through my hair frustratedly. "I need to contact the lawyer. I need some air and time away from this room right now." I would wallow in my own head the longer I sat around, and my head was not in a good space right now.

I wanted to go back to the comfort of home, but Nikolai wouldn't let me. I might have complained a bit initially, but after he forced me to the restaurant and made me eat, it was clear it was a needed thing. Even if I didn't have much of an appetite, the quick little impromptu lunch date with my handsome husband was very much needed and appreciated.

Unfortunately, the blip of bliss didn't keep the storm at bay.

We weren't even home for a full five minutes before there was a pounding at the door. "*Đù má!*" I cursed under my breath when I saw who it was on the security screen.

I had hoped for some more time before dealing with my wicked witch of a stepmother. Unfortunately, I couldn't keep her from knowing about my father's status because she was his spouse and my father never filed the paper to bar her from such privileges. Granted, I probably could pull some strings, bribe a few people, and get things settled how I wanted, but that was too much at this point.

I wasn't worried about my stepmother pulling something over my head regarding my father's health decisions after dabbling in some rather very illegal business to override her power of attorney as my father's medical proxy. So, unless she planned and wanted to pull more illegal shit behind my back, there was no way she would gain control again. Of course, it didn't stop her from being a total witch to me about it all.

Before I could tell the housekeeper to not open the door, it was thrown open from the other side. With no respect, my stepmother barged her way in with an angry scowl on her face. "Why didn't you pull the plug?! He's already dead! It's sick that you are keeping him just so you stay in charge!"

Keeping a stern expression, I narrowed my eyes at her. "Wow at least make up a believable reason. You and I both know that I stand to inherit nearly all of his assets and estate in the event of his passing. I don't see why any of this concerns you, so turn around and put yourself right back out that door before I order the guards to throw you out." I was not in the mood to deal with her right now. Yes, I was curious as to why she was here because I couldn't think of a good reason for her presence currently. But I really wasn't in the mood.

Then the kicker came. With a smirk, my stepmother pulled out some papers out of her satchel and practically threw it at my feet. She didn't have to say it, but I could see her triumphant expression clear as day: read it and weep.

Refusing to bend down to pick up the papers, I glanced down quickly to skim over the strewn out pages. "I am not going to have you disrespect me like that in my own home. You can either pick those papers up and hand them to me like a proper adult, or leave." They were some legal documents, recent legal documents. Although, something about them felt and seemed off.

"You wouldn't even have this home if it weren't for me." She seethed back, holding her nose up high.

"Sorry, I don't recall seeing your name on the deed or anything about you giving me permission to live here in *my* husband's house. Now, like I said, either talk to me like a grown adult, or leave before I have you thrown out." I'm really tempted to go with the latter right now.

"I do not appreciate your disrespect towards my wife, Lady Qing. Say your piece and leave or I will let my wife handle you to her discretion." At least Nikolai had my back, and I was surprised to see him speak up for me rather than stay out of this whole mess.

"You need to control her." Now she was just being rude by ignoring me and trying to bypass my authority with my husband.

I watched Nikolai's chest rise and fall with his deep breaths. I don't know if my stepmother could see it from a slight distance, but I could see the tension in Nikolai's face as his jaw clenched and his eyebrows furrowed together slightly. "My wife is my equal, I do not need to control her. I do not appreciate you disrespecting her in her own home that *I* provided for her. This is your final warning to say your piece and leave, or else."

Smiling gratefully, I reached out and slipped my hand into his, giving it a small squeeze to show my gratitude.

Replacing my smile with flat expression, I turned my attention back to my stepmother, "We've been overly generous with you, so speak and leave. I am not going to tell you another time." Hell, I'll personally grab her by the scruff of her neck and chuck her out the door myself.

"You can read it all yourself and figure it out. I am going to be signing papers at 7 PM later. Whether you are there or not is up to you." With a haughty smile, she left as if she'd won, pissing me off immensely.

"Remind me to never let our kids get married, I can't imagine playing nice with in-laws who are absolute assholes." Nikolai joked dryly with a scoffing chuckle before leaning down and kissing the top of my head.

"This bitch better be lying out of her bleeding ass." I grumbled, leaning down and picking up the scattered papers.

Gritting my teeth, I pulled my phone out after flipping through the papers. "I'll be a moment." I muttered to Nikolai with a quick kiss, taking off to the office afterwards as the phone continued to ring.

Much to my relief after a good hour or so on the phone with the lawyer, my father was safe from my stepmother's claws. Although the documents she produced were legit, they were superseded by my father's own written and videotaped documents that were literally days before he fell into a coma.

Well, my stepmother was definitely going to be in shock when she showed up at the hospital and got all of this slapped in her face. If only I could be there to smile smugly. Too bad I have to prepare for the next day with everyone else. Not counting today, we had one more day until the event. So, I'll let the lawyer handle my stepmother later.

Chapter 40

Nikolai

"No caffeine today?" I was prepared for the struggle which happened nearly every morning with Angel, but not today, shockingly.

Grumpily, and tiredly, she let out a sigh with a pout. "No, I need to cut down the caffeine and nearly all together for a while until my health decides to figure itself out. I'll still eat, don't worry, you won't have to bribe me with my caffeine, I'll be good." Usually I'd call bullshit, knowing how much she fought me on eating an actual breakfast nearly every day, but the seriousness in her voice told me otherwise.

Setting the coffee mug down by the sink, I walked over to her and pulled her into my arms. "Are you sure you're fine to pick up a shift like this? The event is tomorrow, are you sure you need this added stress?" Relaxing before a big assignment or mission sounded ideal, so I was very surprised when Angel told me she picked up a shift last minute.

Everything was all prepared and ready to go for tomorrow's event. The vans were packed with the equipment needed, our main plans and backup plans were all sorted and solid; there was nothing else to do but to wait for tomorrow night to come. So, I wasn't wanting to keep her around for anything last minute regarding tomorrow, just worried about her doing too much.

"It's just a half shift to keep my mind off of everything. Trust me, if I sit around the house, the only thing that's gonna happen is that I'm gonna stress myself out more about tomorrow. Also, if I stay around and stress around too much, you might fuck me senseless to where I'm sleeping most of the day away, which would piss me off later because you know how much I hate wasting a day away sleeping or doing nothing too productive." She replied with a long groan and roll of her eyes.

Chuckling softly, I shook my head at her before leaning down and kissing her softly. "You are the strangest woman I've ever met. I've never met or been with anyone who has ever complained about being fucked too much." To be fair, it was a form of distraction I used too often with her.

"Well, not my fault my husband is a fucking sex machine that wears me out completely. As much as I love being screwed stupid by you, *anh*, I can't spend my days bed bound." She never did complain about the quality, just the fact she couldn't do anything but lay around to recover.

The women I've been with in the past—flings nothing long-term—never would have complained about being able to do nothing, especially after a satisfying session in bed. Hell, most of the women I've entertained in the past would have begged to be a stay at home trophy wife, and some did try. So, it surprised and amused me that Angel didn't fall into the mold. She even threatened me on our second day of marriage that if I ever tried to force her out of her career and life then she would cut a limb off—hinting a lot towards my buddy downstairs being the likely victim.

She was a strong and independent woman, and I didn't want to change her. Sure, she was my wife, but not like there were many requirements for her to fulfill there. We had staff around the house, so it wasn't like she had to do those 'wifely' duties. As far as family planning went, we had that sorted out too.

Angel wasn't the traditional mafia wife, and I appreciated that. It was nice to have the option of not keeping her in the dark, to keep her sheltered from the mafia life and the shit that goes on in it. I made the conscious decision to keep things from her though, not wanting to drag her much into the business because she wanted to keep out of it as much as possible.

It was a little difficult to navigate the mafia world with Angel being not so traditional, and not everyone was used to the fact I allowed her to be as involved as I do. Most were still in the notion of women being uninvolved, that they're there to sit pretty and provide support on the sidelines.

I wouldn't mind it if that's what Angel wanted, but she didn't want to play the ignorant and helpless wife.

"*Anh*, I'm going to be late if you don't let me go." Angel whined softly, jabbing at my cheek with her finger. Yes, jab, not poke.

"Think if I keep you long enough then they'd just mark you as a no show?" I grinned sheepishly as I held her tighter in my arms, making her giggle and hit my shoulders playfully.

Grinning softly, I looked down at her lovingly for a moment before patting her bottom playfully. "I'll take you and drop you off at work. I need to head that way because I have business in the city I need to take care of, and I need to swing by the new club too."

Breakfast went by in a blur, and the rest of the time until I could pick Angel up from work went by at a snail's pace.

Mafia life wasn't all knives and bullets like the movies made them out to be. Most of the job consisted of meetings and playing peacekeeper. Well, it could be a lot more violent, but I never liked unnecessary violence. So, I never punched before asking questions; it was also more of Lev's thing.

There haven't been many fights between our bratva and the other mafia groups bordering us, most choosing to keep their head low to avoid our wrath. Those who dared to try their hand often lost it when push came to shove.

The thought of expanding has occurred to me, but I wanted our business to be more stable before we expanded our territory. Eventually I want all of Nespin and the outlying towns under our control, but I want a steady stream of income from our legal and legit businesses in case things went belly side up.

Well, I can easily acquire another good chunk of the city through Angel. Something I still have to talk to her about. Ideally I wanted to wait a while longer before having more territory under my feet, but with how things were going, it would happen sooner than later.

After speaking with her lawyer, Angel found out her father willed everything over to her. So, once she cut her father off life support, it would all go into her hands. Technically, she could do the handover without her father completely out of the picture, but it would be a little messy since her father's wishes only applied upon his death. So, we would have to deal with her stepmother fighting us every step of the way.

Well, that can be a conversation for later. I didn't want to add any more stress to my lovely little wife who looked rather disheveled currently. No matter how immaculate she looked leaving the house, she always came home looking like a trainwreck. A beautiful trainwreck, but a trainwreck nonetheless.

No matter how messy she looked though, I would never stop smiling at the sight of her.

"Hope wherever you're taking us ain't fancy 'cause I look and feel like shit. Pretty sure I have actual shit on me somewhere too." She joked with a tired chuckle as she walked up to me at the nurse's station.

"We can stop by Guilty to clean up." I suggested with a playful smile.

Chuckling, she looked at me knowingly. "Honey, every time we've stopped by Guilty it's never just a quick stop." She replied with a roll of her eyes.

"Hey, you're the one who wanted to see the ropes last time." I reminded her with a soft chuckle, smirking when I saw her face flush.

"Oh shut up, someone will hear you." She scolded me with a small scowl, smacking my arm softly. "Either way, let's go? And can we get something carb heavy? I think I just ran through what I ate earlier and need to reload."

Smiling, I reached out and rubbed her head. "We can get whatever your little heart desires, *lisichka*." Lord knows how cranky she gets if she doesn't get her way with food.

With a giggle, she grabbed my hand and eagerly dragged me out of the hospital. "I'm thinking maybe pasta? Sandwiches? Oooh maybe a nice burger or some Korean street food. Oh man, a cheesy corn dog sounds so amazing right now. Maybe we should just get something heavily fried instead." Angel started to ramble on and on about possible food choices as the two of us made our way to my car parked at the curb.

"You know what, maybe we should just hit the food trucks and—" Her eagerness came to an abrupt stop.

BANG! BANG!

Our bodies instantly ducked to the ground. My hand instinctively grabbed and pulled Angel close to me so that I could use my body as a shield while my other hand drew out my gun from its holster.

If it weren't for the bullets that bounced at our feet, I could have maybe thought the shots weren't aimed at us. Not like these streets were the halls of Heaven, crime happened every now and then, guns included.

"You fucking kidding me..." I grumbled to myself when a van pulled up the curb and onto the sidewalk a few feet from us.

Pulling Angel up, I shoved the keys into her hand and gave her a firm shove towards the car. "Go, I'll cover you." I told her as four men spilled out of the van with guns drawn.

"Go!" I urged, raising the gun and shooting down one of the men. I wasn't going to wait around to be shot at.

The other three were quick to shoot at us in retaliation. But something was off. We were all out on an open sidewalk, none of us ducking for cover—not like there was any—so the enemy should be having an easy time nailing us. Yet, they weren't. Their bullets were barely grazing us.

"Give me your spare, I can take down the other and the driver!" Angel shouted from behind me, tugging at the back of my suit jacket.

"No! Get out of here! I am not risking you getting shot!" I rather take the damn bullets myself than see a scratch on her.

"I'm not leaving you here to face off against that many gunmen!" She argued as I felt her hands patting at my body, most likely looking for my spare piece.

Reaching back, I grabbed her hand, stopping her. "*Lisichka*! For once listen! Get to the damn car, and I'll catch up! It won't take me long to dispose of them." I may be outgunned, but the odds weren't bad—I've been in worse situations.

"But—"

"Angel!" I only had a split second to turn my head to give her my stern look before my attention had to go back to the shooters who had stopped shooting.

Glaring at them, I kept my aim trained on one of them. "Who do you work for and why are you here?" Who dared to try and gun me and Angel down? Who's the fucker with a death wish?

"Drop the gun and come with us, no one has to get hurt." One of the men spoke up. "Both of you."

"You and I both know that's not happening. So, might as well answer my questions and get a swift death rather than a torturous one once I get my hands on you." I narrowed my eyes at the one who spoke, my finger pulling against the trigger of my gun to the point where a slight twitch would set it off.

"Angel. Car. Now." I ordered through gritted teeth, nudging at her with the back of my heel.

A soft shuffle could be heard when Angel started to move, but she stopped dead in her tracks when one of the other men trained his gun on her. "Nah ah, you're not going anywhere *suka*. One more step and I will put a bullet in your pretty little legs."

"Call me a bitch again and I'll cut your tongue out." Angel bit back feistily with a glare. "*Thằng khốn ngu ngốc*." She uttered with a scowl.

"Last warning, put your gun down and come with us. We don't want to hurt you." The guy who spoke before spoke again, turning his gun to Angel while he spoke.

"Don't do it, *anh*. They're bluffing." It was one gamble I was willing to take.

If they wanted to kill us then they could have easily done so by now. They had us outnumbered and outgunned, and they could have easily killed us seconds ago. Clearly they wanted or needed us alive.

Slowly, I released my hand from my gun after flicking the safety on. Holding my hands out in surrender, I glanced over at Angel who looked at me as if I just sprouted a second head.

"I'm going to put my gun down, so don't shoot." I spoke in a slow and calm manner, slowly bending down to set my gun on the ground. "I'm going over to my wife, so don't shoot."

Carefully, I moved over to Angel with my hands in the air. Once I stood next to her, I glanced down at her. "Take the right, I'll take the left. The one in the middle spent his chamber already." The memory was fleeting, but I remember him pulling the trigger a few times only to have nothing come out of it when they shot at us before. Revolvers only held so many bullets. Not the best gun to bring into a fight.

"You are so not getting laid if I get shot by him." She grumbled, holding her hands up in surrender and following my lead as I led the two of us towards the three men.

"Go!"

The two of us moved in a blink of an eye when we were right in front of the men. Our hands shot out and grabbed at their outstretched ones, disarming them easily with a twist of their wrists and a jab to the elbow.

Just as I recalled, the center gunman had an empty one; the distinct clicking could be clearly heard through our little scuffle with the other two. The third started to panic when I turned my attention to him, discarding his empty gun and making a run for the van.

Unfortunately, before I could go after him, another van pulled up behind us. "*Lisichka*! Go! The car!" I threw myself at one of the new men who filed out of the second van, tackling him into another with a grunt.

Out of the corner of my eye, I saw Angel hesitate for a split second, her body jerking towards me before she reluctantly turned around and took off towards my car.

As she ran, another man went after her. He wouldn't get his hands on her though, not while I still breathed.

Getting up, I ran after the man, grabbing the back of his shirt and tackling him to the ground. I kept him pinned to the ground with a knee to his chest before throwing a punch at the man's face, breaking his nose with a sickening crack.

A high pitched scream made my head shoot up towards Angel who ducked to the side and ran erratically to avoid the bullets that flew her way.

Gritting my teeth, I stilled my anger to keep myself from going on a rampage at the men shooting at her.

Stealing the gun from the man below me, I quickly shot at those who had their gun aimed in Angel's direction, taking out two of the four before I was tackled to the ground by three men.

My struggle to throw the men off was cut short with a sharp prick to my neck.

Damn it.

My head grew heavy quickly as my vision faded into darkness. No matter how hard I tried to keep my focus trained on Angel, I couldn't fight the heavy fog as it descended upon me.

At least my little vixen was safe. I faintly remember seeing her body disappear around the car before I blacked out completely.

Chapter 41

Nikolai

MY BODY FELT SO heavy, as if a sack of bricks sat on top of me. I had no idea how long I was out, and the dark place I woke up in didn't have a window for me to gauge the time of day. The only light in the place was a flickering overhead lamp which dimly lit the place enough for me to make out my small concrete prison.

Groaning, I twist my groggy body into a sitting position. Any hope I had of breaking my restraints disappeared when I felt and heard the heavy chains clink with my movements. My hands were bound behind my back, and there were shackles around my ankles.

Whoever wanted me really didn't want me to escape. They weren't even giving me a sliver of a chance. *"Blyat'."* I would have to wait for my captor to show up, see what they wanted, and try to talk my way out of this shit hole. Or at the very least, bide my time until help came.

It didn't feel long until the sound of a heavy door creaking open snapped me out of limbo, but I couldn't precisely gauged the amount of time I had zoned out because the lack of a clock.

I couldn't help but curse at the unwelcomed sight of Ivan and his children. *"Ty chertov ublyudok."* I highly doubted they were here to save me.

With a soft shake of his head, and a few 'tut tut tut' of his tongue, Ivan looked at me arrogantly. "Your mother should have taught you better. Such a mouth on you, don't know if I want that near my dear Natalia." Ivan spoke down to me like some parent scolding their child, which pissed me off.

"Well you'll never have to worry about that because I'll never go near her." Even if I wasn't married to Angel, I wouldn't touch his daughter with a hundred foot pole, and that's being generous. This woman was a damn grenade.

"That's a rude way to talk about your future wife." Igor scoffed with a twisted smirk, introducing his foot to my stomach harshly.

A sharp, wheezing cough squeezed at my throat from getting the wind knocked out of me. "*Idi na khuy*!" I squeezed out through my coughing fit. glaring up at Igor who still looked down at me with a stupid arrogant smirk like his father.

Gritting my teeth, I glared up at Igor who stared down at me with a stupid, arrogant smirk like his father.

After catching my breath, I let my face twist with a dark smirk which made me look a little crazy. "Take these fucking chains off, then we'll see whose smiling." My words made his tough guy image falter briefly before another kick was sent into my gut.

The feeling of Natalia's hands on my face sent shivers—the bad kind—down my spine. "Stop it Igor! Just give him a chance." I think I'd rather get kicked again ten times over than have her hands on me. "Kolyenka, you don't have to pretend with that little halfling chink anymore, you can finally leave her, belong to me like how it's supposed to be like our fathers wanted. We can overtake the triad, together. You don't need some sham of a marriage to dig your nails into triad territory to pluck it."

Disgusted, I jerked my head out of her hands with a nasty scowl. "Do not call me that, you have no right to it. I'm not the one here who has to get their head out of their ass. I don't give half of a fucking shit what our fathers agreed upon *if* they even did. It was their business between them, and I carried nothing on of my father's business." He was only tied to the bratva now by name.

I had to burn down the bratva my father built and ran with an iron fist and rebuild from a speck of dust. The network I had came from my own blood, sweat, and tears. Everyone all but up and left the moment they heard news of my father's death. Fear kept them hanging around my father's arms, and the moment the threat was gone, they all scattered like rats.

Old business partners slowly crawled out of the woodworks after hearing about the changes under my rule. They respected the fact I wouldn't twist their arm behind their backs and force their cooperation.

Yes, I was well aware my allies could turn on me, but they knew better. The Volkov Bratva remained ruthless and brutal, but we were also more sophisticated than my father. Sadly, the few who mistook my generosity for weakness and tested me learned the hard way.

Word on the street before our reform was that we were a pack of rabid and feral dogs, which was an accurate description of how things were when my father was the Pakhan. Now though, we were known as a deadly pack of wolves, rightfully so. We were strategic with our movements and actions, patient with the hunt. We had order and controlled chaos.

My father always lashed out at the slightest insolence, creating more trouble than necessary. I, on the other hand, struck with deadly precision and only when necessary. With every snake there is a head. Attacking the body without taking out the head does nothing, something my father never seemed to care about as long as he got his dose of bloodshed.

Striking down the right targets made it clear to my enemies and allies that I wasn't one to be trifled with, that I knew the game and how to play it very well. I didn't fuck around like my father; I didn't let greed and power rule and motivate me. I had a straight head and a working brain, that's what made me dangerous to everyone else. They allied themselves with me because they rather me a friend than a foe.

If anyone ever ended up on the wrong end of my gun then it was on them, and everyone knew it. Anyone and everyone I've targeted and killed brought it upon themselves.

Just like how Ivan here deserved a death fitting of his betrayal, and Igor for his insolence. When my wife and brothers come for me, I'll be sure to make the father and son pay for all of this.

"I don't know what lies and shit your father has filled your little brain with, but I will never marry you." I would never wed any woman after Angel, even if I were to become a widow in the next hour, I would never remarry.

My answer and thought process might have been different before meeting Angel, but I became a changed man ever since I agreed to be betrothed to my lovely bride.

There was no one else in the world I wanted to be with than Angel. *My* Angel. I'll never love anyone else. Hell, I never wanted to feel anything for anyone until Angel. I'd already resigned myself to the single life after getting in deep with the bratva. I didn't have time to date, just flings here and there. I couldn't let anyone close in this profession, and I was fine with that. Taking on a partner meant exposing myself, giving my enemy a weakness I couldn't fully cover and control.

I didn't care much for an heir to this empire. I had planned on giving it to whoever I deemed acceptable amongst my men or any of my nephews and nieces if my brothers were to ever have children of their own. I already had enough of a headache dealing with the bratva, and the thought of tossing my own children into the mix was overwhelming.

Sure, I could be an absent father and let my wife raise the children on her own and force one of them to take over, but I didn't want to be that kind of father. I didn't want my own children to grow up distant from me, or God forbid grow up to resent me.

Besides all of that, finding the right partner was a feat in itself. Marrying for the sake of the business—to form new ties and expand—always irked me. Yes, it could be a necessary evil of the mafia game, but I refused to partake in it because of what happened with my sister. She was carted off to some pig for the sake of expansion and making new ties for the bratva by my father, and she ended up dead in a ditch in Russia after months of abuse.

I would never raise my hand against a woman ever, let alone my own spouse. I also didn't want to take away a person's choice in a partner by forcing them into an arranged marriage. Sure, most people in this life accept a facet of it; most people accept there are parts which are out of their control.

Still, if it were anyone but Angel, I would have denied the marriage. What I did with Angel was a little selfish on my end, but I wanted her so badly I wouldn't let her slip.

Sighing disappointedly, Ivan slowly shook his head at me. "Nikolai, be reasonable. This is the only chance you'll get to get out of here peacefully."

The nerve Ivan had right now astounded me. "The triad is nothing, they will be nothing. Join me and we'll have all of the city under my thumb. With your forces and mine, we'll be unstoppable. The whole underground market will be ours! The triad will belong to me as well soon enough. Come on Nikolai, you know better than to turn down a good deal when you see one. Just give up that little play thing of yours and do what's needed and right."

"Even if I wasn't married, I still wouldn't agree to one between me and your daughter. I don't do business with people who traffic humans." He was lucky I hadn't cut things off with him yet because we couldn't risk losing track of him if he fled. Once I got the all clear from Dmitri though, all bets were off.

Laughing like the little delusional psychopath he was, he replied, "That's hilarious that you have a moral compass being the Pakhan of one of the biggest bratvas here and in Moscow. You won't be too bothered by it once you see how much net it brings us." He sounded convinced of my allegiance with him, a grand delusion.

With a firm scowl, I narrowed my eyes at him. "I am not leaving my wife and marrying your spawn." Even if I was held at gunpoint, I would never.

"You want to stay with your cheating wife?" The uptick in Ivan's voice made it hard to read his smug face.

Angel would never do such a thing. Scoffing in disbelief, I faintly rolled my eyes at him. "Of all the lies that you conjure up, you go with the least believable?" But the seed of the doubt was sowed.

"You've never found it odd how well she got along with your little brother? The doctor, Alexei I believe." Ivan continued to speak with a smug smirk on his face which made him hard to read. I couldn't tell if he lied or not with the glint in his eyes. He wanted to hurt me. The malice in his eyes was clear.

I couldn't believe him though, he made lies to try and stir a reaction from me. Angel was faithful. She would never have an affair with my own damn brother. No matter how well they got along, it was because they worked in the same field and could easily relate to each other. There was no attraction between them, not even the faintest spark existed.

Keeping my lips tightly pressed together, I kept my hard glare trained on Ivan, watching as he pulled out a phone and tapped at it a few times.

There was a sound akin to shuffling clothes along with a soft grunt before Angel's voice could be heard through the phone. "Alexei, just shut up and do it, just put it in—oh fuck! God damn it, a warning next time?! Fuck!" There was a sharp gasp and a deep groan that followed, one I knew well.

A deeper voice chuckled, "And have you tense up? It's better that I just did it. It's in now, so you're welcome." It was Alexei's voice, I'd recognize his jovial tone anywhere.

"Fucking hell, I swear, never doing this again." Angel breathed heavily as the sound of shuffling could be heard again.

"Angel, that's what you said the other four times. Yet I still get a call from you. Now relax and let me work it." Alexei replied with a soft chuckle.

Angel groaned for a good moment before speaking again, "And that's why you're the best and I love you. Oh right there, a little deeper, fuck." There was a pause, a muted smack filled the brief silence before a groan—not Angel's or Alexei's—could be heard. "We are so not telling Kolya about this."

"Don't make this a common thing and he'll never find out. I'm surprised he hasn't yet." There was a brief chuckle and sharp intake of breath from Alexei before the recording ended.

"Guess your little wife is spreading her legs for more than just you. Can't deny hard evidence, you just heard it loud and clear." Igor sounded like he had too much fun rubbing it in my face. I should have clocked him that night at my club when I had the chance.

"It's okay, I can make you forget all about them." Natalia's sickly sweet voice whispered in my ear, making me cringe away.

No. No way.

Every fiber of my being denied it—Angel and Alexei together. At the very least, my own brother wouldn't do that to me, especially Alexei.

Maybe the voice was altered? But no, names were used, and unless it was one hell of a coincidence that the names just happened to be my wife and brother's, it was them. There wasn't that underlying buzz that came with altered voices, and I knew too well how my family sounded.

"Kolyenka." Natalia settled her hand on my heaving chest, pulling a deep scowl from me. "I'm sorry."

Jerking myself away from her with a scowl, I glared at her. "I told you, don't call me that." It didn't sound sweet like it did coming from Angel's lips. If anything, it was akin to nails on a chalkboard.

"Where the hell did you even get such a recording? It could be faked for all I know." My eyes drifted over to Ivan who still held the phone in his hand.

Ivan's cocky voice made me want to roll my eyes at him. "I have men everywhere. You're too soft unlike your father. You trust your men too much. You could benefit from learning from me, you know?" Was that true? Did I have another mole? I'd thoroughly vetted through my men again, each and every single one of them, after the little office incident a while back. Everyone was solid.

Was the house bugged?

"Who?" The underlying anger to my voice surprised me slightly when I heard how controlled it came out.

"Big guy, always around your little thing, Benjamin. You really have to be more generous with your money, all I had to do was offer higher than your pay and he was putty in my hands." The moment I heard the name slip from his mouth, my anger ebbed, but I kept the act up to deter him from prodding.

I still had my doubts, but there had to be something else going on because Benjamin would have informed me of any infidelity instantly. He was my most trusted guard, and he was also one of my closest friends. We've been through a lot of shit together, and I trusted him as much as I did my own brothers. So, there had to be something else going on.

Keeping my expression calm, I leered up at Ivan, "So, you just came here to rub it in my face and see if I'll go back on my own morals and form an alliance with you?" I deadpanned.

"If you want to see it that way, I suppose. But all I'm really doing is offering you a chance at something greater. Come on Nikolai, think about it, really think about it." Ivan urged with a widening smirk.

"And if I say no?" I already knew what my answer would be, but I was curious.

Ivan replied to me nonchalantly, "Then we just leave you here for your fate to be decided in the auction tomorrow. A lot of men out there want you as their bitch or dead. At least with me you'll have some rank. It's a no brainer, Nikolai." If I didn't know any better, then yes, it would have been that simple of a solution.

"What were you planning on doing with Angel? The men who captured me wanted to capture Angel as well. Why did you want her? What use do you have for her if it's my allegiance that you want?" It didn't occur to me until now when my brain was fully awake.

"Her stepmother wanted her, I don't meddle with Lady Qing's business, but she wanted my men to take the girl along with you, and said your little *suka* was to belong to me after she was done with her. I don't care about her and her plans, Lady Qing has already promised me the triad territory once the marriage between her daughter and Nikita goes through. I was just going to give your used goods to Igor since he's still hung over on her and has some anger to take out on her." Ivan gave a small shrug of his shoulders when he finished speaking. Then, he turned around and headed for the door.

Gritting my teeth, I tugged at the chains, jerking my limbs in hopes of slipping out of my bindings by some miracle. "If any of you touch a hair on my Angel's body, I will skin you alive and toss you in boiling acid." A threat I would make good on if any harm came to my wife from them. I didn't buy their revelation about Angel and Alexei.

I can't. I won't.

Opening the door, he stood there and turned his head back at me. "I'll give you some time to think about my offer. There's still a good amount of time before the auction starts. I'll leave you to your own devices and hope you give me the right answer when I come back later." With that, he left with Igor on his tail.

Unfortunately, Natalia remained, and I did not have a good feeling about this.

Chapter 42

Angel

THE AMOUNT OF CONTROL I had to exert to keep myself from chasing Nikolai down after finding his location was something I didn't think was possible for me. My husband was out there, being held in some warehouse a half-hour drive away. It would have been simple to throw together a rescue team and charge in, and I wanted to do that, but Stepan advised against it.

If it weren't for Benjamin's assurance that Nikolai would be safe for the time being, then I would have disregarded Stepan's advice to stay put. The event was too close, and we'd put in too much preparation and planning into it for it to be half assed. Stepan was confident Nikolai's kidnapping and my attempted kidnapping were connected to the event. So, the fact one of us got away meant I needed to ensure the plan was carried out successfully.

I still wanted to shove it all back into Stepan's face because I wouldn't let my husband sit in limbo. Who knows what's happening to him there. Being kidnapped and held at a mafia owned warehouse was never a good thing; you either left there dead, in pieces, or broken.

Benjamin assured me Nikolai's life was safe because Ivan had no plans on killing off his future son-in-law. Ivan refused to divulge further when Benjamin pressed about his plans, only ever assuring Nikolai's life, for now. I also didn't want Benjamin pushing too much and risk being made. We never planned for Benjamin to be our mole with Ivan, but when Benjamin came to Nikolai about how Ivan offered him a job, we decided to take the opportunity to plant our own man who we knew would remain completely loyal to us.

Breathing deeply, I rubbed my temples to ease away the headache that squeezed at my brain.

Please be fine, please be alive out there.

The blinking red dot on the map did nothing to ease my worries. It didn't matter that we had a location; the little chip in his ring could only give us a location, not proof of life. He could be dead in a body bag or six-feet underground for all I knew. This stupid red dot could be pinpointing his last known location too if they figured out his ring had a locator chip in it and tossed it.

Yes, I chipped my husband, but he chipped me. So, it was a fair exchange. Besides, not like I cared for him tracking my location, I've nothing to hide from him. The only thing he'd see were my trips to and from work and me around the house ninety-percent of the time. On the other hand, in cases like this where one of us gets yanked randomly off the street, at least the other could locate them. I really didn't give a shit, and neither did Nikolai when I told him I wanted to track his ass too.

"Ange." I sucked in a deep breath when I felt a hand on my shoulder. "We'll get him back." Hanna assured me with a soft smile and squeeze. "Nikolai's tough, he's not going to let himself get killed that easily."

"Well, not much he can do if he's incapacitated." I was being pessimistic, but it was easier to think of the bad than to give myself false hope by thinking of the positives. Last thing I wanted was to believe he was alive and be crushed when I'd find his lifeless body.

Sighing, Hanna reached over, locked my phone, and pocketed it. "Stop, you can't be distracted right now. We'll save Nikolai, let Benjamin and Timothy handle it, they're more than capable. You need to focus on the mission tonight. You need to show the others that you are capable of stepping up to run the business in Nikolai's absence."

"Fucking hell. How did I get roped into this shit. Is it so hard to ask for a perfect man with no strings attached?" I joked with a dry chuckle. "Fuck man." I sighed frustratedly.

His brothers and men trusted me because I was Nikolai's wife, but it was clear they respected his authority more than they did me. They respected—more like tolerated—me because of Nikolai. Granted, some of the men, like Benjamin and Timothy, have come to respect me as my own person. Still, a lot of them were partial towards Nikolai.

I could see the reluctance amongst the men when they showed up for the mission at the estate and it was announced I was in charge during Nikolai's absence. No one complained or spoke out, but I could see their wariness.

"You got this, I believe in you. I know you hate being in charge, but you got this in the bag. Just think of it as another shitty ED shift." At least Hanna's attempts at easing me started to work from the smile I cracked. "You've had a rough day and a half, so worry about one less thing."

Saying it's been rough was a very gross understatement. I couldn't sleep at all last night because I became too worried about Nikolai. Alexei had to sedate me, much against my wishes. I've been basically kept prisoner inside the estate for everyone's sake because I've been trying to make a break for Nikolai the moment I woke.

Then, I got a little cherry on top of this fucked up sundae. The heavy, clunky, extravagant, jade dragon ring served as a suffocating reminder around my left index finger—even though it was a few sizes too big.

Sighing, I asked for an update, "How's everyone taking the news?" There would be push back, a lot of push back.

"Well, the last report I got from our men is that those who didn't default are being rounded up, no deaths yet." Hanna reported after checking her phone.

"Good. And I'm assuming everyone knows of the change at this point?" It's been a few hours since news of my role had been made, and shit spread like wildfire in triad territory.

Fuck. I can't believe it's been a few hours since I signed my father's life away.

I wanted to wait until Nikolai was back so he'd be by my side for support when I would end my father's life support. However, I couldn't wait when I received word about Lady Qing trying to move everything she could and pull what strings she had left. She got desperate, and I had to stop her before she made too big of a mess.

I'd already lost a quarter of triad territory because of her, and if I didn't act when I did then it would have been over half the territory. I'd deal with everything later once I let Nikolai know about the merge.

It just sucked that I would dump this all onto him right after saving his ass. *'Hey love, great to see you alive, oh here's another quarter of the city for you to rule, good luck!'* Granted I would help him somewhat, it would just be a dick move to just dump and bail.

"Well, it's nearing the time. Let's regroup one last time before we head out." Hanna suggested with a few pats of my shoulder.

Well, guess I had no choice in the matter because Bao called for me as well. "Angel! Your husband's for sale!" Well, those were words I'd never thought I'd hear in my life.

With a sigh, I left the office with Hanna and went back to the living room where everyone gathered around. "Bao, I'm really hoping that I misheard you very badly." Honestly, half my mind was barely present, so maybe, just maybe.

Pushing his glasses up, Bao turned his laptop around, showing me the screen. It was messed up. The screen displayed what looked like a shopping catalog, only instead of actual items of clothing or physical goods, it was humans with Nikolai right at the very top.

"Sneak peek of tonight's goods." I read the title of the page with a disgusted scowl.

Nikolai looked scuffed up, disheveled, his clothing untucked and visibly dirty. At least he was still dressed unlike the other people who were displayed in nothing but their underwear or torn clothing that did little to nothing to hide their body.

"If they're going to put him in the auction then that means he's going to be moved from the warehouse he's being kept at." I noted out loud, chewing my bottom lip softly as I pulled my phone out from Hanna's back pocket.

Pulling the tracking app back up, I watched the moving red dot. "They're moving him already." I said while showing everyone my phone.

"What are you thinking?" Hanna asked with a quizzical look. "You have that look on your face, so spit it out." She knew me too well.

"Slight change of plans." Was it a stupid change? Maybe, but I might as well make my fucking name known if I can't escape the mafia life. "The teams will remain the same save for one change. I won't be heading Team Alpha, Benjamin will."

Everyone looked at me with wide eyes, probably wondering if I stroked out. "I'm going in. I want and need to lay my own eyes on Kolya myself. I'm going to stir up some shit as well. It's time that my dear ol' stepmother knows clearly that she has lost. Also, I think it's about time everyone knows who's the new head in charge." And that I am not one to be fucked with.

Looking over at Hanna with a smirk, "Hanna, call our boys and tell them to grab Lady Qing's children before they meet up with us at The Catacombs."

"What are you going to do with them?" Hanna gave me a wary look as she pulled out her phone to do what I told her.

"Leverage. At least she somewhat cares about her pathetic kids, especially her damn son. I just need them to ensure she complies with me." I had no beef with my step siblings, at the moment. We left each other alone for the most part, avoiding each other unless necessary, and we acted mostly civil towards each other.

It was just Lady Qing I had bones to pick with today. I disliked my step siblings because they were insufferable, but they were raised by a monster of a mother. So, I couldn't hold it against them... Much.

"I'm not going to hurt them, I'm not that much of a psychopath." At least tonight I wouldn't unless they interfered with my plans.

"Bao, can you hack their network and falsify an entry for me?" Yes, I planned on waltzing right in. No one there should recognize me. From the roster Bao pulled up, all the guards who worked the event were new and wouldn't know me unless Lady Qing had put out a bulletin on me, which she didn't because she was too arrogant for her own good.

"Yeah, child's play." Bao replied, turning his laptop back around and typing away at it.

"Are you sure this is a good idea? Someone could easily make you and that would just be messy." Stepan spoke up with a concerned voice.

"No one will make me, and I'm not just saying that because I'm being a cocky bitch but because it's true. No one there knows me well enough to blow things up besides Lady Qing. To others, I am just the head's little princess, the clueless and harmless little princess." My father kept me hidden enough so I flew under everyone's radar.

No one, not even my stepmother, knew the extent of the damage I could inflict. They only see and know the act I put up because that's what I wanted. I wanted them all to underestimate me. If people didn't see me as a threat then they'd drop their guard enough for me to strike when the moment was right.

"I don't like it, but I have a feeling you weren't making a suggestion." At least Stepan knew when to throw in the towel.

"Stepan, can you, Greg, and Arseny do one last check to make sure everything is accounted for? I'm going to change into something more appropriate." Barging in wearing full tactical gear to a formal event was probably a bad way to draw attention to myself.

Stepan nodded in response with a soft hum. "We'll handle it, go get ready." Stepan replied with a half convinced smile.

After rushing upstairs, I stripped myself of my tactical gear and threw on a navy blue evening gown with a sweetheart neckline, ruching around the waist with a drop down length that ended at my feet, and the high slit ran up to my mid-thigh did little to hide the garter belt that wrapped around my leg. My gun remained strapped to the right side with a thigh holster, and the left hid a knife on my inner thigh.

The last weapon lay hidden in my bun. The golden hairpin kept my silky locks up in a bun with the ends of my hair falling naturally down the length of my back. A gift from my father that I've never felt the need to use. The golden hairpin was carefully crafted to hide a switchblade in it at my father's request when he commissioned it.

It was a lovely gift, and I really did love and appreciate it. Just a shame I have little to no use for it. I couldn't use it every day at work. Carrying around an expensive hairpin that patients could easily rip out and turn against me wasn't ideal. I couldn't use it out on assignments either because it could easily be tracked back to me. So, the pin had been sitting in its box collecting dust.

Well, at least it would see some use today.

I couldn't help but let out a little laugh as I traced the intricate pattern of the wings on the hairpin. My parents really danced around the whole angel idea as much as they could.

My mother always told me she named me Angel because the moment she held me in her arms for the first time she knew that's what I was, an angel. My mother would probably be shaking her head in shame and digging herself deeper into her grave if she saw how I turned out.

I am the furthest thing from an angel, or anything holy and good for that matter.

If only they could see me now.

Chapter 43

Nikolai

"Ohmpf!" The pained grunt caught my cough when my body hunched over from the kick to my stomach.

"Oi! They said to not damage the goods. He still needs to be alive and relatively unharmed. No one wants a beat up body." One of the guards assigned to me scolded the one who kicked me.

"No one will notice that, he's just being a baby. I didn't even kick him that hard." The other guard argued back with a scowl. "Hope whoever buys him tosses him in the cage."

"Oh please, that'd be a waste. As fun as it would be to beat him to death, it'd be more beneficial to have a bratva boss under your thumb than have him dead after a short burst of entertainment." The first guard wasn't exactly putting any ease in me.

It was unclear whether I would make it out of this night alive or not. I'd signed my uncertain end the moment I refused Ivan's horrendous offer again a little while ago. Even if I still questioned the loyalties of my wife and brother, I wouldn't hand over my bratva to him and have him drag it through the fires of hell and ruin all I've built and fixed.

What would happen next was unclear. All I knew was that I would partake—very unwillingly—in this stupid black market auction. Like hell I would let some fat politician pull my strings. I was going to rain hellfire on everyone the moment these chains came loose.

There was a brief period of travel from where I was being held to—what I assumed to be—The Catacombs, where I was tossed into another cage along with some other people who were fortunate enough to not be bound up.

"*Nyet!*"

My body moved on its own in response to the distressed cry. The sudden impact of my body against another jarred me enough to realize what I had done.

One of the guards made a grab at one of the girls—who did not look legal—and I had body slammed him out of instinct when I heard her cry.

Looking over to the sobbing girl, I gave her a once over to make sure she was fine as I twisted my body back upright. "*Ty v poryadke?*" I asked in a concerned voice.

The girl looked at me with grateful eyes, nodding in response before letting out a shriek when I was tackled over onto the ground with a grunt.

"You're in no position to play hero, bratva scum." I could feel cold metal digging into my side along with the scathing voice of a guard.

"Hey! Put your damn piece away! You know what Lady Qing's orders are. She's already not happy with how scuffed up he looks, don't make it worse. Just forget the bitch, she's not worth the trouble right now, or go to a different cage." Another guard scolded the one who attacked me, pulling him off and shoving him away from me.

With a scowl, the guard who attacked me gave my midsection a firm kick and spat on my face before trudging off to a different caged area. "You're all going to pay for this." I seethed through gritted teeth, glaring at the other guard who had a new victim by her hair. I couldn't do anything to save her because she was in a different area, which made the rage boil in me.

Warily, the girl I saved crawled over to me and slowly wiped the spit off my face with her ratted up sleeve. Whether she knew English or not was unknown to me, but she spoke to me in Russian. "You're with the bratva?" The girl sounded scared, not like I could blame her.

Switching to my native tongue was an easy feat. "Yes, but I won't hurt you. I'll get you all out of here and back home." The strike was tonight, so I had to hang on until the calvary got here.

"No, I don't want to go back home. Please don't send me back home, they'll just sell me again." Another girl spoke frantically, drawing my attention to her by scurrying backwards into the wall.

"Then you won't go home. Those who do want to go home will be provided a safe means of return, but those who want to remain to make a life here will receive the proper help as well." It would be a huge mess, but I rather go through the trouble and make sure these people don't end up in the same situation again. Immigration and papers were going to be a bitch to work with, but I would rather them remain than to send them back to their captors and sellers.

"How are you going to save us if you're stuck here with us? Why are you even helping us?" The girl who wiped my face asked with a frown. "You're with the bratva, so why?"

Looking at the guards, I could see they paid no attention to us. So, I responded in a hushed voice, "We're not all bad." Ironic given the illegal nature of our business. "My people are coming, so we just have to survive until they breach. As for why I'm helping, it's because I don't condone human trafficking or anything of that nature. It's also just the right thing to do." Again, hilarious coming from me. Talking about what's right or wrong being in the position that I am, how ironic.

Sitting back on my hunches, I looked around the area, counting the number of guards, noting their positions and equipment, comfort habits to try and control what I could of the situation.

I assumed this to be the holding area, considering the amount of cages and people in them. The cages weren't big, each section being maybe around 20x20 with multiple people crammed in.

Leaning against the cage door, I eased my weight into it, listening to the hinges creak and feeling the slight give.

If my hands and ankles weren't bound then I could do it. Bust the door down, steal a guard's gun, shoot my way out. If they were under orders not to harm the prisoners then I should be safe, in theory.

As tempting as the idea of escape was, it wasn't feasible the more I thought about it. I had no idea how the situation was beyond the hallway into the main area. So, unfortunately, I had to bide my time and wait for a rescue at the very least. If no one reached me in time, I would figure out another means to escape my buyer once I was taken off the property. If I was tossed in this cage match though, well, I didn't want to think about that.

Frustrated, I let out a small huff, letting my head fall back against the bars of the cage and stared up at the cement ceiling.

Staring off into space, I let my mind wander to the potential lies Ivan had fed me for hours. I couldn't get it out of my mind no matter how hard I tried. Deep down I knew it was all bullshit.

Was our marriage perfect? No, but no marriage was ever truly perfect with no faults. We were still learning the curves together, petty arguments here and there, but all together we loved each other through it all.

But what if?

I couldn't lie to myself and deny the fact Angel and Alexei got along well; those two clicked like two peas in a pod. It was the fact their friendship came so naturally that had my doubts rearing its ugly head. There were times when I wished Angel and I could get along swimmingly like she did with Alexei. I can't help but think if I gave her the choice then would she choose Alexei over me without a second thought?

Goosebumps erupted over my body when I felt the sickly cold touch of a snake. I didn't even have to look to know who touched me. "Rethinking your decision yet Kolyenka?" Her voice still sounded like nails on a chalkboard too.

"I don't know whether to cut your tongue out myself or let my wife do it." I would gladly make an exception to my rule of not hurting women for Natalia. After she tried—and failed—to force herself on me before, I would have no qualms about teaching her some basic manners through violence.

"What does she have over me, hm? She's just a stupid little nurse who's way over her head. She's probably gone and ran off with your little brother at this point after you've been missing a whole day and a half. Why can't you just see reason and divorce her and be with me where we can rule papa's kingdom together in the years to come?" I started to wonder if this crazy bitch had problems with her two little brain cells.

Scowling with gritted teeth, I glared harshly at her. "*My wife* is and will always be a hundred times better than you in every aspect, and at this point, I'd be more worried about what she's going to do to you once she gets her hands on you. I may be a cold hearted killer, but she's got a sadistic streak a thousand miles longer than mine."

Why am I even wasting my breath on her?

Gripping my face, she dug her nails into me. "Last chance. Join us." Sometimes being stubborn was a bad thing. It was cute with Angel, but Natalia made it annoying.

"*Nyet.*" I replied firmly with a glare, scooting myself away from her hand idled in the air through the bars.

My answer didn't please her, and the rough yank of my head against the metal bars as she walked away made it clear.

Damn that bitch.

My fucking head rang from the impact.

"Your wife sounds scary." The same girl from before spoke again in Russian.

Chuckling softly, I shook my head, "She can be, yes, but only to those deserving. Her moral compass is better than mine, but her mean streak is definitely worse than mine. I'm a killer, I won't deny it, but with me people know that they will die. My lovely wife on the other hand, you'll never know with her. Scary or not though, she's not bad, otherwise I wouldn't have fallen in love with her." Even with the doubts in my mind, admitting my love for her came out naturally without an ounce of hesitation.

The thought of waking up next to her soft face, seeing her cheeky little smile, hearing her obnoxiously cheerful laugh, feeling her soft skin beneath my rough hands, and to be able to look into those warm eyes of her to see the adoration and love that reflected my own were the only thoughts keeping me anchored through this ordeal. Those thoughts were my only motivation to make it out of here alive.

God I'd give anything to see her lovely face again. I want to see that uncontrollable smile of hers whenever I'd hold her face before leaning in for a kiss. That genuine smile whenever she looked at me was contagious to where I often found myself smiling like some teenage goofball.

"You must really love her. You're smiling so real, and you look like how my dad looks at my mom." If this kid could see it then I have it worse for Angel than I thought. Not that I complained because what's there to not love about her?

It felt like forever and not when time for the event came. People in the cages were slowly pulled at random once the event was in its midst. This was so fucked up, selling people like cattle. It took a good chunk of my strength to keep myself contained as I watched the guards pull out whoever would be next.

By the time half the people in the cages were gone, it was my turn. It took two guards to drag me out of the cage, and another four escorted me to the main area where I was shoved onto a stage with Lady Qing looking down at me with a sick smile.

My eyes roamed the crowd below, glaring harshly at each and every single person there. They were all going to regret this, and I would make damn sure of it.

"Ladies and gentleman, the prize of the night. I'm sure many of you are acquainted with this *lovely* man here, or at least know of him and his true business. How nice would it be to have all his means at your disposal? To have the Pakhan of the Volkov Bratva under your thumb." Lady Qing's voice echoed throughout the open room with the help of the microphone.

Her voice droned on for a while as she advertised me like some piece of damn meat. I paid no attention to any of it after a small while, her words zoned out completely. My full focus shifted away from everything though in a split second.

For a moment, I thought my eyes were playing tricks on me, that my lack of sleep finally caused me to hallucinate my desire.

Relief filled me for a second before disbelief and anger replaced it. *What the fuck is she doing here!? Alone! Dressed like that too!*

The damn fucker who ogled her would get stabbed if he didn't look away in the next second. I'll make sure it happens. I don't care if I'm chained up, I'll hold a knife between my teeth if I have to.

My eyes followed Angel as she moved graciously behind the large crowd of people, hanging around the shadows and keeping herself obscure as possible. I couldn't help the jealousy boiling in my blood when I watched her lightly brush her hand across an old man's shoulder, smiling flirtatiously and looping her arm around his to turn his body to use as a shield from Lady's Qing's gaze.

Fuck she looked lovely though. I only wished it were my arm around her waist right now instead of that old fart's. The blue stood out so well with her fair skin and made her look like damn royalty.

A swell of pride puffed at my chest as I kept my eyes trained on her. That was my wife. *My wife*. That drop dead vixen was all mine. That proud queen who radiated a deadly aura of power was *my lovely wife*.

I was going to bend her over and take her in that dress after we got out of this shit show. It would look so lovely pooled around her waist while I pound her from behind. Her pretty ass would be marred with my handprints, and possibly some blood from the bastard who slipped his hand down to cup a feel of her bubbly ass. His hands would be the first thing I take from him before I end his life.

In a blink of an eye, I lost her. Panic stripped away the pride as my eyes frantically searched the crowd for my salvation.

Shit, did I really just hallucinate her?!

No, I might be losing it, but I couldn't be that far gone. She's here, somewhere out there.

"Three million, going once. Going twice." Before Lady Qing could end the bid, her body went rigid.

Chapter 44

Nikolai

Smirking, I looked up at Lady Qing, "What? See a ghost?"

Was it a smart idea to poke at my captor? No, probably not, but I couldn't help it. I regretted it though because she proceeded to jab me with a taser. *"Blyat'!"* I hissed under my breath as my muscles ached from the convulsions of the shock.

"You're lucky I'm not tossing you into the cage." Lady Qing seethed with a glare before kicking me off the stage with her heeled foot.

The hard landing knocked the wind out of me when I landed on my back with a pained grunt. I didn't need to say anything to Lady Qing as I glared up at her. She won't get away with this, her days were numbered.

"Do you want him in holding or what do you want to do with him?" Lady Qing's eyes were looking elsewhere, probably my buyer if I had to guess.

Twisting my body upright, I sat on my knees and looked out at the crowd with narrowed eyes, stopping on the man who replied to Lady Qing. "You know, he's been giving me and my family a lot of grief, and I think it's time he gets a taste of his own medicine."

"You're going to regret this later Liam." I recognized the man who won the bid. He was a known politician who did business with the bratva, mainly smuggling drugs and stolen goods, but there was the occasional hit against his opponents when he ran for office. He got all he asked for, but he hadn't been keen on keeping up with the payments. So, I've been sending some of my men to shake him down for what was owed.

"No, I'm not. The only person with regrets between us is going to be you for not leaving me be." Of course he wouldn't admit his own fault with our situation. "Not like it'll matter now because you're my bitch now."

Chuckling amusingly, I shook my head at him, "That's where you're wrong because I am no one's bitch. You think I give a shit that you won that stupid bid? You don't control me, and you won't. I am not going to listen to you and your stupid demands. If you think that buying me will let you control my bratva then you've got a rude awakening coming for you."

At least he'll be easy to kill once I get the opportunity. No way a vermin like him could keep me under his thumb, not in the slightest. If I don't manage an escape then the others would bust me out sooner than later. I doubt it would come to any of that though unless I were to be removed from the premises somehow before the raid tonight happened.

"We'll see if that's still your tone with me once I have your wife under me." That cocky grin of his rubbed me the wrong way with his words. "Cute little thing, maybe I'll just keep her as my personal little nurse."

Gritting my teeth, I swallowed the anger bubbling at my throat. "She's not going to give into your demands." I couldn't help the scowl from forming on my face.

"She will when I have a gun to your head." He seemed so damn sure of himself, and that really ground my gears the wrong way. Angel wouldn't let anything bad happen to me, and we both knew if it came to such a situation then the risk wasn't worth it. Angel would give into his demands if my life were on the line, and it would be the same vice versa.

Although, I held out on his threat because even if he did hold a gun to my head, I doubt he'd pull the trigger. If he wanted control of the bratva then he would have to keep me alive. It wouldn't matter if I implemented him as the head of the bratva, no one would listen to him. The moment he kills me, everyone would turn on him. So, my life was of much importance. Surely Angel would be able to pick up on it and not give into any demands from the corrupted politician if push came to shove.

"Unless she doesn't give a shit about you. I mean, she's got options." Okay, this fucker is going to have a bullet through his brain the moment I get my hands on a gun, after I've removed some limbs.

"Either way, I hope you have some people who can rough him up a bit, Lady Qing. It'd be nice for him to get a beating before I take him back. Maybe he'll change his mind about listening to his new owner after getting a few bones broken." Of course he would have others do his dirty work for him while he stood there with a cocky ass expression.

"You want him in the cage then?" Lady Qing asked, nodding at someone off the stage.

"Yes, and I don't care who you send in with him, as long as they give him a good beating. As long as he's still breathing, I don't care how many bones they break." Liam said with a sadistic grin.

Dropping my body weight, I struggled against the hands that grabbed at my arms and shoulders. Out of the corner of my eyes, I could see the vertical metal bars of a cage rise up from the ground, surrounding the stage I was kicked off of earlier.

It took four guys, but they managed to throw me—literally—into the cage. Not a moment after landing with a grunt, the cage door slammed, and I found myself being surrounded by five men.

A sharp breath and cough was sucked out of me from the abrupt kick to my stomach. Then another kick connected with my face, throwing my head to the side.

This is such bullshit!

This fight wasn't fair one bit. Five men against me while I stayed in shackles. Utter and complete bullshit.

Gritting my teeth, I kicked at the man who stood by my feet, buckling his knees. Actually, I think I might have broken something because his leg was bent at a very awkward angle after my feet connected with him.

Bang!

The gunshot sent the whole place into a frozen silence. Then, the cage rattled violently followed by a grunt.

"*Bratok*!" Never in my life have I ever been more relieved to hear Lev's voice. "*Tashchi svoyu zadnitsu syuda*!"

Another gunshot rang out and one of the men who stood next to me dropped to the floor screaming in pain while holding his knee.

Looking over, I could see Angel standing there behind her stepmother with a smoking gun raised, her dark eyes sharp and locked onto the man she just shot.

With the opening, I jumped to my feet, ignoring the pain that ravaged my body from the sudden movement. Quickly, I scrambled over to the cage door where Lev reached through with a key in hand. The remaining three men snapped out of their stupor and rushed to me when Lev started to unlock my shackles.

"*Blya, potoropis*'!" I rushed my brother, not keen on wanting another beating with my arms and legs tied.

I shook the chains off my arms the moment I felt them slacken. Keeping a tight grip on the links, I quickly wrapped a bit of it around my right hand before throwing my fist out and catching the unlucky man who came too close to it. The man stumbled back, and the other two came at me swinging after sidestepping the man's stumbling.

Raising my arms up, I blocked one and grabbed the other by his wrist, redirecting the punch to the man I blocked and catching the edge of his face. The man stumbled back a little after catching the punch with his face and glared at me.

With my grip still on the man's wrist, I pulled him towards me and punched him—hard—in the gut, causing him to double over and smash his face into my knee that I had brought up.

Then, I twisted his arm behind him until I felt it give under the pressure. Seeing the awkward way the joint popped out, along with the man's scream of pain, made it clear I had dislocated it—what I intended to do.

"Oof!" My breath choked out of me when the man slammed into me because the other two charged at us and slammed into us without a care to the man whose arm I just twisted out of its socket. The man was dead weight slamming into me, knocking the wind out of me when I became sandwiched against the metal bars.

My head rang along with the bars when one of the men grabbed my face and slammed my head back against the cage. "Shit!"

"*Blyat*! I can't get a clear shot!" Lev shouted with his gun in hand, bouncing from target to target.

Glancing over at Lev, I half shouted at him, "I'll be fine, just stick to the plan." Two and a half men against one of me was a fair fight now that I was no longer bound.

Throwing my arm out, I let the chain fly out and wrap around the neck of the man in front of me, ignoring the other two for now. One man was being blocked by an upheld arm while the other one—the one with the dislocated arm—held me against the cage by keeping himself anchored against my waist and hips. So, pulling the chain, I reeled the man towards me and used the momentum to bash my head into his face, making it more bloody.

With him dazed, I grabbed him by the shoulders and threw him into his buddy, causing his buddy to slam into the cage next to me. Using my opening, I threw my hand out and struck the bloody guy in the throat, making him back away—the rest of the chains sliding off my hand and going with the stumbling man.

I wasn't worried about him anymore, the crushed windpipe I gave him would do him in sooner than later. Now to deal with one arm and the other man.

Turning my attention to the man next to me who was still recovering from being slammed into the metal bars, I pulled my arm back and clocked him in the face, making his head bounce against the cage. Throwing an arm across his chest, I held him against the cage. Twisting my body to adjust, I threw punch after punch after punch at him. My attack didn't relent even when he started to hit back. The adrenaline pounding through my body made his attacks feel like nothing against my tense body.

He stood no chance against me, not when he was barely half my size. He was nearly as tall as me, but he lacked the muscular build. So, he lacked the power behind his punches.

My attack on him didn't relent until his body went completely limp and his weight dragged him down to the ground from my hold. Then, my attention went to the man who remained anchored against me.

With a grunt, I brought my elbow down onto his back multiple times to get his grip to ease up enough so I could slide my arms between him and I. Once I managed that, I pried his arms off and shoved him away with a hard push. He was basically a dead man fighting me with one functional arm, the arm that's about to be out of commission the moment I close in on him.

Smirking darkly, I slowly stalked up to the man whose eyes were darting around in panic. "What's wrong? Don't like the wolf outside its cage huh?" I chuckled deeply while wiping away a trail of blood that ran down my eye.

"H-hey man, I was just following orders." His pathetic attempt fell on deaf ears because I really didn't give a shit right now.

All I offered in response was a wicked grin before I charged at him and tackled him against the other side of the cage with a loud rattle, knocking the wind out of him. Then, I grabbed his good arm by the wrist and wretched it behind him when I spun him around and forced him to his knees. With a foot on his back, I pressed him down while pulling his arm until I felt it give and heard him scream. Only then did I let him go, watching as he fell to the ground with his mangled arms.

"Anyone else want to test me tonight?!" I shouted with a glare at the crowd.

No one dared to make a single sound, only looking at me with either wary or down turned eyes.

No one fucks with me or my family and gets away with it.

I might not be retaliating now, but every single one of these fuckers in the room would get their dues.

They crossed the wrong fucking person.

Chapter 45

Angel

CLICK!

The sound of my gun cocking echoed through the pregnant silence.

"Sorry, he's off the market ladies and gentlemen! I'm not really the sharing type. My stepmother here hasn't really gotten the clue to not touch what's mine." I could see my stepmother stiffen at my words, and I could see the way her eyes darted around to see if anyone would come to her aid.

Keeping the gun firmly against her to remind her of who held the high ground, I chuckled softly with a victorious smirk. "I know you never did like your son in law, but even this is a new meaning to monster in law. Seriously? Selling him in a black market auction?" I chided, clicking my tongue and shaking my head softly.

The crowd stayed tensely silent as they stared at me with wide eyes. Soft murmurs slowly filled the air, fingers pointing at me and the cage.

"Guards!" Lady Qing shouted, her body jerking when I threw my arm out and wrapped it around her neck to hold her against me.

Smirking, I pressed the gun against her head more, digging into her temple as I did a quick sweep of the area lazily.

No guards were going to come to her rescue, they were all occupied at this point. Everyone else had pulled off their end of the plan smoothly. And I had taken out the few who were in my way when I entered the place. They weren't dead, but they're out for the count.

"Guards!" The desperation in her voice was amusing.

I wanted to laugh when my stepmother's face filled with hope at the movement of men from the shadows only to have it all shatter the moment she realized it wasn't her men.

Nodding my head at Lev, I watched him say something to his men in Russian. Shortly after, three bound and struggling bodies were dragged before her.

A small gasp could be heard from her. "You wouldn't." Lady Qing glared at me out of the corner of her eye.

"You want to test that? There are worse things than death, don't you forget that. Besides, after trying to kidnap me yesterday, what you did to my father, and what you tried to pull yesterday on top of kidnapping my husband and trying to sell him, you really think I'll hold back when it comes to you, bitch? You took my father and mother away from me, and almost my husband, so it's only fair that I take some things from you, no?" Taunting her and watching her squirm was too much fun to hold back the twisted smile from tugging at my lips.

"Y-your mother? How did you?" She lost her cards, no winning hand in any future for her.

"My father's first wife had a son who just happens to be a detective. And we both figured it was too much of a coincidence that both our mothers met their end by a drunk driver who was never found. He probably would have remained hidden too if you didn't arrange for me and Nikolai and gave me an endless reach of resources." Finding the man who crashed into my mother's car and seeing him dead was the closure I needed.

"The Volkov's have a much farther and deeper reach than the Qing Triad. It only took some effort on Nikolai's part to find and apprehend the slimeball that you hired to commit the vehicular homicide." It was also very satisfying to see Nikolai end that man's life on my whim.

Our relationship really was one made in hell. I never killed but married a killer who was more than happy to do the killing for me. All I had to do was point and say when and how. On the other hand, I handled the tedious business of torture and extraction of information for him. Nikolai had complained about how tasteless he found torture to be, so it was only fair that I contributed my fair share to our marriage.

"He squealed like a pig at the first threat, spilling all about how you paid him and provided the means to carry out both murders, how you told him to make sure that there were no survivors. Fortunately, for Greg and I, there were last minute changes that day so we were not in the car as we should have." Otherwise, my brother and I would be six-feet under right now like how Lady Qing planned.

Greg's existence went under Lady Qing's nose because she thought he had died in the crash, and he was raised outside of our city. So, she never thought to search for him. A big mistake on her part.

"You're done. Your reign ends here. Tonight." Chuckling softly, I shove her to the ground onto her knees.

Looking at the crowd with my head held high, I made my announcement, "From this day forward, Lady Qing is no longer the temporary head of the Qing Triad! By Feng Qing's dying will, I, Angel Vu, am the new dragonhead!" Though I had no microphone, the openness and my position at the front of the room carried my voice well enough. My throat would hate me later for all the shouting, but whatever. "Does anyone here have any problems with this new leadership!?"

Sporadic head shakes waved through the crowd as they slowly tried to back pedal out of this situation, only to be stopped by the teams in place that had executed the pincer movement perfectly. Everyone was trapped in their spot. The only place they could go was forward towards my position which was the back of the room.

My throat would hate me for all the shouting later, but I needed everyone to hear what I had to say. "Glad to see no one has any problem with this shift in position! First off, I'd like to apologize for the shit that my stepmother here has pulled in my absence! This event was, and is not, authorized under triad rule! Everyone in attendance here today will be free to go with their lives intact, as long as they do not try anything stupid! Furthermore, any and all purchases made tonight will be made invalid!" Now that got a rouse from the crowd.

The room quickly filled with the crowd's grievances, some even took a few steps towards the stage which earned them a point of a gun which quickly stopped them. Even with dozens of guns pointed at them, they still got rowdier and rowdier until my head started buzzing from their complaints.

Letting out a deep breath, I let out a single shot at the ceiling, silencing everyone again. "Count your fucking blessings that I am not giving an order to execute you all right now! There are only two options: leave empty handed and alive, or leave in a body bag! Your choice! I also highly advise you don't test me any further tonight because I am not in a patient mood right now!" I warned them all in a loud and stern voice.

Killing the whole room would be easy like breathing, but the mess would be too much to clean up. Like Nikolai said at the meeting, one or two prominent figures we could get away with, but nearly the whole state would not be in any way possible.

We were going to send the state into a turmoil, but it would be on our count and control. All of California will be at the mercy of the Volkov Bratva within a year or so's time if we played our cards right, which included letting these cockroaches live, for now.

Looking over at Nikolai, I couldn't help but give a smile of relief and excitement. Was it wrong to be turned on right now at the sight of him all sweaty and bloody? God the way he took out those men was so arousing to watch. The part where he got kicked around on the ground and got injured wasn't exciting, but seeing him beat those men with his bare hands was something else.

God, am I really that fucked up to find bloody violence arousing?

Snapping out of my thoughts, my eyes softened with worry. "Are you okay, *anh*?" Or at least relatively okay. He looked like he's seen better days right now. His face would be bruised up good, a split eyebrow, busted lip, probably a few bruised ribs from how and where they kicked him earlier. A little bloody too, but nothing like the guys he beat up.

"I'll be fine." He grunted, rolling the sleeves of his shirt up to his elbows, revealing more bruises.

"*Anh*?" I looked at Nikolai with a confused expression when he kicked open the cage door, jumped down from the stage, and walked over to the small group of guards who were kneeling on the ground with our men surrounding them.

"These people came here for a show tonight, so it'd be rude to let them leave unsatisfied, wouldn't you agree, *lisichka*? They wanted to work me up into a mood, so now they'll get their damn wish." The dark edge to his voice made me shiver out of fear and excitement. I could tell by his voice that he had a murderous look to him.

If I was on the receiving end of his murderous gaze then I'd probably be pissing myself. The fear I felt was my base instinct trying to do some self-preservation. Excitement shouldn't even be a feeling in a moment like this, but I couldn't help it. Knowing my husband would let loose excited the side of me that craved a savage man.

The guard let out a high pitched yelp when Nikolai's hands landed hard on his shoulders to drag him up. Pathetically, the guard pleaded with Nikolai when he shoved the guard to the foot of the stage.

"Tonight will also serve as a stern reminder that I am not one to be trifled with." Nikolai faced the crowd, the one who had taken a few steps back to give him room. "It appears that some of you have mistaken my generosity for weakness. Just because I am not the violent idiot that my father was does not indicate weakness, and a lot of you seem to be under the impression that I am growing incapable and complacent because I have been enjoying the peace and quiet that I have garnered through the blood I have spilt."

Oh, he seethed with silent rage—the kind that should be feared more than a loud outburst. And by the way the crowd shrunk away with fear in their wide eyes indicated that they knew they fucked up.

"It's easy to talk about a caged animal from the other side isn't it? But once that barrier is gone, you all tuck your tails between your asses and cower. You all spat your shit at me while I was chained up. Well, where's all that now? Hm? Where's all the talk about how far I've fallen? How soft I got? How I was growing incapable of holding down my own business? And don't even get me started on the disgusting things some of you said about my wife. Mark my words, you will all feel my wrath in the days to come." There was so much conviction in his voice. It was no veiled threat; it was a promise.

With a deep breath, Nikolai picked the guard up by the front of his shirt, holding him up in the air. "I'm going to deal with you first." The guard landed with a grunt when Nikolai threw him onto the ground. "Get up, tough guy. Or do you only pick on little girls half your size and men who are incapable of fighting back? You seemed rather feisty earlier wanting to take me on, so here's your chance." Nikolai held his arms out to the side, goading the guard to strike.

The guard scrambled to his feet, looking at Nikolai fearfully briefly before charging at him with a fist pulled back. Nikolai easily caught the punch with a dark grin and scoffing chuckle. "Pathetic." There was a sickening crack when Nikolai's fist met the guard's face.

"*Lisichka*, give me your knife." He demanded, holding his hand out towards me.

Looking over at Hanna, I nodded towards my stepmother and waited for Hanna to take my position before going over to my husband's side.

"Don't have too much fun now." I said with a dark smirk, pulling out the knife from my thigh holster and placing the handle of the knife into Nikolai's open hand.

Leaning back against the stage, I watched as Nikolai severed the guard's fingers before he spoke. "That's what gets for touching and forcing himself on the girls earlier." His eyes glared at the crowd with an edge of darkness and anger. "This is what will happen if you dare go through with your pathetic threats about touching my wife. If any of you even think about touching my wife then it'll be your fingers that get hacked like this poor bastard. If any of you dare try to lay a finger on my wife then it'll be your damn hands that I take off."

There was a moment of pause as Nikoli took in a few deep breaths, his body relaxing a little with the act. "It's going to be your eyes next if you don't quit looking at her." He snarled, narrowing his eyes at a few men who let their eyes linger on me much too long.

Fuck, I love it when he gets a little jealous and possessive. Even if I was more than capable of handling myself, just something about him wanting to protect me was sweet and sexy. Yes, I would condone him for gouging out the lingering eyes of a pervert.

Amusingly, I chuckled with a fake smile. "Anyone else have anything they want to say about me or my husband? Speak now or forever hold your peace."

No one dared to twitch their mouth, most of them hanging their head in shame or shaking their heads in response. With an overly exaggerated smile, I spoke, "Glad to see we've come to an understanding. Now, as I said, you're all free to go, just no funny business. Although, I would implore you all to think twice about leaving on an impromptu vacation for a while. You might be walking away with your lives tonight, but that doesn't mean that my husband or I are done with you. We'll be in touch, so make sure you stay available. Otherwise, I would hate to see what would happen to you or your loved ones."

Slowly, the crowd thinned out as everyone was escorted out of the facility in a single file line. All who remained in the empty area were Lady Qing, her children, Nikolai, and me.

"Where are your partners in crime you witch?" Was it a coincidence the other three heads weren't here? Or had she managed to warn them somehow?

We were hoping to strike down the major players with this operation, but there were no signs of Ivan, Lilian, or Ramon. Natalia was here, and we managed to snag her when she tried to escape. But no signs of her siblings or father, who we really wanted.

"You'll never get them. Once they catch wind of this, they'll go under until they're ready to strike you down. So, enjoy your rule while it lasts." I wanted to slap the cocky smirk off her face, and the sensation itched at my twitching hand. "You think anyone is going to follow your lead? You're just a little girl in way over her head!"

"Well, if they don't want to follow then they'll face the consequences." The cops were going to have their hands full throughout the next week or two with how much I would throw at them.

"We both know you don't have what it takes." Lady Qing sneered with a short chuckle.

Well, I couldn't argue with her there. Chuckling softly, I shook my head lightly as I walked over to Nikolai. "But my husband does." Twisting the ring off my finger, I held it out to Nikolai with a confident smile. "There will be a formal announcement tomorrow with the council, but from this day forward, the Qing Triad will be merged under the Volkov Bratva and be under their rule."

"You! You can't do that!" I knew it would piss her off. Everything precious to her fell away from her hands in a blink of an eye. "No one will follow the rule of a damn Russian! He knows nothing about us or our ways or operations!"

I couldn't help but smile delightfully at the sight of her cracking. "But I do, and I am going to be by his side every step of the way through hell and back. And I can do whatever the hell I want, that power was given to me the moment my father passed and his will was enacted. You've lost because you let your hubris get ahead of you. You thought you played the game your way, but my father saw through it in the end and made damn sure you would lose it all."

"So, what now? You're just going to kill me and my children?" The situation was finally sinking into her thick skull.

"No. I told you that I wouldn't harm your children as long as you behaved, and as insufferable as they are, they're innocent in this matter. They'll be free to go as long as they promise to disappear from the state, forever. But as for you dear ol' stepmother, I've got other plans for you that require you to be alive, for now." She may be a bitch, but she had useful information we could extract.

Pulling out my hairpin, I flicked open the blade as I walked over to my step siblings. "Two choices: disappear forever from the state and you'll go free right now, or decline and suffer the same fate as your mother. Your choice." The latter was a bluff, I wouldn't harm them unless they gave me reason nor would I ever subject them to anything I would do to their mother. But I had to put fear in them.

"We'll go! You won't ever see our faces again! We promise!" The eldest daughter responded with no hesitation, the other two nodding in agreement.

Honestly, if it weren't for their mother giving them a poor upbringing, they probably wouldn't be too bad of people. Not going to lie, I did pity them. Well, they'll find their way eventually, their bank accounts were cushy enough to keep them sustained for a long while as long as they didn't blow through it.

A few flicks of my wrist and the ropes fell to the ground, and the three of them scrambled to their feet and ran, not bothering to spare their mother a glance as they disappeared.

"Damn, not even a 'bye' from either of them." I rubbed it into her face with a chuckle and shake of my head.

"Everyone is cleared from the building, victims included." I heard Alexei report to me over my ear piece.

"Alright, everyone clear out. We're about done here. We'll re-group at the estate." I said over the communications system before reaching down and yanking my stepmother up by her arm.

Smiling wickedly at my stepmother, I gripped her arm tightly and dug my nails into her until I drew blood. "You and I have a car ride to take."

My words were empty, but Lady Qing didn't see it that way because they seemed to spur her into action. Her hand darted across my face, catching my cheek with her overly long nails.

"*Con đĩ*!" I hissed in pain while pressing the back of my hand against it because I still had my hairpin tightly gripped in it.

Lady Qing quickly dug her nails into my forearm, causing me to release her reflexively. Then, she turned and tried to make a run for it, but she only made it three decent steps before Nikolai placed himself in her path, stopping her.

With her escape cut off, she turned her attention back to me, lunging at me with her nails aimed towards my face.

Backstepping, I reached out with my free hand and grabbed her wrist to pull her off to the side to redirect her forward motion away from me. As she veered off to the side of me, I brought my hairpin down and sliced her face in a downward motion when I twisted my body towards her.

A second slice was placed across her bleeding face as I swung my arm back up in order to plunge the hairpin down into her deltoid. Burying the blade deep into her muscle, I sliced the blade down the full length of her arm to her wrist, making her scream in agony.

"You're lucky I have other plans to torment you, otherwise I'd kill you right here and now or even slice your spine to paralyze you. I want you to suffer like my mother did along with all your other victims." An evil snake like her didn't deserve an easy way out, not in the slightest.

I would stick her in a car, make her drive off only to have a truck crash into her. I wanted to see the panic and horror on her face. I wanted to watch her crawl out of the wreckage like the pathetic worm she is. I wanted her to beg for mercy, for even just a chance of it, only to deny her of it. I wanted to break her until she became no use to us, only then would I stab her through her black heart.

Wickedly grinning, I held the blade up to her neck after pulling it out of her arm. "I am going to enjoy driving this hairpin into you over the years. Even when it dulls out, I'll continue to use it until I draw your last breath with it."

Chapter 46

Nikolai

THE TWO WEEKS THAT followed the night at The Catacombs flew by in a blur. The majority of the time was spent cleaning up the mess that Lady Qing had created. A majority of the men who were employed under Lady Qing were disposed of in bits and pieces into the river, and those who were blackmailed into giving her loyalty were given two options: leave the business completely, or work for us. Surprisingly, a lot of them chose to follow Angel with the merge after she assured them I was a fair employer.

Lady Qing was currently being held in one of our bunkers, her reluctant help to keep herself alive being more helpful than not. Angel made it clear to her the moment she outlived her use then she would be disposed of, and the threat itself seemed to do the trick.

The meeting with the major players in the triad went as we expected. Nearly all of them weren't happy with Angel handing over leadership to an outsider like me, and they weren't happy with the merge either. But given their options, they were eager enough to fall into line. We were going to keep a close eye on them for a while until we could determine their credibility.

Establishing bratva presence in our newly acquired territory was met with a lot of resistance, which was expected. A new rule meant uncertainty, so I didn't expect everyone's cooperation up front, especially after the reputation my father had given the Volkov Bratva. Many were still stuck with what my father had built and fronted, and they thought I was the same.

"Kolyenka?" The headache that ate at me faded at the sound of her soft and soothing voice. "Dinner's ready, and everyone's outside and ready to dig in."

Breathing deeply, I stretch my arms above my head with a groan before standing up from my desk. "Sorry, I guess I lost track of time... Again." There was so much to do still. I know not all of it had to be done right away, but I didn't like to leave loose ends.

"No more tonight *anh*. You need to relax a little before you blow a blood vessel." Angel chuckled softly, walking up to me and kissing my cheek. "Also, it's not every day that you'll turn forty. So, get your ass downstairs."

Chuckling softly, I wrapped my arms around Angel and held her tightly. Not a day has gone by that I've thought about how close I came to losing my precious wife. It probably wouldn't be the last time given the mafia life. The fact she had an attempt on her life with the bomb, which we found out was ordered by Natalia, paired with her near kidnapping, everything was too close together. If she had been kidnapped with me that day, well, I didn't even want to imagine what could have transpired.

Picking Angel up, I set her on my desk and kissed her deeply as I took her hands in mine. Breaking the kiss, I took her left hand in mine, slipped her ring off her finger, and pocketed it.

"What'd you do that for?" She looked at me with a confused and concerned expression, searching my face and eyes for an answer when I remained silent.

"Only my wife can wear my ring." I was probably going to get punched in the face for messing with her like this, but she's been an asshole recently and needed to have a taste of her own medicine.

"Did you hit your head somewhere or had too many drinks while you were cooped up in here? I am your wife." It was hard not to smile at her pouting glare as she crossed her arms across her chest.

"No, you're not. I never married you. You exist, my wife doesn't." The small, little black box in my pocket felt like the size of a moving box that bulged out, and it started to feel like it weighed a ton.

"Nikolai, what the hell is going on?" She looked ready to pull her hand back and land one on my face.

"You're not my wife, Angel Vu, not yet anyways." Slowly, I got down on my knee in front of her. "Just like the car crash, we came into this life out of the blue and haphazardly. I know I'm not perfect and that I've still got a lot of growth when it comes to relationships, but there's no one else in this world that I would want to grow with besides you. There's no denying the fire between us. I knew from that first night that you were special, and I still regret not acting on my feelings and talking to you sooner, but I am going to spend the rest of our lives to make up for that lost time if you'll let me. So, let's start this over properly. Angel Vu, and that better be your real name, will you marry me?"

Worry twisted at my face when Angel started to laugh and cry. Did I fuck this up somehow?

"Oh my God, yes! Yes! Oh God I thought you were going to divorce me and kick me out or something, God don't scare me like that! But yes, oh God yes I'll marry you, again." Angel slid off the desk and threw her arms around me, leaning down and kissing me deeply before holding her hand out for me to slip the new ring onto her finger.

Unlike the first ring, this one actually had thought put into it. The delicate platinum band had small vines of roses twisting off of it with smaller pink diamonds embedded in the center. The centerpiece was a round black diamond that wasn't big, but it was cut so intricately that it sparkled and glimmered brightly.

The thought of getting a big diamond ring had crossed my mind, but Angel wasn't that kind of woman. She also made it vehemently clear that if I were to ever gift her a big diamond ring then she'd throw it back in my face. Also, her friends were very helpful in vetoing ring ideas I sent their way when I came up with the idea of proposing to Angel.

"Any chance I can convince you to change your name this time? Mrs. Volkov has a nice ring to it." She never did fall onboard with changing her last name the first time around, but that was understandable given the circumstances.

"Hmm say it again a few times, it might start to grow on me." She giggled against my lips, kissing me playfully.

"I'll say it however many times you want." I loved the sound of it, but I was biased. The thought of her having my last name stirred that possessive side of me awake. It was just another way for the world to know who she belonged to.

"You can fuck me later, we really have to eat dinner." With a roll of her eyes, she patted the front of my pants where I began to strain against it. Before I could grab her and try to change her mind, she slipped away from me and darted over to the door.

It was hard to keep from talking business during the dinner party, but all of us managed to keep it at bay for now by talking about moments in our past. But some still managed to slip in.

Surprisingly, Stepan was the one to bring it up this time. "God, I can't believe you thought Alexei and Angel would go behind your back like that. Granted, that was a nice trick they pulled, very well executed, I'll have to give them that." The recording that had been shown to me during my capture was quickly debunked when I'd gotten ahold of it from Natalia's phone and showed the others.

Yes, it was Alexei and Angel I had heard in the recording, but it was taken way out of context. The recording had come from Benjamin, and he showed me the full recording when we were all trying to smooth the situation out. Apparently, Lev and Angel were sparring with each other and one wrong tackle landed Angel with a dislocated shoulder. In which Alexei was called in to fix.

"You'll never have to worry about Angel and Alexei, not with Angel's little rules of P with all the other nurses." Hanna commented with a soft chuckle.

"Rules of P? The heck is that?" Alexei sounded genuinely curious, as with the rest of us I'm pretty sure. "And the heck does it have to do with Angel not dating me?"

I wouldn't voice it, but I was genuinely curious and wanted to know about this little rule of hers. Although, I'm pretty sure the quizzical look on my face would make it clear to Angel I wanted answers along with everyone else who poked and prodded at her.

With a roll of her eyes, she chuckled softly before satisfying everyone with an answer. "It's just a silly little made up rule by us nurses on who not to date. Basically, if their job title begins with a 'P' then don't date them. So basically, the list so far: physicians, providers, policemen, paramedics, politicians, prisoners, psychos, and pfirefighters. Yes, firefighters but we added a 'p' in front because those guys are dangerous. Because let me tell you, I would gladly be a serial arsonist or petty criminal to have some of those guys come kicking down my door."

Narrowing my eyes playfully at Angel, I questioned her with a knowing voice. "Oh really?" I shouldn't be getting jealous and possessive, but I couldn't help the little nagging tug at my chest when I thought about Angel eyeing other men lustfully. "Am I going to need to replace all the policemen and firefighters out there?" I half joked with a half serious smile. I would seriously replace them if it meant keeping my wife's eyes on me only.

Giggling, she stuck her tongue out at me. "Oh please, the only man I need or want to look at is you. Besides, I already broke the rule by marrying you, so of course I am going to give you everything." Angel grinned at me cheekily.

"How exactly does Kolya fit on that list?" Alexei asked with a raised brow.

"He would fit under psycho because, well, no sane person would ever willingly choose to be with me, let alone marry me, twice." Well, she wasn't wrong there. Any typical man would have ran for the hills or tried to get Angel tossed into a psych ward if they ever found out how crazy she was underneath all her sexiness.

Chuckling softly, Angel shook her head. "Can't believe they put in so much effort to try and get you to agree to them. Still can't believe they're still in the wind either." Angel said with a sigh, relaxing against me after she sat down in my lap.

Unfortunately, Ivan still gave us trouble and evaded our grasp. We've managed to shut down his incoming and outgoing shipments, but he still had a small operation based in the city itself that we have yet to discover and shut down. Natalia was still with us, locked away in a bunker until we revamped The Catacombs to our new holding and torture area.

Angel wasn't too happy with waiting to get her hands on Natalia though. My little hellion wanted to tear the poor woman at the joints for laying her hands on me during my capture. She also wasn't happy about not being able to kill Natalia because I figured we could try to use her to get Ivan, but I promised Angel that if it turned out to not be the case then Natalia's life was hers to snuff out.

"We'll get them eventually, but let's not think more about that tonight on Kolya's birthday. I say it's time for presents to keep our mind off of things." Stepan suggested with a smile, sliding over the first box of many in front of me.

A new car to replace the one that met its unfortunate end with Angel, a lot of high end liquor, and a brand new state of the art phone from Bao. One by one I opened the presents and set them aside until only one remained.

Angel eagerly handed me the box, the corners of her lips curling upwards uncontrollably in a smile. "What could you have gotten me?" I've never made any indication of wanting anything with her, and the box was too light to indicate that its content was more booze.

"Just open it and see for yourself. Don't worry, you'll love it." An excited smile brightened her face as she looked at me lovingly, which only made me more curious about the contents of the box.

Carefully, I opened the small box, and I nearly dropped it when the contents flashed at me. "*Lisichka*." I looked at her in disbelief as I held the little note and the strip of pictures.

Happy birthday dad!
See you next year!
Love,
Your boys

Besides the note and ultrasound pictures, there were two pairs of blue shoes, two onesies with the numbers 1 and 2 marked on the front, and a piece of paper with the concluding result of her pregnancy along with confirmation of the genders.

It seemed to have come as a surprise to everyone, just as it had to me, because they all crowded around me to look at the contents of the box with their own expressions of disbelief and excitement. Then, the endless congratulations patted my back and shoulders, and Angel was swarmed by tight hugs.

Everything just blurred by for me though as I was too busy in my own head. With a protective hand over Angel's stomach, I held her close while smiling like an idiot.

We were going to be parents. I was going to be a father. The love of my life carried our children. Soon, she would grow round with our love, then we'll have two little bundles in our arms. God, the thought of her getting bigger aroused me so much. I never understood it when men would say their pregnant wife is so sexy, but now that I had a pregnant wife, just the notion of her getting big and round with our combined love was a whole other feeling I couldn't describe properly with words.

Then, the bliss flew out the window when the realization hit me. "You went through everything pregnant? I am so happy right now but I'm also so pissed that you would be so reckless." The estimation on the pictures stated she was a little over six weeks pregnant, and the operation and attempted murder and kidnapping happened right in the middle of that timeframe.

"Well, to be fair, I didn't know I was pregnant until two weeks ago, at least it wasn't confirmed officially until two weeks ago. The levels were too low and off when I went to the doctor initially because of my little bouts of exhaustion, and the fact that I still had my IUD in me didn't give me much hope because typically pregnancies like that don't last. The results didn't come back until two days after the operation stating that the levels were looking good. I didn't want to say anything about my first appointment either because the doctor had said to not be too hopeful coming in because of the circumstances. So, it was a huge surprise when the twins appeared to be healthy. I wanted to tell you last week when I received the news, but I wanted to wait until the blood tests came back with the genders." Angel explained herself with a small smile.

I couldn't hold it against her after hearing her explanation. The initial tests showed the babies wouldn't likely be viable, so I understood her persistence with keeping her involvement in the mission. But still, I wasn't happy with it, but I couldn't do anything about it now since everything already happened.

At least we had an answer for her exhaustion the past few weeks. I just wish she had told me so I could have been there to comfort her. She took on all the stress of uncertainty by herself, and even if the outcome would have been less than ideal, I would rather be there for her than not. She was mine to love and care for, for better or worse.

"*Anh*?" There was an edge of concern to her voice as she held my face in her hands.

"Hm? Yes, love?" Now I was worried because this moment felt too perfect, so why the concern? She was still smiling happily at me, but there was a worried edge to it.

Chewing her bottom lip, she let her eyes wander away for a second before locking them back onto mine. "You still remember how you owe me that favor for saving your ass?" Why was she bringing this up?

"Yes, and I am still honoring it." I don't know what she could ask for now. We were going to be married again, she was going to have the wedding of her dreams, she could buy the whole damn world with the amount of money in my bank account, and we were going to have two wonderful boys in a few months. She had everything and if she didn't then she easily had the means to get whatever she desired. So, what would the favor even be?

"I know you've got a lot on your plate, we both do technically, but what do you say to opening up like a little shelter of sorts for victims of trafficking? I mean, we'd probably do a lot of illegal shit, but at least we could protect the victims better than the police and system in place right now." She sounded hesitant as she posed the idea to me.

It was true, our plates being as full as they are, but there's no way I could deny my wife's request, not when it was something actually good. Also, not like I could deny her anything.

"By illegal shit you mean?" I prodded with a smirk and short chuckle, curious as to what illegal activities she had in mind.

Giggling sheepishly, she tapped her chin in thought. "Uhh it might involve talking to some people... With weapons... I mean, some people just wait for the girls to get out before snatching them again, so maybe they just need to be taught a hard lesson of when to quit it." Well, that would definitely fall under the illegal umbrella.

"So basically, you want to have a safe haven shelter with hitmen on standby for hits on pimps? The last part obviously is not going on the papers." I summed it up with a chuckle, looking at her amusingly.

Rolling her eyes, she gave my arm a soft whack. "Well, if you want to put it that way, yes. But I mean, I want to actually help them too, not just provide a safe roof over their heads."

"I know what you meant and want the moment you asked, *lisichka*." Maybe it would be a good idea to have a legit business in helping victims. It would make assisting them a lot easier if we went through mostly legal means.

"You sure that's the favor you want to ask of me? Nothing for yourself?" As if she needed anything else, but I just wanted to be sure.

"Well, would it be too much to ask for you to not be an asshole to me while I am pregnant?" She asked with a playful chuckle and glare.

"When am I ever an asshole to you in general? Besides, how would I even be an asshole to you while you're pregnant?" That was the last thing on my mind. Sure, I might give her a hard time here and there just to see her get worked up—she looked too cute when she was mad—but I would dial it back now that she's pregnant.

Huffing, she scrunched her face up in a cute pout. "You're always an asshole to me, but that's beside the point. What I meant is for you to not get all over protective, controlling, and bossy. And don't you dare deny it either because I can already see it in your eyes. I don't want anything to change between us, and I sure as hell don't want you treating me like some precious little egg. I am not quitting my job in the ED nor am I going to transfer to some other department that's less strenuous, and I am not going to stop partaking in our mafia business. I will, however, stop with the raids and won't be in the field until I'm fully recovered after giving birth." Her voice took a serious edge after the first sentence.

"You know I can just tie you to the bed." I joked with a chuckle, holding up my hand to catch hers when she threw it out to hit me playfully.

With a warm smile, I threw my arms around her and held her tightly against me. "I'm not going to step on your toes, lord knows you'd make me regret it severely if I do. As I said in the past to your dangerous activities, I don't like it, but nothing I say or do will change your stubborn mind." At least she would dial it back with the field activities, so I'll take that win.

"Just promise me you'll be extremely careful. I know you're more than capable of handling the shit that life throws at you, but you are pregnant now." For my sake, I might just risk her wrath and chain her to the bed if she wasn't cautious from now on.

"Of course, I'm stubborn, not stupid." She chuckled with a roll of her eyes.

Grinning happily, she leaned in and kissed me deeply with a sigh of pleasure. "But you'll be fine with granting me those favors?" She asked in a soft voice after breaking the kiss, letting her lips linger against mine as her eyes looked up into mine.

Chuckling softly, I kissed her with a smile. "*Lisichka*, I'll grant you any favor you want from here on out." Can't say no to my lovely wife.

Chapter 47

Angel

"Girl, he loved it, so stop fretting." Hanna assured me, grabbing my nervous hands to stop them from fidgeting. "You saw the way his face lit up in the video. Besides, who wouldn't love a sexy little boudoir album from their fiancé as their wedding day gift?"

"If I looked sexy and hot then yeah." No matter how much Nikolai doted on me and my new body, I still felt very self-conscious about it.

"Girl, quit it. He *loved* it! He was still flipping through it when I left with a huge smile on his face. You're a bomb ass bitch, so hold that head back up and fuck everyone else." Hanna encouraged me with a grin, hugging me tightly with a contented sigh.

Having kids really changes your body. I knew that fact, but to have it happen personally was a jarring experience. Especially after having twins, my body really wasn't how it was before pregnancy. Nikolai constantly reassured me that he didn't see me any differently, that he actually loved my body more than before because this was the body that brought our children into this world. He also didn't complain about how much bigger my ass got.

Hanna stood behind me with an annoyed glare, probably tired of my complaints about my insecurities like Nikolai has been. "Come on, finish up, it's almost time for you to become Mrs. Volkov, officially this time." She rushed with a chortle.

Looking at my reflection in the mirror, I couldn't help but smile. Hanna was right, I needed to quit it. It was my wedding day for God's sake, I should be happy and elated—nothing else.

The fact I was getting married didn't fully hit me until I was standing at the end of the aisle, staring ahead at Nikolai's grinning face when he got his first look at me in my ball gown wedding dress, embellished with embroidered flowers with sparkles that flowed the skirt of the dress down to the long train.

I felt like a fucking Disney princess, which was something I never thought I'd want in my life until I went wedding dress shopping. I always associated being a princess to being weak and useless, just sitting around until my prince charming swept me off my feet. I didn't belong in a fairytale; I belonged in a Grimm story. But now, being a princess didn't mean you were some helpless romantic hoping for happiness to come along. A princess could be a warrior who made her own happy ending.

And now, I would be a fucking queen with Nikolai by my side.

Standing at the altar, I let my eyes sweep over the crowd. The small chapel filled with our closest families and friends, all who were looking at us with genuine happy smiles. Then, in the front row, were our sons—Anatoli and Anton Volkov.

The twins were close to being two years in age, both of them nearly spitting images of Nikolai with their enchanting blue eyes, which I was more than elated to see. As much as I loved my brown eyes, they were plain in my opinion. The only thing they got from me were my lips and slight uptick to their eyes that made them a little sharper looking. Well, and I'm pretty sure they got a majority of my personality.

Anatoli and Anton were two very lively, and loud, babies. A curious bunch who wreaked havoc wherever they went. Especially now since they're more mobile on their tiny little legs, nothing was safe from them. They were very stubborn too, though I try to blame that more on Nikolai because I felt like he had a harder head than me—he liked to argue otherwise though.

"*Ty takaya krasivaya. Ne mogu poverit', chto ty budesh' moyey na vsyu zhizn'.*" I had no idea what he said, at least not fully. Something about being beautiful, I think. I really needed to start picking back up with my Russian lessons. "You are so fucking beautiful baby. I can't believe how lucky I am to have you." He whispered to me with a big smile as he reached out and placed his hands on my waist. "Words can't describe how I feel right now seeing you like this."

Noticing the glassiness of his tearing eyes, I giggled softly as I reached up and held his face lovingly. "Don't you dare start crying on me, I spent way too long on this makeup to ruin it." I joked with tearful eyes and a happy smile. "You look quite dashing yourself in an all-white suit." This was probably the only time I would see him in any color other than black, gray, or dark blue. So, I was going to savor this image and burn it into my mind for all of eternity.

The ceremony proceeded smoothly, and soon it was time for our vows.

"Kolyenka, from the moment I hauled your huge ass out of the car, I knew deep down that I was going to meet my match in you. Though our relationship started off unconventionally, I am grateful for the time it gave us to grow to love each other. I am grateful that you are such a wonderful man, one whom I'll be more than proud to call my husband until the end of time. I promise that I will forever remain by your side, through the good and the bad, through sickness and health, for rich or poor, and for better or worse. I promise that I will continue to be the best mother that I can to our children, and I promise to be that little wild vixen you signed your life away to over two years ago." Forever and an eternity with Nikolai was going to be a dream come true and paradise.

"Angel, my *lisichka*, I promise I won't crash into your life more than I already have. From the moment I laid my eyes on you and mistook you for an actual angel, I've never been able to get you out of my mind. And now that I am going to have you now and forever, I can't even begin to describe how grateful and wonderful I feel. I know

I'm not perfect, but you make me want to be the best, and I promise you that I will only give you my best for as long as we live. I swear to you that I will remain by your side through it all, through the bad and the good, through sickness and health, for rich or poor, and for better or worse. I promise to be the best husband to you, and the best father to our children. I'll never ask you to change for me, all I ask is you never let your little fire fade. You'll always be my *lisichka*, for now and ever."

Fuck, I didn't want to cry on my own wedding day, but I couldn't help it. My husband was too much of a sap sometimes. "God I love you so much." I giggled through my tears.

"I know." He replied with a cocky grin. "I love you so much too, *lisichka*."

"Well then, let's move onto the good part then." The officiant this time wasn't some random person snatched in the middle of the night. Instead, it was Greg, who was apparently an ordained minister; yeah, this came as a shock to all of us when he offered to ordain our wedding. "Do you, Nikolai Volkov, take my lovely little sister, Angel Vu, to be your lawfully wedded wife, to have and to hold until the end of time and eternity? To cherish and love?"

"I do." Nikolai replied without an ounce of hesitation.

Turning to me Greg repeated the same questions. "I do." Never in my life had I been so sure of two simple words. Funny how those two words held such different feelings now than two years ago when they were said under duress.

"Well then, I pronounce you husband and wife... Again and officially. Now, lay one on each other so we can get to the good part." Greg said with a chuckle, shutting his little book and urging for us to come together.

"Don't mind if I do." Nikolai chuckled, pulling me flush against his strong body and kissing me deeply, dipping slightly and making me squeal and giggle into the kiss as I kept my arms tightly around his neck.

"Well then! Mr. and Mrs. Volkov everyone! Officially this time!" Everyone in the place knew about the little marriage from before and how it got nulled and voided because of the fact it wasn't my real identity on the papers. It's become a running joke for the wedding really.

"Shall we, Mrs. Volkov?" Nikolai offered me his hand with a loving smile.

"We shall, Mr. Volkov." I replied with a giggle, taking his hand and walking down the aisle with him and out of the chapel.

The reception was held at the estate in the backyard, and the whole thing went by in a blur. From all the pictures, greetings, food, drinks, and dancing, time just flew by. The night was over by the time we knew it—afterparty included.

Exhausted after the long night, Nikolai and I retired to our bedroom after checking on the slumbering twins who had been put to bed by Lev and his girlfriend.

"God, your family is huge. Not gonna lie, I barely remember half their names." Nikolai's family flew in from Russia, and even if he was estranged from some, there were still a shit ton who were still on good terms with him or were really close.

"Dima is really nice though, good head on his shoulders." I imagined his cousin who was the head of the bratva over in Russia to be brooding and serious like Nikolai sometimes, but the man was almost a ball of sunshine.

"Why do you think I trust him to run our operations in Moscow? He's a natural born leader, much better than me. Even if he may not seem like it, when he's working, he gets serious." Nikolai chuckled softly as he loosened his tie and unbuttoned the first few buttons from his shirt. "Now, no more talk. I believe we have a marriage to consummate."

"Uhh think that ship's long far—ah!" Squealing and giggling, I lightly smacked Nikolai's back when he threw me over his shoulder to carry me over to the bed. Well, at least I had a nice view of his ass.

"Don't get too loud now, *lisichka*, wouldn't want to wake everyone up." Nikolai chuckled darkly as he threw me onto the bed and caged me between him. "My lovely bride. My wife." He groaned deeply into the kiss, his hand tangling into my loosely curled hair.

With his lips locked with mine, tongue deep in my mouth, his free hand slid behind me, finding the zipper to my dress and undoing it. "You're so lucky I didn't go with a corset or buttons." I joked with a giggle, sitting up a little to let him fully pull my dress down to reveal the lacy little piece I had on under.

"*Trakhni menya*." He groaned, his hungry eyes devouring my body that was scantily clad in the strapless lingerie piece.

Biting my bottom lip, I reached a hand down to my parted legs and ran a finger down my inner thigh. "Make love to me Kolyenka, make love to me then fuck me." I whispered wantonly, looking at him with lustful eyes as I rubbed my clit through the crotchless lingerie bodysuit.

Getting off the bed, he started to work off his layers of clothing. "Finger yourself, keep yourself nice and wet for me, *lisichka*." He said with a groan. "That's it, good girl." His praise sent shivers down my spine as I buried my fingers deep inside of myself.

My eyes lazily followed him as he moved to his nightstand, opening the bottom drawer and pulling out the leather cuffs and tossing them next to me on the bed. Then, he stood at the edge of the bed, grabbed me by my ankles and pulled me until my ass hung off the bed. Grabbing my wrist, he pulled my hand away from my aching pussy and slipped my fingers into his mouth, licking and sucking them clean with a low groan before getting down on the floor to level his face with my pussy and digging in.

"Oh fuck!" He wasn't playing nice. I anticipated some soft licks and kisses, but he went ahead and latched himself onto me and sucked hard. Shuddering, I fisted the sheets when I felt him plunge two of his fingers into me, moaning deeply while I bucked my hips against his hand. "Please, let me come, please."

"You don't need any permission tonight, *lisichka*. Come to your heart's desire tonight." His words rumbled against me, making me whimper softly. "Don't hold back." That usually meant he planned on making me orgasm until I couldn't form a coherent thought.

His fingers dug into the sweet spot deep within me while his tongue swept and lashed against my clit, causing the pleasure to rise quickly within me. His arm wrapped around my hips, preparing to keep me firmly planted against him when I would try to pull away from him in the throes of pleasure.

"Kolyenka!" My body ached from how hard I tensed my tired muscles. The moans of pleasure quickly turned into cries and whimpers of anguish as he forced a second and third orgasm out of me following my first. "*Anh!* Oh God!" I could feel the tears spilling out of the corner of my eyes as I whimpered and struggled against him.

"Fuck!" I gasped, my moan getting caught in my throat when Nikolai suddenly stood up and thrust himself into me with no warning. "Fuck, you're still so big." I'd already resigned to the fact I would never fully adjust to his huge size even after two years with him. There was always that pleasureful burn of his huge member stretching at my tight cunt whenever he'd enter me, and it was a feeling I've come to welcome each and every time.

Leaning down, his lips captured mine in a soft and loving kiss as his hips moved in long strokes, letting me feel every little inch of his length from tip to base. "You have no idea how badly I wanted to barge into the bridal suite and take you when I saw that little album. I wanted to fuck you and fill you so that you'd be walking down the aisle with my cum dripping down your thighs." He growled softly, gripping the plush of my thighs with his large hands and pushing my legs down flat onto the bed to the side of me.

"*Moya seksual'naya malen'kaya zhena.*" His words made me shiver with pleasure and moan loudly as another orgasm washed over my aching body. "That's it baby, ride it out, keep squeezing me like that."

"*Detka, bol'she. Trakhni menya sil'neye.*" I'm surprised I managed to say the words without tripping over any of it between my moaning.

"*Vse, chto khochet moya zhena.*" Nikolai chuckled in response, picking up his pace.

Bracing myself using his shoulders, I gripped at him as his hips started to pound into me. "Fuck, right there, hit that spot again babe." The tremble of pleasure that shook at my body when his fat tip hit my sweet spot was delightful. "*Anh*, harder, please." I was so close to another orgasm; it teetered right at the edge.

With a deep growl, he pressed me harder into the bed and angled his hips to get my sweet spot with every thrust. "Come on, be a good girl for me, *lisichka*, let feel that cunt of yours milk me." His teeth grazed at my earlobe before pinching it between them with a firm tug.

"Come with me Kolyenka, please. I want you to fill me with your cum." The thought of his hot seed spilling into me brought a shiver of pleasure to my wound up body.

"Trying to get out of your fucking after this, *lisichka*?" He asked with a chuckle as his hips met my body more violently.

"Oh please, don't act as if you're a once and done man." The amount of times he's ran me ragged and still had it in him to go another round was more than I wanted to admit.

"Weren't you the one teasing me about keeping up with a youngling like you in my old age?" He retorted with a teasing grin and a raised brow.

"Oh shut up and fuck me *anh*." I scoffed with a playful smack of his shoulders.

"With pleasure." The hard slam of his hips nearly had me screaming with pleasure as I felt myself starting to tighten around him. "Not yet *lisichka*, just a little more."

He was close, I could feel him throbbing the more I tightened myself around him to coax his own release out. "Kolyenka." God I don't know how much longer I could hold out with him slamming into my sweet spot like this.

"Come for me *lisichka*, let me feel you." He groaned with a pant, letting out a roar when his hips became more erratic for a few thrusts before seating himself fully within me at the height of his own release.

Throwing my arms around his neck, I buried my face into the crease of his neck to muffle my scream of pleasure as my body shook from the immense pleasure of my orgasm.

"*Blyat', ya tak tebya lyublyu.*" He strained against my lips.

Panting softly, I kissed him with my trembling lips. *"YA tozhe sil'no tebya lyublyu."* I giggled softly, resting my forehead against his and looking into his loving eyes.

As the wave of bliss rolled over, his eyes turned dark again with a smirk. "On your hands and knees, *lisichka*."

Giggling with a huge grin, I quickly scrambled from under him. *"Da, ser."*

EPILOGUE

Angel

~15 YEARS LATER~

My body tensed for a split second when I felt something sling across my shoulders. "Mom, you look so lovely tonight, have I ever told you how good you always look?"

Not even bothering to look at my son, I rolled my eyes and continued to look through my purse. "What did you do? Or what do you want?" Compliments in that loaded tone around this house were never empty.

"Wha? What do you mean? Can't I just tell my mom how lovely she looks?" A quick glance out of the corner of my eyes was all I needed to confirm that my son was up to something by the sheepish grin on his face.

The cheekiness in his eyes was all I needed to tell which of the twins was buttering up to me. "Anton Nikolayevich Volkov, spit it out. If that shit doesn't work with your father, what makes you think you could pull it off?" I asked my son with a raised brow, turning my head to look up at him with narrowed eyes.

"Okay, fine, it's about the car..." He didn't even bother finishing his sentence, letting his voice trail out.

"You are not getting the Aston, nor are you going to get the Porsche, or the Bentley, and if you keep bringing this shit back up then so help me God I will find a 1990 Honda Civic for you to drive in."

Okay, so maybe promising the boys one of the cars as a gift for college was a mistake without specifications.

Pouting overly so, he swayed back and forth with me. "Oh come on mom, how come Anatoli gets one but I don't? Is it because he's older? I knew you had your favorite!" He playfully accused me in a whining voice.

"Anatoli gets one because that's the one he chose and didn't crash. You wrecked the damn Ferrari within an hour of getting the keys to it." I retorted with a saccharine smile, throwing my son's arm off my shoulders to go grab my coat from the coat closet.

"Oh come on, it's not my fault you passed on the bad Asian driver genes to me." Anton joked with a roll of his eyes. "Besides, I don't hear dad complaining or cutting you off every time you wreck your car. I mean, this is what? The fourth Aston this year? And it's only been six months into the new year. I don't see dad not replacing it or cutting you off from all the other cars." Anton stuck his tongue out at me with his arms crossed.

"The accidents weren't my fault. Did I choose to have a bomb placed under my car? No. Did I ask for a murder attempt in the form of a semi-truck or SUV? No. None of it was ever my fault, so therefore invalid in your argument because *you* crashed your car into a fire hydrant yourself after trying to impress your fifth girlfriend of the month." Okay, I have to admit, my luck with cars was shit, but I couldn't control murder attempts on my head because I was the Pakhan's wife.

"I think he was trying to pull a dad. Said he saw a cute girl in scrubs walking and thought that it'd be nice to crash into her life like dad did to yours." And there was my other son, making a jab at his younger twin.

"Haven't your dad and I drilled into your stubborn skulls to do as we say and not what we do?" Not saying we were bad parents, we raised our kids well, and they've grown into wonderful people. But the mafia life was a brutal one, and being born into it meant they were tied to our lives whether they wanted to or not.

Nikolai and I kept our children away from any kind of mafia business until their late teens, and even then we never forced anything on them. We always taught them to be good with a straight head and strong morals, and we made it very clear they should not follow us as examples because that would be a very violent outcome. Either they would be brutal killers like Nikolai or sadistic torturers like me. Both which neither of us wanted for our children.

"Where is dad anyways? I wanted to talk to him before you and him go on your little date." Anatoli asked, looking around to see if he could spot his father.

"He's outside with your uncle Lev and the twins. I think they're sparring with each other back there, or shooting." They have been out there a while, probably best if I check on them before date night gets canceled again because someone got a little too into it.

With a deep breath, I made my way out back with my sons in tow. "Oh lordy." I groaned, pinching the bridge of my nose at the sight of my daughter choking out Lev while my other son held him down. Of course, Nikolai wasn't doing anything to stop the madness. He just sat there in his chair sipping on some whiskey while on his phone.

Sighing heavily, I clicked my tongue out of annoyance. "Natasha! Misha! Get off your uncle before you actually kill him! And why is he bleeding!?" Well, so much for date night.

Natasha and Mikhail—who we called Misha—were our other two children. We were trying for a third and ended up with twins, again. They were unexpected, but they were both loved equally just as much as Anatoli and Anton. Misha looked exactly like me but with slightly lighter hair similar to Nikolai's, but he definitely had Nikolai's personality. Natasha was the opposite, looking like Nikolai with slightly darkened hair and my fiery personality, which got her into trouble more often than not.

"He popped his stitches, he's fine," Misha said with a wave of his hand as he got off his uncle with a huff. "It's just a minor flesh wound."

"I'll call Uncle Alexei," Anatoli said with a sigh, pulling out his phone and stepping off to the side. "Don't cancel date night again, you and dad need it, more so you mom," my son said with a wave of his free hand as he held his phone up to his ear with his other.

"You need to lock your arms more, gives a tighter hold and less wiggle room for your opponent." Anton advised his sister, demonstrating using his own arms with the air.

My eye twitched from my growing irritation. Turning to Anton, I whack him over the head with my purse. With a small, playful scowl, I scolded my son, "Don't fucking help her kill your damn uncle."

Nikolai's snicker made my head turn towards him, "And you, you're supposed to be supervising." I scolded my husband with a soft glare as I pointed and jabbed a finger his direction.

"I was, Lev was fine, and the twins were doing great. I would have stepped in if Lev actually passed out," Nikolai said nonchalantly with a shrug of his shoulders before downing the rest of his drink and standing up.

"*Trakhni tebya, muzhik*," Lev groaned, still laying there on the ground. Slowly, his head turned towards me, "Your kids are monsters."

"Oh, like yours are any better? Last I checked, it wasn't my door that was busted down by the feds because someone hacked them." I retorted with a knowing look.

"How'd I do dad?" Natasha was definitely a daddy's girl, and she knew she had Nikolai wrapped around her little fingers. She was also pretty aware about having brothers at her disposal also because she was the youngest.

"Good, but remember, you gotta learn to do things without much help from Misha. He's not always going to be there by your side to assist you." Nikolai commented with a proud smile. "Keep it up along with your studies and you'll be ready to take my position as Pakhan sooner than later, *malysh*."

Out of all our children, only Natasha had shown any interest in taking over Nikolai's mantle when time would come. If I had a choice then I wouldn't want either of our children to take over, but the Volkov Bratva legacy had to continue somehow. All our boys were prepared to step in if something were to happen, but they were more than eager to let their little sister take the lead when she showed interest.

"You kids behave, your mother and I are going out." Nikolai told the kids with a sigh before looking at me with a soft and loving smile, the same one that always pulled at his lips whenever he looked at me, even after nearly two decades of being together.

"Anatoli wanted to talk to you before we go," I said, looking over at my oldest who waved us off with a shake of his head and dismissive wave of his hand, letting us know it could wait.

With a smile, I leaned into Nikolai when he placed his hand on the small of my back and led us inside. "I love you." And like always, I grinned like a love struck idiot when I uttered those words and looked up at my husband.

"As I love you too, my lovely wife." He replied with a smile and kiss.

"Thank you for loving me." I murmured against his lips after breaking the kiss.

"Thank you for agreeing to stay in my life and putting up with my bullshit. I couldn't have asked for anyone better. I'll always love you forever and always, *lisichka*."

GLOSSARY

- **Anh:** A Vietnamese term of endearment for a male.

- **Ba:** Dad.

- **Blya, potoropis':** Fuck, hurry up.

- **Blyat':** Fuck.

- **Bozhe, ya na sekundu zabespokoilsya:** God I was worried for a second.

- **Bratok:** Brother.

- **Con đĩ:** Bitch.

- **Con đĩ đó. Tôi sẽ giết nó:** That bitch. I will kill her.

- **Detka, bol'she. Trakhni menya sil'neye:** Baby, more. Fuck me harder.

- **Derzhu pari, on chuvstvuyet sebya ublyudkom seychas:** I bet he feels like a bastard now.

- **Đù má:** Fuck.

- **Govno:** Shit.

- **Iisus chertov Khristos:** Jesus fucking Christ.

- **Idi na khuy:** Fuck you.

- **Malysh:** Little one.

- **Moy malen'kiy otrod'ye:** My little brat.

- **Moya seksual'naya malen'kaya zhena:** My sexy little wife.

- **Nyet:** No.

- **Pokatay menya, detka. Osedlay moy chlen, kak budto ot etogo zavisit tvoya zhizn':** Ride me baby. Ride my cock like your life depends on it.

- **Segodnya tebe ne sbezhat':** You can't escape today.

- **Spasibo, ser:** Thank you, sir.

- **Suka:** Bitch.

- **Takhchi svoyu zadnitsu syuda:** Get your ass over here.

- **Takaya khoroshaya malen'kaya shlyushka:** Such a good little slut.

- **Thằng khốn ngu ngốc:** Stupid bastard.

- **Tol'ko dlya tebya moya lyubov':** Only for you my love.

- **Trakhni tebya, muzhik:** Fuck you, man.

- **Trakhni menya:** Fuck me.

- **Ty chertov ublyudok:** You're a fucking bastard.

- **Ty tak khorosho postupila, lyubov'. YA tak gorzhus' toboy:** You did so well, love. I am so proud of you.

- **Ty takoy vkusnyy. YA nikogda ne nasytlyus' toboy:** You're so delicious. I will never get enough of you.

- **Ty tozhe sil'no tebya lyublyu:** I love you too much.

- **Ty v poryadke:** Are you okay?

- **Ty tozhe tebya lyublyu:** I love you too.

- **Ty takaya krasivaya. Ne mogu poverit', chto ty budesh' moyey na vsyu zhizn':** You're so beautiful. I can't believe that you'll be mine for life.

- **Ublyudok:** Bastard.

- **YA tebya lyublyu:** I love you.

- **YA tozhe sil'no tebya lyublyu:** I love you very much too.

- **YA tozhe tebya lyublyu:** I love you too.

- **Yebat'! Tak chertovski plotno i khorosho:** Fuck! So damn tight and good.

THANK YOU

Thank you so much for reading the first installment of the Volkov Bratva series! I really hoped you enjoyed Nikolai and Angel's story, and I hope you are ready for more down the line. The series is going to continue with each brother's story with their own love interest.

The series will continue with Stepan and Hanna's dark desires and adventures in The Bratva's Beast. Another dark mafia romance with plenty of spice.

If you guys want to see extras, sneak peaks, and other tid bits or just wanna have a peak at my antics I go through then follow me on my social media handles!

tiktok.com/@rose.chase.author

instagram.com/rose.chase.author/

facebook.com/rose.chase.author

amazon.com/author/rose.chase

About the Author

R OSE C HASE IS A dedicated writer who has been crafting stories since her middle school days, where she first found her passion for storytelling on online forums and Wattpad. In addition to her creative pursuits, Rose is a loving mother to two wonderful boys and a full-time nurse, demonstrating her unwavering commitment to both her family and her profession.

Her writing journey has taken her into the realm of contemporary romance, with a particular fascination for the complexities of dark romance and morally gray characters. Rose's storytelling skill shines as she delves into the intricate dance between love, desire, and the shadows of human nature.

When she's not busy saving lives and caring for her family, Rose immerses herself in the world of fiction, where her words breathe life into captivating narratives that leave readers yearning for more. With each story, she invites you to explore the depths of love and passion while confronting the complexities of the human heart.

www.ingramcontent.com/pod-product-compliance
Lightning Source LLC
Chambersburg PA
CBHW031830310726
48972CB00005B/1227